wolfsgate

CAT PORTER

WILDFLOWER INK, LLC

WOLFSGATE

Cover Design
Najla Qamber
Najla Qamber Designs

Editor
Jennifer Roberts-Hall

Interior Design
Cat Porter

ISBN: 978-0990308515

Visit my website at www.catporter.eu

CONTENTS

For
R & D
and
Eugenia & Stella

PROLOGUE

England, 1790

HE WAITED FOR IT. It was coming now. His skin was icy cold from the inside out. His eyes rolled back in his head. That prickle fizzled down his spine once more, and the familiar gentleness seeped over every inch of his flesh. And finally...

Oh yes.

He floated, swathed in a gentle blur, wafting on a thick cloud.

That's it...bloody marvelous.

Fingers slid through his hair, and tingles spread across his scalp and needled his neck. His blood backed up in his veins for a painful split second.

A touch? Who's touching me?

"Brandon," a soft voice whispered like a warm breeze over his face. The shadow inside him shifted, and he turned towards that sudden promise radiating over him.

My name?

"Dearest Brandon." The sweet voice poured over him like warm honey easing the fizzle in his veins. A hand settled on his shoulder and slid down his arm, then squeezed once. He gasped, his insides flinched.

Muffled voices then choked breathing lingered over him like smoke.

Come back...please, more.

He forced his eyes open, pleading with his lids to function just this once. He had to see the voice, the touch. Had to...

"I told you. This is all that's left of him. If you were hoping on his return, you were hoping in vain," came a sharp masculine voice. A voice he knew.

"But we thought he was dead—"

"He's as good as dead. You call this being alive?" the man cut her off.

"Mightn't we take him home?" she asked.

Home?

"Are you mad? He's dying for God's sake. Best to leave him here for however long he lasts under the doctor's care."

"This is care?"

"Shut up, Justine."

Justine.

The name vibrated in his brain, and a bittersweet emotion he could not name shimmered against the hollow walls of his chest. Images flickered through him: Desolate brown eyes desperately holding back tears, innocent laughter ringing out, an outstretched hand in a dark corner, an anxious girl sitting in a big saddle on a large horse...his horse? Now, there on his chest where this peculiar sensation ached there came a light caress, a pressing in of a hand.

Oh yes...just there.

"For Christ's sake, stop touching him!"

He tilted his head and managed to open one eye.

Finally.

And the breath sucked out of his lungs.

Velvet. Chocolate. Silken earth.

Those same beautiful, large brown eyes from his memory beckoned him.

2

"Brandon?"

"Come away," said the man.

That voice. I know that harsh tone.

The man gripped the woman's arm. She tried to pull away, but stumbled back against him. "Do you understand now?" He scowled, shaking her arm slightly. The young woman only nodded, her chin trembling. "Come now, don't make this more difficult. He won't last long. Do it, and we'll be done with this."

The man let go of her and moved away. She leaned closer, and a scent of lavender drifted over him. His lips parted on a whimper pleading to inhale that magic.

"I promise you, Brandon," came her voice, steady this time. The muscles of her face were tight, her brow furrowed over those velvet eyes. "I won't leave it like this. By everything I am, everything I have left, I swear I won't leave you here all alone, I won't let them destroy you."

The velvet gleamed now, and a shining heat radiated right through him as his lungs contracted painfully. A drop of wet fell onto the skin at the base of his throat, and then another fell on the torn grooves of skin on his face. The drops of warm liquid trickled over his flesh, stinging his skin, and a moan escaped his chest. He wanted to see her, to feel her touch on him again.

He tried to reach for her, but it was too much of a struggle. His arms wouldn't listen to his commands, and his eyelids sank with the effort, his eyeballs swimming in his head as muffled voices and footsteps thudded around him.

He was adrift once more. Gone.

CHAPTER ONE

Two Years Later

"THERE IS YOUR HUSBAND, MADAM." The doctor's lips settled in a firm line.

Justine fought the wave of nausea rising in her throat, holding her breath against the stench of sickness and desolation in this large hospital room full of forgotten patients.

Her gaze followed his outstretched hand pointing towards one of the many ill, diseased, and infirm lying in unclean beds.

Her heart skipped a beat at the sight of him. Straggly black hair and a beard made him a fierce-looking creature, even though he was incapacitated in a hospital bed, mumbling to himself quietly like a helpless child, his eyes glazed. His thin frame lay twisted on the dirty linens, his bearded face gaunt, his eyes seeing something far from reality, his mind engaged in the clouds. This was Brandon Treharne, Baron of Graven.

He was not the Brandon she remembered—that Brandon was a fine young gentleman, bursting with vitality and searing good looks. This was a scarred shell of a man, clinging to a half-life, not the dashing older step-cousin who had once wiped her tears and lied to their nanny on her behalf when she had fallen and ripped yet another hole in her dress. Nor was he the energetic creature who roared with laughter as he would chase her and her step-sister like a tiger through the great hall of Wolfsgate until they could no longer breathe nor laugh any harder.

Justine leveled her eyes at the Doctor. "We are taking him home."

His eyes bulged, his mouth fell open. "Are you quite sure, ma'am?"

"Quite." Justine squared her shoulders and cast him a quick, cool glance. Disdain. Impatience. Irritation. The way a noble-woman would respond to an insolent remark. She'd practiced for this moment. Justine raised an eyebrow at the medico in his old powdered wig. "I have made all the necessary arrangements. There is a doctor waiting."

The doctor's eyes pinched together. "I mean no disrespect, ma'am, but I have my instructions from his uncle—"

"I've come here with my uncle on several occasions to see my husband."

"Yes, my lady. I remember." The doctor frowned at them both. "This is most irregular."

Justine tilted her head at him, eyes narrowing. "My coach is waiting." She snapped the words. Lady Graven would tolerate no denial.

Davidson, the beefy estate manager who had accompanied Justine on this mad quest to London leaned forward at her side and glowered at the man.

The doctor heaved a sigh. "As you wish." The doctor motioned to two of his lackeys to unchain the patient from his bed and escort him out to his wife's hired coach.

Davidson surged ahead of her to assist the men with their charge who now groaned and grunted at the sudden, sharp movements his body was being forced to make. Brandon twisted and shrugged away at the contact forced upon him.

"You will have to sign for him, Lady Graven." The doctor directed her to his office.

Justine's chest stiffened at the sound of the title. She desperately needed fresh air, itched to get out of this building as soon as possible. However, the thought that Brandon had languished here for two long years and would finally be free fueled her restraint. The doctor placed a document in front of her. She quickly perused the discharge form with a show of cool irritation and signed her name where he indicated. Dropping the quill on his desk, she swept out of the room.

Davidson reached into the coach and grabbed one of the blankets they had brought, wrapping his young master with it. He shook his head as he took in the young man's haunted eyes and haggard face. The men shoved Brandon into the carriage, and he howled softly, curling himself up into the corner. Davidson rewarded them with a few coins each. He helped Justine into the coach, threw himself in, slammed the door shut, then banged on the roof. The coach jolted forward, and they were off.

It was done. Finally.

The planning, the deceptions, the posturing for the doctor—and now here was the stark reality before her in the coach.

"Dear God, he's a sight," Justine said, trying to ignore the sting in the back of her throat and the pitch of her stomach.

"Caw, he stinks!" Davidson's face twisted.

"Yes, he does." Justine leaned towards the beleaguered Brandon and touched the blanket over his arm. His eyes jumped, and he flinched back from her, crouching in the corner like a trapped animal. "If only that were his sole problem." She squeezed his knee. "Brandon, it's Justine. We're going home to Wolfsgate. Do you understand? Mr. Davidson is here with us, you remember him? Your father's steward."

She searched his eyes for a response, but there was none. "Brandon?" He only retreated from her, staring aimlessly out the window, his head rocking with the movement of the coach. She sank back in her seat, biting her lip.

7

"It will take time, ma'am. This will be difficult, but you'll see, he'll get better. May not be the same man ever again, but—"

"Anything would be better than this."

"This next bit will be the hard part. Are you ready?"

"Absolutely, Davidson." Her steady gaze slid back to Brandon. "Absolutely."

Hours later the carriage exchanged horses at a coaching inn where they took a room, washed Brandon, changed his clothes, clipped his hair and nails, and shaved his beard. Brandon had moaned like a child. He was quite thin, his bones jutting out, his sinewy muscles visible. They were gentle and very careful while handling him so as not to upset him too much. Luckily he did not fight them. In fact he only stared up at Justine, his grey-green eyes soft. She could look for hours into those eyes, eyes the colour of seawater just before it pools on the shore.

"Velvet," he murmured over and over again. A shiver swept the back of her neck. By the time they were finished Justine began to recognise Brandon Treharne once again. Still a shell of his former self, but it was he.

Davidson had a quick meal while Justine stayed with Brandon, then they got on the next coach and continued on towards Gloucestershire. She supposed Brandon had been given a heavy dose first thing in the morning at the hospital for he was very quiet and still the entire journey, which was lucky, but nevertheless, disturbing. The rocking motion of the coach lulled him to sleep right away.

They would have at least ten days alone at Wolfsgate before her stepbrother and stepfather returned from Edinburgh, and they desperately needed that time to get Brandon strong and back on his feet.

They disembarked in the village before theirs where a friend of Davidson's awaited them with a carriage to take them the rest of the way home without the possibility of recognition. Finally, very late into the night, the rolling hills of Wolfsgate began. She took in a deep breath as the carriage at long last drove through the high black iron gate.

The ancient manor rose before her against a star-filled inky sky. As a young girl, when she had first lain eyes on the great historical stone residence, it had impressed her greatly, and became a glorious retreat to her. But as a young woman, it had become more like a prison.

Tonight as Justine stepped down from the carriage and glanced up at the manor's high central tower and then across the flowering vines that climbed the massive stone walls of the old Tudor house, her every muscle tightened; she felt taller, bigger, stronger, like she was a part of the very stones of this house. A fullness rose through her chest. She had kept her promise. She had done the right thing. The planets and stars would realign once again for Wolfsgate. They must.

Davidson helped Brandon out of the carriage who only moaned in protest. Justine pushed opened the great front door. Molly, the old housekeeper, waited for them with a huge lit candelabrum on the polished chest in the entryway. The thick flames flickered in the rush of cold air, and the ends of the Flemish tapestries flapped against the stone walls of the hall. The old woman's eyes were round under her bonnet, her hands clutched together.

"You've brought him home," Molly whispered. "Bless you, child. Bless you!"

CHAPTER TWO

DAVIDSON HELD the rope between his big, stocky hands. "When he awakens it will be rough. We don't know yet how his body will react to not having that poison."

Justine nodded, her lips set in a stiff line. He tied Brandon's wrists to the sides of her bed while her fingers twisted in the folds of her skirt. She felt a twinge inside her at the sight of Brandon so helpless, so vulnerable, his large frame filling her bed. Yes, *her* bed. Brandon would stay in her bedchamber for the time being as there hadn't been time to prepare one for him before they'd left for London lest she arouse suspicion in her stepfather.

Davidson loosened his necktie, flung off his frock coat, and slumped on the armchair rubbing his eyes. Justine kicked off her shoes and sank back into the chaise opposite the bed, curling her legs under her skirts. She let out a heavy exhale, and her eyes fluttered closed.

Someone was barking orders, a deep voice, argumentative and mean. She unstuck her eyelids and jolted upright. Davidson stood at the end of the bed, his arms crossed. Brandon was pulling at the ropes, growling out every obscenity known to mankind, his legs kicking, his torso twisting. He stopped at the sight of her, his eyes bulging, his arms still tugging at the rope, his chest heaving for air. He suddenly collapsed back onto the bed and let out a groan. A wild creature shackled, trapped against his will.

And so it went for days. Davidson would either respond to Brandon's wild exclamations or make no attempt at all to reason with him. Brandon would quiet down, and then it would begin all over again for hours at a time, the quiet then the restless and loud behavior.

Brandon slept fitfully, his legs convulsing now and again. She wiped the cold sweat from his brow and decided to change his nightshirt which was drenched in perspiration.

His eyes flew open, and he tried to reach out a restrained hand to touch her. "Velvet," he groaned.

"Brandon? It's me—"

"No, no, no." Confusion swept his clouded eyes, and he fell back against the pillows again, the side of his mouth twitched, his hands pulled on the restraints.

Once Davidson awoke, he helped her change Brandon out of his wet nightshirt, wash him with a cloth, and dress him in a fresh gown. She changed the soiled sheets turning his body to either side as she worked, placed a clean bucket at his side for his bouts of nausea, and made sure a chamber pot was at the ready.

Justine knew he wouldn't eat, but she could try and offer him some bread at least. Maybe today he would take it, but she was wrong. Today, he threw the dish and the cup which shattered against the cabinet, then shouted a string of curses at her, cursed himself, and tried to rip the rope off his hands.

"Stay away from me! Damn you, I don't know who the hell you are! A demon? A pretty devil in disguise? A siren sent to torture me?"

Davidson stormed into the room with a cup of whiskey and put it to his lips. Brandon smelled the liquor and drank it greedily like a thirst-crazed animal after an interminable trek. His glassy eyes were a deeper hue of green now, and they pierced hers making her insides squirm. He turned to Davidson and spit a shower of whiskey at him. Justine flinched and stumbled back a few steps. Davidson only grabbed a folded square of linen on the side table and mopped his face. Brandon threw his head back on the pillow suddenly and wept, his feet thrashing against the mattress.

"Davidson, are you all right?"

"I am, he's not." Davidson wiped off his hands, dropped the linen on the washstand, and quit the room.

Brandon's extreme moods continued for days. He would carry on about everything and nothing, then he would stop suddenly and look right through her and Davidson, sink back onto the bed and mutter to himself. Justine would sit with him, giving Davidson a much-deserved break from the confines of that room. Now, ten days later, he was calmer and seemed to have turned a corner.

Who could possibly know the dark recesses Brandon now travelled through in his overtaxed brain or the thousand different pains his body was experiencing? Now that he slept she stroked his hair to try to chase some part of his misery away. He hissed and moaned in his sleep at the contact. She took his cold hand in hers, the hand that used to hold her small one years ago, lifetimes ago.

Her first time at the estate she had gotten lost walking to the creek on her own, and Brandon had been the one to find her. He had taken her hand in his and brought her home and, thankfully, did not inform her mother about her carelessness. When her stepbrother, William had gotten mad at her for touching his books and had shoved her, Brandon had defended her, leading her away by the hand and rolled his eyes at William to make her giggle.

Now all these years later, it was her turn to provide him

comfort and safety. She rubbed his cold fingers between her hands and could not resist brushing her lips across the prominent knuckles.

The last time Brandon had taken her hand it was to say goodbye when he had left for Jamaica four years ago, and she had known she wouldn't see him again for a very long time. He had kissed her cheek and stroked the side of her face, the edges of his lips curling into a wistful smile just for her.

She took in a breath of air, thanking Providence that William had decided to take his father to Edinburgh on business with him at the last moment, hoping the change of scenery would do his addled senses some good. Luck had truly shined on her, for such a long absence for both of them was extremely rare.

Justine had wasted no time in dashing to London with Davidson and bringing Brandon home, but that wasn't the only reason. She daren't think about William's reaction to what he would learn in Edinburgh when he realized how she had lied to him.

All for Brandon, all for Wolfsgate.

Her fingertips brushed over his cold hands now freed from the rope. Justine covered him with a blanket, and his eyes fluttered open. "Siren, do not leave me." He trembled, his skin was so very pale, his lips a strange shade of blue, his eyes a cool grey. Justine's chest constricted. She ran her hand up and down his back under the covers. His teeth chattered, he rolled up in a ball.

She kicked off her shoes, opened the blanket and got in beside him. Justine smoothed his hair off his forehead, and he leaned into her touch. She took him in her arms like she would a child, and he immediately curled up around her, his cold face rubbing her upper chest, his long arms wrapping tightly around her. Soon enough his breathing evened out, and her own tense muscles relaxed to the soothing sound. Her gaze flicked down. His eyes were closed, he slept.

Justine slid her fingers through his black hair which still smelled of the nutmeg scented soap she had used to wash it yesterday. Her body settled into his solid weight at her side, her own slow, even breaths matching his.

CHAPTER THREE

THE SCENT of flowers mixed with that of warm skin stirred a forgotten ache within Brandon. He unglued his eyes and was met with the face of a woman. He took in the full, dark lashes, contoured brows, the elegant nose. Long, thick, springy locks of coppery brown hair tickled his shoulders and his cheek. Her heart beat swelled in his ear, her bare arms were draped around his shoulders sheltering him in her warm embrace. He was pressed fully into her chest, the tops of her smooth breasts peeking up from her bodice rose and fell with each breath under his very lips.

Fantastic.

Where the hell was he?

Aside from the beautiful young woman holding him close, he was in a bed with clean linens. That was certainly unusual. Well, both situations were quite unusual.

The woman stirred under his weight, and he pulled his head back to focus his still-dazed vision on her face. Her fetching pink lips pressed together then released on a small breath and fell slightly apart. Her body squirmed under his, flexing, stretching. He was mesmerized.

Her eyes opened, and they looked directly into his. His lungs squeezed together. Rich brown eyes, the colour of the finest French molten chocolate he had drunk once in Paris as a boy. His mouth watered for that smooth, lush richness right this very second. Maybe if he...

He knew these eyes.

There was something familiar about them, about her, something he had an instinct to preserve. He pressed his body into hers, the need to keep her soft warmth close overwhelming, to absorb more of it, more of her. She stiffened, her dark orbs widening under his unfiltered examination. They stared at each other as his hand travelled up her waist, her lower back arching in its wake. Her sensuous lips only parted further. He leaned in closer to her face, barely an inch from that mouth. His gaze was riveted on those lips.

"Such hospitality," he murmured.

She squirmed and planted a hand on his chest. "Brandon!" she stuttered. He blinked up at his name. "Do you not recognise me?" she asked.

"Unfortunately, no." His nose moved along her jaw, his lips brushed her skin. He was an animal sensing her blood, her heat, her aroma. Delicious. His veins pounded. "But we can surely remedy that." He nipped the side of her throat, and her body jolted in his embrace. She twisted in the other direction, but she only revealed more of that delicate throat to him. His hand cupped the fantastic swell of her breast, and a sigh escaped him. So soft, bloody perfect. She pushed at his chest with both hands.

"Brandon—" She struggled to catch her breath. "I'm Justine. Your Uncle Richard's stepdaughter."

His body stilled. "Justine?"

"Yes. Yes, it's me."

The last time he had seen Justine, his little step-cousin with the shy smile and easy laugh, she had been a young, budding girl. He studied her face once again. "Christ." He exhaled and released her from his grasp. "You're all grown up, aren't you?" Was he expressing surprise or admiration? He wasn't sure. Maybe both. His body was at full attention, that was certain. Yes, definitely admiration.

"It's been a very long time," she murmured.

His gaze flickered down her torso. "Obviously," he muttered sinking back onto the pillow. She wriggled out of the bed, the mattress shifting, and a chill swept over him right away. A sudden heaviness settled in his limbs as he watched her smooth down her skirts. Something sharp pricked his shoulder. Four hairpins lay on the pillow. He held them out to her as she tucked the blanket around him. She bit her lip and plucked them from his fingers.

A gold ring on her left hand caught his eye. "You're married?" Her gaze snapped up at him, and she stopped fiddling with the blanket. "Your ring," Brandon said gesturing to her hand. "Damn, I've been gone a very long time then." She didn't answer and only collected the remaining hairpins that were on the bed.

"How long has it been, Justine? What's going on?" His lips pressed into a hard line. God, my head is killing me, actually my whole body is killing me, every joint, every muscle." His palms rubbed over his eyes.

Justine cleared her throat. "You were in a shipwreck coming back from Jamaica. We thought you were dead, but you survived. You've been in hospital in London for quite some time."

His breath tightened in his lungs. Broken images swarmed through his brain—shouting, battering wind and rain, wood cracking, breaking apart, huge waves of icy sea water squashing him, engulfing everything.

The end of the world.

"Define 'quite some time' would you?"

"You've been missing for almost two years."

The blood drained from his head. "Two years?"

"Mr. Davidson, the estate manager, and I came to get you and bring you home. We arrived at Wolfsgate almost ten days ago. The physic they were giving you at hospital made you ill." She averted her gaze.

"What does that mean?"

"You had serious injuries and have been in a lot of pain over a long period of time, and they gave you a special remedy for it, too much of it. Over time, your body became accustomed to it."

"Accustomed to it?"

"Yes."

"What sort of special remedy?"

Justine exhaled, her hands clasped together. "Opium."

Opium?

He clenched his jaw and moved to sit up, grunting with the effort. Justine wrapped her hands around his bicep to help him. His penetrating gaze darted up at her, and her skin heated again.

"And why did you come? Where are Father and William?"

"They're in Edinburgh on business. They're due back shortly," she replied.

He sat up and finally noticed the heavy green velvet drapes hanging from the bed canopy, a woman's looking glass sitting upon a toilette table next to a large Jacobean chest that looked like it might contain forgotten treasures. An old cane-backed armchair that had seen better days with a small table next to it, and a worn green velvet chaise with a blanket tossed carelessly over it on the other side.

"Is this your bedchamber?"

Justine only nodded, her tongue darted out and swiped at her lips.

"Why in the hell—?"

The door shoved open and Davidson entered holding a tray with a steaming bowl of broth. "Ah! You're a fine sight, that you are Master Brandon!" He grinned. Justine took the tray from him and placed it on the table. Davidson grabbed Brandon's arm and squeezed it.

"Davidson," Brandon murmured.

Davidson grinned. "You're doing well, my boy. Very well." He glanced at Justine, his eyes squinting at her momentarily. Justine's hand went to her hair which now swirled around her shoulders. She stood up straighter and pushed the unruly, heavy locks behind her ears.

"I've brought you some food. Had some meself downstairs," said Davidson.

Brandon scowled. "What is it?"

"A simple broth, nothing extraordinary," said Justine. "You need to eat Brandon." She brought the tray to his bed. His dark gaze darted to the murky liquid.

"I doubt you tucked into this, Davidson," Brandon muttered. Davidson only smirked.

"Come now," Justine said. "Molly cooked it just for you."

He leaned his head back against the headboard, his eyes trained on her. "What will you do if I don't eat it?"

A delicate smile crept across her lips. His stomach dipped at the sight. "Oh, I'm glad you have the energy to display your wit today," she said.

"I haven't woken up next to a pretty face and such an appealing body in a very, very long time. Maybe that has something to do with it." His heavy gaze locked with hers. "Lucky man, your husband." Justine's face flushed scarlet, and a flicker of warmth spread through his body at the sight. She returned her attention to the bowl, stirring the spoon in the hot broth.

"What are you on about?" asked Davidson from the armchair at the other side of the room.

Justine grinned as she held a spoonful of soup to his lips. "He's being cheeky." His nerve endings tingled as her face lit up. He took the spoon between his lips, and she dipped it in his mouth.

Davidson chuckled. "Then we are well on the road to recovery, I should say."

Justine held a cloth underneath his chin as he swallowed the warm liquid. "Not very horrible, I hope."

He made a face, his lips tipping up. "A little horrible."

"Oh good, more then." She grinned as she lifted another steaming spoonful of broth from the bowl. His pelvis stirred under the quilts. He could do this all day with her.

Brandon managed to eat half the soup and a few bites of the crusty bread. He took the napkin and wiped his mouth. He stared at her as he settled back on the pillow, his eyelids drooping.

Hours later after he woke from his nap, he surrendered to a bout of nausea. Justine sat at the edge of the bed wiping his brow with a cool, wet cloth, keeping his damp hair away from his face.

"Perhaps you'd like to take a turn about the room, get accustomed to moving and walking once again?" she asked.

"You're trying to sound very bright and positive, I must say, Justine." He coughed, adjusting himself back on his pillows.

"Could you try? Davidson and I will help you steady yourself."

He studied her face again. "You are a woman on a mission, eh?"

She shrugged her shoulders. "You have been stuck in this bed without much regular exercise. Your body needs to move again. I don't like seeing you like this Brandon, and I'm sure you don't like how it feels, either." She pulled back the bedcovers. "You need your strength back. Let's try. Please."

"So polite, how could I refuse?"

"Too right. I wouldn't if I were you, sir," Davidson said. He came to the other side of him. He and Justine held Brandon by the arms and around his middle as he put his weight on his feet. He inhaled a deep breath and his body swayed. His foot took one step forward, then another. He teetered and leaned heavily on Justine. Darts of pain shot up his right leg, and he let out a hiss.

"Take a moment, take in a breath," Justine said. "We're not going to let you go."

Brandon took in her determined gaze and sucked in air again. He took another heavy step forward, then another, letting loose a string of curses as the three of them hobbled around the small room. He shifted his weight and winced.

"We can get you a cane for this side, just until you're stronger," said Justine.

"Won't that be the height of fashion, though?" Brandon grimaced as they led him back to the bed. Suddenly he stopped, his body stiffening. "What the bloody..."

Justine followed his gaze. He stared at his reflection in her small mirror, tilting his head left then right, assessing the damage. Trembling fingers traced over the two long scars that ran from his temple down his right cheek.

"Your souvenirs from the shipwreck," said Davidson.

"The gashes were once quite deep, but they've healed," Justine said her hand firmly around his middle. "The doctor in Cornwall did a good job. Over time, they may become less prominent."

Brandon only shook his head at his strange, foreign reflection, his eyes clouding. He turned from the mirror. "They are harsh reminders of a life lost."

"Yes, Brandon. But you are found."

CHAPTER FOUR

BRANDON STILL ERUPTED into a charge of unpredictable highs and lows, exploding into a fierce rage then later lapsing into a brooding melancholy. Justine had sent Davidson out to purchase a smart cane for him to use, which he hated, but soon enough admitted it helped. He hobbled about the bedchamber at regular intervals. Then he finally left the room and conquered the long hallway. Eventually he tackled descending the staircase and then later on in the day, went back up the staircase.

Thankfully the worst of his recovery had passed, for there was another sort of storm ahead of them.

Justine crossed the front hall carrying a tray with a pot of tea and cups to bring into the parlour in time for Brandon's morning descent downstairs. As she crossed the hall, she glanced up at the top of the staircase and her breath caught. The twenty-six year old man towering before her was more like the Brandon Treharne she remembered.

He was not quite bursting with the vitality of his charmed youth, but it was Brandon, fully dressed, hair neatly pulled back in a tie, with his cane in one hand. He managed the stairs on his own without stopping, only some wincing, three curses, and his eyes on her all the while.

She smiled at him, her fingers tightening around the handles of the tray.

The front door burst open with a harsh scrape and bang.

"Bloody hell!"

She flinched, scalded by the the acid tone of the familiar deep voice exploding behind her. Justine dropped the tray on the oak sideboard. Brandon froze at the bottom of the stairs.

Her stepbrother, William stood at the entrance, his cold black gaze sweeping over her. Her stomach hardened as his dark eyes shot to Brandon, then back to her.

"What have you done, you little idiot?" William's voice thundered.

Luck was no longer with her now. She took in a deep breath, forcing her thoughts and emotions to unscramble.

Brandon's eyes trained on the choleric figure before him. "William, you've come to welcome me home?" The edges of her lips tipped up. It was oddly comforting that Brandon's wit had not faded after all these years.

William's body snapped towards her. "How dare you?"

She picked up the tea tray and swept past him into the parlour.

"What's this? What's the to do all about?" Richard staggered into the parlour after his stepdaughter and son, his dated grey wig teetering on his head. Molly appeared, her wrinkled face ashen. The old man threw his cloak on a chair, and she rushed to swoop it up.

"Look who's returned home, father," William said.

"Who, my boy?" Richard asked, his eyes scrunched at the figures across the room as he scratched under his wig. He flung himself into the nearest armchair, his legs stretched out.

"She's brought Brandon back."

"It cannot be. It cannot be..." Richard blinked at Brandon, glowered at Justine. "Oh, you stupid cow."

"Yes, he's home where he belongs," Justine said through gritted teeth, ignoring her churning stomach.

William's eyes narrowed over her. "You foolish chit. I could wring your little neck. First, what I learned in Edinburgh, and now this."

"What are you arguing about? You're doing my head in," Brandon's voice rose.

William's lips rolled as he continued to pin Justine with his glare. "You lying bitch." His voice was low, cold, seething. Justine poured Brandon a cup of tea.

"Are you not pleased to see me, cousin?" Brandon asked. "You really seem quite annoyed. Time and events have not softened your heart toward me?"

"You were fine where you were."

"I'm sure you thought so."

"I made sure of it, cousin. Obviously they did a fine job keeping you alive. We were told you were at death's door."

"How long ago was that, I wonder?" Brandon's eyes flashed. "You're disappointed I'm home, aren't you?"

A cold grin stole across William's lips.

"Disappointed I actually survived the shipwreck, disappointed I did well in Jamaica. The list is endless."

William's lips curled. "Oh no, I'm quite pleased, really."

Justine pressed her cold hands together. The facetious tone in her stepbrother's voice set her nerves on edge as it always did. She could practically hear the wheels of invention turning and clacking in William's mind at this turn of events.

"Two whole years of my life, missing, gone, lost."

"We thought you were dead, Brandon," Justine said. "Barely anyone survived that shipwreck."

"I survived, but I'm still confused as to the after part."

William smirked. "Confused, eh?"

"Justine still hasn't explained everything."

"Oh, hasn't she?" A snide smile marred William's handsome features. "This is all very entertaining." His hard gaze darted to Justine. "Does he know?"

"Please, William. Not like this."

"Know what?" Brandon asked from behind his tea cup. "What's going on?"

Richard laughed. "Oh, this is such fun. Pour us a drink, girl." Justine ignored him.

William leaned into her and pulled her chin up with a finger. "What did I promise you? You and I had an understanding, did we not? Yet you have broken that understanding in not one, but two treacherous ways. You know what that means, don't you?"

Justine's jaw clenched. He released her, but his cold gaze remained riveted on her. "She didn't tell you, Brandon, did she?"

"Let me explain it to him," Justine said. William's fingers flicked up at her as he moved towards Brandon. Justine's pulse pounded. "William, please."

"What are the two of you on about?" Brandon exhaled settling on the edge of the sofa, stretching out his bad leg.

Richard's thin laughter filled the room as Justine's lungs constricted. There was no going back now, no stopping William. Brandon had to find out sometime, but it wasn't supposed to be like this.

"Ah, cousin." William leaned an arm against the carved stone mantel and let out a small laugh. "Justine is your wife."

CHAPTER FIVE

THE BLOOD DRAINED from Justine's face.

Now it all begins.

Brandon's eyebrows slammed together. His head jerked at William as if his cousin were suddenly and inexplicably speaking a foreign tongue. "What did you say?"

"Oh, I think you heard me." William's eyes gleamed. "*You* are married to *her*."

Brandon's dark gaze fell on Justine, and her heart plunged like a lead weight inside her chest under its sharp severity. She lowered her head and focused on the worn hem of her dress.

"How can I possibly be married?" Brandon asked, his voice tight.

"You were too overwhelmed by your medicinal fog to notice," William said.

Brandon's gaze darted between them. "Is this some sort of joke?"

"I don't joke about marriage." William snatched Justine by the arm and threw her down at Brandon's feet. Justine gasped, her palms smacking against the cold, hard floor. "The little stray is yours, to have and to hold until the end of your days." She didn't

29

dare look up at Brandon, she only wanted to melt right through the floor.

"No." Brandon sat up straight, his neck stiffened. "Ridiculous."

"Yes, that's the word for it. Ridiculous!" Richard snorted. "There was a parson, a sniveling bride, several witnesses, and a special license. All done quietly and quickly at your bedside at hospital." He snapped his fingers in the air.

Brandon's eyes blazed. "When?"

"Almost two years ago, after you were found," William answered. "We put the quill in your hand, and you signed your name as best you could. You were humming some tune at the time, staring at your bride, spittle coming out of the side of your mouth. It was quite touching." William studied Brandon carefully, enjoying his cousin's response immensely.

"Why? Why would you do this?" Brandon's voice quaked. "Where is my father? He would never—"

"We'd found out you were alive, after months of thinking you were at the bottom of the sea," William said. "But instead, you were degenerating away in hospital in the throes of a strong restorative to help you through your severe injuries from that shipwreck," William said. "By the time we found you, we were told you weren't to last too much longer. Bloody hell, the state of you then. Eh, Justine?"

"How convenient." Brandon rubbed the back of his neck.

"But in the meantime the estate was at a standstill," William said.

"What do you mean, standstill? Where's father? Where is he? He would never have—Justine? You said he was with them in Edinburgh." Brandon's face tightened, making his scars more prominent. Justine, still on the floor before him, raised her head, tears spilling down her flushed cheeks, her lower lip trembling.

"No," he breathed.

"He passed away soon after the news of your shipwreck,"

Justine whispered, smoothing her hands down her skirts. She had wanted to be the one to tell him, but not like this.

"You are the only legal heir to Wolfsgate. Quite unfair. In your absence, your wife here has been taking care of things on the family's behalf," Richard said, a cackle lining his words.

Brandon planted his elbows on his shaky legs. A low moan escaped his chest. Justine moved towards him, her hand touching his knee. He shoved it away.

"How?" he managed, his voice hoarse, his eyes covered. "How did my father die?"

"The doctor told us his heart had been weak for some time," she said quietly. "He grew old before us. He wasn't in any pain really. One morning, he did not awaken. He'd left us in his sleep."

"Why did you not tell me? Why did you hide it from me?" Brandon's red, glassy eyes were positively savage.

Her insides twisted. "You needed to recover first. I did not want to upset you. I thought—"

Brandon's wet, fierce gaze slid to William. "You wanted to have your way with Wolfsgate? Is there anything left?"

"Oh, some," William said.

"Do you hate me that much?"

"I don't consider you, cousin. I've gotten on with my life. In fact, I'm a married man now. And a father."

Justine winced at the smug grin growing on William's face. *Here it comes.*

"I married Amanda Blakelock. We have a son," William said.

A moment passed in stunned silence. Brandon flew at William, and the two of them crashed to the floor. Brandon threw a punch in William's face, another to his stomach. William grunted and stumbled to regain his footing, raising his hands. Fists thudded against flesh. William flung a chair at Brandon, and Brandon heaved himself out of its path by knocking over Richard.

"Goddamn you! Get out of my house!" Brandon yelled. A

desperate scramble of feet. Doors pulled open, slammed closed. Brandon's laboured breathing filled the otherwise silent room.

"Justine." Brandon stood before her, his eyes fierce, his body bent to the side. "Explain this."

She wiped at the wetness on her cheeks. "Which part?"

A bitter laugh tore from him. "Ah now, that is certainly rich."

She picked his cane up from the floor and placed it on the sofa. "It's true. We are married. Richard has the certificate to prove it." She straightened a chair, picked up cushions from the floor.

"For God's sake, leave it!"

"There are no servants here anymore, Brandon. Only Molly, and she can only do so much." She shoved the cushions back on the settee one after the other.

"Why? Where are they?"

"William fired them all. No 'unnecessary expenditures' he said."

"Of course, my uncle and cousin had you to do their bidding?"

"I do what I can." She pushed the winged armchair in its proper place.

"I'm sure you do." Brandon planted his hands on the sideboard and took in a deep breath.

"They forced me into this marriage, Brandon. I had nothing to do with their deception. I've brought you back to fight them. You must believe me."

"I cannot believe all that father had is gone!" He pounded his fist on the wood. His eyes darted over the faded brocade drapes, the scratched table in between the four worn armchairs and the tired settee, and the empty, smudged wall where three small paintings used to hang. The peeling plaster trimming the decorative ceiling was an eyesore. Only the larger sofa, and the Persian carpet on the floor still looked respectable.

"Abandoned and forgotten," he said. "Their lust knows no

bounds. And you let them do it, didn't you? You helped them." She didn't answer. "How did you agree to this marriage farce, Justine? Why?" His voice was laced with disappointment and that stung.

She took in a deep breath. "Over the past several years, your uncle has become somewhat eccentric and unstable, and William has never been agreeable or obliging. As you know, I have no other family. I have nowhere else to go.

"After your father passed away, they had decided on a husband for me, an older man, much older. They were preparing for the engagement, but then they discovered you were alive, in hospital, sunk into oblivion. They then decided that my marrying you was a better course of action, that I would be more useful to them this way because they would gain control of the estate. William wanted control."

He only nodded and poured himself another drink, gulping it down. "And he married Amanda? How the hell did that happen?"

"He is persistent. He wooed her for some time after you had left for Jamaica, and one day she agreed. They live at Crestdown with her father and brother." Justine chewed on her lower lip. "I do not know more than that. I do not see them, and Amanda and I were never close."

"Obviously neither were she and I." He brushed a hand down his face. "And what do you get out of this, Justine?"

"Pardon?"

"You heard me, answer the question." His face was immobile, her insides tightened under the harshness of his glare.

"You think I wanted this? To be forced to marry you in order to let them steal from you and Wolfsgate?"

"How much did they promise you? What is it you want of me? My name? My title? What?"

"You don't believe me then? That they forced me?"

"Why should I? You are their pawn. As my wife you gave them access to my inheritance."

Justine's skin prickled. All the stress and fatigue of the last months strangled her every nerve. She never imagined Brandon would believe the worst of her.

He raised his glass at her. "Well done, Lady Graven."

The blood roared in her head, and something snapped inside her. "Indeed. I am living the high life here at Wolfsgate. Not a care in the world. Fancy frocks, servants, parties, and this magnificent estate to show off and call my own."

"Enough!" His pale green eyes flashed at her.

"I am not profiting from this arrangement, Brandon." She planted her hands on her hips. "I didn't want this for you or for me, but I had no choice."

Brandon's weary eyes shifted over her, darted around the room like a caged animal desperate for an escape route. His right hand shook slightly. That needy compulsion gnawed at him.

Justine poured him a glass of brandy. She raised the glass in his direction, and he took it from her. He gulped the liquor, his dull eyes never leaving hers. "Another," he muttered, his voice flat. She took the glass, filled it halfway and returned it to his shaking hand.

He drained it then leaned closer, his warm breath fanning her cheek, the fumes of the liquor between them. "Why shouldn't I just turn you out the door, eh? This very minute." His lips hung open as if they would bare his teeth at any moment.

She held her breath. "You could."

He cocked an eyebrow. "Yes, I could."

"But, frankly, I'm all you have at present."

Brandon's chin shot up. "Who says I need anyone?"

"Look at you."

His jaw stiffened. He drew himself up and held the glass out to her. "Another." She poured only a little in his glass and handed it back to him. "If all is as you say, we make the perfect pair." He saluted her with his glass. "To us then, Justine—the manipulated, the tossed off, the rejected." He drank, then held the glass out to her. "I think you had better have some yourself. You are going to need it, wife."

She took the brandy from him, her cold fingers brushing his warm ones. She swallowed what was left in one go, because she knew what he was thinking.

The inevitable.

Would he use *that* as punishment? His eyes glittered over her, and a shiver raced down her spine. He was considering the possibilities, wasn't he?

"I wanted to wait and explain everything to you once you were more yourself, but—"

"I am no longer myself," he breathed.

"There's more you need to know."

"More? God no, not now." His mouth twisted in a grimace. "Leave it. I've heard enough for one night. Tomorrow is sure to come, and it won't change anything, will it?" He threw himself into the nearest armchair, let out a sigh and rubbed his eyes.

"Brandon, please. You must hear—"

"Go, dammit." He sighed heavily. "Leave me the hell alone."

CHAPTER SIX

EVENING CAME, but Justine was in no mood for sleep. She hadn't even changed into her night clothes, only managed to release her hair from the pins that held it, tugging her fingers through the thick mass as she chewed on a thousand anxieties. It had all gone badly, very wrong. What had she expected though? She had to focus on the fact that she did manage to get Brandon out of that hospital, helped him get his strength back, and now he could take his place as rightful heir of Wolfsgate.

She shook her head at the memory of the wild look in Brandon's eyes when learning of their forced marriage and of Amanda's marriage to William. His desolation at the news of his father's death had been brutal to witness, and a nagging fear that he would do something extreme ate at her insides.

The front door slammed, and Justine darted to the window. Brandon marched across the front lawn toward the stables, his hair whipping about his face, his cloak flying behind him.

"No, no, no!" her voice drummed against the thick glass. She knew where he was headed. She was sure of it.

Justine flew down the stairs, fastened on her boots, threw on her cloak, and ran out the door toward the stables, but she was too late. The pummeling of horse's hooves rumbled in the distance.

"Brandon! Wait!" But the dark figure on the horse took no notice of her as he bolted into the night. He had to be headed for Crestdown, Amanda's family home where she and William resided.

She had to go after him.

Justine ran to the stables and saddled her horse. Her cold fingers pulled and secured the leather straps over the animal in the dark. Thank God she had realized from very early on that being self-sufficient was paramount to survival at Wolfsgate. Several years ago she had hired Martin, a young tenant from nearby, to tend to the horses, teach her to ride properly, and show her how to deal with a saddle. She finally felt confident on a horse thanks to his instruction and encouragement and plenty of practice on her own.

She mounted her mare and urged the horse onwards. She quickly cleared the pathway through the thick dark woods and then the maze of trees that circled Crestdown's park. Justine's straining eyes finally caught sight of the rider and his powerful horse charging ahead of her. She urged her horse forward faster. She didn't want the inhabitants of the house to hear them and come outside. She had to get to Brandon before he stormed the front door or worse.

Crestdown was a much grander, polished, and more modern structure than Wolfsgate, which was modest in comparison. But then again, Wolfsgate was almost two hundred years older and had been built by a Graven ancestor with only a few renovations over the years.

Justine slowed down her horse, slid down off the saddle, and tied her reins to the nearest tree. A rush of pure energy pumped through her, making her more determined with every quick step to get Brandon out of there.

Light glowed from a high window at the ground floor and the

heavy drapes were partly open. She stole a glance up into the house. William and Amanda stood by their fireplace talking. She wore a dark dressing gown, her long golden hair spilling over her shoulders. William leaned close to his wife's side and whispered in her ear. Amanda laughed. He grinned at her and planted kisses against her throat.

Brandon emerged from behind a tree and stood watching them. She ran to him.

"Brandon!" she whispered. He didn't seem to notice her. His demeanor was forbidding, but it didn't stop her from wrapping her hand around his taut bicep. A haze of misty rain shrouded over them.

"Come away, Brandon. Don't do this."

"The bastard."

Justine returned her gaze to the window. William folded Amanda in his embrace, and her neck arched up as she laughed once again. Brandon's arm shook in Justine's tight grip.

"I had to see it for myself," his voice rasped.

"She thought you were dead. We all did. Had you been engaged to marry?"

"No, but 'tis no matter any longer."

"It matters to you."

The rain drops began to fall heavier, fatter, faster. Brandon's jaw clenched, his wet hair matted against his face. "He probably knew I was alive all along."

"No, Brandon, we were told you were dead. William grieved for you. It was a few months later that he found out you were alive, and then the lies and deception began."

He said nothing but continued to stare at William and Amanda. The rain's persistent beating on the leaves and the grass pounded in Justine's ears. Icy coldness seeped through her veins. She had to get him to leave here before they were seen. More importantly, before Brandon sank further into a pit of black humour or rage.

His face was ashen. "This is the life I would have had, isn't it? This is what was expected of us: the comforts of a fine house, a fitting spouse, a child? This is what our parents planned for all of us." His gaze fell to the ground, his scars glistening in the rain. "And what home do I have now, Justine?" His voice was rougher now. "An empty shell of an estate. No father. A wife I had no knowledge of borne from a girl I no longer seem to know. And what family I do have left is stealing from me and plotting my demise." His chest expanded as he took in air. "All in ruins, all of it. I will destroy William. I swear it."

"He's not worth the effort." Her fingers clutched at his wet cloak.

"Why not? He's stolen everything from me."

"No, he hasn't. You have Wolfsgate. Hurting William won't bring back Lord Jeremy or time lost or your full health. I beg you, Brandon. Do not take rash action."

"Do you think I cannot take on William?"

"I have no doubts on that score, but I would not want you to get hurt in any way. Get stronger, bring the estate back to its full strength—that alone will destroy his pride. That is your best course of revenge."

"You must be an expert of all things William by now." Brandon smashed his lips together and returned his gaze to the window. "I want to make him suffer."

Justine's heart thudded in her chest. "Please, let's go back to the house. *Your* house."

"It's odd how all this feels foreign to me."

"What do you mean?"

"Society, relations, home." His head tilted back, and he exhaled heavily, his wet hair in slick locks around his temple. "I'm flailing in the dark here, licking my wounds like some pathetic animal. Yet it's absurd, for I can't even make sense of what it is I'm feeling." His aching voice trailed off in the cold, humid air.

"Loss?" she asked settling her hands on his trembling chest.

Brandon nodded. "You, too, know loss well." His eyes were heavy, his cold fingers tightened around hers.

She squeezed his hand. "I do, and I can tell you it will probably hurt for a long while yet. But you're alive Brandon, and you're healing. You must give yourself time."

"He took time from me! Time I will never have back."

Justine leaned into him. "Yes, he did. So better for you to get stronger and claim your rightful place at Wolfsgate. I shall help you."

"You cannot help me." He released her hands from his grip. "You should stay away from me, for I am full of poison, always will be."

"No, you aren't. That's over now, Brandon. That poison is out of your system. You are in control of your life again."

"It will always control me, Justine. I can feel the need for it blistering inside my veins right now. But it's not just the opium." His fierce eyes pierced hers, and the tangle in her stomach twisted into a knot. "You shouldn't look to me for anything." His voice was rough, low.

Brandon's severe, dark face took her breath away. It brought to mind the ghostly tales William would tell them as children of the lone black wolf who allegedly lived in the woods surrounding Wolfsgate, howling his despair into the winds of every storm. The last black wolf remaining in England was cursed to haunt the Traherne family forever.

Brandon's ancestors had been given their lands and title by a Norman king in the twelfth century as a reward for hunting and killing as many wolves as possible. Here, in the nearby forests which bordered Wales, the wolves had been quite numerous and were a constant threat to livestock and travelers. The fearsome creatures even desecrated graves. Over the years, the Trahernes proved themselves to be worthy hunters. By King Edward I's reign in the thirteenth century the order for the animal's total extermination had been given, and over a hundred years later, they had become practically extinct.

William had always enjoyed telling the ominous family legend. Over the centuries, the spirit of one lone wolf had remained trapped in the woods which surrounded Wolfsgate and would appear on moonlit nights howling for his revenge on the Trahernes. No matter how many times it was told, they had always been completely absorbed by the tale. Listening to it would make Brandon unusually quiet and Justine melancholy. Only Annie, William's sister and Justine's stepsister, would roll her eyes and giggle.

Justine blinked. Here he was before her; her tragic, howling, lone wolf.

"I have nothing to give you." Brandon's long fingers gripped her face, his nostrils flared. "Not like any normal husband should."

She covered his hands with hers. If only it were as simple to comfort him now as it was when he was overwhelmed with fever or chills during those first days, and she had held him in bed keeping him warm. But it wasn't simple. Now, he'd probably only push her away. It wasn't her he wanted anyway. Wasn't Amanda what had brought him to Crestdown in the middle of the night in the rain?

"There is nothing normal about this entire situation, now is there?" she asked.

"Why the hell did you bring me back?" The words wrenched from him.

"Because you are alive and you are the heir of Wolfsgate. God's blood, it was the right thing to do."

"And what do you want from me? How is my return good for you?" Brandon's jaw tightened. "Now you are saddled with a deranged, deformed husband. There has to be a reason you risked their wrath. Tell me."

"You're not deranged and deformed!" Her voice scraped from her aching throat. "Oh please, let's go."

His fingers gripped her arm. "Tell me."

"To be free of them once and for all," she whispered in the darkness against the pattering of the raindrops falling harder, faster. "I can bear no more." The tension in her upper back and shoulders suddenly released. It felt good to say those words out loud at long last to someone who actually understood. Brandon closed his eyes for a moment. His hand slid up to the side of her face, and she leaned into his touch. He pulled her cloak tighter around her shoulders, his gaze flickering down her body.

"You're cold and wet," he murmured.

"As are you."

His lips twitched, his thumb stroked her cheek. "Did you saddle your own horse and follow me all the way here?" She only nodded, her teeth clenching against the frigid air. His cool hands smoothed the wet locks of hair from her face, and she let her head fall back slightly, letting out a sigh. "You mean to tell me that the girl who was once so afraid of horses can now saddle one on her own and ride in the dark of night?" Justine only grinned at him. "Christ! You *have* grown up and changed. Not too much though, I hope." His voice had lowered, and a soft, searching look passed over his eyes for a moment. "Come on then." He tugged on her hand and led her toward his horse. Her hand tingled within his grip. "Ride with me, we're both too cold to go it alone."

"You must be exhausted."

"All of today's excitement provided me with a natural delirium, not to mention the artificial delirium that is my norm. Although I can feel it draining through me now. Go, bring your horse."

She brought her mare over to where he stood with his animal. She opened her mouth to protest, but he swiftly lifted her up into his saddle, and then his solid frame was at her back. His arms stretched around her, his hands firmly on the reins. He leaned over and took hold of her horse's reins, and they rode away from Crestdown in silence. Justine's muscles tightened as she tried to hold onto the pommel without falling back onto his chest or risk falling off the horse altogether and landing in the mud.

"Lean into me." Brandon's lips brushed against her ear, his deep voice rumbling through her. Heat fanned her face as she adjusted herself and eased back slightly against him, his long legs pressed against hers. Brandon dipped his chin close to her face. "Justine." Her breath hitched at the teasing tone of his voice. She leaned her weight more fully into him, finally relaxing her muscles and nestling into the heat of his chest. The aroma of the liquor on his breath mingled with the very masculine scent of his sweat and the wet leather from the reins in his hands. She breathed it in.

Is that what comfort and safety felt like?

Their horses steadily made their way towards home in the wet blackness. Justine wasn't sure if she'd prefer the ride to end quickly or not at all.

CHAPTER SEVEN

"ARE YOU FEELING ALL RIGHT, MA'AM?"

"Fine, Molly. Nothing another cup of tea won't cure." Justine pulled her shawl tighter around her shoulders against the morning chill and sank back in the old chair at the large servants' table in the centre of the kitchen, staring at the steam rising from her cup. Molly bent over the breakfast tray she prepared for Brandon. She had been in service at the estate since Brandon had been a boy. After William had fired all the servants, Molly had shuffled about the large, empty manor house on her own, dusting and arranging where she was able and cooking meals with Justine's assistance. Justine couldn't imagine Wolfsgate without her.

Justine and Brandon had been soaked through by the time they had returned home last night. Brandon had insisted she go into the house and get warm and dry while he took care of the horses, but she had refused. They had taken care of the horses together, then ran back to the house in the driving rain hand in hand.

Once inside she had tried to help him change, but he had

barked at her to leave him be, stripping off all his clothes right there in the hall to underscore his point. Justine had bolted up the stairs to her room and he'd remained in the parlor.

She swallowed more tea and stared at the fire roaring in the kitchen hearth. She knew that as the official Lady of the house she should be sitting in the formal dining room having her breakfast along with the Lord of said house, but she couldn't bring herself to break familiar habits. At least not yet. The informal kitchen was warm, cozy and safe to her.

William and Richard had liked the fact that she had stopped joining them for most meals. They had rarely deigned to step foot in the kitchen, so it had become her retreat over the years, and she found she actually enjoyed helping Molly with the household chores. She had learned a variety of new things about managing a house under her tutelage and could even bake bread herself. Justine smirked at the thought of her mother's certain horror at such a scene.

Brandon had spent the night in the parlour. At one point she'd heard him walking about, cursing, breaking glass, then silence. She had gone to her door, but she stopped herself from opening it. He needed to be alone, and the last thing she wanted to do was to pressure him in any way. So she climbed back into her bed. He was grieving the loss of his father on top of coping with all the lies and betrayals by members of his own family.

Today would be a new opportunity, a new start between them, wouldn't it? However, she had to brace herself for more of his bitterness and mistrust.

"Why did you not tell me? Why did you hide it from me?"

The pain in his eyes when he learned of his father's death haunted her still. Justine did not want to have to hide anything from him.

"There you are!" Richard's thin raspy voice cut through her musings. "Where have you been, Lady of the Manor?" Her stepfather's bony finger poked at her shoulder, his body wavered, and his eyes were red. "I can't get a decent meal in this house now that your husband is home? When I call you, I expect you to come at once. Imagine, I had to come after you in the kitchen of all places."

"There are more important things that need attending to today than your stomach, sir," she said.

"Ah, looking after your Lord and Master, are ye? Giving your husband special attention? You best think of something fast, sweet pea, something more elaborate than a breakfast tray, before he throws you out the door. Like what's between your legs, eh?" Richard laughed.

Justine's face heated, and she turned her face away from the sour smell of his breath.

"Ah, what's this? Tsk, tsk. Was it not to your liking?" He let out another shriek of laughter. "Or was there no wedding night still after all this time? Not up for the task, was he?" Richard cackled in her ear. The old familiar pressure closed in on her lungs and the bile rose in the back of her throat. He pinched her shoulder and her body flinched. "You're a married woman now. You have responsibilities."

"Leave her alone, old man," a deep voice boomed through the kitchen.

Justine's eyes widened. Brandon stood in the doorway, his face stony, his body rigid. Richard cowered a few steps back and stumbled on his dressing gown.

"Ah, there is the fortunate bridegroom," Richard said. "Not satisfied, eh my boy? Come for breakfast, have you?" Richard tittered and flopped his hand back in Justine's direction, losing his balance. He gripped a chair to steady himself. "Here's your wife, ready and willing."

Brandon's eyes blazed, and he didn't move a muscle, yet the room filled with his anger. "I want you out of my house, Uncle. I will have you delivered to your son within the hour, so pack your belongings. Do you understand me?"

Molly and Justine shared a quick glance.

"What?" Richard spluttered through rubbery lips, studying Brandon as if he remembered finally who his nephew was.

"And I want that marriage document before you go, do you hear?"

"Oh. That." Richard's eyes sunk into his face once more.

"Molly, take my uncle to his room, help him pack up his belongings as he is leaving us today," said Brandon. "And get the marriage certificate from him."

"Yes, sir." Molly nodded at her master, a slight smile etched on her face. She took Richard by the arm and scooted him out of the kitchen.

Brandon's sober gaze fell on Justine. Steam rose from her every pore. "Are you all right?" he asked, his voice gentle.

She nodded, a hand going to her throat. "T'was nothing."

"T'was ugly." He studied her, but she turned her burning face away from him. He let out a heavy sigh. "Have no fear. The true Master of Wolfsgate has returned, and everything is changing for the better."

A small smile lit her face. "And so it is."

"Such faith." Brandon ran his fingers through his unkempt hair.

Justine went to the side table. "Molly just prepared this tray for you. I'll bring it into the dining room."

"I don't want anything." He straightened himself up and leaned on his cane again. "Bring me the marriage document and please arrange for Uncle Richard to be taken to William's." He turned and left the room.

Justine deposited the tray back on the table. This was going to be difficult.

Over an hour later Richard left in a clamor of shouting and whining protestations. Justine heaved a sigh of relief the moment

Martin picked up the reins of the old carriage loaded with Richard's trunks and led the horses and Richard away from the house. She could only imagine the scene that would take place at Amanda and William's house upon Richard's surprise arrival. She truly hoped Amanda enjoyed her father-in-law's singular company.

She leaned her forehead against the cool pane of leaded glass. Her stepfather and stepbrother no longer had any control over her. Brandon was reviewing their marriage document this very moment confirming its legitimacy. She had to speak with him. She quit her room and went down the long stone staircase.

Justine held her breath as she knocked on the parlour door. No response. She pushed it open slowly. The marriage document lay on the worn settee, and Brandon was slumped in the large seat of the bay window which faced his mother's rose garden. His eyes were closed, his legs stretched out before him. The brocade curtains were open and warm light streamed over his figure. His shirt was untied at the neck and untucked from his breeches. The long, sturdy column of his throat glistened with perspiration.

The room was stifling. Justine leaned over him, raised herself on her toes, and unhitched the latch, pushing open the casement window. A gust of fresh air washed over her. Brandon's eyes flashed open. He glared at her, his lips set into a firm line.

"You need fresh air," she said quietly. "Richard's just left."

He grabbed her arm pulling her towards him, and her hand instinctively flew out landing on his knee to keep herself from falling on him. He clasped her fingers, his eyes smoldering over her. "Where's your wedding ring now, Lady Graven?"

"I-I used my mother's old ring for the trip to London."

"What a fine masquerade," he muttered. Brandon released her and she stumbled back. He jerked his head toward the window glaring at the roses, the coloured shrubbery, and hedges that created the serpentine walk. His head fell back against the wood panelling, the lines of his face tightening. He was angry.

Angry they were married, angry he had been cheated out of so much.

Angry at her.

Justine slipped from the room and closed the door behind her.

CHAPTER EIGHT

JUSTINE DIDN'T SEE BRANDON AGAIN FOR TWO DAYS. She had Molly check on him and leave him trays of food, but they would be left mostly untouched. He did, however, order her to fetch him more liquor.

"So be it," she muttered to herself as she packed away another empty brandy bottle in the kitchen. He was so very stubborn and wallowing in self-pity which she could most certainly understand. But what gnawed at her was that he likely wouldn't be able to survive this emotional mire without desiring the opium once more. All this liquor was certainly not helping.

Justine wiped her hands on her long apron which she wore over her oldest dimity skirts. Today she planned on tackling the kitchen garden which she had abandoned for her trip to London and its aftermath. She went through the back door of the kitchen and surveyed the overgrown, wild stringy mess. The reedy weeds seemed to mock her as they shook in the breeze. She wrapped her thick, wavy hair in her large kerchief keeping it out of her way and grabbed her shovel digging into the ground determined to do battle with the tenacious roots. She shoveled, hoed and pulled at the offending weeds until the entire garden was clear.

Hours later Justine was tired and sore, but she knew it hadn't really helped. She didn't feel that pleasure of accomplishment as she usually did when doing such work. She arranged her tools on the side of the low garden wall, and wiped the perspiration from her brow. It was quite warm today. and now it was hours past midday. The only thing she wanted to do was have a quick swim in the creek. She marched off through the stone archway to the rose garden and onto the serpentine walk.

Much ahead of her time, Brandon's mother, Lady Caroline had eschewed the organised linear gardens of her day in favour of a more natural and spontaneous landscape for Wolfsgate. She had created a unique, unstudied world beginning with the shady and intriguing serpentine walkway bursting with borders of luxurious rose blossoms, pale pink begonias, scarlet dahlias, dusky pink and purple riots of hydrangeas. In the summer sweeps of lavender and large-leafed greenery ran into taller flowering shrubs and hanging trees.

Even though this exuberant, impetuous garden had not seen a proper gardener's care in quite some time, Justine did her best to prune and trim, but she liked the organised chaos. It had a kind of rough, sumptuous magic all its own. This lush, sheltered walk remained a sensual pleasure of a different kind of beauty— vivid and dramatic, wild and unsorted. Meandering on this walkway was a meditative release and delightful restorative unlike any other.

The stone walkway led directly to Lady Caroline's folly, but Justine turned right onto another well-worn path for the creek. Ten minutes later she reached the water with a loose smile on her face, her body relaxed. She unfastened her kerchief, released her hair, and removed her corset and soiled skirts, leaving on her thin chemise. She entered the cold water and sighed deeply as it wrapped around her ankles, her calves, her thighs. She plunged in.

Justine swam to the opposite shore and back. She floated on

the surface with her eyes closed, her hands paddling aimlessly through the cool water, soaking in the golden warmth of the sun on her skin. The breeze murmured through the leafy trees overhead.

A forceful splash of water crashed next to her, and Justine flinched, wiping at her eyes. Brandon. His slick, wet hair, bare shoulders and contoured back gleamed in the golden light.

"Oh. Brandon." She swallowed hard and immediately submerged herself lower in the water. "H-How are you feeling?"

He let out a groan. "At this very moment, much better, however long that lasts." He wiped the water from his face. "I was suffocating in the house. My head ached. I went outside and saw you walking this way through the woods. I figured it must be to come here. My head is so muddled, it's no wonder I hadn't thought of it myself."

They paddled around each other in the water, his pale green eyes never leaving hers, his thick, black lashes glistening with drops of water. Justine dipped lower under the surface of the water.

"Do you often work in the garden?" he asked.

A flutter went off in her belly at the thought that he had been watching her. "I enjoy it. I've managed to grow quite a few herbs and vegetables over the years, mostly by trial and error."

"Did Richard and William appreciate your efforts?"

"Oh, I don't think they even noticed. It served to keep me out of their way though, more than anything. That, I am sure they appreciated. Have you seen Lady Caroline's roses? They are still thriving."

"Yes, I saw them." A smile wafted across his lips at the mention of his mother, then faded just as quickly.

Justine twisted away from his heavy gaze and dove under the water. She came up and Brandon stood perfectly still, his gaze fixed on the rocks where years ago his cousin and her stepsister, Annie, only fourteen years old at the time, had met her death.

They were all so much younger then and under the canopy of what they had considered to be a family.

"It seems like a hundred years ago, I swear," his hoarse voice broke the eerie silence. A shadow crossed his features, his mouth downturned.

"Yes, it does," she said softly. "You did everything possible to save her."

He rubbed at his chest. "That is at the root of all of this, isn't it? His sister's death at my hands secured William's anger toward me forever."

"Annie was already dead when you got here, Brandon. Stuck in the rocks, taken under in the floodwaters." Justine chewed her lip. "And anyway, we all know I was to blame."

"Justine!"

"It's true, isn't it? I knew she wanted to go see the frogs in the middle of the night, and she had sworn me to secrecy. We were to go together, but I had fallen asleep, so she went on her own. I woke up, her bed was empty, and I just knew. I was too terrified to go to Richard or to William."

"You came to me," Brandon said, his voice low.

"Yes. Somehow I found the nerve to go to your chamber and wake you, tell you that she was missing and most likely at the creek. You took off immediately, we barely got your boots on you. I shall never forget standing in the pouring rain on the front steps watching you fly off down the muddy hill. I shall never forget it."

"But I was too late."

"If only I hadn't fallen asleep, or if I'd woken up earlier, or hadn't tarried in coming to you."

"Stop it, Justine." He swam closer to her, his brow furrowed. "Annie was quite impetuous. She was a smart girl, but so damned impulsive. Even if you had been awake, you couldn't have stopped her. I warrant she would have had you out here in the floodwaters with her. We would have lost you as well, but thank Providence you're here." His heavy gaze held hers. "I couldn't get her loose no matter what I did. Her foot had gotten stuck between those two bloody boulders, her dress had twisted around her, pulling her down like a lead weight."

"Brandon..." She laid her hand on his bare arm.

"I will never forget finding her face down in the rushing water, bobbing like a lifeless object." His wet hand quickly covered hers, gripping it tightly. "Our very own Ophelia."

She released her hold on his arm. "Annie was no Ophelia. There was not a sullen or gloomy bone in her body. She was a good soul. From the moment I'd entered their house upon my mother's marriage to Richard, she never once showed me any resentment or wickedness. Ever," Justine breathed. "From the very first, she treated me as a true sister. Annie was my best friend, and I will never forget her. Her death changed everything for me, even more so than my own mother's passing."

What had come over her? She'd never said these words aloud before, not to anyone. Not even to herself.

CHAPTER NINE

A TWINGE ACHED in the hollow of Brandon's chest. After Annie's death, everything had indeed changed in their house, just as it had when his mother had died a few years before that. It was as if that same noose had tightened around them all once more.

Justine, who had always been a smiling, affectionate young girl, had suddenly transformed into a shy and withdrawn creature who rarely laughed in the forthright way she always had.

Justine's mother had passed away the year before Annie's sudden death, and after that Justine spent most of her time with her governess rather than with Brandon and William. On occasion, Amanda's younger brother Andrew would draw her out, but it was generally frowned upon.

William had grown cold and churlish after the shocking loss of his beloved sister. After that, he never had a kind word for Justine and wouldn't allow her to play with their circle of friends. It was then that Uncle Richard began a slow degeneration into his own strange world.

Thereafter, Uncle Richard barely registered Justine's presence and often left her on her own at Wolfsgate, relinquishing responsibility of her under the pretense of the country being a better place for her to grow up. Richard and William would spend many months at a time in London on their own enjoying society and its entertainments. They would return to the country whenever it pleased them, which was seldom, and Justine would only accompany them to town on rare occasions. Brandon winced at the memory.

He had left England then and gone on his tour of Venice, Rome, and Florence with his good friend, Charles, and Justine had stayed on at Wolfsgate with only his father and her governess for company.

"Brandon, do you remember when Annie and I found you and William here swimming, and you wouldn't let us swim with you?" Justine's voice was light, her face upturned, her eyes relaxed. "It was so very hot that day, and we were desperate for a swim."

"Yes, I do." The edges of Brandon's mouth curled up. "Annie got quite annoyed, and you both took our clothes. You saw us naked." He let out a loud laugh. It felt good to remember a summer afternoon when children's pranks and swimming in a cool creek were their only cares. "Ah, the look on both your faces!

"I was frozen to the spot, I couldn't move." Justine's unfettered laughter rang out over the surface of the water, and an unfamiliar warmth spiraled in his chest. "William was so angry with us— yelling and carrying on, all the while completely forgetting he stood there before us without a stitch on him!"

"Annie only made faces at him."

"Yes, she did, then she threw all your clothes in the water, grabbed my hand, and we ran all the way home. Laughing, laughing..."

"Such silly girls." He splashed water at her.

"Oh!" Justine splashed him back. He splashed her again, moving closer towards her. Justine let out a squeal and smashed her hand through the water in his direction. "Brandon! Stop it!"

"You stop! Or I will have to resort to extreme measures."

She only laughed harder, and he launched toward her. His hands gripped her shoulders, and she turned to twist out of his grasp, but only twisted deeper into his body. She shoved at him, but her hands slipped against the wet skin of his bare chest. He held her fast, and she bit her lower lip. His gaze fell on her mouth inches away from his own, then it dropped lower.

Her wet bosom was plainly obvious through the sheer wet fabric of her chemise which now clung to her body. His nerve endings lit up like a flame, and he broke away from her, diving under the cool water. Within moments, he came back up for air, but Justine was no longer in the water. She now stood on the shore by their pile of clothing.

"Justine? Are you leaving?"

She turned to answer him, and his eyes flared. She instantly blushed, realizing too late that her naked body was visible to him under her soaked chemise. Softly cursing under her breath, she quickly turned, offering him a full view of her rear. His pulse ticked harder, faster.

"I'm cold." She snatched up her skirts and got into them, then wrapped her corset around her torso, quickly fixing the stays. She tucked and smoothed the clingy, damp fabric around her fetching body.

Brandon floated on his back on the water as he enjoyed the view of his wife. He took in her full breasts, her shapely bottom, the curve of her hips. Justine was no longer a girl. She had grown into a woman. A very desirable woman.

His body tightened, his hand smoothing over his hardened cock. It had been a long time since he had been aware of that particular reflex and was pleasantly surprised by it. In fact, that distinct burn now flared all through him. Maybe it was one of his body's strange new reactions to having been finally drained of the opium. Maybe it was all this rejuvenation and fresh country air.

Maybe it was simply Justine.

Brandon got out of the water. She was hunched over on the

ground buttoning her boots. He tossed his head and squeezed the excess water from his hair, knowing the cool drops would fall on her.

Justine blinked up at him. "I should go. Molly may need my help. I didn't tell her I was coming here." She stood up and scrambled away from him.

"Wait for me. I'll come with you." His body quaked with silent laughter at his bride's obvious discomposure over his nakedness. "Could you hand me my shirt, Justine?"

She darted to his mound of clothes, and, averting her gaze, handed him his shirt. She was nervous, and he liked that. He could take advantage of it. No, he still didn't trust her motives.

Although he had known Justine since she was a child, the last time he had spent any time with her she had been a girl of maybe fifteen or sixteen years. She was a woman of twenty now, having lived with William and Richard. Surely, a different person. How could he be certain of her true character? How could he be certain of her role in William and Richard's plot that had entwined him?

Justine peeked over her shoulder at him. "I thought perhaps you might like to visit your father's grave. May I take you there tomorrow morning?"

He pulled up his boots, his eyes remaining on her. "Yes."

She smiled. "Good."

He stood up, and his ankles wobbled, his body swayed. His hand shot out to grab the tree trunk near him. Justine was next to him in seconds, her arm around his waist. His wet hair splattered her face and neck with water as her body pressed against his.

She placed a warm hand on his chest. "What is it?"

"Dizzy...I don't know." He grimaced. "Too much bloody excitement, I suppose. And that damned knee again."

"Do you want to sit?"

"No, no, I don't think I'd be able to stand up again. Let's walk slowly." He tucked his free hand around her shoulder and pulled her closer. The warmth of her body seared him to her side. She waited as he took a few more deep breaths. Maybe his pulse would ease, and he could go back to feeling normal again.

No, normal was most certainly over.

"Better?" she asked. He didn't answer. His muscles remained tense. "You don't have to be embarrassed with me, Brandon." Her voice had softened. "I saw you in that hospital. I know what you've been through, and I know the effort this is taking. It will be some time before you will be fully strong again."

His gaze slid to her face. Her head was tilted back, there was a gleam in her velvety brown eyes. Was that hope? Confidence? Did this girl ever waver in her belief that all would be well?

"Ready?"

He clasped her hand on his chest in reply. They walked slowly, his breathing laboured, his limp pronounced.

"When we get home, you will eat something, even if I have to feed you myself, do you hear, my Lord?"

"Stop bothering me about bloody food," he said through clenched teeth.

"You cannot heal completely without sustenance. God knows what evil swill they fed you at that hospital, and you wasted away. And your current diet of spirits will not do. It will only set you back."

"You take your role as the overbearing wife most seriously, Lady Graven."

"I'm not overbearing!" Her eyes searched his. "Am I?

He let out a chuckle and squeezed her shoulder. "I'm teasing you. I forgot how easy it was to tease you, and how much I enjoyed it."

"I don't mean to irritate you, Brandon. I'm only concerned for your well-being."

"I'll eat something, I promise. Do stop talking though, my head is doing me in." His arm trembled around her body, and he tightened his grip on her flesh. He was uncomfortable again, rattled and unnerved. The aftereffects of the opiate still poured over him in waves every so often. Would this damned torture ever end?

Once home, Justine settled him in the armchair in the parlour and brought him a change of clothes. She crouched before him and removed his boots, then stood over him to remove his shirt.

He scowled, pushing away her hands. "I can do this myself. I'm a grown man, you know." He stretched to remove the shirt, but sparks of pain raced over his muscles and he grimaced. He cursed, his arms falling back down to his sides.

Justine's lips set firmly together. "Who do you think helped Davidson change and bathe you when we got you out of hospital? I did. Don't fight me, let me help you."

He was exhausted, and her touching him would feel bloody good, wouldn't it?

Oh, let her play nursemaid.

He uncurled his fingers from his shirt, and she quickly peeled the wet fabric off his torso, then wrapped a thin cotton blanket over his cool skin, rubbing him with it. Their faces were inches away from each other. Her short breaths fanned his chest. That heat swirled in his veins again.

"You should change too," he murmured.

"I will, after. Now let's get on with it."

His jaw tensed as he searched her unsmiling eyes. She was so soft one moment, almost fragile, as if she could break in your very hands. Then she transformed into a determined and reso- lute worker.

Justine's fingers undid the fastenings at his breeches. He lifted his eyebrows. Well, no sign of the blushing virgin bride here. His flesh prickled with heat, and he pushed her fingers away, raised his hips and lowered the wet breeches himself, then sank down onto the seat again, and she yanked them the rest of the way down his legs. He covered himself with the blanket, and she rubbed it over his legs and feet without removing it from him. She was all smart efficiency now. His young bride's hesitant touch and violent blushing were gone.

She put the clean nightshirt over his head as he sat, his face level with her chest. His pulse thudded in his neck as he took in the golden colour of her skin dotted with freckles, the curves of her full breasts straining against the wet material of her dress. He had a savage urge to bury his face in those round, firm globes of flesh. He shut his eyes in a small attempt to gain control of himself, yet her scent filled his nostrils. Clean and fresh like dewy green woods in the morning. His cock stiffened, and he groaned inwardly.

He studied her as she folded his wet shirt and added it to the pile of his damp clothes on the floor. Wavy tendrils of her hair had fallen in wisps about her neck. A girl who enjoyed the outdoors and didn't care that she wasn't fashionably pale but kissed by the sun? Yes, he liked her raw brand of beauty.

He liked her.

For God's sake, this is Justine.

And so?

She wasn't his sister, nor his cousin; not a drop of familial blood between them. Only bonds of legality. She was his wife. He certainly could have plenty of unclean thoughts about Justine.

She stood before him again smoothing the sleeves of his nightshirt over his shoulders, her hands spreading their warmth down his arms. Then came the fine wool gown gliding down his torso and over his legs, and a very comfortable, warm sock on each foot.

"I feel like an old man." A rueful smile curled his lips.

One of her elegant eyebrows arched up. "You are most certainly not an old man, Brandon."

"Oh?" He had to make her blush again. Had to see that pink bloom across her gorgeous skin. "Do I please you?"

Her gaze darted up at him, and there it was. Warmth seeped

through him at the sight. Her face reddened, but she ignored the comment otherwise as she busied herself putting his arms through a dressing gown and tying the belt about his waist. He put his hands over hers as she finished with the belt. "Thank you, Justine."

"You're welcome," she murmured.

He brought her hands to his mouth and brushed them with his lips. Her eyes shone, but she averted her gaze. He released her hands. "Go take those wet clothes off and have Molly bring us her tasty supper."

She gave him a small smile and made her way up the stairs. "I will."

CHAPTER TEN

HIS SCREAMS WOKE HER. Desperate, wild.

"The mast! The mast is breaking!"

Justine dashed down the stairs in the dark, holding her night-dress close, almost tumbling down the last two steps, and charged into the parlour. Brandon thrashed on the floor from side to side, gulping for air, his features twisted in the moonlight which streamed through the partially opened curtains.

"Give me your hand...give me..." he choked, his every muscle straining, his back arched, the veins in his neck corded.

Justine bent over him and tried to take hold of his flailing arms. "Brandon!"

He fought her attempts to stop his movement and shoved her to the side. She placed a cool hand on his forehead. "Brandon, wake up. It's only a dream. Wake up!"

He shuddered and his shoulders fell back, his chest rising and falling rapidly. His eyebrows were deeply knit, his skin covered in a sheen of cold perspiration.

"Brandon, t'was just a dream, a bad dream." She wiped locks of damp hair from his scarred temple.

His eyes twitched opened, and he rubbed them with his

palms as he tried to focus on her in the darkness. "Justine?" he choked out through ragged breaths.

"Yes, Brandon, you're all right." She rubbed his arms. You were having a nightmare about the shipwreck, I think."

"God...yes," he stammered through short breaths. He pressed his eyes closed and reopened them. "Bloody hell, it was so real." He gulped in air, his head rolled to the side.

She darted to the kitchen and brought back a wet cloth and wiped his face with it. He moaned softly as she stroked his shoulders, neck and chest.

He pushed himself up and leaned against the settee. She wiped the curls of damp hair back from his face, and he pulled her down next to him. His arm wrapped around her tightly, and her oversized nightdress slipped off her shoulder. He slid his hand down over her ribs settling just under the swell of her breast for a moment then back up to her bare shoulder. His breath began to steady.

Hers was racing.

"I haven't thought about that night for a very long time. Images here and there, sounds, but not the whole of it."

Justine wrapped her arms around his trembling torso, her fingertips pressing into his damp flesh. "It must have been horrible," she breathed against his throat.

"Did many people survive, Justine? Did you ever hear?"

"Only a few." Her one hand roamed over his taut abdomen in an effort to soothe him. "The ship got caught in a storm and the crew lost control of her. It's truly a miracle that you survived, and finding you was another." She pressed herself deeper into him as the memories of those horrible days snaked through her.

The servants whispering and crying in the hallways; Molly bent over her kitchen table, her head in her hands, her bony body racked with sobs; Richard wandering around the house aimlessly gibbering to himself—everyone had stopped paying him any mind.

William had drunk himself into a stupor, planting himself in a chair in the centre of the drawing room and staring out the large main window the entire day. Justine had weaved around them all as if everything were happening in slow motion in a land of fantasy. She couldn't face Lord Jeremy bedridden in his room just then, none of them could, but she knew they expected her to do it.

Instead, she had run outside to escape from them, to escape from the suffocating hopelessness of death once more. She had run as fast as her legs could take her up and down the long hills until she had reached the sheep pasture. There she had screamed wildly to the fluffy clouds and the ridiculously tranquil blue sky. She had pulled at her hair and fallen to the grass, ripping clumps of earth and green out from the ground, kicking and crying. Martin had found her and listened to her laments and weeping until she had gotten herself under control, then taking her hand in his, he had walked her home. But the heaviness had remained in her heart and her soul.

All that was over now, wasn't it?

Justine's hand skimmed over the cool, smooth skin of Brandon's firm chest. "It's done, all that pain and grief is over. Thank God, you are alive and safe." She inhaled his warm scent at the base of his throat. His other arm snaked around her middle and stroked her side flooding her body with liquid heat. She shifted in his embrace, and Brandon's eyes glinted at hers in the moonlight. His hand wrapped around her neck tilting her head to the side, and her breath caught. His lips dragged against the delicate skin of her throat, and she jerked in his arms letting out a low whimper.

His mouth blazed a path over her cheek and took her parted lips, her body trembling in his hold. His fingertips dug into her flesh through the flimsy fabric of her nightdress as he swallowed her soft cry, his tongue delving deep inside her mouth. She stiffened at the invasion, but then she opened for him, welcoming his onslaught.

Her fingers swept up to the side of his face then lost themselves in his hair. A groan escaped his chest, and Justine's body arched against his at the sound. He tugged her chemise down until his fingers found the soft skin of her breasts. She cried out as he gently cupped one in his cool hand.

"Oh, Justine..." He groaned as his lips burned a trail down her throat to her chest.

A cool draft swept over her exposed flesh and stung her skin, a foreign, searing ache igniting between her legs. Her hand gripped his shoulder tighter, and her lungs squeezed for air as his mouth suckled on the fulness of a breast then took it in his mouth. The sensation ripped through her.

Her eyes squeezed shut, and a moan uncurled in her throat as his fingers toyed with the sensitive nipple of her other breast. He clutched her hand and brought it down between his legs. Her heart stuttered as he guided her fingers under his long nightshirt to his smooth hard length. She buried her face in his chest, her lips nuzzling his smooth flesh, as her small fingers wrapped around his shaft.

"Bloody hell." His stiff cock pulsating in her hand. He pressed his hips up and moved both their hands against his hard length. "Yes, like that..." Brandon moaned in her ear. "Oh..."

The raw timbre in his deep voice sent sharp, scorching tingles searing through her. He crushed her even closer to his chest, and she inhaled the sweet, woodsy alcohol fumes from his warm breath. His body stiffened against hers, and he let out a string of undecipherable words in her ear, his savage tone leaving her breathless. Underneath their hands, his throbbing cock sent bursts of fire straight to her belly, pooling in her very centre.

Brandon clasped her hand in an iron grip against his pulsating hardness and showed her how he wanted her to stroke him. He buried his face in her hair and groaned, his fingers digging into her skin.

Justine's lungs constricted as needy, primitive sensations racked his body. His cock spasmed in her hand, filling it with a warm, thick, sticky substance. Brandon's body slackened against hers, and his breathing relaxed and deepened. Justine peeked up at his face. His eyelids were closed, his lips parted. He had found rest.

She, on the other hand, needed a brandy.

Justine reached for the wet cloth she'd left in the tray on the end table and wiped her hand and his abdomen. Her gaze swept over his peaceful features; only the scars gave witness to any turmoil that lay within him.

Her finger outlined the edge of his jaw, and the image of him at the creek this afternoon immediately invaded her brain. Naked, the water falling off him in sheets, his wet skin glistening in the sunlight. Yes, quite a different picture from when he was a boy that summer day with William and Annie.

This afternoon Justine had stopped breathing as her eyes had been helplessly glued to the image of bare, beautiful manhood before her. Even though he still was not eating that much food, he had filled out since he had come home and seemed more a man his age. His lean form was quite simply perfect, like the ancient Greek and Roman statues she had seen at an art exhibition in London years ago.

She rolled her eyes at herself on a sigh, her finger tracing a line down his warm arm. Brandon wasn't made of marble or stone, and neither was she. Justine leaned over him and brushed his lips with hers.

She most certainly needed a brandy.

CHAPTER ELEVEN

JUSTINE POKED at the wheat cake and jam in her dish. She had no appetite whatsoever. The sideboard was laden with food this morning, but none of it enticed her in the least. Her stomach was tied in knots.

Last night she had indulged in some brandy, then fallen asleep at Brandon's side. She had woken up when the first glow of dawn had begun to flood the parlour, their bodies still curled together in blankets on the Persian rug. But the stiffness in her upper back was not the only ache shooting through her. Her chest had stung with the memory of the sensual fever of hours before. It stung still.

Never had she experienced anything of that physical intensity. That sort of craving, that rush of wild feeling, of need, that was passion, desire, was it not? That was far, far beyond any of the dramatic romantic novels she had read or what she had gleaned from the womanly chats she had overheard among the servants and the tenants. It was far beyond the brief kisses, warm glances, and hand-holding she had once shared with Andrew.

Gripping her cup, she gulped the last of her tea. No, this was quite different, this passion with Brandon.

The recollection of his enflamed body shuddering and finding release in her arms, his moans filling her ears, his hands caressing her breasts, his lips nuzzling her skin, his tongue dancing with hers, his carnal mumblings in her ear, his warm, masculine scent...all of it rushed through her once more. All of it transfixed her still.

She didn't feel ashamed about the experience, but she did feel awkward. Would Brandon remember it? Or would he ignore it? Perhaps even worse, he might comment on it flippantly or tease her? All these possibilities twisted her insides even tighter.

"Good morning." Brandon sailed into the dining room, his tone bright. Her throat constricted at the sight of him, freshly dressed, the lines of his face relaxed.

He headed directly to the sideboard and filled a plate with bread, ham, a wedge of cheese, a cold fillet of beef. He took his seat opposite her at the table. Her back was stick straight and her fingers curled tightly around her plate as he consumed every last morsel. A famished wolf taking his fill.

"Not hungry?" He sat back, wiped at his sharp grin, and tossed his napkin on the table.

"I..."

He rose from his chair, closing the distance between them. Justine's breath caught as Brandon took her hand in his and brushed her cheek with a gentle kiss. His lips lingered by her mouth like the illicit touch of a feather. He pulled back slightly and gazed at her. She blinked up at him, her body utterly still as his seawater eyes bathed her in their softness. He brought her hand to his lips sending sparks through her. "Shall we leave for the cemetery in ten minutes. Will you be ready?"

"Oh yes. Ten minutes."

"Very well." His knuckles stroked the side of her face as the edges of his mouth tipped up into another smile, this one slow, warm. Scorching. Devastating. He let go of her hand and strode from the dining room, taking her breath with him.

That wasn't a mere good-morning-and-thank-you-for-break-fast smile. Oh, he remembered. He had liked it.

Perhaps today would be a good day for her to try to explain everything with Richard and William to him, and hopefully gain some measure of his trust. She rose from the table.

He insisted they ride their horses to the village church cemetery.

"Are you sure?"

"Quite sure." He settled onto the saddle, taking the reins in hand. "Ha!" His horse charged forward.

He galloped ahead and Justine followed on her horse. He stole a look back at her and grinned. Her lungs squeezed, and she urged her horse faster. She finally caught up with him. "Are you sure you're all right?"

"Stop worrying, woman!"

"Very well!" She galloped ahead of him, his loud laughter roaring behind her.

They entered the outskirts of the village where the old stone church and cemetery were located. He took the reins of her horse, and his large hands slid about her waist and pulled her close as his sober eyes studied her face. His fragrance, a scent which reminded her of freshly washed linens having dried in the breeze, drifted over her, and she bit the inside of her cheek.

She was unaccustomed to a man assisting her. She was also unaccustomed to a man constantly staring at her as if he were trying to read her mind or make sense of her. Brandon seemed to have no sense of discretion now, no filter for the finer points of appropriate behavior. He did or said just as he felt in that moment, be it a wry observation or an unabashed and pene-trating gaze.

She didn't find it unsettling, though; she found it intriguing.

CHAPTER TWELVE

BRANDON TOOK JUSTINE'S ARM, and she led the way behind the ivy-covered stone church to the gated cemetery. The stone angel, blackened and discoloured with age, loomed over the family tomb, eyes gazing heavenward, great wings outstretched behind her.

As a boy she had frightened him. Her austere face was one of victory and hope, his father had explained. *"She should be an inspiration to you."* Yet Brandon remained alarmed by her severe expression.

When he had been forced to bid his mother a bitter farewell, he was sure the angel was mocking him. His beloved mother now belonged to that angel, not to him. Surely she was frightened by the angel as well?

His lips had quivered, his hands in tight fists at his side. He hated that statue. He hated the baby that was stuck in his mother's womb, leaving her body bloody and torn instead of bringing them great joy as she had promised him over and over.

Justine removed her gloves and touched the smaller stone angel at the side of his parents' grave. This more delicate figure was draped over in grief over a small headstone engraved with

75

the name *Anne Treharne*. Justine placed the roses she had picked earlier this morning into the grieving angel's hands, stroking its weathered stone fingers. His heart thudded in his chest.

His parents' names were engraved in the large stone: *Jeremiah Treharne, Caroline Treharne*. He exhaled loudly and flexed his hands at his sides. A sharp ache unlike anything he had ever felt before pierced his heart and scratched over his skin.

Justine moved closer to him and slipped her small hand into his. Brandon immediately entwined their fingers and pulled her close to his side, blinking back the wetness filling his eyes. They stood together in silence for a long while.

"He did not suffer in the end, Brandon," she said, and his cold hand tightened its grip on her warm one. "I was with him his last days. He slept mostly. Then one morning, he did not wake." Justine opened his palm and placed a small hard object in his hand.

His eyes narrowed at the glint of gold. "Father's ring? Where did you...?"

She pulled on the silken drawstring of her small, beaded reticule. "Lord Graven gave it to me. He asked me to keep it safe for you until you returned. He knew you would return. He insisted that he would have known if you had died. He assured me you would be back. And here you are, Brandon. Just as he knew you would be."

He let go of her hand and slid the antique gold ring inscribed with a medieval "G" on his finger.

"Shall I leave you for a moment?" Justine asked.

Brandon only nodded. She moved forward and laid her hand over Lord Jeremy's name and closed her eyes. "Rest now, my lord."

Brandon's head bowed at the roughness of her whisper.

"Rest, he is finally home."

CHAPTER THIRTEEN

JUSTINE RETREATED from the grave and moved toward the horses.

"Justine?"

A familiar male voice filled the crisp autumn air, and her feet doubled back. Andrew Blakelock, Amanda's brother, stood before her. Last she had heard he had left England to travel on the Continent. It had been over two years since she had last seen Andrew, and not under the best of circumstances.

Justine bowed her head. He swiftly removed his hat, and bowed before her. His blue eyes and blond hair shone brightly in the sun. She cleared her throat and smiled back at him. Andrew darted forward and took her hand in his, planting an enthusiastic kiss on her skin. He glanced up at her and grinned. His familiar bergamot cologne wafted over her, and Justine rocked back slightly. He released her hand, but not before his thumb caressed the spot where he had kissed her.

"It's so very good to see you again, Justine." Andrew's clear blue eyes danced over her. "Brandon is back, I hear. "

"Yes, he is. He survived the shipwreck after all." Justine turned away from his warm gaze. She stepped back two paces trying to avoid the waves of eagerness and expectation rolling off him, but it was no use, no use at all. She clasped her hands. "He had been in hospital in London, unknown to us all this time."

"How extraordinary."

"Yes, quite extraordinary. Luckily our own Dr. Langham happened to be visiting at that hospital and recognised him." She blinked up at Andrew. That old comfortable familiarity between them rose up, but Justine pushed it away. Here was the kind, fine gentleman who once held her affections. The attractive young man she had once yearned for, the one who had been forbidden to her, the one whom she had cried over. Now he finally stood before her once again like he had done in her dreams. But that dream had come true too late. Now there was no joy in her chest, but only a sinking, ripping feeling.

"When William's father arrived at our house there was quite a to do. Yet, Justine, you remain at Wolfsgate with Brandon?" His eyes widened over her as if searching for a clue to a puzzle.

But Justine had no answer. Her mouth opened, but she could not will her voice to function. Her brain could not form words, logical words to answer his most logical question: Why she, an unmarried young lady, was living at an unmarried gentleman's house who was not a blood relative instead of residing with her stepfather and stepbrother?

Andrew moved closer to her, his face suddenly blocking the sun's glare from her vision. "Forgive me for seeming forward." His voice was lower, a blond eyebrow lifted. "But how can that be if your stepfather is now at ours? Surely, you must come as well?"

Dear Lord, just the thought of her living with all of them at Crestdown was so dreadful, so strange, so truly awful. Justine's gaze darted over at her and Brandon's horses feeding on the grass in utter contentment.

"Justine?" Andrew's pressing tone squashed her spiraling thoughts. "Are you assisting your Brandon in some way?"

"Yes, yes I am. He remains still rather weak, and he is somewhat ill. I could not—"

"Oh, I see, yes, of course." Andrew tossed his head back, his lips curving into a slight smile. "Very kind, indeed. One would expect nothing less from you. Indeed, I was surprised that William said nothing regarding your absence when his father arrived yesterday, but Amanda and I were quite taken aback. Therefore, I thought perhaps I would offer you my assistance in some way, in order to expedite..." He tilted his head at her. "Dash, Justine! It's wonderful to have bumped into you this way. I planned on coming by Wolfsgate this afternoon in any event."

"Mr. Blakelock, that is most considerate of you. Truly." Andrew's brow furrowed at her formality. "However, I must tell you—"

"Justine?" Brandon's deep, sharp voice resonated behind them. She turned on her heel. He stood a few feet away from them leaning on his cane, his head cocked to the side, a scowl darkening his face.

"Brandon, you remember Andrew Blakelock?" She swiped a stray lock of hair from her brow and forced her body to move to the side.

"Of course." Brandon remained still. His eyes narrowed in the glare of the sun.

"Graven." Andrew bowed his head.

"Mr. Blakelock was telling me that your uncle arrived safely at Crestdown," said Justine.

"I'm so relieved." Justine knew Andrew couldn't possibly understand the brittle tone in Brandon's voice like she did.

A smile brightened Andrew's face.

No, he definitely did not understand.

Andrew gestured at Justine. "We were, of course, expecting Justine as well, now that her stepfather is living at ours."

A query lit Brandon's eyes. The edges of his lips tipped up. "I don't understand. Why would you think Justine would follow Uncle Richard?"

"Well, it's just...that..." The smile faded from Andrew's lips. His round eyes shot to Justine's pleading for assistance.

"Why would Lady Justine leave my house, Blakelock?" Brandon's voice cut like a knife between them. "When she is my wife?"

Justine froze. There it was, for the very first time, Brandon's acceptance of their marriage and his public declaration of it.

Andrew's face turned different shades of grey and white. He shifted his weight, he looked away. Brandon's stony gaze remained locked on Andrew, his scars tightening over his face, his fingers gripping his cane.

"You...are married?" Andrew sputtered. "I did not know."

Her heart pounded wildly outside her chest. Could they both hear it?

A bitter grin lashed Brandon's lips. "My cousin and my uncle did not tell you?" Brandon emphasized his words slowly, relishing them, as he moved toward Justine. "How odd."

"When did this happen?" Andrew said. "You've only just returned. I thought—"

"What is it you thought?" Brandon asked.

Justine clasped her hands together. She had to intervene. "T'was in London, in fact. We spent time together in London after Lord Graven's release from hospital."

"I see. Well." Andrew cleared his throat. "Congratulations to you both." His lips smashed together.

"Very kind of you." Brandon took Justine's hand in his. Andrew's eyes darted to the movement, his face tightening. The Graven ring Brandon wore ground into Justine's knuckles, and she grit her teeth.

"Well. I shall take my leave." Andrew bowed his head sharply. "Amanda will surely want to see you."

"Will she?" asked Brandon.

Justine's body stilled. She was quite sure Amanda would be fascinated by the news.

Andrew's eyes flashed at Brandon. "Yes, of course. You'll come

to Crestdown for dinner. We'll arrange it. We are family after all."
Andrew shot one last glance at Justine, and turned stiffly, strode off, dry leaves crunching in his wake.

Brandon cursed under his breath. "Did he really just say we are family? Damn me, this homecoming becomes more entertaining every day."

CHAPTER FOURTEEN

BRANDON GRIPPED Justine's waist with his hand and twisted her toward him. His eyes burned into hers, and she let out a gasp. He really should control his temper, but to hell with that. "What was that really about then?"

"He must have seen me from the road and came over to say hello."

"He came for more than hello, Justine." He'd seen Blakelock kissing her hand, savoring it, and he'd seen her pleased smile beaming back at him at which point something in his head had detonated.

"He did not know about our marriage," Justine said. "There has been no formal announcement, after all, and William must not have—"

"Of course he hasn't!" His voice rose sharply. "You didn't answer my question, Justine. What is between the two of you?"

"Nothing." A shadow flickered over her flushed face. "Well, not anymore."

"Ah—is that honesty? How refreshing." His shoulders stiffened as he loosened his grip on her waist. "Tell me."

"There has always been a certain fondness between us over the years."

"A certain fondness?" Icy stabs raced down his spine. *Dear God, what now?* Had they been secretly engaged? That prickling over his skin intensified. "Did he ever ask you to marry him?" He tried to restrain the thoughts rioting in his brain, the fire sparking in his veins.

"No."

"I don't believe you. Why the hell not?"

She shifted her weight on her other foot. "Well, not formally, no."

Brandon winced. "Not formally?"

"We had, once or twice, discussed the possibility, in the most indirect of terms, but..."

"But?" His breath came in shallow now, a cold sweat beading on his brow. His pulse raced in his temple. He knew Andrew and Justine had always been close as children, but dammit they hadn't been children for quite some time, now had they?

"William wouldn't allow it," she said.

His cold fingers were on her chin, drawing her face toward his in a firm grip. "William? But such a match would have been ideal, would it not?"

"So I thought. But he wanted Amanda, you see."

"And so?"

"He did not want me connected to her family in any way. We would have been brother and sister yet again."

"So he refused Andrew?"

"No, he found another way."

"What other way?"

"He made me tell Andrew no without any explanation and forbade me to ever see him again."

Brandon scowled. William had forced Justine into rejecting Andrew for seemingly no reason, putting her into the role of the capricious, flighty girl, which she was not. The poor boy must have been gutted by it. And Justine?

Oh, sod it all!

"Did you love him?" he asked. Her gaze shot up at him, and he took in her clouded eyes, her stiff jaw. An ache tore through his bad leg. "Or is the better question do you love him still?"

"I had a great affection for him, Brandon. He was a source of brightness for me, my only constant, and a dear friend for quite some time."

Brandon's rioting thoughts broke free from any restraint and made him dizzy with their chaos. He was not the only one confused by this marriage. What an arrogant, egotistical ass he'd been, assuming Justine had gladly and willingly agreed to their marriage as if she were desperate to hang onto him for his money or his title or simply desperate for a husband. Her thoughts and feelings lay elsewhere all this time.

He stepped back, his grip tightening over his cane.

Of course, he was no longer the great catch he used to be; his present looks and behavior left much to be desired. God, he was a pathetic fool, wasn't he? Justine didn't want this either. She too was a casualty of William's war against him. What she really wanted had been denied her, taken away from her.

His head pounded and a scraping feeling gnawed over his skin, his lungs constricted. Damn, he needed a fix.

Right the hell now.

"I didn't let it go on, Brandon," Justine's voice interrupted his swirling thoughts. "After William insisted it end, I stopped accepting his attentions, and I requested my letters be returned. They were, and I destroyed them, and I returned his letters. I avoided Andrew after that, in fact, I barely left the house in all that time. Since then he has been traveling on the Continent. This is the first I have seen him since...all of that." She inhaled a short breath through her pale lips.

Attentions.

Letters.

Destroying.

Avoiding.

The words whirled through his fried brain from the second they left her sweet mouth. Andrew had left England for an extended tour of the Continent? Apparently, he had not taken the rejection lightly. Blakelock had loved her all right, and from what he had just witnessed, he loved her still.

"And then you and I were married." Justine's strained voice sheared through his haze.

The fingers of his one hand traced a trail up the side of her soft throat. Her pulse drummed under his touch, her strained gaze pinned on his. He was making her anxious, uncomfortable, apprehensive. This delicate, sweet creature who was pulsing with life should belong to a kind, blond boy like Andrew Blakelock.

As children Blakelock had always had a special affection for Justine and Annie. He would insist on including the younger girls in their games and would take the time to entertain them by making silly drawings of animals or caricatures of people they knew. Oftentimes he stole sweets from the dessert trays in the kitchen for the girls when they hadn't been allowed downstairs during a dinner party.

After Annie's death, if William went too far in his perpetual annoyance with Justine, Andrew would step in and come to her defence. Andrew would pull the girl out of William's way and send her off in the opposite direction, often following her himself. Amanda, not one for confrontations, never paid much attention and tended to drift away during these incidents. Brandon would chastise William for his cold spitefulness. Justine would often look up at Brandon and Andrew with her soft, brown eyes, a slow smile lighting her face, then turn and run off. No pouting self-pity, only genuine gratitude would shine in that innocent face.

He took in a deep breath. Yes, he was not for a girl like her; he was ill, used up, a strain. His existence had robbed her of her ideal knight in shining armor. Here she was putting on a brave face for him and for Andrew.

Even now he could still feel her heart beating through his chest when he had held her tight in his arms last night, when he acted like an animal in heat. Justine hadn't pulled away from him, though. She hadn't shown any disgust. She had tensed for a brief moment, but then she had opened to him, and he had drowned himself in her. Her innocent, breathy noises had cut through his selfish, libidinous fog and made his release all the sweeter, all the more powerful. In fact, the memory of them was making him hard right this very minute.

The lavender from the soap she had used in her hair still lingered, as did the sensation of her full breasts and hardened nipples pressing against his chest. A thousand currents had roared through his veins straight to his demanding cock which had flourished under her tight grip. When she had groaned his name, her hand cuffing him, her softness melting around him, that's when he'd spent himself. He hadn't even seen to her pleasure, imagine when...

Had he been dreaming? Was last night real? Did she truly feel that good in his arms? The desperate need to taste her again erupted within him.

His hands wrapped firmly around her neck, and he tugged her to him. She let out a soft cry as his mouth crushed hers, his tongue sliding between her full lips. Her hands pressed into his chest, keeping them apart. Her beautiful brown eyes searched his, as his thumb stroked her now swollen lower lip.

He hadn't been dreaming. She bloody well felt amazing.

The thought of Justine holding someone else's hand, sharing stolen kisses with...

He wanted to possess her, claim her, be the one to make her desperate with fire. Greed took hold of him, and he tilted her head closer to his face. His tongue plundered her warm mouth, and she whimpered softly. Sweet Jesus, that sound was the most beautiful thing he had ever heard. Her hands glided around his middle and pressed into his back. The ache in his chest spiraled.

Yes.

"Graven, you hound! Respect for the dead, man!"

Throaty laughter rose behind them and Justine froze, her fingers curling into his frock coat. Brandon muttered a curse as he twisted around. His face lit up. "Charles?" His close childhood friend, Charles Montclare.

"You bastard, alive and kicking are you? The rumours are true. And there we all were, mourning your loss for some time. Ironic, though, finding you now in a graveyard, don't you think?" Charles laughed. His suede eyes swooped over Justine and settled on her face. "And who is this adorable creature?"

Justine lifted her chin, her cheeks still pink, her lips swollen from Brandon's kiss. Charles raised an eyebrow, and a wicked smiled curled the edges of his mouth.

"Come now, Montclare, you remember Justine?" Brandon said. "William's stepsister."

"I'll be damned." He bowed his head and a grin brightened his fine sharp features. "Just a slip of a girl last time I laid eyes on you. Have they been hiding you in the attic all this time, my dear, because I haven't seen you about at all? Nor in London...no, I haven't seen you. I would have remembered." He bowed his head.

Justine bowed her head. "I have been home at Wolfsgate, Mr. Montclare."

"Under lock and key then." His eyes glinted at her. "What a waste."

Charles Montclare hadn't changed one bit. He was as tall as Brandon, with light brown eyes, and dark golden hair. The bastard still used that polished charm of his to great effect. There was a time when the two of them had been the most popular and appreciated young gentlemen in the county. Only Charles's brand of charm was a bit chillier, more sardonic than Brandon's, and his flirtations knew no bounds. Brandon used to find Charles's *esprit* amusing. Right now, however, he didn't find it amusing in the least, and his palm itched to smack the smirk off Montclare's handsome face.

"Justine and I are married," Brandon's voice cut through Charles's thick attention on Justine.

"What?" Charles shook his gaze from Justine to Brandon and back to Brandon again. "How did I miss the wedding of the year? Did I not merit an invitation?"

"We were in London and had a quiet, low-key affair," Brandon said.

Charles tilted his head at Justine and grinned. "Well, one less fine local lady for me. Congratulations to you both."

"Thank you. Come by the house, Charles, let's catch up."

"Indeed I will. Just got in from town myself. Errands for father, don't you know. It's never ending. I'll be by soon. Though I wouldn't want to interrupt the newlyweds." He let out a short laugh, his hand clapping on Brandon's shoulder. "I'm damned glad you made it out of that shipwreck alive and came back to us, old friend. Nothing like a resurrection."

CHAPTER FIFTEEN

IT WAS past ten o'clock at night, and Brandon found himself at the Fang & Feather. Again. He would come to the tavern often in the wilder days of his youth with Charles, William, and others at his side. Now he was alone. Alone yet married.

Pathetic.

He threw himself onto a bench in a corner and signaled for an ale.

"Lord Graven t'is you? I'd heard, but seeing is believin', sir!" The tavern owner, John, had stood before him when he had first made his entrance some nights ago, his big belly shaking, his hands held high. From the moment Brandon had walked through the door that first time, they had all stared at him. The din had diminished then rose up again with cheering and some confusion as they'd raised their mugs of ale in his direction, the word "resurrection" rustling about the hot room. Buxom, sweaty girls took turns refilling his mug, smiling at him. He laughed at their saucy quips. Yes, it was good, all this noise, diversion, merriment.

Hurrah.

He brushed a hand down his face. He would've enjoyed this years ago. It used to be a right party. He stretched out his legs under the table. Even that was painful, blasted knee. No, nothing was the same. Nothing would ever be again.

He had been coming to the Fang & Feather every night this week, but it was not proving to be the diversion he had hoped. In fact it was tedious beyond belief. However, it was a damn sight better than being in that house and seeing his unsightly reflection in the looking glass or staring at the walls, walls that needed maintenance. So much of it needed maintenance, upkeep, requiring his decisions, his commands. All of Wolfsgate waited on him, on his word. And who was he to give it? Ah, yes. Divine heir. Lord and Master.

But something else gnawed at him too. Ever since his discovery of Justine's former relationship with Blakelock he had been in a pique. Was it humiliation? Or simply the sting of his manly pride having been knocked down a peg? He wasn't sure. Taking Justine in that kiss hadn't been the cure. Quite the opposite, in fact. It had only caused the vile humours coursing through his veins to simmer and pitch him in an unusual fever.

He distracted himself with riding all hours of the day, hiking over his property, and drinking as much as possible every night, then slinking back into the house undetected. He didn't want to look her in the eyes. He knew it was childish, but it couldn't be helped.

Those eyes.

At noon today Justine had found him in the parlour just having woken up from his spot on the floor, cushions under his head.

"Are you ever going to leave this room?" She had pressed her lips firmly together, her hands at her hips. "How can you possibly be comfortable in here? I will clean your bedchamber today, and you will sleep in there."

"You will do no such thing."

"Gaw!" she'd spat out, her face red. She'd marched out of the parlour, but moments later charged back in to face him, planting her feet on the floor.

"Do you not want to use the stairs, is that it?"

"What?"

"You heard me!"

"You obviously have no understanding of physical discomfort, Justine."

"You're being lazy," she retorted.

"Don't be ridiculous!" Brandon raised himself up.

"And perhaps feeling sorry for yourself?"

"Justine—" he growled.

"Shall I send for more brandy then, my lord?" She crossed her arms in front of her chest and tilted her head at him, then swiftly marched out of the room once more, and this time slammed the door behind her.

She had returned not half an hour later bearing a tray of tea and biscuits. He stood smoothing down his shirt, tucking it into his breeches, his gaze locked on her cool one. She plonked the tray on the table as he fastened his buttons, then curtsied at him and swept out of the room. He stood there riveted. Was he impressed or annoyed?

Damn her, definitely impressed.

Doors slammed open, footsteps boomed overhead. He had swallowed down a cup of tea, grabbed a few biscuits, and left.

The tavern was quite crowded and noisy this evening making the fetid air even more insufferable. He rubbed at the side of his face and waved a girl over for another drink.

A heavy, burly arm settled on his shoulder, and his head jerked to the side. Davidson, dark eyes twinkling in the dim light, slid onto the bench beside him, plonking his own mug on the table.

"How are you doin', sir?" Davidson asked, sweeping a stray strand of his grey-brown hair behind a protruding ear. The girl brought Brandon his drink and hovered over him, a smile pasted on her shiny face. Davidson shoved her off, swatting at her with his hand. "I heard ye been here most nights."

Brandon only gave him a dull stare and leaned his back against the wall. He took his pipe out of his coat.

"Lady Graven is well, sir?"

Brandon only let out a dry laugh and drained his mug.

Davidson leaned his arms on the table. "On our way to London to get you out of hospital, Lady Graven had told me how you came to be married. I imagine it must be difficult for you to deal with the wrongs your uncle and cousin have perpetrated against the two of you."

Brandon filled his pipe with tobacco.

Davidson frowned. "Lady Justine is a fine girl and not a stranger to you. God only knows what those two thieving bastards put her through all these years. And she having to live with them alone at that great house once your father passed on. I would see her about on her regular visits to the tenants. A bit elsewhere, she was, yet always doing her best not to look sad. She got good at it, I daresay."

"Regular visits to the tenants?" Brandon gulped down more ale.

"That's right. Always goin' round bringing food, offering a friendly chat," Davidson replied. "She helped a lot of families through the sickness a while back." He let out a sigh. "She was a companion to your father at the end, reading to him, feeding him, listening to his stories. He didn't want to talk with no one else. And since Lord Jeremy passed—God bless him—she's been trying to keep up all on her own."

"Wasn't her place." Brandon scratched at his prickly arms.

Davidson slammed down his mug on the scarred table. "I don't think you quite understand the sacrifices she's made, sir." The sudden sharp tone of his voice sent barbs up Brandon's neck, and he glared at his groundskeeper.

Davidson did not cower. "Her plotting to get you out of hospital, her leaving that house, was a mighty risk. If they had known, they would have put an end to it at once, and there's no telling what they would have done to you and to her, I reckon."

Brandon's eyes strained to focus on Davidson. He still couldn't get the image out of his dazed mind of Justine walking all the way to the tenants' cottages in winter, in summer, showing kindness to them on his family's behalf. "What do you mean 'what they would've done to her?' Has she been in danger from them?"

"I can't say exactly, but they certainly don't treat her as they should do a daughter or a sister. Do you think she's been living the high society life since she's come of age? Bah." Davidson scoffed.

"Have they been hiding you in the attic, my dear?" Isn't that what Charles had said when he feasted his eyes on Justine at the churchyard? He had barely recognised her.

"Pardon my saying, sir, but I wouldn't put nothing past those two."

"Well, they got her to agree to the marriage, didn't they?" Brandon lit his clay pipe, inhaling the smoke it offered him.

Davidson leaned across the table, his eyes tight. "What's a sweet girl against the likes of them, eh? She's never spoken about that to me and I never asked. But I'm sure no one would have been the wiser while they ate through your inheritance. She decided to do something about it. And she did it." Davidson's dark eyes pierced Brandon's as if trying to impale his words straight into his master's skull. "I wouldn't let her go alone to London, knew she'd be needing help getting you out and back on your feet. And forgive me for saying, sir, but I have known you since you were a young lad, and here ye are cocking yourself up. Bloody shame that. Bloody waste for all of us." Davidson drained his mug, slamming it once more on the table.

"She shouldn't have bothered with me as there's nothing grand left of me or the estate."

Davidson's head tilted. "You think that's what matters to 'er?"

"Well, I can't say I know my wife very well."

"Go home and get to know her!" Davidson exclaimed. Brandon only cast him a dark glance as he inhaled more smoke from his pipe, letting it burn in his lungs.

"Oh, I see, this is you feeling sorry for yerself? Drowning yer sorrows? Ah, such sorrows!" Davidson planted his hands on the table. "Has she not told you then?"

Brandon's eyes narrowed as he exhaled a plume of smoke. "Told me what?"

"Oh, damn me." His fingers gripped Brandon's arm, and he yanked him close. Brandon's eyes flared. "It's all there and more," Davidson said in his ear. "She's been hiding it from them for a long while now."

Brandon's face twitched. He gripped the edges of the table to keep himself steady as an eerie lightness rushed to his head. "What did you say?" Brandon breathed.

Scowling, Davidson smoothed down the sleeve of Brandon's frock coat. "'Bout two years ago when your cousin curtailed my running of the estate, she came to me and asked me to show her how to keep the books. And then a few months later she asked me about the enterprise in Jamaica. She was in a panic."

Brandon tugged his hands through his hair in an effort to feel pain, feel something, anything. A leaden weight pressed in on his stomach, and that heaviness travelled up his torso settling in his chest.

The other night he had woken up in a sweat and gone into the study with a lit candle. He had pulled open the desk drawers and found the estate accounting ledgers. Going through them, he'd been astonished by the sudden drop in income and the great rise in expenditures written out to his cousin and uncle. Nothing significant was noted for maintenance or upkeep or food. And nothing for Justine. His fingers had circled over figures on the paper as his brain tried to make sense of the fact that Justine might possibly be telling him the truth about her role in William's scheme.

"She's not told you then?" Davidson rubbed a hand across his stubbly jaw. "Or maybe you haven't given her a chance to tell you? Stubborn boy! I told her this would be difficult, but this is beyond —" He exhaled through his nose. "I should have checked in on the two of you, but I didn't want to intrude or seem forward. More fool am I!" He followed Brandon's troubled gaze down to the Graven signet ring on his hand and shook his head. "Your wife has single-handedly saved your precious inheritance and your life, Lord Graven."

Brandon clutched at Davidson's arm. "Help me get home."

CHAPTER SIXTEEN

AFTER A LONG, restless, and unsuccessful attempt at sleep, she'd decided to have a bit of brandy, that was if Brandon hadn't finished it all yet. She'd found both the drawing room and the parlour empty, cold, dark.

The front door grated opened and frigid air rushed into the hall, swarming over her skin. Brandon stood in the doorway, his face pale and worn, his neck bent to the side, his head leaning against the door jamb.

"Brandon? Are you all right? You look..."

"Terrible, I know."

Justine set the brass candle holder on the console table and shoved the great door closed behind him. She peeled the heavy cloak off his shoulders, tossed it on the chest of drawers next to her, and led him to the bench in the hall. Crouching before him, she began removing his boots. "I'm glad you're in one piece at the very least." She tugged off his right boot with both hands.

"I don't feel like I am." His voice was hoarse. "I feel more like a thousand broken pieces, and I'm not sure what to try to mend first." She stole a look up at him. Tears streamed down his face, and her heart twisted.

"One thing at a time, Brandon. That's all you can do." Her hands reached up towards his face, but he grabbed her wrists and held them fast, his grip firm despite his fatigue.

"Don't. I need to feel this." He released her hands and wiped at his face himself. "It's been happening frequently since the poison cleaned out of my system. Quite inconvenient for a man, eh?"

Taking a breath, Justine returned her attention to removing his other boot. His chest heaved for air as if trying to rid itself of the dullness embedded there. The silence fell heavy between them.

"Justine, I need to apologise to you. I've been such a bastard." A pained expression shadowed his features. "Davidson found me at the Fang & Feather tonight. He explained a few things to me. Things I wasn't aware of."

She set the boot aside and met his gaze. "I've wanted to explain to you since we came home, but there never seemed to be a good time."

"I don't know how can I ever thank you for taking on such a burden for my family."

"You don't have to."

"Yes, I do."

"It's all right, Brandon."

"No, it is not. I've been indulging in self-pity and self-absorption at your expense."

"Well, you're entitled, after everything you've been through." She swept the hair from his face. "And the after-effects of the opium only make it worse."

"You deserve better from me, my girl. Much better." His voice was raw, barely above a whisper. "I'm sorry I snapped at you. I get carried away at times and—"

His murky grey-green eyes held hers as his hands cradled her face and drew her closer to him. Her pulse raced as he bent down and touched his cool lips to her forehead. His heavy gaze fell to her mouth, and the flutter in her stomach rose through her chest.

Brandon bent his head down closer, and his lips brushed hers. She gasped softly at the gentleness of his touch, heat coiling though her insides. His eyebrows knit together as if a new thought suddenly perplexed him. A noise muffled in his throat, and he bent and kissed her again, his hands sliding down around her neck keeping her close. His tongue snaked through her lips, seeking hers, and Justine let out a small cry as she opened her mouth to him.

His thighs pressed around her, and her hands skimmed over the hard muscles, sliding up around his taut middle. She tasted the ale in his mouth, inhaled the tobacco that clung to him along with an undeniable masculine musk, all of it unwinding that knot within her. His tongue lashed against hers, and a molten warmth seeped through her, seizing her core.

He suddenly pulled away, his forehead resting against hers. "Christ," he breathed. "Forgive me, Justine."

Her fingers caressed his cool cheek. "For what? For...that?"

"No, not for *that*." He smiled against her skin, his thumb tracing her swollen lips. "Forgive me for being a difficult bastard."

His burning gaze was dissolving her like sugar crystals in a hot cup of tea. "I forgive you." Her lips brushed the underside of his jaw. "Let me take your coat from you." She rose, absently placing a hand on his thigh to steady herself. His muscles hardened under her touch. Brandon stretched his arms out, and she tugged off his frock coat. His shirt clung to his smooth broad back in perspiration, and he fidgeted, his shoulders twitching.

Justine frowned as she touched his arm. "Brandon, would you like a bath? It might help. The tub is in the kitchen, I'm afraid."

He cast a glance at her. "That's fine. I'll help you."

"No, you sit. I'll let you know when it's ready."

"I need to move, do something." He rose to his feet and rested one arm on her shoulder, and they slowly walked into the kitchen together.

She showed Brandon the tub in the anteroom, and he helped her pull it out before the fireplace. He lit a fire as Justine filled pots with water, took out a clean bath cloth and a larger one for him to step on.

Once the water heated, he filled the tub himself. Before the tub was even halfway full, he began to strip his clothes off and climbed into it. Justine's cheeks inflamed once more. She brought over a smaller bowl of warm water for him to pour over his head.

"Oh, that feels good." He groaned and the rich satisfaction in his voice warmed her insides. She licked her lips as she held out the soap and a small cloth to him. He took them and began to scrub his skin. She dried her hands and headed for the door.

"Justine, wait. Sit with me."

She turned, her eyes wide and went to Molly's chair by the hearth. He reached back to his neck with the soapy cloth. "Oh, let me." She rose and took the cloth from his wet fingers and, lifting his hair, scrubbed the back of his neck and down over his shoulders. She worked in small circular motions rubbing the soapy cloth gently around his throat, around his ears, the hard angles of his jaw relaxing under her fingers. She dipped the cloth in the water to rinse it and went over his face and neck again washing away the soap from his skin.

"Very efficient, Lady Graven."

She let out a small laugh. "Years of training under Nanny's care." His languid eyes remained on hers, and the thumping in her chest continued. "You've gotten some sun I see. Not as pale as the moon any longer."

"I've been riding and walking quite a bit lately."

"Yes, you have. Your leg is better?"

"Better, but still not completely right. I'm not sure it ever will be."

This bath was much, much different from the other times she

had washed him. He was no longer a helpless, ill patient. No, this was a vibrant man in all his glory, perhaps tired and drunk and weary, but still a vibrant man.

A man who had just kissed her.

Soapy water dripped down the firm contours of his chest. She took in a deep breath and rubbed the cloth down his chest which was peppered with dark hair. She rubbed down his long lean arms, where powerful veins seemed sculpted into his skin.

"Justine?"

"Hmm?"

"Feels very good." His voice was smooth as silk.

"I'm glad you like it," suddenly rolled out of her mouth.

His lips curled into a trace of that familiar, devastating smile once more. "I do." His voice dropped, the smile vanished, and his eyes closed. Only the splashes of the bathwater filled the silence between them.

"Could you lean forward?" she asked. "Your back…"

He leaned forward, and she rubbed the soapy cloth over his neck, sweeping it down over the long lines of his back. Another low groan escaped his throat. The loaded silence crushed her, as she scrubbed across his back once more.

"Now I feel revived," he murmured. He leaned back suddenly, the water sloshing around him. He gazed up at her face.

Justine swallowed hard. He was so very handsome, every bit as handsome as she remembered him, but she had not paid too much attention to it back then, had she? He had been an older brother figure to her, and she had valued that and liked it tremendously. William had hardly been the kind, warm sibling she had hoped he would be.

She had been thrilled to be a part of their family. After Justine's father had died suddenly in a coach accident, sadness, apprehension, and uncertainty had defined her life. A year later, her mother married Richard, and suddenly Justine became part of a new family. She had an older brother and sister who had an impressive house in town along with a titled uncle, aunt, and cousin who owned a beautiful country estate.

Brandon was her elder step-cousin. *He is my husband now.*

That sensuous half-smile faded from his lips, and his impenetrable stare bored a hole through her. Droplets of water dripped from his slick, raven hair down his forehead. On an impulse, she reached out and wiped at one with her fingertips. He grabbed her wrist with his hand and pulled her close to him. She gasped as hot, soapy water rushed down her arms soaking her sleeves. His eyes narrowed over her. "I'm still not sure if I can trust you, Justine."

She held his gaze. "That is for you to decide."

"Yes, it is. Well said." Brandon drew her hand to his mouth and kissed the back of it. She wasn't sure if that kiss signaled an *entente* or if it was the sophisticated gesture of a predator softening its prey before the kill. He brought his fingers to her jaw, his thumb stroking her lower lip. Heat jabbed through her. He seemed to like doing that.

She liked it too.

"Tell me," he asked. "I'm not ruined?"

"No, you are not ruined." A smile lit up her face, and she wiped a tendril of hair from her eyes.

He reached out to smooth back another unruly lock of her hair. His fingers lingered on the edge of her ear tickling the delicate skin. "Why would you do this for me, Justine?"

"What do you mean?" Her eyes searched his. "Why would I not?"

"Not many people would. Selfishness reigns in our day and age."

"Brandon, your life and your family's legacy were in jeopardy. I couldn't be a part of your destruction. Yes, I did play a role in their plan, but not willingly." Her head dipped toward him. "I could never harm you intentionally. You were always kind to me, and your father was very good to me. He was more a father to me than I have ever known." She twisted the cloth in her hands. "How could I allow for you, for Wolfsgate to be destroyed?"

"My father obviously trusted you."

"I loved Lord Jeremy." Tears pricked her eyes.

Brandon's thumb stroked the soft skin of her jaw. Her cheeks heated, and she bit her lip. Letting out a sigh he took back his hand, and Justine quickly dipped the washcloth in the water again and scrubbed his knee with it. He stretched the leg out and leaned his foot against the rim of the tub, and she brought the washcloth down his calf.

Justine went to the other side of the tub. A rivulet of perspiration trickled down her chest as she leaned over and scrubbed his thigh, bringing the cloth down his leg to his foot. He let out a low chuckle and leaned forward, plucking the washcloth from her hand and bringing it all the way up his thigh under the water to his pelvis. Justine shot up and filled another bowl with hot water. She held it out to him, and he poured it over his head groaning as the warm waterfall streamed down over his body. She stilled, the image burning into her brain. He handed her back the bowl, and her fingers gripped it tightly.

"It's such a huge relief to know there is money in the estate," Brandon said. "This changes everything."

"Money always does."

His eyes darted up at her. "William and Richard are not yet aware of your deception?"

"Good God, no. They believe the only source of income now is what little they have allowed Davidson to generate on the estate."

"And you've kept up this masquerade for some time? Over a year? That's why you've continued on without servants or new clothes or much upkeep around here?"

Justine smoothed a hand down her damp front. He had noticed that she wore the same two dresses over and over again. "Yes."

His somber gaze settled on her. "That all changes immediately."

She wasn't sure what that meant. She opened the bath sheet
for him, and he stood up from the tub and took the cloth from
her, a small smile forming on his lips. With their gazes locked on
each other, he dried his upper body with the cloth. He wrapped
the linen about his waist and climbed out of the tub with his
warm hand clamped onto her shoulder for support.

"Leave the tub for tomorrow, Justine, and help me to my
chamber. I want a proper bed tonight," he said as he headed for
the door.

She stopped in her tracks.

"What is the matter?" he asked. "Do I no longer have a room?"

"Of course you do, it's just that I haven't had a chance to
prepare it properly."

"I thought that's what you were doing today, banging away up
there."

Her cheeks reddened. "I was annoyed with you, so I left it,
and took more time with Richard's old room instead. Yours needs
dusting, airing, has no bedlinen, furniture is missing...Oh, do
stop laughing, Brandon."

"I am a very clean boy right now, Justine."

"Yes." Her gaze swept over his gleaming skin, his contoured
form. "You are."

"I'm also quite tired and somewhat drunk, and I'm getting
cold standing here debating this with you. Take me to your room.
Your bed, I'm sure, is pristine and fresh. I've already lain in your
bed, haven't I? Come."

She walked before him up the stairs, gripping the brass
candle holder, her knuckles white. The light cast its soft glow on
the paintings of Graven ancestors hanging on the walls of the
grand staircase. The stern light-coloured eyes of Brandon's grandfather and great-grandfather seemed illuminated in the dim light,
following their steady progress up the stairs.

Justine's favourite was of Lady Caroline as a young mother, her hair long, full and flowing, the same rich dark colour as her son's. She held the hand of a three-year-old Brandon, who was pressed at her side, a blazing, satisfied smile lighting her lips. It was Brandon's smile, his mother's, the one he rarely wore any longer. Justine had caught him staring at the portrait the other day when she had been rushing up the stairs, but he had turned away immediately without a word and tramped out of the house.

His bare feet padded on the stairs behind her now, his clean soapy scent drifting over her like a fine cologne teasing her senses, sounding an alarm. They walked down the long landing towards the last door on the right. Her fingers clasped the handle tightly as she pushed open the door to her room. Brandon immediately peeled off the bath sheet from his body, tossed it on the floor, stripped the quilted coverlet aside, and flung himself face-down onto the bed.

He let out a long groan. "Wonderful."

Justine's eyes flared at the sight of a naked Brandon on her bed. *What a beautiful rear he has.* A current sparked through her insides. She put the candle down carefully on her dresser across from the bed.

"Where are you?" his deep voice rolled through the darkness.

"Here, I—"

"Come to bed, Justine."

She untied her robe with cold fingers, shrugging it off her shoulders and flicking off her slippers. She took heavy steps to the bed and climbed in, the linens cool against her heated skin. He turned his head on the pillow, and his eyes studied her in the dim light. She could hardly breathe. Her brain worked overtime to convince her this arrangement was perfectly ordinary, perfectly natural. They were husband and wife now. She could breathe again, relax.

Impossible.

Might conversation help?

"Brandon, remember when I first came to Wolfsgate and there was this terrible storm full of howling winds and thunder and lightning? And all of us were so very frightened? The walls were practically shaking with the thunder. Nanny had gotten us all into one big bed together and—"

"And told us mad ghost stories and sang old Cornish ditties she really shouldn't have shared with children?" He chuckled darkly. "Yes, I remember."

Justine smiled, her muscles finally relaxing. "I didn't understand the ditties."

"No, of course you didn't."

"But Annie explained them to me later."

They both laughed. "Good God, nothing escaped that girl," Brandon turned on his side. "The last time I saw you was when I left for Jamaica, wasn't it? You had brought me one of my mother's roses to say goodbye." He wound a strand of her coppery brown hair around his finger. "You had petals in your hair."

Justine's scalp tingled. "You and your father had been fighting. You were so upset. I thought if I brought you the rose you would—I don't know—be less upset, I suppose. I was a young girl then, what did I know?"

"You understood how I was feeling, and you tried to do something to make it better. How old were you then?"

"Sixteen."

"Hmm. Not so very young." He released her hair and turned over once more, folding his arms under his head, the firm contours of his shoulders visible in the waning firelight. His heavy eyes remained on hers. "This was your bedchamber back then too, wasn't it?"

"Yes."

"And now we're all grown up, and here I am in your bed," he said in a low tone which quickened her pulse. Rougher, richer than a whisper. "I have to get to know the girl I left behind years ago. That girl who is now my grown-up wife." His eyes drifted closed, and his breathing deepened. He was asleep.

She pulled the coverlet higher around them. Justine remained awake for a long while, studying the relaxed face of her husband, his words still echoing around her.

CHAPTER SEVENTEEN

BRANDON'S HAND sifted through her hair which slid like thick ropes of silk through his fingers. He had woken to find her head on his chest, her hands curled into her body at his side like a child's, her legs bent by his waist. He pulled the bedcovers over her shoulders in a sudden surge of protectiveness.

Moments ago he had been gripping Justine's waist, crumpling her nightdress in his hand, his lungs squeezing for air. Fragments of another nightmare had torn him from sleep. Luckily he hadn't woken her. He smoothed the thin garment down over her warm skin and then sank his fingers back into her mane of thick hair letting out a sigh.

How she bewildered him.

"I'm still not sure if I can trust you," he had said to her during his bath.

There had been no pleading on her part, no teary-eyed imploring, no batting of those beautiful, long eyelashes. None of the usual feminine tricks that were catalogued in his memory. And no attempt at a seduction with him naked in a tub under her very hands. No, no typical feminine maneuvers whatsoever. He had waited for the signs, yet they never came. She had even answered his accusatory questions with genuine frankness.

His head sank back into the pillow. Even as a young girl Justine had been guileless, and he and Annie had been protective of her. He exhaled, his hand stroking over his painful erection. Now he was lying in her bed next to her, feeling something other than brotherly protectiveness, something fervent and dark.

Annie had always said she couldn't fool anyone, as Justine often unwittingly spoiled many of the schemes she frequently planned against the rest of them. Justine had apologised. *"No, Justine. It's a gift. You mustn't change. Not ever. Dissembling has become second nature for us. We need you.'* Annie had said hugging her stepsister close.

Any sort of lying or pretense had always been a challenge for the young Justine. *'You're shy,'* he had told her once when he had sensed her irritation with herself. *'But that simply means you're sensitive. You see and understand things others don't.'*

His father had trusted her on his deathbed, hadn't he? Lord Jeremy was not a man easily fooled. He had certainly kept his brother Richard, a weak character whom he barely tolerated, at bay for years, making sure his visits to Wolfsgate were few and far between. That was probably why he had agreed to let Justine stay at Wolfsgate for longer patches after her mother had died. He had offered the innocent girl a respite from a stepfather and step-brother who obviously never gave much of a damn about her and much preferred London society to the country.

And now years later, this orphaned, abandoned girl had saved his bloody life, nursed him back to health, and protected his inheritance all the while.

One artless, unworldly young woman.

Well, not too artless, for she must have had guile to have gotten him released from that hospital. It couldn't have been easy. He would have liked to have seen it. She had even used a borrowed wedding ring to play her part. And the clandestine accounting with Davidson behind William and Richard's backs? No, this girl had done a lot of growing up over the years out of grim necessity.

He had to trust her.

His finger coiled around a lock of her hair. He wanted to.

CHAPTER EIGHTEEN

JUSTINE'S LIPS brushed against a wall of warmth. She burrowed closer to the soft solidity surrounding her as she licked her dry lips. Her tongue swiped against something taut and smooth; it pulsed under her touch. There was movement over her bare thigh, which was trapped in between two massive legs and...

Justine's eyes flew open and her breath stuck in her chest. The room was engulfed in inky darkness. It was still the middle of the night, and her body was entwined with Brandon's. She tried to extract her leg from his as gracefully as possible, which proved to be impossible. Thankfully, he shifted slightly and his legs released hers. She twisted away from his very appealing, very naked, heat-saturated form never having been more grateful for the darkness. Justine eased back against her pillow once more.

The mattress moved beneath her. Brandon let out a groan and drew his body up against the headboard, adjusting the pillows behind him. Warm fingers drifted across her bare shoulder, down her back. Her eyes flew open once more.

"Justine? Are you awake?" His fingers swept the hair from her neck sending tingles skittering across her skin.

"Yes."

"Tell me more of what has been going on here since I left for the Indies," he said, his voice low, gentle.

She turned onto her back. His face loomed over her, his loose, dark hair almost touching his shoulders. Clearing her throat, Justine pushed herself up. "Can you not sleep?"

He rubbed his eyes. "I'm always dreaming, always waking."

"You need a bedtime story then?"

"Yes, that's it." He let out a soft chuckle. "Give us a fairytale, would you? Ah—why don't you tell me about our wedding?"

Justine let out a laugh and he smiled at her. She drew her knees up to her chest and faced him. "That sounds rather bizarre, does it not?"

"It does, but I think we should embrace it. We are living most peculiar circumstances. Tell me."

"Once upon a time the brother of the king and his son explained to their ward that the prince of the castle, feared lost at sea in a horrible shipwreck, had been found in a dark dungeon in the great city. He was, however, physically frail, scarred, and considered insane." She drew out her voice as if she were recounting a horror tale. Brandon laughed.

"They took her to see the young prince in his misery. He was in oblivion, muttering to himself, dirty and disheveled in this cavern of horrors. He was so changed, so utterly different from the prince she had known. It frightened the young lady, made her sad. Then it made her angry."

"I remember her eyes, her voice," Brandon murmured. "She made an oath, did she not?"

"She did," Justine breathed.

"Say it."

"She promised the prince she would not leave him there alone, that she would come back for him, that she would not let them destroy him."

"You kept that promise," he whispered.

Her fingers curled into the bedlinen at his side.

"Go on."

"The doctor told the young lady that the prince's heart was no longer strong. 'See,' they assured her, 'he's dying. You shall marry him and you will shortly be a widow. You shall marry and Wolfsgate will be ours.'"

"Is that what they said?"

"That is what they said. But the young lady felt horrible for she knew agreeing to this would mean betraying the prince and the king, his father. She pleaded with them, but they only laughed at the idea that procuring a wife for such a prince was proving to be so difficult."

"Yes. Quite comical," he murmured.

"They said if she did not marry the prince, they would find someone else for her, someone she would surely not like. They reminded her that they could have turned her out after her mother had died, but they had not been so cruel. They had taken care of her and allowed her to thrive at Wolfsgate as part of their noble family. Therefore, she was obliged to do as they bid her.

"They purchased a special license to marry without the usual bans and arranged for a parson to officiate at the prince's bed. The prince only mumbled something about velvet. The parson took that as an 'I will.' They put a quill in the prince's hand, and with some assistance, he scratched on the registrar's document, then they handed it to the young lady to sign. Thus, the young prince and the young lady were married and became Prince and Princess of Wolfsgate Castle. The End."

"Ah, quite the remarkable tale." He rolled onto his back and let out a dry laugh, a hand in his hair.

Justine glanced at him. "After that I stayed home and only left the house to visit the tenants, the cemetery, or for the rare errand in the village, to attend church on holy days. William declined any invitations I received, telling everyone I had taken ill over your loss and Lord Jeremy's death."

A twist of images and emotions billowed in the shadowy darkness of the room, twisting around them both.

Justine let out a sigh. "Through all of this I clung to the fact that you were still alive, and it was within my power to change their game, if only I would take the risk and try. Like you had tried to find Annie in the dark rain. You left your warm bed in the early hours of that cold and rainy morning and ran down to the creek half-dressed to find her." She blinked at him. "Perhaps that is why William resents you so much. It's not that he blames you for her death, but he blames himself for not having tried to save her. You were the one who ran to find his sister before he could even get himself out of bed. Because I had gone to you."

His teeth dragged across his lower lip. "What would Annie say if she could see us together now?"

"Oh, she'd have a right laugh, I expect."

"Well, we owe this all to medieval Traherne tradition," Brandon muttered. "With me alive yet unfit, and with you as my wife under their thumb, they did what they wanted with my money and my holdings."

"The very day after I became your wife William demanded a large sum of money from the estate and I complied. Once I he took some of your parents' jewels and several paintings."

"Does he have a problem with gaming?"

"I never had that impression, but, frankly, I'm not sure. He rarely allowed me to go out socially with him and Richard. William kept Davidson on so the estate would continue to generate its most basic income, but I wasn't allowed to spend much on maintaining Wolfsgate or to keep a servant other than Molly. I kept in touch with the tenants and the basic goings-on with Mr. Davidson's assistance."

"You did very well considering the circumstances," Brandon said.

"All this time I felt tremendously guilty that you were languishing in hospital. I wanted to figure out a way to bring you back." Her fingers twisted in the sheets. "Recently, William demanded money again, a lot of money, and I did something."

"What did you do?" The bedding rustled as he moved.

"I forged a letter from your broker in Jamaica saying that a drought had wiped out most of the sugar cane crop that year and any financial reserves you and your partners had were used to cover the losses."

Brandon's eyes widened.

"They'd had a dry season there, I had read about it in the papers. That's what gave me the idea, made it believable. I needed time to figure out a way to get you back, see how ill you really were. Davidson and I even managed to intercept a letter that arrived from the partners in Jamaica where they wrote that they had been lucky and the drought hadn't wiped out their crop. Imagine!" Justine shook her head. "I was desperate to convince William that things were falling apart here without you."

His fingers stroked the side of her face. "You did the right thing, Justine."

"William was livid," she said. "I knew that he was considering renting the house. Eventually he would find some other way to drain it until there was nothing left."

"And you would outlive your usefulness."

"I wrote to the hospital, and they said you were doing better, but under heavy sedation. Dying, indeed. Hope I had not known for so very long was suddenly very real.

"In the meantime, through a friend at his club in London, William heard that your Jamaica partners were having their annual meeting in Edinburgh. He decided to go and introduce himself in your stead and took his father with him. I knew he would find out that the letter I had produced about the money lost in the drought was a fake. It was now or certain doom. I left for London immediately with Davidson, hoping we would return before they did." She gripped his arm. "Forgive me, Brandon, for not having tried sooner. You suffered, and I let it go on."

"This has nothing to do with you, you brave girl. There is nothing to forgive." His fingers skimmed her face. "This is all on William."

She bit her lip and leaned over her side of the bed, sticking her hand under the mattress and removing a small satin pouch. Folding her legs under her, she opened the pouch, and took out a key.

"What's this?"

"A key to a cabinet in the kitchen."

Brandon's brow creased. "A cabinet in the kitchen?"

"Yes. It's where I keep those documents safe." She yawned and sank back against her pillow again. "I'll show you everything in the morning." Her gaze fell to his bare chest and lingered there. "I'm quite tired now," she murmured.

He took the key and the pouch and deposited them on the small table by the bed. "That was quite a tale you told." He pulled the covers around her. "Quite a tale."

"All true. All true."

CHAPTER NINETEEN

"WHAT ARE YOU DOING?" Brandon's voice echoed through his childhood bedchamber.

Justine's head snapped up. Her breath caught at the sight of him leaning against the doorjamb, his arms folded at his chest. Dear God in heaven, he was like the formidable full-size portrait of his stern-faced grandfather which hung in the stairwell. The same grey-green eyes, now cold and unreadable, the same broad shoulders and chest, the same casual elegance and sophisticated bearing, salted with recklessness.

But this younger Lord Graven before her was a more modern, rugged figure. He wore his white shirt opened at the neck over close fitting breeches and high boots, his dark hair loose, almost grazing his shoulders, his scars clearly visible.

She turned back to the heavy blue brocaded panel before her and swatted at it with a great straw paddle. A cloud of dust released over her. "What does it look like I'm doing?" she said.

The morning sun streamed in from the open leaded glass windows through a thick haze of dust. The massive, dark Jacobean oak bed with the heavy cornices and deep blue canopy was stripped bare, the thick inlay and elaborate carved posts gleaming in the light. Justine batted at the large panels of ancient fabric once more.

"It looks like you are hell-bent on kicking me out of your bed," he said. Her eyes flashed at him, yet she continued to swat the fabric. "Stop it, Justine."

"Whatever for?"

"I don't want to use this room again, ever."

She stopped bashing the thick blue hanging, its gold edges worn and dark in the harsh light. A great puff of dust settled about her. "Why?"

He shifted his weight and leaned against the other side of the doorjamb. His eyes rested on the tall, heavy dresser as he cleared his throat. "This room represents a whole other existence to me. I'm not that person anymore. So don't bother." His gaze darted to the bulky canopied bed that once belonged to his great grandfather. "Please, Justine."

"Very well." Justine shoved the thick hangings to the side. "Of course, you should be in the master bedroom." She rolled her eyes at herself. "What was I thinking? I will prepare Lord Jeremy's room for you directly." His eyes tightened and he clenched his jaw. She stopped at the sight. "Brandon, surely you would prefer the master's bedchamber? Your own room, a room to yourself?"

"No."

"But Brandon—"

"Unless, of course I'm bothering you?" His eyes pierced hers.

"No, you aren't bothering me—"

"Your room. With you."

Her heart skidded to an abrupt halt. She couldn't tear her gaze away from his pale eyes, so like some sort of exotic sea in a country far away. "Very well. As you wish."

"Thank you for the clean clothes you left for me," he said, his voice more controlled now. His gaze darted to the right once more in the direction of the massive chest of drawers.

"You're welcome." She turned her head slightly. "What is it?"

"Hmm?"

"What were you looking at?"

"Nothing." He re-crossed his arms and stood erect.

Justine turned her head in the direction of his gaze. "I had found something in this dresser last year, stuffed in between old clothes in the first drawer. I think you'd like to see it." She opened the first drawer and removed a small black silk pouch. She opened it and took out a gold box the size of her palm. "It's a snuff box, isn't it?" She put it in his hands. Elaborate swirls of ornate foliage were etched on its shiny surface.

"No, it's not a snuff box. There should be a key in the pouch."

She found the tiny key and he aligned it inside a groove on the underside of the box, and mechanical strains of a melody erupted from it.

Her eyes flickered up at him, a smile lighting over her face. "Oh, it's wonderful, isn't it? Was this yours?"

Brandon shook his head. "It was Mother's. My father had found it in Switzerland for her. One of the first ever made."

"Unfortunately, I don't remember Lady Caroline very well. I had come to Wolfsgate just before she—"

He twisted the key from the box and the music abruptly ceased.

"Shall I put it somewhere else in the house for you?"

His eyebrows slammed together. "No, leave it where you found it."

"Oh. But—"

He gave Justine the music box and key, and she slipped them both back in the pouch and returned it to the drawer. "Do you have the key I gave you last night?" she asked.

"Yes, I do."

"Good. Since I'm finished here for now, let me show you the documents." She moved to the windows and reaching up on her toes, leaned forward to take hold of the handle.

"Here, let me." He moved forward and shut the great, heavy window himself, latching the casement closed.

"Molly has been cooking since early this morning. She's inspired now that Richard's gone and you're home."

"I'm not hungry."

"You have to eat, Brandon."

"Giving orders again, wife?"

"If I must, yes."

"Very well then." He gestured grandly outside the room. "After you, my lady."

CHAPTER TWENTY

HE LIKED TO WATCH HER.

That glorious chestnut hair peeked out from her kerchief, its coppery tones glinting in the morning sunlight as she'd worked in his old bedroom.

Even when trying to close a goddamn window she was graceful. He groaned inwardly and the blood hammered in his veins. Her supple movements had become a source of fascination to him.

When another dream had woken him up again in the middle of the night he'd found her pressed against him once more. He hadn't moved her away, he hadn't wanted to. He also couldn't stop himself from exploring the gentle lines of her body. Merely the simple act of his fingertips tracing her legs, the curve of her hips, the dip of her waist and then up her smooth back over her chemise, nothing more, had aroused him intensely. Now, as he followed her down the stairs, he grew hard. He knew the sensuous curves that lay under those layers of clothing she wore today. A hidden feast.

Brandon glanced at the paintings hanging on the thick wood

paneled wall. He stopped before the towering portrait of his paternal great-great-grandfather.

"Brandon?"

"I'm looking for the wolf." The edges of his lips tipped up. "Do you remember?"

"Of course."

In every formal portrait of a Graven male, there was hidden a figure of a black wolf somewhere in the landscape. As children they had loved searching for the hidden creature in every painting that lined the grand staircase, each one a sinister reminder of the ancient Graven past.

"Is it the honor these Gravens thought it was to have slain so many creatures or is it a burden on their souls and now on mine?" he murmured.

He reached up, his index finger tracing the fierce animal with the glowing yellow eyes crouched in the distant trees at the left edge of the painting. "Is not the wolf a metaphor for evil Man who has a never-ending lust for power and dishonest gain? That wild, savage, murderous beast which lurks in all of us?"

"Well, yes," said Justine. "But in northern mythology, the wolf is a symbol of a persevering, loyal warrior."

"Hmm." He lifted an eyebrow. "Which am I, I wonder?"

In the kitchen they found Molly preparing a pot of tea.

"Good morning, Molly."

"Good morning, sir," said the woman, her crinkly face beamed at her young master and mistress. "I was just saving a plate for you from breakfast, my Lord."

"I slept late today, Molly, didn't I?"

"No matter, sir." She uncovered a dish with cheese, ham, and freshly baked rolls, jam tarts.

"Ah, one of my favorites. Well done, Molly." Brandon munched on the small tart. "Hmm. I'm looking forward to dinner today."

Molly's face broke into a huge smile, her cheeks flushing. "Glad to hear it, milord."

Brandon wiped at his mouth, brushed the crumbs from his fingers. "First order of business around here is to hire servants, what do you say, Molly?"

Molly's small eyes sparkled and she dug her hands in her skirts. "A proper cook? A footman? A manservant for you, milord? A few others to clean all the house top to bottom?"

"That sounds right, dear. You know best, Molly." He winked at her.

Molly had been in service to the family since Brandon was a young boy. She had risen the ranks to housekeeper and was quite attached to the family, and the family to her. Her shiny blue eyes and the old-fashioned white cap she still wore reminded Brandon of the good things in this house. The way they used to be with Father, Mother, no life and death decisions, no cares for tomorrow. Only iced cakes and apple tarts and a multitude of games with his cousins in the gardens and at the creek.

Bloody simplicity.

"I'll go to the tenants today and inquire," Justine said. "Molly, could we have our tea in the study?"

"Yes, ma'am." Molly prepared cups and saucers on a small tray. The old teapot.

"Thank you. We'll be there directly."

Molly took her tray and left the kitchen.

"The key?" She held out her palm before him.

Brandon placed the key in her hand, and she headed to the back pantry. She returned with a leather folder thick with documents and a worn blue velvet jewelry box.

"What's this?" Brandon tapped on the box with a long finger.

"Open it."

He clipped open the fastening and pushed back the lid. Something burned in the back of his throat. His mother's ruby and diamond earrings and matching bracelet glinted at him in the morning light. A hundred memories of her beautiful face flooded him, the feel of her touch, the warmth of her voice.

Her clasping his hands as they danced together in the parlour.

Her rich, unaffected laughter at something his father had said over dinner.

Her wearing these very earrings which always hung fluidly by her long, elegant neck.

He could still feel the drop rubies of her bracelet knocking against his fingers when he held her hand at a formal party. The glorious feel of her full silk skirts against their joined hands. He was her 'little gentleman,' she had declared to all her guests.

"Brandon?"

"I haven't seen these in a very long time." His voice was quiet, yet thick with emotion. Lady Caroline's death was a tragedy that had marked him and his father, disjointed their relationship, and altered the entire rhythm of the household forever on.

"Your father had them hidden. He'd told me where to find them in his room," Justine said. "I'm afraid it's all that's left. Richard went through almost everything." Her fingertip poked at a small yellowed paper with faded ink nestled underneath the bracelet. "There's a note just under here. He'd pointed it out to me."

Brandon removed it carefully, unfolded it. He read the familiar hand. A short love note from his father to his mother. His heart thudded in his chest. He folded the delicate piece of paper and tucked it back inside the velvet box, snapping it shut.

"I'm so sorry I wasn't able to save anything else." She rubbed her hands together. "There was your father's gold watch, a small cross on a chain, rings, and Lady Caroline's lovely long pearl necklace."

Brandon winced, giving her a slight wave of his fingers, begging her to stop. "Thank you. This means so very much to me, Justine."

"You're welcome." She averted her eyes from his piercing gaze.

They went to the study where Brandon settled in behind his father's desk and Justine unfastened the worn leather folder spilling with documents. After a short while, Brandon looked up at her from the piles of papers before him. "This was a lot of work on your part, very smart. Bold, in fact." He eased back in his chair, his hooded eyes settling on her as she refilled their tea cups.

"Thank you." She handed him his tea. "I have an idea, Brandon."

"What is it?"

"I think you should come with me to see the tenants. They are your tenants, and they should see that you are alive and doing well."

"Yes, you're absolutely right. I should. I need to see them. Also, I should sit down and confer with Davidson straight away, and communicate with the partners and the manager in Jamaica. There's plenty of work to be done."

"Yes, there is."

He gathered the papers into the binder. "That makes you happy, Justine?"

"It does."

She handed him the last pile of documents. "I could help with correspondence, or whatever you like."

"I would like that." The two of them working together for the good of Wolfsgate pleased her. It pleased him too. He locked the leather binder and the jewelry box away in one of the desk drawers and tucked the key in his pocket.

Her face beamed, her smile so genuine that it lit up something inside him, an ember that he thought had long since burned out, but now flared once more in the dark cave that was his soul. Whatever it was it felt foreign, but at this very moment it was an unexpected pleasure warming him.

Perhaps he ought to savor it.

CHAPTER TWENTY-ONE

AFTER A LONG WALK over the hills by the sheep pasture, they'd finally arrived at the tenants' cottages. They were met with much enthusiasm. Justine led Brandon to the Archer's home.

"Oh, Miss Justine—oh begging your pardon—Lady Graven— we're that pleased for ye, truly we are!" The young red-haired Archer girl hopped on her toes with the news of Justine's marriage to Brandon.

"Thank you, Lizzie," said Justine . "So you'll come and work at the house?"

"Oh, yes, anything for you, ma'am!" Lizzie let out a laugh.

"Indeed, girl!" Mrs. Archer shot a stern look at her daughter who stilled immediately. "Lizzie has some experience as a lady's maid now. She worked for a bit for Mrs. Treharne."

"Ah yes, that's right, you were in service at Crestdown for a time." said Justine.

"For a short time, yes. But Lizzie had to come home and mind her father and brother and sister when my aunt took sick and I needed to go to her." Mrs Archer folded her hands together.

"Now auntie is right as rain, Mum has returned, and we are all home together." Lizzie's hands shuffled through her skirts.

Mrs. Archer bowed her head at Brandon who filled the small dark room with his height. "This is most kind, your Lordship. An honor."

But Brandon only had eyes for Justine. This was the third house they had visited. Each family was more pleased than the last to see their master back in his family seat, yet even more pleased to hear that he and Justine had wed. Justine knew every one of his tenants, and they had greeted her with a singular ease and warmth.

It was obvious that over the years she had put in the time and effort to build relationships with these people, something that perhaps a lesser woman would not have done. A lesser woman who thought herself grand would have stayed within her grand house, only associated with her particular circle of grand friends, pampered herself in trivial indulgences, and ignored the real world which moved and shifted around her.

But not Justine.

Justine felt an obligation toward the tenants which was impressive as she had not been the official heir or representative of Wolfsgate, not even a blood relative of the family. And yet she had not only recognised that responsibility, but she had taken it up as her own obligation. Indeed, seeing her amongst them now, she betrayed no physical discomfort with the lower classes.

They left the Archer cottage and walked toward the cottage belonging to the widow Shaw.

"This will be our last visit Brandon, I promise." Justine pressed her hand on his arm. "You must be tired by now, and we still have the walk home." A lightness floated through his chest at the soft tone in her voice, her concern for him, at her planning ahead and reassuring him that she understood his limits.

At Mrs. Shaw's table they were seated across from each other. Brandon sat still as the women chattered and Mrs. Shaw brought forth a dish of pasties.

"Mrs. Shaw, your meat pie never disappoints." Justine said.

"Do try it Brandon, it will take you back to our childhood, I promise you." She grinned and bit into the pastry. Her tongue swiped a golden flake of crust from the edge of her lower lip. "Delicious."

That mouth of hers.

Brandon crossed his legs, his grip on his cane tightening. He tried to will away the pounding in his head, not to mention in his groin, but it was impossible. He couldn't tear his eyes away from Justine's lips. Silence fell in the room, and his gaze jumped between the women. They stared at him. Mrs. Shaw's hands fussed with her skirts.

What the devil was wrong? Was he drooling? Maybe he was, he had been obsessing again over his wife's lips wrapped around his...

Justine tilted her head at the dish.

"Ah," Brandon exhaled. He took a large bite of one of the pies before him. The flavor and texture melted in his mouth. "My wife is absolutely correct, Mrs. Shaw. Delicious." He nodded at her.

The woman's face flushed, and she bobbed her head at him. "Thank'e, sir."

"Mizzy Justine!" A dark, scruffy boy, his hair standing on end, his face smudged with streaks of dirt, burst into the cottage and threw his arms about Justine. "You said you'd be back long before this!"

"It's Lady Justine, John," said his mother. "Mind yer manners, love."

"Oh my, oh my!" John blinked up at her, mouth hanging open. "Milady? Fancy that! And what makes ye a proper lady now, Mizzy Justine?"

"I do."

The boy's head jerked in the direction of Brandon's rich, low voice. His eyes widened at Brandon.

"I have married, John." Justine smoothed the hair over the boy's head. "This is my husband, Lord Graven of Wolfsgate."

The boy's eyes scrunched together and widened as he examined Brandon from head to toe, his neck and shoulders stiffening. "But yer supposed to be dead. Ain't that right?"

Mrs. Shaw gasped. "John Shaw!"

Brandon grinned. "That's how the story goes, John. But as you can see, I'm very much alive and married to your Mizzy Justine, which now makes her my Lady Graven." He liked how that sounded the second it rolled off his lips—*my Lady Graven*. Justine stared at him. Did she like that, too? He leaned back in the uncomfortable wood chair.

With a small hand at her cheek, the boy peered into Justine's face. "Guess you can't marry me then, eh? But seein' as his Lordship come back from the darkness o' death for you, that's somethin', I expect."

"Oh, Lord, deliver me," muttered Mrs. Shaw.

Justine smiled, her hand touching his. "You could very well say that, John."

"That's all right then," the boy mumbled, frowning at Brandon.

"Have my pasty, John." Justine pushed the plate towards him. "I couldn't possibly finish it." John lunged at the food and took off with it outside.

"Forgive the boy, Lord Graven." Mrs. Shaw flushed once more.

"Ah, he knows his mind, Mrs. Shaw, and he's outright. That's a gift. Let's hope he never loses it."

The door was pushed opened, and in strode a tall, muscular young man with long dark hair. "Auntie Keren—oh, pardon." He hung his hands at his hips. His brooding, dark eyes took in Justine.

"Lord Graven's been waiting to see you, Martin," Mrs. Shaw said.

That dark gaze shifted to Brandon.

"Martin, do you remember Lord Graven?" asked Justine.

Martin stood very still before the table and nodded at Brandon. "Sir," he said just above a whisper.

"Lady Graven tells me you are a fine hand with horses, and that you've helped her quite a lot at Wolfsgate, even with her riding," said Brandon.

Martin's eyes slid to Justine. She nodded at him. "Yes, sir," Martin said.

"I'd like to keep you on formally as groomsman." Brandon straightened his spine. We're cleaning up the house and making repairs, and we need the help. What do you say?"

The muscles around Martin's jaw tensed. "Thank you sir. Yes."

"Very good then, come to the house tomorrow morning," Brandon said.

Martin dipped his head at Brandon. His gaze slid back to Justine. "Ma'am." His hand touched Mrs. Shaw's arm, and he left the house.

"He's a good boy, our Martin," Mrs. Shaw said. "Became very quiet after his parents and sisters were taken away with the sickness. Doesn't have any family left, but us. We took him in then. Loves horses, just loves them. I believe he'll do well by ye, sir."

"So my wife tells me, Mrs. Shaw. I'm sure he will."

A slight smile curved Justine's lips. She raised a chipped cup to those remarkable lips and drank. Listening to yet another story Mrs. Shaw told her about her children, Justine grinned, her head tipping back, exposing her creamy throat. Her easy laughter filled the cramped space and lapped around him like soothing, fragrant bathwater.

He could not remember such a sultry, inviting sound nor feeling the velvet smoothness which now passed through his chest upon hearing it. Yes, an untroubled, simple pleasure. He pressed his palm down his thigh. For the first time, he sensed his limbs were not tense, nor were his muscles coiled. Unusual, really. At this moment, he was actually content to sit in this dark, stuffy cottage on this battered hard wooden chair and watch a friendly young woman with sparkling eyes, a woman who happened to be his wife, simply discourse with another woman about daily nothings.

Brandon's attention drifted from the women's trail of chatter. The cuff of his shirt poking out of the sleeve of his frock coat fascinated him. Irritated him. His fingers tugged at the offending fabric. Cold perspiration beaded on his forehead. He curled and uncurled his fingers into a fist until his knuckles whitened. His skin begged to be scratched. Begged.

A touch on his shoulder.

His body jolted, his eyes darted up. Justine's warm fingers stroked his tight jaw, and he let out a short breath.

"Shall we go home?" she whispered.

Home?

Her smooth, rich voice flowed over his weary muscles like warm oil, a balm, and his shoulders eased. She stayed close to him as he rose from the chair, faltered, her arm sliding around his middle. He leaned on her for a moment. "Thank you," Brandon murmured against her hair. He hated being dependent on Justine physically. She didn't look like she had the strength to help him, but her determination was nothing short of iron. Strands of her curly hair slid against his lips, and her lavender scent filled his nostrils. His eyelids sank for a moment.

In silence, they walked slowly back towards the house, his limp more pronounced from his fatigue. In the distance, just over the roll of the green hill before them, the darkened medieval stone towers of Wolfsgate were visible.

Yes, home.

CHAPTER TWENTY-TWO

BRANDON DID NOT PROTEST when she helped him out of his outer-wear and boots. He settled into the sofa before the fire and loosened his neck cloth.

Molly had drawn the heavy midnight blue curtains, lit a fire, and had a cold supper ready for them. A tray of cheese, chicken, and bread as well as a bottle of wine and two glasses spread before them on the low table.

"They like you, all of them, very much." He opened the bottle of wine.

"The tenants?" She sat next to him. "I enjoy visiting with them, having a woman's chat, playing with the children. I enjoy their company."

"My uncle was surely not good company, especially for one such as you."

"I began visiting them regularly when the fever hit. Dr. Langham had come to check on Richard and Lord Jeremy. I asked him how the village was faring, and he told me about the children being ill and underfed. I begged him to let me accompany him on his visits with supplies and be of assistance to him, but he refused, saying it would be unseemly and much too dangerous."

Brandon's arm stretched out around her shoulders. He pulled her close and dipped his head to hers. "Let me guess." His breath mingled with her own. "You went on your own with a cartful of food and supplies?"

Justine grinned. "I did. Then one day he caught me feeding little John soup, and he was quite cross with me. I begged him not to say a word to my stepfather or William, and he relented after seeing all the food and the bed linens I had brought. I also gave him money for medicines."

He planted his lips on the side of her temple and held her for a moment. His fingers squeezed her shoulder, lingering on the side of her arm. "I am full of admiration, Lady Graven."

A spiral of warmth rose inside her. It had been a great joke to William and Richard that she was now Lady Graven. It had been a bitter joke to her as well; a forced marriage to a phantom husband who would soon be dead. But now, with Brandon alive and here and saying her title himself, it was no longer a hoax, a travesty, meaningless and empty.

Yet it was real on paper only.

Brandon poured the wine and offered her a glass of the ruby liquid. He drank, winced, and sucked in his cheeks. "Ach, not a good vintage." He put down the glass.

Justine grinned. "No, my lord," she said. "The good bottles are long gone, I'm afraid."

"And yet you let me drink it?"

"I felt your expert opinion and judgement were required, Lord Graven. You are the Lord of all here at Wolfsgate."

"Duplicitous fox." He wiped at the edge of his mouth with his thumb. "What happened to the girl who blushed at the mere mention of a pretence?"

"Gone."

"I think I know how I can still make that girl blush."

I'm sure he would. "Would you like a brandy instead?"

"Please. Damn me, I do remember my father always kept a

very good wine cellar. I'll have to re-stock right away. This just won't do."

"You and William and your friends spent plenty of time down there educating yourselves about wine, did you not not?"

Brandon grinned. "You knew about that, eh? We did, indeed. We educated ourselves very well with quite a variety of bottles."

Justine remembered another time in the wine cellar one rainy afternoon when she and Annie had been re-enacting ghost stories for each other in its crypt-like atmosphere. She had heard murmurings in the stone corridor and chanced upon Brandon and Amanda kissing. It was the first time she had ever seen such a kiss between a man and a woman.

Amanda was in Brandon's embrace, standing on her toes, her delicate hands against his chest, his fingers gripping her upper arms, keeping her close. Their mouths were latched onto each other, and it was obvious that their tongues were moving together. Justine had stood frozen by the wall witnessing their... hunger. That was the only way to describe it. Brandon and Amanda hungered for each other, and Justine had watched them in utter fascination.

"What is it?" Brandon's relaxed voice broke her reverie.

"I was just remembering the games we used to play in the cellar: haunted castle, imperial spies, the ghostly dungeon." Her teeth gnawed on the inside of her cheek.

"Hmm." Brandon leaned his head back against the edge of the sofa and stared into the fire. Was he remembering now as well? Remembering those hungry kisses? Those feelings of passion with Amanda?

At that time, Brandon had only just returned from Italy. Amanda had probably expected to have been proposed to then. But instead his father had immediately sent him off once more, this time across the great ocean to the island of Jamaica for two long years. Those two years had turned into four after a ship-wreck and William's fateful strategy. Now Brandon had finally returned home to find he was married to her, the little nobody, and his exquisite Amanda was married to William.

She slid the wine bottle out of the way. Fate certainly was sour.

He had to be curious to see Amanda again. The idea pierced her sides. And when he did, how would he react? Perhaps that passion he once felt for her had never faded?

Justine couldn't imagine being in love with Brandon and then marrying someone else. William was quite a striking and attractive man, yet with a more solid form than Brandon's present trim frame. William's handsome luster, however, was edged with a cool harshness.

Justine hadn't had much contact with William and Amanda since they had married. Only once had she accompanied Richard to dinner at their home. Andrew was already abroad at the time. The dinner had been a stiff affair with William conversing with his father, and Amanda finding Justine woefully uneducated about the current goings-on of London theatre and fashion. However, Amanda's father had been most appreciative that he had a willing listener in Justine. Mr. Blakelock had set about educating her on Whig politics and then on his ideas about farming in their county and husbandry. It had been a long evening.

Justine sank deeper into the sofa. She was sure Amanda would be quite eager to see Brandon again.

"Justine, have the brandy." Brandon offered her his glass, and the sweet, potent vapors of the liquor dissolved her daydream. She took the glass from him and brought it to her lips. His gaze remained on her as she drank from his glass. "Do you like it?" he asked, his voice low.

She nodded slightly, unable to tear her gaze from his.

Oh, I like it very much.

CHAPTER TWENTY-THREE

A SHARP THRILL coursed through Brandon's blood and shot straight to his cock as Justine swallowed his brandy slowly, the delicate skin on her throat moving with the action. These erotic feelings for her were coming harder and fiercer each day.

He was surprised at how at ease he felt in her company. With Justine he felt no pressure to be the Brandon Treharne he once was, the one everyone still expected him to be. He had seen that expectation at the Fang & Feather each night and in his tenants' eyes today. He knew they had been taken aback by his moody and withdrawn demeanor. They seemed uncomfortable in his presence and had focussed on Justine.

Thankfully, Justine let him be in his tangle of moods and extreme humours. If she intervened in his twisted train of thought, it was with a logical, practical purpose that he later appreciated. She wasn't afraid of his sudden, wild tempers either. In fact, she had a temper herself and sometimes unleashed it.

He liked that, too.

Would his jagged edges ever ease? Would he ever feel that the fragmented pieces of his self were mended or in some sort of order at the very least? In his current irregular and mercurial state Justine was becoming his touchstone.

Touchstone.

His forehead creased with the memory of that word. His father had once used it in reference to his late mother. *"She kept me sane, my boy. It's a rare thing. Perhaps one day you'll be blessed and find yours,"* he had told him.

With Amanda he remembered feeling a keen excitement and a raw, boyish eagerness. She would flirt shamelessly with him one moment and then behave demurely the next. Her girlish games entertained him because he had always been beguiled by her physical beauty and itched to claim it, and he knew she was enthralled by him in turn. She was the prize of the neighbourhood would one day be his.

But was Amanda ever his touchstone?

He never given that much thought back then, not at that age. He he had indeed felt a wave of anger upon learning of her marriage to his cousin; his ego had been bruised that he'd been so easily forgotten, that life had moved on without him.

Amanda was still beautiful and alluring from what he had seen through the window that rainy night at Crestdown, however, it was Justine who intrigued him, Justine who invaded his thoughts at every turn.

Traces of the sadness and loneliness he remembered about the girl still clung to the young woman, but they only shrouded a deep, innocent delight in life and a practical inner strength; a strength on which he found he relied more and more.

Yes, his touchstone.

His jaw tightened as he watched her finish his brandy.

A touchstone he badly wanted to taste.

His arousal was stronger than ever these days. The girl whom he had always felt protective of, he now wanted to possess; be in her, on top of her, under her, the lot of it. They were married after all, but this was Justine. Her feelings actually mattered to him.

With her beside him in bed he was finally getting quality rest. Before falling asleep they would banter about the estate, she would tell a tale about a local, the minister's snobbish wife, the changes in the village shops, make an observation, or a joke or two. He would inquire about his friends and how their lives had changed since he had been gone. He had never had this ease and restfulness, this sort of friendship or companionship before with a woman.

Justine usually fell asleep long before he did, curling up into a ball at his side clutching a pillow. He would put his arm around her, draw her close until she released the pillow and clutched him.

He had told her she wasn't alone anymore, and he had meant it. Every night he would sink his fingers into that incredible hair of hers. Touching her relaxed him. Keeping her body close and safe from the cold pleased him somehow. Marriage had a certain appeal after all.

Last night he had woken up with another nightmare. He teased himself with the memory.

She had instantly rolled into his body, wrapped herself around his shaking frame, her hand stroking his heaving, damp chest. He took her in his arms and pressed his face against her throat. She had kissed his temple and dragged her fingers through his hair and over his shoulders. The tension in his strained muscles began to fade.

"Was it the shipwreck?"

"No, the hospital this time."

"Did they harm you there? Did you remember something particular?"

"No, the dream was more about how I felt there.

"Tell me."

He sucked in air. "Desolate and abandoned. Broken. Helpless and alone. All of that laced with the ethereal effect of the opium. Quite a desperate combination. Two years of that, Justine. And just now it had me in its grip again. I couldn't breathe. Felt as if I were drowning."

"It's over, Brandon. You're here now. You're home." She rubbed her legs against his. If she did more of that, he was going to pull her under his aching body and drown himself inside her.

"Justine, you're cold." He hooked her knees with his hands and brought her legs up towards his hips. He rubbed her icy feet, then stroked a path up her bare legs. She shivered—from the cold or his touch? Her body slackened into his, and he took in a deep breath, his lips brushing her forehead. He pulled the covers around her, his hand drifting down her lower back over her nightdress, but stopped before the beautiful curve of her rear. They lay there in silence listening to the wind roaring outside the window.

"Do you think he's out there?" she asked.

"The wolf?"

"I like to think he is."

"Really? You were always the one crying for his release from his supernatural bonds."

"He's been a part of your lives from the beginning, a part of Wolfsgate. Without him there would be no Barons of Graven, would there? And you have been a part of him. You are forever entwined. I like to think he needs us as we need him."

"Do we? He's not simply a ghostly menace?"

"No, he's not, Brandon. I don't think he stays to haunt you. I think he stays to keep you on the straight and narrow, my Lord Graven.

"There's a thought." He planted another kiss on her forehead.

She snuggled into his side. "You're naked."

He chuckled. "I enjoy the feeling of clean, soft bedlinen against my skin and a real bed under me after so many years. Would you prefer I wore a nightdress in future?" She'd only smiled against his skin, breathed deeply, and drifted back to sleep.

Now, sitting here in the parlour, both of them drinking before the fire, another memory ignited a flame inside him. That of his cock throbbing in her delicate hands while they had lain on this very floor. His hand rubbed down his torso at the recollection.

That night his uncontrollable lust, his drive for release, his need to feel her touch had been all-consuming. Frankly, he was surprised she hadn't pulled away or protested. Justine had embraced him, let him guide her hand to his salvation and shuddered in his arms when his mouth had finally found her magnificent breasts. The following morning he'd only wanted to show her affection.

Fancy that.

With every laugh, smile, casual touch or graze of their hands, arms, and legs in their early morning tangle of sheets or the sight of her fabulous hair on his pillow, on his chest, it was there, charging through his veins, heating his blood, filling him with need. Flashes of the same tension were obvious in her eyes, in the sound of her irregular breathing when she'd first climb into bed with him. Even in the dark he could sense it, smell it.

"More brandy?" Her rich brown eyes swept over him. Brandon exhaled, but it didn't help. That brutal need only coiled tighter inside him.

"Bring the bottle."

CHAPTER TWENTY-FOUR

THEY HAD FINISHED THE BOTTLE.

Holding onto each other, they managed to climb that interminable staircase and get to Justine's room. She wrestled with her stays and her corset and skirts, while Brandon peeled off his clothes and belted a thin wool robe about himself.

He crouched by the hearth adjusting the logs with the iron poker, making the flames blaze once again. "What was it you used to say when we would played Kings and Queens?"

"'Thank you, m'aaaaaaaam'—in my finest northern accent." Justine repeated it, drawing out the vowels even more this time. Brandon's body shook with laughter. Justine fell back on the bed.

"You made a fine lady-in-waiting for Queen Annie." He placed the poker back in its stand.

"Yes, I did."

"And I the finest King, I must say."

"Oh, of course." Justine let out a soft laugh.

"And William was some sort of Lancelot? Was that it?" He went to the basin to rinse off his hands.

"Yes, albeit a wicked one." She sighed. "And if Andrew was about, he was his lackey or spy."

He grit his teeth at hearing the Adonis's name cross her lips. "Yes, poor Andrew," he muttered, drying his hands.

Justine sprang from the bed and darted toward the large Jacobean trunk in the opposite corner of the room. She jerked it opened and rummaged through layers of clothing and objects.

"Annie and I loved dressing up in your mother's old gowns that she'd given us to play with. We would trip over those huge skirts everywhere we went. And these *faux* jewels of hers, too. Look, Brandon." She held up a long strand of coloured glass beads putting it over her head.

"Quite regal."

"What did you take us for, sir?" She curtsied and let out another soft laugh. An unusually eager sensation spiked through him at the carefree sound. His eyes met her bright ones, and it was as if a flaming arrow pierced his chest. His body stilled, his lips parted. Her long thick waves of hair tumbled over her naked shoulders which peeked out from her nightdress, her taut nipples searing through the delicate fabric, the necklace falling between her breasts. A surge of heat flashed through his body, filled the room, and squashed his ability to breathe.

She turned back to the trunk. "I've saved a few souvenirs from our childhood." She spun to face him wearing a worn dark blue tricorn hat on her head. "Does this look familiar?"

He grinned. "That was my pirate captain's hat."

"Indeed it was, Captain. I think it was your grandfather's before that, was it not? And here we have your weapon of choice." She brandished a thin wooden sword. "There's one more for you here somewhere." She dropped the sword on the bed and bent over the trunk again digging through its contents. She shot up. "Here it is. Your majesty, may I present, the royal crown." She flourished a fabric crown in the air that Molly had sewn for him out of several layers of thick gold material.

Justine sprang across the bed to get to Brandon who stood on the other side. His breath jammed in his throat at the sight. She would be the death of him tonight. She sat up on her knees at the edge of the bed before him and propped the crown on his head. Her lips parted as her hands slid down his arms. He was under the spell of her relaxed, pleasure-filled eyes.

"Christ." Brandon tossed the crown to the bed. Her eyes widened as his hand stroked her flushed cheek. "It would seem the lady-in-waiting is actually a Pirate Princess in disguise," he breathed. His lips brushed the corner of her mouth, and she let out a small moan.

Hunger for her flared all through him. Years worth of hunger that demanded its fill. Raw need combusted in his veins igniting small explosions through his entire body. He couldn't stop it, and he didn't want to.

He had to have her.

"And this Pirate Princess—" His thumb rubbed over her lower lip, slipping inside her mouth ever so slightly, brushing her tongue. "—has taken the King prisoner."

His fingers slid down the slope of her throat, then back up around her neck. He scattered tiny soft kisses next to her mouth then pulled back to look at her for just a moment. Yes, she was speechless. His hands fisted in her hair, and his mouth crushed hers. The old tricorn hat tumbled to the bed.

His fingers stole over a breast and captured the nipple through the light fabric of her chemise. So beautiful, so soft, other worldly even. His tongue explored her mouth, tasting her, demanding of her. She let out a moan and arched against his chest. He growled in her mouth as he pressed her back on the bed, the mattress shifting under their weight. His hands skimmed down her sides and swept under the thin fabric of her nightdress. Finally, her silky, naked flesh was in his hands.

"Oh, Brandon—"

He pressed his hard length in between her legs, nestling it

there. She whimpered. That was encouraging. His wool dressing gown had opened, exposing his bare chest and abdomen. "Take it off me," he whispered roughly. She tugged on the belt until it untied, slid the robe off his shoulders, pulling it down his arms, her warm hands stinging his skin. The damn robe finally fell away. Justine's fingertips skimmed over his bare chest as her breathing grew deeper, ragged like his own.

Brandon tore the chemise from her body. His entire being seized at the sight of her bareness, the glass bead necklace laying over her breasts. She was an odalisque of the Orient. An exotic creature. Familiar yet foreign.

All expectation. All promise. All for him.

She was his.

He licked at her throat, drinking in her faint scent of lavender and the sweetness of the brandy on her breath. She was maddening. He was mad. Stark raving mad. For her.

He rubbed the glass bead necklace over her nipples and sucked on them both together. She writhed and let out soft cries at the friction, at his hands caressing her flesh. He squeezed her breasts together and suckled and adored them. Everything spun into a blur. He was a hungry, greedy beast. His one hand glided down over the delectable, smooth curve of her hip until it sank into the most private part of her.

"Oh, Justine," he groaned in her ear softly biting on her ear lobe as his fingers explored her wet silken heat. He found her pearl and teased it, caressed it. A soft cry heaved from her lips.

"Brandon—" Her raspy voice sent a shiver down his spine.

"So wet for me." His fingers moved more insistently. He raised his head and watched his hand working, her hips squirming. Then his gaze returned to her face, and his eyes melted with hers. "I want you, Justine. Do you want me?" Her fingers dug into his arms, her breaths came faster. "Tell me," he whispered through ragged breaths. He had to hear her say it, needed to hear her say it.

"Yes. I want you."

Brandon kissed her like a famished beast, his lips then dragged across her jaw and down her throat. He wanted nothing more than to make her as insane with need as he was. He removed the necklace from her throat and brought it between her legs, running the beads up and down over her wet slit. "Brandon!" Her back arched, her legs squeezed together, her body twisted, trembled, her pelvis tipped up, pleading for more.

"Yes..." He dragged the necklace over her, teasing her, then laced it over her breasts. She grasped it, kneading the beads into her soft flesh. His finger entered her silky wetness slowly, and her body quaked at his invasion, her mouth falling open. Brandon let out a groan. Her eyes exploded with feeling, and she cried out.

"Christ, so beautiful, my beautiful Justine," he murmured against her skin. He took the end of the necklace in his mouth, tasting her, and her eyes flashed at him. He let it drop from his lips and licked a nipple. "I have to taste more of you, my delicious girl." She arched her body into his like a kitten eager for play, her hands sweeping up into his hair, tugging at it.

Oh she wanted more, too.

He raised himself up and nudged apart her thighs. She blinked up at him and let out a whimper. His mouth sank over her, his tongue swirling through her. She cried out, and her hands pulled at the necklace, and it broke apart, blue and green beads popping over her pale skin, skipping over the bed.

"Holy..."

The sweet and salty tang of her secret flesh on his tongue made his insides explode. He glanced up at her. Her head thrashed against the pillows, and her hands reached out to grip his hair once more. He caught her wrists and pinned them to the bed at her sides. His fingers entwined in hers holding her hands firmly down in the twisted sheets, and her upper body finally stilled. Her moans drummed in his ears like a siren's call.

This was heaven.

Pure, bloody heaven.

What had come over him? He had never done this before to a woman, never been enticed by it, but now, now he was lost in Justine, sucking, swirling, his tongue pressing round, darting inside her. Her hips rocked to their own needy rhythm against his mouth urging him on. Her body shuddered in his ruthless hold, and she cried out sharply coming to a frenzied, pulsing release against his tongue.

He licked at her, his heartbeat hammering in his chest. "My tongue will never be the same," he murmured against her inner thigh. A moan escaped her throat.

He needed to be inside her right this minute. This wasn't just his body screaming for release, but the desire to completely consume Justine. He got a hold of his senses and his cock as he grit his teeth. Her eyes snapped open at the promise of his rigid length at her opening. He only wanted to explode, but he didn't want to hurt her. He was determined to make it good for her. Very good. Damn well amazing.

He wanted her to like it. A lot.

He entered her, sinking inside her.

Her eyes pleaded with him one moment, then softened the next, her jaw slackening. She took in a breath, then lifted her hips up to meet his, her hands on his biceps, pulling him closer, deeper. Brandon gasped and closed his eyes for a moment, groaning over her as he filled her inch by devastating inch.

There was no breathing now, no thinking. Time stopped.

His lips touched hers, and his one hand brushed the hair from her damp face. Her glassy eyes were fixed on his. Her body stiffened.

"Am I hurting you?" he whispered hoarsely. She only shook her head.

He shifted himself and sank deeper inside her, then pulled himself out just a bit and slowly thrust in again. Their heavy breathing hung over them, the musky, warm scent of their arousal filled the room. His face loomed over hers. Justine's eyes practically glowed. His lower lip quivered, his lungs tightened painfully, his throat thickened. His entire body throbbed, begging for one thing only.

Her body took his in, offering him the world.

His eyes tried to focus on hers through the blur of sensation, this maelstrom of foreign emotion that had him in its grip, but he couldn't. The breath choked in his throat.

His heart banged a drumbeat in his chest. He stopped moving inside her.

Justine's one hand reached up and gently swept back his hair then slid down and wrapped around his neck. Her other hand cradled his face. What a soothing touch she had. How did she know he needed...

"What is it, Brandon?" she whispered.

"You feel so good, so good. I want to..." He swallowed. "I want to stay right here." He was drowning in Justine's large eyes. If he could stay sheathed inside her forever, this luxurious, safe haven, he would. Here was a bliss he had never known before, and it wasn't artificially induced. It was something else, he didn't know what exactly. Had coupling ever been like this before?

Justine's warm hand rubbed the straining muscles of his neck. She licked her lips. "Bran." Her voice was soft, beckoning, seeping right through his pores, offering him sanctuary. The knuckles of her other hand delicately skimmed his hard, stubbled jaw until the harsh lines eased.

She bent her knees and brought her legs close to his sides, pressing them around his hips, rocking her pelvis up against his. With that one graceful, generous movement she took his breath away as her body took his cock deeper. A soft cry escaped her lips as she rocked against him once more, taking him in again. His eyes squeezed shut against the rapid fire detonation in his veins.

The air hissed from his mouth, and his head arched back for an instant.

A savage force inside him wanted nothing more than to slam into her hard and fast, but he did his damnedest to control the raging impulse to transform into a blood thirsty animal. He should control himself, shouldn't he?

Damn.

His cock stroked in and out slowly as her fingers dug into his flesh. He dipped his face into her neck, the powdery scent of her damp skin driving him mad. His jaw clenched. "Jus?"

"Don't stop," she said through ragged breaths.

He lost whatever control he had left. His thrusts quickened, driving him forward in his search for more of this, more of *her*. The hair hung in his eyes as he watched her. He desperately wanted to pleasure her again, and, this time, to see that pleasure wash over her face. His insides tightened at the thought.

Justine's hands swept down his damp back clasping him over the surging muscles of his rear. Her erotic little breathy noises came quicker. He needed to elicit more of them.

He hunted inside her, chased. She turned her head away, and her muscles tensed around him, but she clung to him, taking him all in, taking whatever he gave her. He finally went off, shuddering deep inside her, releasing himself into the embrace of her beautiful body.

"Justine," his hoarse voice rumbled through the silence. "You..." his voice trailed off. She only stroked his back. He collapsed to her side, clinging to her. His mind was lost in a haze, floating somewhere in the hot room.

∾

BRANDON AWOKE WITH A START. His eyes blinked in the darkness. Sweat pooled underneath his cheek, his head laying on her chest.

A thought had pinned itself in his hazed mind and wouldn't let go.

What the devil was it?

He raised himself up over her sleeping form.

Ah, yes.

His wife had not been a virgin. Someone had gotten there before him.

CHAPTER TWENTY-FIVE

HE WASN'T HER FIRST.

His head sank back against the pillow.

Fascinating, for a girl who had spent most of her life practically cloistered on a country estate. Cloistered, yet her *affections* had flourished for a certain young gentleman as she had so delicately phrased it. The memory of Andrew Blakelock looking like a young Adonis at the village church the other morning, his pretty blue eyes sparkling over Justine flashed through his brain.

He scrubbed his face with his hand. Was it a celebration swive in honor of their secret engagement? Or maybe a goodbye swive before William and Richard dragged her to London and married her off to him, the scarred, addled cripple?

She had lied to him, and that stung as much as the lie itself.

When the early morning rays of light peeked between the drapes, he half-heartedly tugged at the sheets twisted between them and inspected the linens. There were no signs of blood.

His mouth pressed into a firm line. He had no right to be angry or even jealous. She had fallen in love with the boy and wanted to marry him, and it would have been a very good match. William and Richard had shattered Justine's dreams, destroyed her hopes for her future, saddled her with a thousand responsibilities and obligations no better than a common servant. Then they chained her to him.

It was, however, a rash act for a girl like Justine. Was she so deeply in love with Andrew, her desire for him so intense that she could not help but indulge, thinking they were to be married shortly? Still, a great risk. Or perhaps Andrew had forced himself on her when she had been made to reject him? He raked his hands through his hair and sucked in a deep breath. No, Adonis didn't seem the type, and Justine had been pleased to see him at the cemetery, not upset or afraid. More likely they had had a torrid reunion in secret before Adonis left for his Grand Tour.

He couldn't be sure of course, but any scenario made his brain pound as he imagined Justine in the arms of another man, foreign hands exploring her flesh, her spreading her legs wide with anticipation and finishing to full pleasure at the movement of someone else inside her.

Did she finish off with him last night?

Just before he burst inside her, she had turned her face away, half-buried in her pillow, her neck strained, her legs stiff at his sides. There were no cries or moans as there had been earlier with his mouth on her. No, goddammit, she hadn't finished, in fact, she had fought against it at the last minute. She had urged him on in the beginning, enjoyed it, even. But then it was as if she had purposely decided against it.

He rubbed his chest in a futile attempt to ease the tension surging through his muscles. She didn't want him then? Had she simply put up with it, put up with his need like a dutiful wife?

No, she did want him. He had read the signs correctly, he wasn't that far gone. Maybe she had felt she was betraying the Adonis and held herself back at the last moment out of guilt? Because she had been enjoying it a hell of a lot before he had even entered her.

Brandon closed his eyes and the usual pains pummeled his head, scraped over his flesh once more.

His gaze fell on her delectable body next to him on the bed. Although he had felt no barrier once he was inside her, she had been extremely tight even when so wet. Perhaps it had been only once and some time ago. The smooth skin of her back shimmered in the glow of dawn. His pulse tripped at the memory of her softness wrapped around him, clinging to him, her moans erupting in his kisses. She had given herself to him without pushing him away or exhibiting fear in the face of his desire, a moment or two of anxiety perhaps, but that was natural.

When he had tasted her, her experience of such pleasure had obviously been a surprise to her. She went wild for that, and so did he; it had nearly done him in. He smiled to himself remembering how he had to hold her down. All her verbal responses to his sucking on her, licking her, had been whimpers and cries teeming with desire and vulnerability. Then that raw moan just before she...

Oh, yes. That would remain branded on his soul forever.

He leaned over and kissed her bare back, his hand roaming over her hips to the smooth curves of her rear. Had she regretted that experience?

Whatever first experience she had had, it must have left her with a mistrust of her own self and perhaps hints of shame. His fingertips trailed over a silky thigh. He was going to change all of that for her. He would be the one to give her that bloody ecstasy, and she would damned well remember it and want more.

Much, much more. Just like he did.

Since he'd returned home, he realized his senses and emotions had both dulled and intensified after the trauma of the shipwreck and the use of the opiate. Such sharp polar opposites would drive anyone mad. This was his strange new reality, his special madness.

Bedding Justine was a fantastic cure for his ills.

He rubbed his jaw. Who would have thought? The young girl who had peppered his youth with smiles and a thousand kindnesses was now his wife. A wife he wanted to swive, possess, consume.

As often as possible.

Repeatedly.

Bedding Justine was his new compulsion.

He had to still those black thoughts regarding her first time for now. He would find out more later when he had the energy to deal with it. In the meantime, he would demand her attention and pleasure her over and over again until he was sure there was nothing left of any romantic sentimentality or wistfulness she may still harbor for the blond Adonis.

Yes, he wanted to feel that fervor grip her and know that he was the cause of it. And she would know it too. He wanted to hear her plead for more, to need it just as much as he did.

He nestled against her, his hand tucked around the fulness of her breasts, his groin pressed into her spectacular rear, his mouth at the delicate nape of her neck, and he closed his eyes.

Yes. That was a fine plan.

CHAPTER TWENTY-SIX

I CAN'T BREATHE.

Can't breathe.

"Justine!" a muffled voice reached her as if through a long tunnel with her stuck at the opposite end. "Justine, wake up!"

Large warm hands gripped her stiff arms. The sheet which had bound her legs was torn off of her. Cold. Exposed.

She jerked her hands before her face. "No!" She flinched in his arms.

"Justine—you've had a nightmare." One of his hands was at her neck, the other rubbed the back of her head.

She blinked at him. *Brandon.* Slowly her body began to relax in his arms. He brushed the hair off her face, stroked her cheek. Her eyes tried to focus on his face, the cold sweat beaded on her temple.

"You seemed so frightened," he said in a gentle tone. His hand swept over her chest to where her heart hammered. "You're still upset."

Her body stiffened and her chest caved in. The cold air in the room swept over her exposed breasts and tummy. Her eyes widened. She was naked in bed with Brandon's arms around her, and they had...

She pulled at the sheet to cover herself.

"What was the dream about?" Brandon asked tucking the sheet and coverlet around her.

"Pardon?"

"I dream of a sinking ship and a hideous hospital. What do you dream of?"

She looked away, anywhere but in those beautiful sea-coloured eyes of his that held a secret knowledge of her.

"Tell me." He stroked her arm.

"It's a dream I sometimes have." She cleared her throat. "A brigand dressed all in black hunts for me through the house at night."

His gaze searched hers and knots twisted in the pit of her stomach. She darted out of bed, desperate for her chemise, but he pulled her back into his arms. She took a deep breath, but her muscles remained taut. He caressed her cheek with his warm hand, and the aroma of him drifted over her. That same heady scent was all over her skin and the bedding.

"If you don't relax I will find another, more interesting way to make you relax." Brandon's hips pressed against hers. She swallowed hard and sank back into his embrace. The taut smoothness of his body around her flooded her with memories of last night.

"Does this brigand ever catch you?"

"No. He comes close though. It's the same dream I've had since your father died. I felt truly alone in this house after he passed away. Even with Richard and Molly here. It's a big house. It can be particularly frightening at night."

His fingers stroked the side of her cheek. "You are not alone anymore, my girl." Her pulse quickened as the heat of his gaze poured over her. "And as my wife, Richard and William have no hold over you any longer. I promise you that. Do you understand?"

He sat up and gathered her in his arms, bringing her up between his legs, against his chest. He brushed the hair from her neck and dragged his lips over her cool skin across her shoulder and her neck. She shivered in his arms. His hot hands slid over her bare thighs spreading them apart. Her belly dipped.

"When I was inside you last night, you fought your pleasure. Why?" His fingers trailed up her torso until they found the soft underside of her breasts.

Her head pressed back into his chest. "What do you mean?" she whispered.

His hands gently caressed her breasts, and she held her breath as sparks of pleasure shimmered over her flesh. "The first time, with my mouth on you, you finished. When I was inside you though, at the end, I felt you trying to push it away. Tell me why. You don't have to be embarrassed with me. Not after last night, surely."

Her face heated, and she twisted her head towards his shoulder. There he was using her own words against her.

"Tell me."

"It was...overwhelming. I'd never felt anything like that before."

"Like what?"

"Like I would be shattered and swallowed whole at the same time." She let out a small gasp as his fingertips teased her nipples, and a tingling sensation shimmered through her. "You were watching me, and all I could think—"

"Too much thinking. You wanted to hide, like you're doing now. Don't hide from me, Justine, not you." He lightly pinched a nipple, and she gasped. The other hand slid down her torso to the soft inside of her thigh as his lips nipped at her earlobe.

"Touch yourself," he said, his voice husky and low at her ear.

Her throat burned. He took her hand in his and led it to the wet silkiness between her legs. With his hand guiding hers, her fingers swirled over her sensitive, secret flesh. His tongue flicked a delirious path across her neck and back up to her ear. She shivered, squirming against him. His hand continued to guide her finger in swirling motions, and her body slackened against his, her hips tilting as his other fingers rolled one of her agitated nipples. Wetness flooded her centre, and she moaned, her body shifting in his arms.

"Do you feel that, Jus? That's yours." His lips brushed her temple.

"Brandon—"

"Let me give this to you. Let go, love."

"Let go?" she asked.

"Yes, sweet girl, let go."

"It's too overwhelming."

"As it should be. That's good." His warm breath fanned her cheek. "You won't break or go under. I promise, you won't. I'm holding you, I'm right here to ride it with you."

Brandon brought their fingers to his mouth and sucked on them. Her eyes widened at the sight, her heart tripping at the soft, tugging pressure of his hot, wet mouth on her fingers. He was tasting her. An impossible ache surged through her. His lips released their suction, and their wet fingers luxuriously sank between her legs once again. Insanity. Ecstasy.

"Tell me how it feels, Jus," he whispered.

"Brandon..."

"Do you like our fingers touching you?"

"Yes." She twisted in his arms again, her free hand slid up around his hard bicep.

"Do you want more?" He increased the rhythm and pressure of their fingers and she panted. "Tell me what you want, Justine."

"Yes," she rasped. "More."

Her slickness began to collect around their fingers, making erotic sounds that seemed to echo over her skin. He slid their fingers inside her, and her inner walls pulsed around them.

"Look, Jus. Look at what we're doing. You're so beautiful like this." His lips brushed the side of her face. She held her breath and cast a glance down her body, connecting the chaos coursing through her with what their hands were actually doing.

"Breathe. Welcome it. Let go."

"Let go? And go where?" she asked through choppy breaths, her eyes shut.

His lips curled against her skin. He nipped her earlobe, tugged on a hard nipple, and her eyes fluttered open. Oh, he was determined to overload her with sensation and get her over the edge, and she was at his mercy.

"Come to me, Jus. Surrender to it," he breathed. She drew her knees up pressing back further into his chest. Her hips began to grind on their hands, her eyes were jammed shut. His tongue flicked at her ear. "Stop thinking."

Her face twisted in his arm. "I want to please you."

"Oh, sweet thing, you please me. And it pleases me greatly to give this to you. There's no right or wrong here, Justine." His mouth nuzzled her neck where her pulse galloped wildly under his lips. "I want you to feel it. Feel it all the way inside your beautiful quim." His fingers curved inside her, moving in a new and unforgiving rhythm. She let out a deep moan, her legs stiffening.

"I have you." His voice was thick, the tip of his tongue tracing the skin behind her ear once more.

Her hand released its tight grip on his bicep and reached up to clutch at his hair. Her head flung back. "Brandon!" Her body spasmed, her release rippling through her.

"There it is...yes," he murmured, his voice raw, his one hand tightly cupping a breast, the other still inside her. "Don't turn away from me again Justine. Or I'll find other such ways to get you to let go, do you understand?"

She nodded. Words, her voice, all failed her.

"Look at me." She turned to face him, and he kissed her hard holding her close. She settled in his embrace.

Her husband's embrace.

CHAPTER TWENTY-SEVEN

BRANDON FOUND her in the kitchen the next morning. He took her hand from the slices of bread she was arranging on a dish, raised it to his lips and kissed it. He then pushed his mother's velvet jewelry box toward her on the kitchen table and tapped it. "These are yours."

Justine's eyes flicked down at the box then back up at his determined face.

"You are Lady Graven now, are you not?"

Her lips pursed, yet she said nothing.

His head tilted at her, his eyes tightening as his long fingers went under her chin and raised her head to face him. "Are you not Lady Graven *now*?"

"Yes," Justine's face heated. "I am now."

"They are yours."

She sucked in air. *They had to have this conversation.* Of course, they should have had it in the very beginning and much before last night. She had to say it to him, though. She removed her hand from his and swallowed, wondering how in the world to form the words.

The thought of him staying with her out of a sense of obligation pained her. What if last night was simply an expression of that obligation or a fleeting impulse? Justine wanted him to feel free, not like a prisoner. No, not a prisoner. She knew too well what that felt like.

He chewed on a crust of bread. "You're over thinking again."

"Brandon, wouldn't you prefer to arrange for something else?"

"Something else?"

"I know a divorce is impossible, but there must be some other arrangement you would prefer?"

His head snapped up at her, his eyes a dark shade of green. "Oh?" He tossed the crust of bread on the table. "What would you prefer, Justine?"

"What I mean is you are back from the dead. A whole new life is ahead of you. You should be able to decide for yourself who you want to marry, instead of being burdened with Richard and William's scheme. It is quite unjust and unfair."

A muscle in his cheek tensed. "Aren't those lovely sentiments? Do you feel guilty?"

"I don't want you to be trapped. I was trapped as well."

"How is it you say these things to me now after last night?" His gaze swept over her. "You either think very lowly of me or very lowly of yourself."

Her insides stung, her mouth dried. "Last night was—"

"Yes?"

Steam rose from her chest and heated her face. She could still smell him on her skin, feel his tongue on her flesh, the fulness of him inside her. "Last night was wonderful," she breathed.

His fingers traced a trail along her collarbone and her body gave a start at the contact, her skin flushing. He lifted an eyebrow. "These are not ideal circumstances and all of it quite unfair to the both of us. Yet you think you are a burden to me? Aren't I the burden in this equation?"

"I think you are hurt and angry, and you have every right to be." She leveled her eyes at him. "You've been deceived by your own family. I only wonder if you may feel different over time once things settle in your head. I wouldn't want you to feel bound to me when you do not have to be."

His eyes blazed. "Regardless of how this marriage came about, you are not a burden to me, Justine. Perhaps this marriage is holding you back?" His neck stiffened, the tone of his voice icy. "Holding you back from someone else or from another life you had planned for yourself?" The angles of his face hardened making the scars seem more pale and prominent over his skin.

"No, Brandon, this marriage is not holding me back from anyone or anything else. It is an honour to be your wife."

He sucked in a breath. Picking up her half empty tea cup that was on the table, he drained it of the now cool liquid then slammed the cup back in its saucer. He licked his lips, his gaze jumped around the room. "My frock coat?" he asked, his voice flat, his face ashen. "Where is it?"

"Your frock coat?"

"Yes."

Her heart sank. "Is that where it is?"

"Hmm?"

"The laudanum, Brandon."

Davidson was right to warn her that the first months would be extremes of up and down; that he might seek out a substitute for the opium on his own.

"Smart girl." A frozen smile hardened Brandon's face. "The local apothecary is full of it. A most virtuous tincture, the man told me, a highly recommended panacea for every ailment. It's a lesser form, of course, but it provides an acceptable haze to stem the tides that overwhelm me still."

"A haze? Is that what you seek?"

"As you keep pointing out, Justine, trying to come to terms with over two years of your life having been stolen by your own

169

uncle and cousin is a lot to take in. It's all left a bitter taste in my mouth. Got to wash it away somehow."

"Don't give into that bitterness, Brandon, to that temptation."

His eyes squinted at her, his brows bunched. "Why the hell not? It appeases this sizzle in my veins quite nicely. I've tried the past few days, I really have. But dealing with one's own resurrection is proving to be a tad trying."

"This difficulty shouldn't be for too much longer. Don't waste yourself to this poison."

"Pretty words." His nostrils flared. "Are you going to save me now, my girl?"

"These tides—what do they feel like?"

He swallowed. "My head buzzes, my fingertips go numb. A wet chill clings to my flesh like a tight veil of slimy ice, and I'm nauseated, thank you very much."

"I understand this is difficult, unbearable. But 'tis temporary, 'twill pass."

"Just give me the goddamn laudanum, Justine!" he roared.

She remained still. Her voice calm. "I wish I could save you somehow, but only you can save yourself. I think if you want it badly enough, you can accomplish anything. You're strong that way, Brandon."

"How inspirational, Lady Graven, but I'm not strong. I'm simply vile."

"Do you have any idea how this all began? I do."

He scratched at his arm, his face stony. "You said it was my pain remedy in hospital."

"At first, yes. But you were provided with a steady supply. More than necessary. William and Richard made sure that plenty was available for you, because they paid for it, Brandon. I overheard them discussing it in the study last year and with the doctor who was in charge of you at hospital. They were quite pleased with themselves."

His cold eyes clamped on hers.

"Your coat is over there." She pointed to the garment draped over a chair in the corner. "Molly was going to sew a tear on the pocket this morning." They stared at each other in silence. "Go get it then."

He sprang at the chair and groped at the frock coat, finally extracting a small glass bottle from a pocket. His shoulders drooped as he rubbed the bottle with his thumb. "I've been trying Justine, fighting this for days. It's not working." His lips tightened. "More tea."

She poured tea in her cup. The muscle in his cheek twitched again. "A few drops will dull this bloody sting right now. It's weaker than the opium I'm accustomed to. I can wean myself off it like baby's milk."

"You've been weaning for a while now, haven't you?" she asked. He only scowled at her. Justine crossed her arms. "My mother took laudanum, Brandon. She was a very unhappy woman, and it offered her that acceptable, artificial haze of contentment you speak of. But underneath that fleeting bliss, her bleak disappointments with life, with herself, with me were still painful for her. I must say, now I understand that lost and agitated demeanor of hers. Those are my memories of her."

He raised his head. His eyes were fevered, bloodshot.

"You wish to go backwards? To be stuck in that haze?" Justine asked, her voice cool. "Isn't that what William wants?"

He placed the small bottle on the table with a clank, letting out a guttural moan. She wrapped her arms around him, her body pressing into his. "You can do this."

Brandon's hands clasped hers at his back. "Lock the bloody doors." A command.

His hard, dark gaze followed her as she stepped back toward the door which led out to the dining room and twisted the key, then to the other door which led to the garden and turned that key.

Clack.

He stalked toward her, the fierce predator, and pulled her into his chest, his lips punished hers in a deep kiss. Her hands clutched at his waist, and the air surged from her system as his tongue plundered her mouth. He groaned, and that heat swirled between her legs at the primitive sound.

He jostled her back across the room until her rear pressed against the hard edge of the table. Her breath hitched in her throat as he lifted her up, and his hand swept over the surface. Tea cups and dishes crashed to the floor, the forks and spoons she had laid out earlier clattered somewhere in the distance, the cacophony adding to the chaos already exploding in her body. Brandon hovered over her like a hungry beast ready to devour her.

He unfastened his breeches, his hands drew up her skirts, and he wrapped her bare legs around his hips, his cold hands sending shivers across her flesh. He spit into his fingers and brought them to her opening. She held her breath as his rigid shaft thrust into her, biting down on her lip as a stinging soreness flared inside her. His dark gaze held hers as he filled her slowly, his lips parting to take in air, his eyes closing.

A thrill seized her. Would it always be like this—this profound, blissful shock when he first entered her? Brandon grunted loudly, the sound echoing through the kitchen. He pinned her hands by her head, his face now closer to hers. "Give me all of you, Jus, I want all of you."

She held his wild gaze. Had she done this to him? Brought him to such hot, menacing desperation? He dragged his cock out and then impaled her body again, another low grunt tearing from his chest. He drove into her over and over, harder, quicker than before. His one hand folded her knees pressing her legs high against his torso. A thousand sensations built and intensified inside her. She was all feeling, all sparks, all fire, burning, burning deep inside.

She could forget like this.

Yes, she could forget the loneliness, the resentment, the bitterness, the anger. This was new and satisfying, and hers, all hers, flowing through Brandon, flowing through her.

This was a kind of joy, but she didn't deserve it. Didn't deserve Brandon.

No. She should swerve out of its way.

She held her breath and tore her eyes from him to fight the tide, but he wrenched her face closer to his, his other hand planted on the table for support. "Look at me, dammit. Don't you dare fight this, Jus. I need you. Need you in it with me." His hips ground against hers, demanding her participation in this primal dance.

A long moan escaped her mouth, and her fingers slid up into the thickness of his unruly hair, their eyes melding. His lips brushed the inside of her wrist as his hand went to her breast claiming her soft flesh. Justine's back arched and she cried out, unable to control the rush of feelings and not wanting to any longer.

"Yes," he hissed. That undisguised hunger in his voice only spurned her on to embrace the mad rush of sensation. She did want this badly, just like Brandon. She wanted to feel alive, wanted to be possessed by him. Her hands clutched the surging muscles of his lower back, her insides squeezed around him.

"Brandon!"

His head reared up, and his body hardened and convulsed into hers. He buried his face in her neck as Justine went limp in his arms, her breathing laboured. His one hand slid down her side to rest over the supple curve of her rear. His other hand tugged the material of her bodice out of the way releasing a nipple to his mouth. He sucked as if his need for her was still unsatisfied, and that tingling sparked over her flesh once again. He slipped his fingers between her legs at their connection.

"Oh, you can't possibly," she whispered hoarsely. "You've melted me already." Her head tossed on the table, her body pinned down by his heavy weight, the shudders still vibrating through her. His mouth continued its attentions to her breast whilst his hand slid around to her rear.

She gasped, her hips jerking. "What are you doing?"

"I want all of you Justine, every inch. And you're going to give it to me." His eyes glinted over her. His finger gently stroked the outside of her tight bud and slid in just a bit. Her entire body tightened then quivered, humming with anticipation. The tip of his tongue slid a wet trail along her jaw.

Justine's head rolled back onto the hard table, her breathing quickened. "You're merciless."

"I am," he murmured against her throat. His cock stirred inside her, gliding in and out of her slowly as his fingers teased her rear. It was a perverse sort of heaven. There could be no more thinking, none at all, only feeling him moving inside her, filling her, filling all of her.

"Look at me," he said. Her eyes swirled in his. "Feel me inside you."

"It's too much, too much." She raised a hand to his cheek as if it were a white flag.

He kissed her palm then bit it gently. "Hold onto me. I'm not letting you go." Brandon rocked deeper inside her. "You inspire me, Jus."

He suddenly released her of the pressure of his fingers, and sharp pleasure tore through them both. A snarl curled his lips as he hissed in air. Justine's body shuddered, her eyelids squeezing shut.

Surrender.

His hands gripped her wrists and fastened them to the table once again. "Don't ever talk to me about separating again." His voice was steady, sharp, like a commanding army officer. "This is where I want to be. With you. Inside you." He ground his cock deeper, and her back arched against him, a cry escaping her lips, her body immobile under his firm grip. "This is all I know right now. And I like it."

Her eyes widened, her breath burst in and out.

"Don't ask me what I might want or what I might think I want. It's very courteous of you really." His voice was like acid, sizzling with bone-melting clarity through the sensual fog. He dipped his face closer to hers, the heady aroma of their desire rising from his throat. She inhaled that holy scent locking it in her memory.

"I do appreciate it, but my brain no longer functions according to the niceties. All I know is that right here and right now, it's you and me and this bloody house. We shall continue to live here together. We shall restore Wolfsgate, get me healthy, deal with my cousin and my uncle, and enjoy each other all the while. Do you understand, Lady Graven?" His tongue flicked against her trembling lower lip. "Do you agree?"

"I agree."

CHAPTER TWENTY-EIGHT

HE STRETCHED out his hand to her. "What do you think? Do you like it?"

"I do. Very much." She placed her hand in his as she stepped up into the new curricle for their trip to the village that afternoon. She settled into the seat next to him, and he signaled the horses with a flash of the reins. The two animals sprang forward, the carriage jostled to life.

In the village, they were rewarded with surprised and appreciative looks from the many passersby. Justine squeezed her gloved hands in her lap tighter together. She sometimes walked to the village to visit Annie's grave, peruse the shop windows or run a few errands like an ordinary, everyday person, going unnoticed except for a few friendly smiles and greetings to those with whom she was acquainted. But she certainly had not made such an entrance in a Graven carriage for a very, very long time.

Her gaze darted at Brandon at the reins, sitting erect, his glossy black hair smoothed back with a tie. He was not paying any mind to the people, his somber focus remained on his horses and the busy road before him.

A stream of wagons and carriages clattered over the cobbled

streets, and the din of merchants' cries advertising their wares and those selling cold and hot viands on the street corners filled Justine's ears. A group of beggar boys pushed through the crowd and splashed in the mud and the many dirty puddles on the road. The bold, colourful signs which hung over each shop front competed with one another for attention.

"The village certainly is no quiet hamlet any longer, eh?" Brandon remarked.

They had an appointment with the tailor which Brandon had insisted upon immediately. Justine was thrilled by the prospect of new clothes at long last and felt the excitement of a child at Christmas bubble through her.

At the shop, Mr. and Mrs. Thompson regaled them with the latest in fashionable materials and designs. Having already come to the house to take their measurements, the tailors needed Brandon and Justine to decide on the final details. "Arrange for anything you want and more," he whispered in her ear, his cool fingers touched her throat and lingered there. "For if you don't, I shall choose for you."

She smiled at him as his thumb rubbed the side of her cheek sending warmth skittering across her skin. Brandon followed Mr. Thompson to the other end of the small shop which was crammed with bolts of fabric and ribbons dangling everywhere.

Aside from truly needing the clothes, Justine wanted to make Brandon proud of her. It was now no longer a dark secret that she was Lady Graven.

She ordered dresses for morning and daytime, for working about the house and the gardens, gowns for dinner parties and balls, outfits for riding, a new winter cloak. Deciding on new dressing gowns and nightdresses made her skin flush when Mrs. Thompson gushed over the fine imported silks and laces that had just arrived. The delicate fabrics flowed softly and coolly under the prickly heat of her hand. Her flesh flared with heat at the thought of Brandon's fingers sliding over such ethereal material on her body.

"Yes, those will do nicely," she murmured cooly ignoring Mrs. Thompson's pointed gaze.

Justine wanted to look elegant and sophisticated, and Mrs. Thompson guided her as to which dimity, muslin, silk and wool fabrics were appropriate for each dress and outfit. Justine didn't tarry long over the endless bolts of fabric and didn't allow Mrs. Thompson to continue fawning over her to choose the most expensive ones. Justine knew which colours flattered her, which did not, and made her choices quickly. She requested that the more everyday pieces and at least one dinner dress be prepared for her as soon as possible. Mrs. Thompson's face beamed as she took notes in her small book.

Brandon sat back in an armchair. His eyes, which seemed almost an opalescent green in the small, crowded shop, were pinned on her. His face was somber, his long legs crossed casually at the knee, his one hand gripped the cane at his side. Other than his thumb twirling his ring, his body was motionless. He reminded her of a wild animal, albeit an elegant one, calculating, assessing, ready to spring.

The Brandon of the past had always been full of movement and energy, unable to sit still. However, the current Lord Graven, with his almost ominous demeanor, epitomized a sort of forbidding, understated, and seasoned elegance.

She tilted her head at him. Was he feeling out of sorts or restless? Perhaps he was just terribly bored, which would have been completely understandable under the circumstances.

Brandon's one hand casually stroked the side of his thigh, and a faint smile curled the edges of his lips. A rush of heat engulfed Justine's chest and glowed there. Her husband was a very handsome, very desirable man indeed.

"Not to worry, my lady." Mrs. Thompson's thin voice deflated

Justine's reverie. "I have it all down. You have made very fine selections."

Justine's eyes remained on Brandon. "Thank you, Mrs. Thompson."

Brandon suddenly rose from the chair, took her hand in his, and led her out of the shop. Justine turned in the direction of their carriage, but his firm hand tugged her back. "I thought you might like to go to the confectioner's and see what's on offer. You think he still makes those fantastic chocolate drops we used to fight over?" His relaxed, throaty laughter made her grin.

"He does. And those sugar biscuits you were always so fond of as well."

"Good. First, there is something else that needs addressing." Brandon's gaze darted across the road. "As we are here, I would like to resolve it."

"Oh?" Her delight over the promise of sweet treats faded instantly. Was he taking her to the solicitor? The bank? He led her across the road to the jeweler's shop.

"Lord Graven, welcome sir! What a great pleasure to see you in such fine form." Mr. Easton's posture straightened and he bowed his head. "How may I be of assistance today?"

"I need a ring, Mr. Easton," Brandon said. "For my wife."

Lightheadedness threatened her, and Justine pressed a hand onto the polished wood table before her.

"Yes, indeed, sir," said Mr. Easton with a wide smile. "Congratulations to you both." Justine leaned slightly on the counter and attempted to take in air, but her lungs did not want to cooperate.

The jeweler presented them with satin-lined trays filled with sparkling gems, like a selection of the finest sweets. Brilliant stones of all colours and shapes set on bands of gold, some ornate, others simpler in design. Justine's mouth went dry. She had never seen anything of the kind in all her life.

"Justine? Which do you like?" Brandon leaned close to her,

his clean fragrance wrapped around her. Her eyes filled with water, her heart thudded inside her chest.

His warm hand covered hers. "A gift from me." His lips twitched. "We can't have you borrowing someone else's ring, can we? Bad luck, that. Want you wearing my ring."

Her eyes stung, and she wrapped her fingers around his arm, unable to meet his gaze.

"Want you wearing my ring."

"You choose," she whispered hoarsely. "Please. I'd like you to choose it."

Brandon gave her hand a slight squeeze. He scanned the trays of jewels and pointed to a gold band with an oblong emerald in its centre surrounded by three smaller emeralds on each side of it. The green gems were set in a vine of delicate gold leaves which flourished between the stones. Brandon took the beautiful ring from Mr. Easton and put it on her finger. She held her breath as he eased it over her knuckle until it settled at the base.

The jeweler bent his head over her hand. "Perfect!"

CHAPTER TWENTY-NINE

JUSTINE'S HEAD twisted on the pillow, her back arched, her hands clawed the coverlet.

"Justine?" Brandon took hold of her wrists, pressing her into the bed. "Justine you're having another nightmare. It's all right, I'm here." His chest constricted at the sight of her struggling. "Jus?" His hand went to her chest and her erratic heartbeat made his eyes tighten.

Her eyelids peeled open and her bleary gaze flitted around the room before settling on his face.

"You're safe, Jus," he said, his tone soft. Her muscles relaxed one by one, and she settled back onto the mattress, her breath choppy. He rubbed over the base of her throat. "Robber pay you another visit?" he asked. His fingers wiped the damp hair from her face, and a hot stab pierced his chest. There was the lost little girl he remembered in those troubled brown eyes pleading with him.

His hand went under her head and rubbed the back of her neck. Her breathing began to slow down, and she licked at her dry lips. "You're not alone at Wolfsgate, Jus. I'm here with you." Her hand came up and wrapped around his neck for a moment then slid down his bare chest, her other hand clinging to his waist.

A shiver travelled up his spine and discharged its keen energy all through his body. "Shall I get you a drink?"

She didn't speak, only her feet tangled in his, her smooth thighs brushing against his legs, pressing against them. Her moist eyes stayed on his in the glow of the dying fire. Eyes filled with need.

He brushed his lips over her mouth then nuzzled her warm cheek. His hand swept down to her hip drawing her body closer to his. She let out a hiss as her fingertips dug into the firm flesh of his rear, and his eyebrows lifted.

"What do you want, sweet thing?" he breathed over her, liquid heat coursing through his veins. "You want me to make it better, chase it away?"

She let out a soft groan and raised her mouth to his. He took it, and her tongue slid through his lips tangling with his, her breasts pressing into his chest. He nudged open her legs with his knee, and his fingers found her wet heat and stroked her. The blood rushed to his head, and his already hard cock practically growled as her one leg hooked around his hip. He thrust inside her and she cried out softly, her neck arching back.

He was intoxicated.

Completely intoxicated.

A shiver stole down his spine as he gave her deep, slow strokes. "Oh, Jus," slipped from between his lips. His cock had never felt so damned blessed. His, until now, utterly superficial understanding of the flesh crumbled as he drove inside Justine, her pelvis rocking up to meet him, her glorious eyes glued to his. This was another kind of pleasure. This was not mere swiving, a meeting of body parts for mutual satisfaction; this was offering, receiving, giving, creating.

She cried out. His balls tightened and his brains blazed like a furnace being fed fresh coals. He licked at the damp saltiness of her throat, whispering endearments and a host of filthy sentiments in her ear. She groaned and hooked both her legs high over his hips.

Her nails raked over his flesh, and the bite of pain only incited his lust. Her gorgeous breasts rubbed against his chest as she moaned loudly, digging her heels into his rear, her body wanting. Insisting. She wasn't over-thinking now, wasn't closing herself off from him, from the pleasure he offered her. She urged him on, faster, harder.

The issue of her virginity flared at him, pecked at him.

No.

He would not think of it now. He would hold off confronting her. Frankly, he didn't think he would be able to control his emotions if he heard the truth, whatever the hell the truth was. No, the virginity conversation could wait. This felt too damned good. That strange sensation unfurled in his veins, smoothing the coarse edges of his soul.

Justine was now his.

His to fuck until kingdom come.

CHAPTER THIRTY

BRANDON DRANK deep from the large mug of cold water she had brought him to the roof where he and a few men worked making repairs. Thank God the wind was blustering over them as she needed the harsh rush of air to whip her out of these endless dreamy reveries.

His skin glistened with perspiration and the muscles of his jaw and neck worked to drain the cool contents of the mug. Justine licked at her lips her fingers gripping the tray handles tighter.

"Thank you." He placed his empty mug on her tray. Her gaze remained on his full, wet lips.

"Thank you, ma'am!" Her sensual absorption with her husband was interrupted by Martin and the other two young men working with him. They loaded her tray with their large mugs.

Justine took a step back, but Brandon's one hand curled around her arm and pulled her close, a cheeky grin lighting his face. "Justine, my father's room, is it being attended to?"

This morning in bed laying on their sides, her back to his front, he had woken her up with kisses along her shoulders and his hands stroking her breasts until her entire body ached for him. He had slid inside her from behind and whispered in her ear that she should prepare the Lord's bedchamber as soon as possible.

"So Lord Graven can plunder his Lady properly," he'd said, thrusting inside her. *"Find it, Jus,"* his voice had been harsh, commanding. That dark tone did her in every time. He craved engaging her in the act, and she craved him doing so. She had moved against him, and his hand had slid between her legs stroking her until she had screamed.

That was a fine, fine way to begin one's day.

She adjusted the suddenly heavier tray in her grip. "The room will be ready today."

"Good." He brushed a strand of hair back from her face and went back to work. Justine quit the roof, her feet springing down the steps to the second floor.

"All the bed chambers are finished ma'am." Lizzie's rosy face tipped up at Justine as she took the tray of mugs from her.

Every window was open, every door, and the cool air rushed and swirled around Justine as she strode through the upper gallery, a wide grin on her face. Rows of washing hung on the sun-filled lawn behind the house. Two girls swept the hallway, another dusted off the paintings on the stairwell, and the oak panelling along the walls gleamed in the midday sun. The hum of loud voices, footsteps, bustling, and the hammering on the roof all surged together like a rousing symphony.

Plenty of work had been done and there was a good deal more to do, and the thought only quickened her pulse. They were moving forward; Wolfsgate was seeing brighter, better days.

She had organised the new staff's duties for the day, first having them clean up the servants' quarters where several of them would eventually stay, and then the kitchen, the dining room, the study, the parlour, and the main bed chambers, and lastly the drawing room at the end of the great hall. She had

Molly direct traffic and make a stew with the new cook and bake plenty of bread so everyone could be fed a proper meal later on.

Brandon and Davidson had reviewed the sorry state of the stables first thing in the morning with Martin in tow. Then they inspected the entry way of the manor, the roof, the cellars. They pored over old maps and charts of the estate, making plans for improvements. They toured the grounds, papers and maps in hand.

Brandon showed little signs of restlessness and instability these days. She knew it must be ever-present inside him, but now that he was fully occupied, both mentally and physically, in tasks he cared for, he seemed to be in good form.

She went outside to tend to Lady Caroline's rose bushes. Justine sank her fingers into the damp, thick soil and smoothed the earth around the plants. A shadow fell over her hands.

"You're prettier than any rose, you know."

Her gaze snapped up at the familiar warm voice. Andrew stood before her, one hand propped on his hip. Her breath caught. She had lived another lifetime since she had seen him last at the church graveyard.

"Hello, Mr. Blakelock." She wiped her hands on her apron, stood up and bowed her head. "How are you?"

He took in air through his nose and shook his head. "Not well.
"

"Oh? I'm sorry to hear that. I hope—"

"I cannot comprehend that you are married to Graven."

"Please, don't."

"Did you ever love me? Ever? Really? Or was it all a game to you?"

Justine's insides knotted. She detested the pain and resentment visible in his eyes that she knew she had caused; pain that Andrew most certainly did not deserve. Justine could never tell him the truth, and never give him some sort of logical explanation for her rejection of him. Now she had to lie to him about her marriage.

"It was most certainly not a game. My feelings were real."

"Were?" He stepped closer to her.

She retreated a step. "Stop, I beg of you or I will have to ask you to leave."

"Did he force you to marry him?" Andrew's brows knit together.

"No, Mr. Blakelock, Lord Graven did not force me."

His eyes flashed. "Did he force himself on you? And now he's playing the gentleman by marrying you?"

"No! How could you—"

"Then why? Why?" His eyes searched hers, his voice rose. "You must have spent all of two minutes with him in London. How did he convince you before you even came home? Were you so enamored of him? Were your circumstances so desperate?"

He would never know how very desperate.

"Please—"

"Did your brother encourage this?" He scowled. "Or perhaps you convinced Graven all on your own. Is that it, Lady Justine? You saw an opportunity and convinced him using your delicate charms?"

Her blood froze at the viciousness in his tone, the coldness in his eyes. He touched her arm, and she shrank back.

"I know I have been gone a long while, yet I always thought that when I returned we would try again, that perhaps it was some immature misunderstanding." He let out a heavy sigh and his face fell. "Oh, Justine, why did you not come to me? If something was wrong, if you needed anything, whatever it was, why did you not come to *me*?" His jaw clenched, his hand clamped onto hers. "I always believed there was a measure of trust between us." The knot twisted further in Justine's belly, and her eyes pricked.

"Blakelock, this is a surprise," Brandon's deep voice bellowed.

They both jerked apart, their hands dropping to their sides. "Interested in what we're planting in the garden this year?"

Justine squinted up at her husband in the glare of the sun. His long black hair moved freely in the cool breeze. His white shirt was smudged with dirt and open at his neck which gleamed with perspiration down his torso, the torso that Justine had eagerly explored with her hands and her lips just this morning.

Brandon's fingers settled on his hips just over his long powerful legs which were stamped in tall, scuffed leather boots. Brandon presented a picture so different from Andrew's refined and polished appearance.

How much had he heard of their conversation?

The snarl on his lips confirmed that he had heard plenty.

CHAPTER THIRTY-ONE

"Graven." Andrew nodded sharply at him. "I was out for a ride and thought I'd stop by. However, I see you are both quite busy. I shall take my leave."

Brandon slid an iron hand around Justine's waist pulling her close to his body. Andrew's gaze immediately followed the gesture, his blue eyes hardening then shifting away.

From the roof where he'd been working, Brandon had been admiring his wife in the distance. He'd been admiring her diligence as she dug her hands in the dirt, her attention to detail, her rounded backside every time she leaned over.

Then he saw Blakelock admiring her too.

"Yes, we're very busy," said Brandon. "New staff, cleaning, fixing, quite a job, the lot of us working together."

"Indeed." Andrew's eyes swept over Justine. She clasped her hands together, her face pale. He turned away, striking his hat on his head. "I'll leave you to it then." He bowed his head. "Good day."

"Next time you visit, be sure to use the front door for a proper welcome," Brandon said.

Andrew's shoulders stiffened as he charged towards his horse and mounted it. They rode off, the animal's hooves pounding the dirt.

"Why was he here?" Brandon's voice snapped.

Her chin dipped down. "He's—"

"He's what?"

"He's confused by our marriage."

"Confused? What is there to be confused about? Maybe we should invite him to our bedchamber to extinguish his confusion once and for all?" His hand gripped her arm. "He obviously still has feelings for you, my girl. And what of yours for him? Such feelings don't evaporate quickly. Look at you, you're positively disturbed."

"If I am disturbed it is because he is upset," Justine replied. "And I've not seen him or heard from him in years, just as I told you. He was simply surprised that we are married."

"He can't get over the fact that he lost you to me?"

She dropped her shoulders. "Is this how it is with you men? A competition?"

"Yes, Justine. It's always a competition—for women, money, horses, and a host of other things." Anger simmered in the pit of his stomach. "Is there anything else you need to tell me about you and Andrew?" A painful twinge cut through his bad leg and he shifted his weight.

"I've told you everything, Brandon." She pinned her arms to her abdomen.

"Everything?"

"Yes, everything." Her eyes narrowed. "What are you asking me?"

"Don't you lie to me, woman!" Flashes of Andrew squeezing her hand, his lips on her skin, their sharing easy laughter, taking walks together, scribbling each other romantic missives, her luscious mouth whispering his name...all roared furiously in his dark imagination blurring his vision, smoldering in his chest.

"I am not lying, Brandon. Andrew and I have never shared more than a kiss. A very innocent kiss. Ever."

He snorted. No, this was too much to deal with now after all the energy he'd wasted on the Adonis's little visit. Justine still refused to confess her little secret. How could she continue pretending? He took in a deep breath. He didn't want to lose any more control. Or maybe deep down inside he didn't want to know, not just yet. She was his now, his wife, in his bed every night. That had to be enough.

He grabbed her arms and pulled her into his chest. Her lavender scent drifted over him reminding him of his fondness for her, his bloody weakness for her, or was it purely a burning, uncontrollable need for her?

"Innocent kisses, eh? If I see him here buzzing about you again, I will break his neck, do you understand?"

"Brandon—" She raised a hand to touch his face.

He pushed her away and marched off, his hair whipping in the breeze. He didn't want to listen to explanations or excuses anymore. His head hammered with every heavy step of his boots on the hard ground, his fingers flexed and curled tightly into fists. He had to regain control over his rage before he did or said something he would later regret. To do that he had to get away from her.

What he really needed was a fix. Hell yes, that would surely help.

CHAPTER THIRTY-TWO

LOCKS of her unruly hair fell loose from her kerchief, and she swatted them out of her face. Trying to appease both Brandon and Andrew had her head spinning.

"Why won't he listen to me?" Justine muttered aloud. "Of course, why should he listen to what I have to say after hearing Andrew's tirade?"

There was no telling what dark, unresponsive mood Brandon might sink into now and then be beyond her reach for some time. She ripped the kerchief from her hair as she replayed the look on his face over and over again in her mind—anger laced with hurt. Her throat closed. Her need to keep him safe overrode her annoyance.

"Brandon! Brandon, wait!" She ran after him and finally stumbled at his side, a hand on his arm, gulping for air. He stopped. A grimace etched his scarred face, his eyes were red and glassy.

"You could have had Andrew, Justine. The young, genteel gentleman." His hands dug into her hair, pulling through the ropy strands, tugging her head back to face him. "You were denied him because of me."

197

His anger had dissolved into guilt in the hundred yards he had marched off from her.

"Not because of you, Brandon. Because of William and Richard."

"Because of me."

"And what are you? An ogre? A hideous, multi-headed dragon breathing fire?"

"Yes, I'm breathing fire." His warm, callused hands cradled her face. "And I'm burning you. My family has burnt your life to ashes."

"I'm not ashes." She had to say it, had to give him something to move forward, like he gave her in their bed over and over again, freeing her, making her feel alive and wanted. She raised herself up on her toes and kissed his lips. "I'm right here, and I need your fire."

He pulled her into his embrace. Justine absorbed his rapid heartbeat into her own chest, and the hardness between his legs pulsed straight to her very centre. He claimed her mouth, and that aching hunger for her husband snaked right through her. He let go of her suddenly, pulling her arm, marching her across the green.

"Brandon, what are you doing? Where are we going?"

He ignored her and kept charging down the hill then through the grove of trees at the edge of the park toward the great oak tree. They entered under the thick green canopy of the enormous ancient oak, its leaves and branches flapping against Justine's face and shoulders. Here, years ago as children they would play house or jungle, or attend imagined masquerade balls with William, Annie, Amanda and Andrew.

Now, within its vast, shrouded shelter, Brandon lifted her up in his arms, hooked her legs around his waist and pushed her up against the massive tree's trunk. His eyes fell to her parted lips taking in air. "You are my wife now."

"Yes. Yes, I'm your..."

He swiftly unfastened his breeches. The harsh, irregular bark of the tree scraped and jabbed her back, but she didn't care about the discomfort. It reminded her she was alive. Her heart pounded, her every muscle tightened. His frenzied, wordless need for her thrilled her. He lifted her higher.

Yes...

There...

Oh, for the love of...

His cock pinned her to the tree, and she groaned out loud, her fingers digging into his shoulders.

"Say it. Say it, dammit," he demanded, his breathing heavy.

"I am your wife."

"Yes." He thrust inside her again, then again.

"Yours Brandon, only yours." Her head jostled against the rough bark as he plunged inside her over and over. Her lungs squeezed for air, her head whirled with a rush of emotion as his grey-green eyes pierced hers.

"They've tried to take everything else from me," he breathed fire.

Not me. Never.

Quicker he drove into her, grinding his hips against hers. She clung to him. The shocking fulness of him, the sting of his frenzy. Pain and wild pleasure stormed inside her, and she rode the storm with him. She needed this too. She needed to let go.

Simply let go.

The cold breeze dried her lips as she cried out with every punishing thrust of Brandon's hips. Her fingers clung to his thick, damp hair at the base of his neck. His breathing grew more ragged and sharp, and his one hand gripped her bare bottom so tightly it throbbed. She welcomed the pain.

She deserved it for years of hurt stamped on Andrew's face.

She deserved it for the eerie shadows haunting Brandon's eyes.

Every thrust burned, inflaming her further, casting her over the edge along with him. Her fingers twisted in his shirt, her heart jamming in her chest as her release ripped through her. Brandon's eyes squeezed shut and he convulsed into her.

They remained suspended together, speechless, unable to move, only clinging to each other through a haze of perspiration and raw satisfaction. Brandon released her from his tight grip and helped her find her footing. He stumbled back. Justine's shaky hands smoothed down her skirts and adjusted her bodice.

"Are you angry with me still?" she asked as she ran her fingers through her hair. He stood rooted to the spot watching her thick mass of coppery tresses tumble past her shoulders. "Brandon?"

"I am having a hard time believing what you say about Andrew for he is behaving as if you spurned him last week and not years ago. If his feelings are still so intense for you, how is it yours are not so for him?" He inhaled deeply and slid his hand up and down his chest. "What is it Justine? A few turns between my legs and you've forgotten all about him? Damn, I must be good."

She drew nearer to him. "You and I are good together, Brandon, that is what I know. I could have said no to you the first time, when you asked me if I wanted you, but I have chosen to live. Your return home is a whole new world for me and for you, especially for you. And even though this union was forced upon us, I have chosen to take this second chance at life, and I am content."

He tilted his head at her, his eyes murky pools of seawater, revealing nothing.

"I enjoy being with you, Brandon," she breathed, her face burning. "Is that wrong?"

The breeze shifted and a cool rush of air swirled between them. He brushed his knuckles across her warm cheek. "No, it's not wrong, Jus. It's very good."

CHAPTER THIRTY-THREE

"WAS THERE NOT a long carpet here in this hallway?"

Brandon and Molly stood outside of Justine's old room surveying the long hall. "The opposite hall has its carpet, but this hallway has none," he said.

"Quite right, sir," Molly replied. "Its twin was here for many years, but Martin had to take it out a long while back."

"Take it out? Why?"

"Said Lady Justine had tripped on it and fallen. It was quite frayed at the edges after all these years, got ripped, he said."

Brandon's mouth settled into a firm line. "Martin has helped out at Wolfsgate quite a lot, eh Molly?"

"Whenever we needed young, strong hands, I would send for him, and he would come right over. Did a fine job with odd repairs, the horses and the stable. Boy's had it hard, sir. His father drunk himself to death with gin, then he lost his mother and sisters to the fever. Whenever he'd come, I'd give him food to take home with him."

Brandon's face tightened. Young, strong hands indeed. "That was good of you, Molly." His gaze returned to the bare wood floor of the hallway. "I will have to buy another carpet then, for the winter is upon us."

"Yes, sir." Her crystal blue eyes widened ever so slightly. "Would you like your tea now, my lord?"

"Yes I would. I'll go wash up and be down shortly. Is Lady Graven about?"

"She's going over a few things in the pantry, sir."

The days had passed with much activity around the estate. Both Brandon and Justine were pleased with the progress that had been made. Every afternoon Molly and Davidson reported to their master and mistress on what had been accomplished that day, all four reviewed what needed to be done the following day, and each tiring week wore into the next.

After they had finished their supper that evening, Brandon and Justine retired to the parlour where Katy, the new parlour maid, had lit a fire for them. Brandon sank back into the old leather armchair and drank a brandy while Justine sat on the settee at his side and went through several pieces of mail that had arrived for them earlier in the day.

A smile curled the edges of her lips. "It would seem word has spread regarding your return."

"Hmm?" Brandon rubbed his eyes. "Do tell."

"Lord and Lady Marchmain send their regards and cordially invite you to a ball on Friday next."

"Remind me?"

"Marchmain House is around the hill from Crestdown. And there reside three unmarried daughters."

"Ah, the ones with the same sounding names, eh?"

"Very good, Lord Graven. Mariah, Mavis, and Marianne."

"There, you see?" He glanced at her. "My brain is not completely boiled."

"No, not completely."

His thumb rubbed the thin rim of the glass. "A ball. Would you like to go?"

"Would you?"

His forehead creased as he took the invitation from her and read it. "Seems they don't know we're married." He tapped the heavy paper which had only his name written on it. "Yes, we should go, make an entrance, and introduce ourselves to proper society." He dropped the invitation on the table at his side. "You can show off one of your new gowns." He offered her his brandy glass. She took it and sipped on the amber liquid as she gazed into the fire. He put his hand on her knee and squeezed it. "We don't have to go if you don't want to."

"I would very much like to go." She swallowed the last of the liquor. "I just hope you are ready for it."

"What do you mean?"

"Seeing William and Amanda again. Remember, you foiled his grand scheme."

"Oh no, not I. You did that all on your own, Lady Graven." A devilish grin played upon his lips as he leaned closer to her, a hand stroking up her thigh.

She met his gaze. "Yes, but you've taken back control of the estate. The money is there. I am sure he is quite annoyed with the both of us."

"Good. I look forward to that annoyance very much."

"That is what I'm concerned about."

"Why? Do you think I will lose my temper?"

"I don't want anything bad to happen, Brandon."

"You're that concerned?"

"I wouldn't be surprised if William were to orchestrate a scene with you in public simply to goad you or slight you socially." She sighed heavily. "Please keep your distance from him. At the very least, don't do or say anything to provoke him."

"He deserves to be punished, Justine. I will find a way."

She refilled the brandy glass and handed it to him. "Brandon—"

"Stop worrying." He leaned back into his armchair again and

stared into the fire. "You had asked me once if Amanda and I were ever engaged. Although I had never asked her, not even made a promise, I had assumed we would marry one day. We all took life for granted then." He let out a low chuckle. "The foolishness of indulged youth. We thought life would simply be what we wanted of it. It showed us, eh? A right kick up the arse and then some."

"You two might have been married now if—"

"Amanda is married to William. She made her choice." Brandon took a swig of his drink.

"She was most distraught when news came to us that you were lost."

"And was William her constant companion in their mutual grief at my death?" Brandon leaned his head back against the sofa.

"I suppose," she murmured.

He stretched out his legs. "She wouldn't have married William if she didn't want him, Justine. She's headstrong that way. Furthermore, she's always liked immediate gratification. Never had much patience. Are they happy together?"

"I can't say as I never really see them. Once briefly here and then a dinner at their home. I've only seen their son at his christening."

"That's uncivil."

A shadow crossed her face. "It suited me just fine."

"Did it?"

"Yes. I was glad to be left in peace."

"I certainly don't leave you in peace."

"That's different." Her velvety eyes softened. "That I like."

Brandon put down his drink and took her hand in his. He pulled her into his lap and kissed her gently, eliciting a soft noise from her throat. His fingers loosened the fichu at her chest and found the swell of her breasts underneath, then yanked at her bodice tugging it loose.

"Your hair," he breathed. "Take down your hair, Jus."

Her hands flew to her hair, and she released the many pins holding up the sides, the curly strands falling over her back. His fingers swept through her thick locks, its flowery fragrance drifting over him.

"I want you naked right now." His hands went underneath her skirts and stroked her warm skin.

"Here?"

"Here. Now, Lady Graven." His fingers worked to unbind her stays, tugging and dragging at the thick ribbon. She looked down to inspect his work, her breath stalling and catching with each sharp movement. "Damn, I can't see!" he muttered and she let out a laugh and turned in the direction of the fire so he would have more light. He glanced up at her, and her eyes glowed in the flickering light, her tongue darting over her lower lip.

His heart pounded as he finally set her free. "Stand up."

She stood with her back against him, and he tugged down her skirts until they dropped to the floor then swiftly pulled the muslin shift over her head and tossed it. He finally slipped his hands around her bare waist and cupped her breasts. They both groaned as she leaned back into his chest, her hands covering his, pressing in.

She turned to undo his necktie, but he pushed her hands away, shaking his head. Her eyes flashed at him as he pulled her down on the carpet. His mouth laid a wet trail of discovery from her breasts down to her belly, as his hands, rough and callused from the work he had been doing, grazed her smooth skin, rasping any diffidence from her.

Brandon reached for the glass of brandy and tipped it over her. Justine gasped as a stream of liquor trickled over her flesh. He licked at the amber liquid pooling across her breasts and spilling down her middle as she writhed under him. He reached again for the glass, and she held her breath as he drank, his eyes catching the light from the fire. He leaned over her and drizzled the brandy from his mouth over her mound down into her silken cleft.

"Brandon..." She moaned and raised her hips. "You are wicked." Her breathing grew ragged as he licked at the amber liquid streaming over her flesh. He sucked on the deliciously swollen button of her core and relished her salty taste which now mingled with the warm, sweet liquor. His hands kneaded her rear, bringing her closer to his mouth, the need to consume her overwhelming.

She shuddered, and that loud, undisguised moan he wanted to hear finally escaped her throat. His hunger for her roared through him, and he shoved her legs apart wider, nipping at the smooth flesh of her thigh. He glanced up at her as he blew air over her lush wetness. Her eyelids fluttered, her lips parted.

His tongue swirled through her delicate flesh. "Beautiful quim. Pink and wet and all mine."

He hadn't had her in days. With all the heavy physical work about the property, he had been too damned exhausted and so had she. He had missed her. Very, very much.

He stripped himself of his shirt. "What do you want, Jus? You tell me what you want, anything, and I'll give it to you."

She sat up and helped him remove his breeches. "I want to pleasure you."

His lungs constricted. His heart vaulted in his chest. Justine pulled herself on top of him, and he adjusted her thighs around his. She looked into his eyes, and he saw it flash across her gorgeous face. Uncertainty.

Brandon to the rescue, my love.

His hands cupped her breasts, his lips nuzzling them gently, exploring, kissing, nipping at the soft flesh. Her body finally relaxed in his hold.

"You're so beautiful," he whispered against her damp skin as he guided her hand to his shaft. His veins screamed to life as his cock pulsed under her firm touch. They stroked him together, and a low moan heaved from his parted lips. "Bloody hell, Justine."

Together they placed him at her very wet opening. "Take me inside you," his voice rasped. Her hands clutched his shoulders as she lowered herself, and he filled her slowly, his hands gripping her hips to control her first movements. She moaned softly, her eyes fluttering closed.

"I'm so hungry for you." Brandon kissed her along the pulse at her throat, and she ground down on him again and again finding her rhythm. That was what she needed to hear; she needed to feel safe and wanted. Bloody hell, that was what he would give her.

His hands squeezed her back. "I can feel you everywhere." His eyes flicked down to take in the heady sight of their union. He slipped his hand over her hip keeping her arse tucked into him. That luscious arse drove him mad. She panted hard, moved quicker, and his flesh combusted all over.

Her lids lowered over her glazed eyes, and a dull pain ached in his chest at the sight. He began to thrust up harder inside her, and she gasped, murmuring against his skin, her hands digging in his hair. He gently settled the tip of his finger in the tight rosette of her rear, and she jolted in his arms. His other hand slid in between her legs, his thumb finding her centre, teasing it.

"Oh, there you go again," she gasped.

"All for you." His lips pressed into her throat.

Justine rocked her body urgently against his, her cries coming quicker. Lord have mercy, he was desperate to finish with her. "Finish with me, Jus, come on."

Justine let out pleading noises from the back of her throat. Every nerve ending in Brandon's body buzzed with force. Her body clenched onto his cock, and she came apart in his hands, her pleasure spiraling right through him as he went off.

The din of their heavy breathing filled the room over the fizz and crack of the burning wood. A raw moan loosened from her throat, and it shot an arrow through him which deepened and expanded the burn in his chest.

He luxuriated in the silken feel of her skin, and his hands slid down her back over her beautiful rear. His fingertips skidded over something unusual on her skin, an irregularity.

"What's this, Justine?"

"Hmm?"

He traced the once angry welt with his fingers. Her body stilled under his touch. "I thought it was some sort of birthmark before." He leaned over her body inspecting her lower hip which gleamed in the firelight. "It's a scar, is it not? How did this happen?"

She lifted up from him, wiping the hair back from her face. "Summer before last I had an accident in the kitchen. I was carrying a heavy platter, lost my balance and fell back on the corner of the table."

He tilted his head. "Were you naked at the time?"

"No. I was wearing my lightest muslin if you must know. It ripped straight through, blood everywhere." She reached for her chemise.

Silence fell between them.

"I don't believe you."

She let out a small laugh. "I can be very clumsy, especially when I'm tired."

"The edges of the kitchen table are worn and rounded with age. They have no sharp edges."

"Are we really going to discuss the state of the kitchen table?" She smoothed the thin chemise down over her body. "There was a broken glass on the edge of it that I had neglected to collect earlier. I learned my lesson to clean up my messes right away after that."

He picked up her skirts and corset from the floor, his gaze meeting hers as he pulled up his breeches. "Are you hiding something from me?"

"Brandon, it was an accident." She shook out his frock coat and folded it over her arm. "Let's go to bed."

CHAPTER THIRTY-FOUR

"Perfect." He was still, his pale grey-green eyes shining over her.

"Do you really think so?"

"Oh yes. Beautiful." His fingertips brushed the ruby and diamond earring dangling from her ear and grazed her neck.

"It's an honour to wear them," she murmured.

His warm fingers stroked the smooth skin of her wrist under the matching bracelet. The swaying and jostling of their refurbished black coach slid Justine closer to Brandon on the firm upholstery. The heady fragrance of his new amber scent filled the coach.

Her dress of lilac silk elegantly draped beautifully over her body, and her new delicate shoes with a slight heel felt comfortable on her feet, at least for now. Lizzie had tamed her hair by pinning most of it up, allowing for several long, thick coils down her back, and she'd accented the crown of her head with a crisscross of thin lilac ribbon.

Lady Caroline's jewels decorated her ears and wrist, and Brandon's ring shone on her finger. All these fine details gave her courage. She would need as much courage as possible this evening.

Justine had not been out socially for ages. She was excited about the music and the dancing, excited to see familiar faces, but she was also nervous. How would William and Amanda react to seeing Brandon and Justine together? That is, *happy* together. Or at least not unhappy.

The more intriguing question was how would Amanda respond to seeing Brandon again? To seeing Brandon married to someone else. To her.

Brandon's fingers tapped out a rhythm on the coach window. The trees flit by as their carriage bore them away from Wolfsgate and hurtled them toward uncharted territory.

Justine pressed her back into the seat cushions once more. Was Brandon thinking of Amanda now, anticipating their reunion?

Amanda was beautiful and she knew it—a blond, blue-eyed angelic doll, utterly feminine, elegant and graceful. Rather unlike her. Justine sighed. Brandon may be feeling attached to her now and grateful to her for getting him out of hospital, saving his fortune, and enjoying all the amorous activity. But when he'd see Amanda tonight in all her glory, what will be going on in his mind, not to mention in his blood?

Justine's relentless thoughts collided and fired off with a vicious rapidity. Her fingers twisted in her cloak. Perhaps all this affection he showed her was an expression of gratitude or simply his fresh hunger and nothing more, and she should accept that. Justine squelched that sour thought as the stately spires of Marchmain House rose before them.

It had been many years since either she or Brandon had been here. The sprawling house was one of the finest in the county. Wolfsgate seemed modest in comparison.

Their coach slowed down over the circular drive which swarmed with carriages emptying out finely dressed ladies and gentlemen. Servants had lit great torches dotting the drive, marking the entrance to the house. Their coach came to a halt, and Justine held her breath.

The door on Brandon's side was thrown wide, and a rush of cold air burst into the compartment. The coach heaved with his exit, and she pressed her legs together, a hand smoothing down her cloak. A few moments later her door swung open and Brandon's hand beckoned her forth. She put her hand in his, and he led her onto firm ground as a rush of excitement shot through her. He tucked her arm in his and together they walked up the steps into the great house. Smartly dressed servants greeted them at the hall, taking her cloak and his great coat.

Marchmain House had been recently renovated in the fashionable Palladian style. A long, sleek stretch of black and white marble floor gleamed before them as Brandon slowly led her into the great saloon at the centre of the house. The edges of the sprawling room were trimmed with proud Roman columns with the requisite Corinthian capitals. Ancient masks, satyrs and scalloped shells moulded out of plaster peeked from every corner. Quite a contrast to the medieval griffins and wolves that were engraved on the original moss-covered stone walls of Wolfsgate.

No, this was a different world indeed. This was a veritable temple to modern opulence and extravagance.

The smaller rooms to the side reminded Justine of the coloured jewels she had seen in the village shop, each flanking the diamond that was the saloon with their green or red velvet wall coverings and matching damask curtains. The fresh, sleek sparkle of the vast interior was so very different from the intimacy of the rich dark woods and natural stone of Wolfsgate.

Her breath stalled at the coffered dome that hovered high above them at the centre of the great room giving the space a magnificent cathedral-like atmosphere. Justine wasn't sure if it was meant to inspire awe or strike humiliation in the piteously underprivileged below.

Brandon's arm stiffened under her hand, and he brought

them both to an abrupt halt. Justine's wide-eyed gaze fell from the architectural astonishment above her to the dread before her.

Hundreds of eyes feasted on them. Here was another kind of theatre, to be sure. Rustling and chattering wound their way around the great room as fast as flames. Her fingernails dug into Brandon's arm.

"Lord Graven, good to see you alive, my boy, I must say." Lord Marchmain lowered his voice and leaned in, "Do forgive us. We did not know you had married when the invitations were prepared." His round belly jiggled with forced laughter.

"Oh dear, truly." Lady Marchmain touched her husband's arm, her powdered face turning rosy as she bobbed her head at Justine.

"Congratulations," said Lord Marchmain.

"Thank you, sir. You know my wife, Lady Justine, my uncle's stepdaughter."

"Yes, of course." Lord and Lady Marchmain smiled at Justine, and Justine bowed her head.

Mariah, Marianne and Mavis Marchmain stood next to their parents, ardent smiles stamped on their young, eager faces. "Welcome. Hello. How lovely to see you!" They each took turns greeting their guests.

Justine smiled and reciprocated their greetings. Brandon stood beside her and nodded at them, a faint smile icing his lips then melting just as quickly as he turned away from them. The three young sisters blushed and frowned under his dismissiveness.

After the barrage of amiable sentiments was completed, Justine and Brandon entered the great saloon. There they were: Amanda, William, Andrew, Richard, and Mr. Blakelock, Amanda and Andrew's father. Their fine clothes accented their rigid postures. Each regarded Brandon and Justine with different degrees of keen interest and cool wariness.

Amanda's blue eyes swept over Brandon from head to toe and

then rested on Justine, one elegant eyebrow arching higher than the other. Justine exhaled as they approached them.

Amanda's pale golden hair was in a loose chignon, with long tight curls draped over her shoulders and falling down her back. Her deep crimson silk dress fell over her slender curves in the modern free style drawn in at the waist which made her porcelain skin positively glow. A matching red ribbon was laced around her neck in a fashionable tribute to the current sufferings of the French nobility. Amanda was certainly a provocative figure *à la mode* this evening. Justine's ribs squeezed tightly as she bowed before them, and they returned the gesture.

"Brandon, it is very good to have you home and safe once more," Amanda remarked, her voice glossy and fluid. Her fingertips touched his arm, then quickly retreated.

"Thank you, Mrs. Treharne. It is good to be home." Her lips pursed together at his reply.

William came forward. "Brandon, don't you look the picture of health? Quite a change from the last time I saw you. Married life must agree with you."

"Yes, it certainly does." Brandon's eyes narrowed, his scars taut and pronounced. "I'm sure you are quite familiar with that feeling." Amanda's eyes darted up at him as William's searing gaze settled on Justine.

"Yes, congratulations are in order, my boy!" Mr. Blakelock broke the thick silence. He shook Brandon's hand.

"Thank you, sir," Brandon said.

"It's a pity your parents aren't here to see you well and finally settled with a wife."

"I agree. They would have been pleased."

William snorted. Brandon drew close to his cousin. "You will be civil this evening at the very least, do you understand? Especially toward my wife." William tilted his head, a hint of amusement sweeping his features. Amanda quirked an eyebrow at Justine, then just as quickly turned away. Andrew remained to the side, his arms crossed at his chest, a muscle at his jaw twitched, his blue eyes positively icy.

"Nice to see you my dear," murmured Mr. Blakelock to Justine. "It has been too long."

"Thank you, sir." Justine bowed. "Indeed, it has been."

Andrew, his cheeks ruddy, stepped up and mumbled his hellos to Justine and Brandon. Brandon nodded at him and immediately tugged at Justine's arm moving her away before she could complete her greeting. He led her to Richard, who was slumped in an armchair slurping from a glass.

"Hello Uncle."

"Well, look at you." Richard's mouth twisted in a lopsided smirk of sorts. "Dressed and presentable for the party!"

"I could say the same for you," Brandon said. Richard scowled and waved his wine glass at his nephew.

"Hello," Justine said to Richard who ignored her, only drinking noisily.

"Enjoying your new home, Uncle?" Brandon asked.

"Bah!"

"There you are, old boy!" A clear, deep voice hung in the air. Charles Montclare led a trail of several other men who Justine recognised as old friends of Brandon's and William's.

Charles took Justine's hand in his and turned her slightly to present her to the rest of the group. "Stephen, Matthew, Thomas, may I present the lovely Lady Justine."

The mens' eyes widened, and they smiled at her bowing their heads. She remembered each one of them as rough and tumble young men, but now they were all polished gentlemen.

"Ma'am." Stephen bowed slightly before her, his eyes dancing.

"Damn ye Graven, very nice," Matthew murmured. "William's stepsister, eh? Forgot about her."

Justine's cheeks reddened.

"I'll be damned," said Thomas. "My sister's around here somewhere. She'll want to see you, Lady Graven, to be sure."

"Georgina is here?" asked Justine. "How wonderful! I'd hoped she would be. We haven't seen each other in ages."

"She's complained of it regularly. She's been at our sister's in Devon for quite some time. Only just returned. I'll go find her."

"Yes, yes, go, off with you." A grin illuminated Charles's handsome features as he kissed Justine's hand, his gaze unfurling over her from head to toe. "Lilac certainly suits you, Lady Justine." He released her hand, as her husband's strong arm wrapped around her waist.

"Enough, you rake, making a show of my wife," Brandon said. "Some things don't change."

"Oh, I've gotten worse, my friend," Charles replied. Stephen and Matthew laughed. "Thank God you're back, Graven. These two have been driving me mad."

Justine glanced at Brandon. He did not seem overwhelmed or bothered by all the fuss made over him. Brandon had once been the centre of attention in local society, and his long absence had no doubt put a damper on the social activities of a great many, especially the ladies.

Justine took in the the bustle of activity around them. Everywhere there were games of chance, a variety of drink, self-important men, and pretty eager ladies. Would all this excitement tonight make Brandon uncomfortable and feed into his need for chemical reinforcement?

Or perhaps it would feed into a vanity that had suffered long years of neglect, but was now ready to ripen once more?

Justine leaned on Brandon's arm and lifted her mouth to his ear. "I see Georgina. I'm going over to say hello." He squeezed her hand and released it.

She left the men to their animated conversation and darted through the crowd. She looked forward to spending time with

Georgina tonight, to converse and laugh with another woman her age. Her friend. She had missed her companionship dearly.

Georgina and Justine hadn't seen each other since before William's marriage to Amanda. Georgina had been absent from her country home for long stretches, but the two friends would write to one another, Georgina amusing her to no end over her adventures in London and Devon.

On her journey through the crowd, several ladies stopped Justine and congratulated her on her marriage to Lord Graven. She conversed with them, then begged off with the usual pleasantries and continued on her course for Georgina through the crowd.

"You are in love with him then?" Andrew's voice was low, his breath on her shoulder. She whipped around. His face strained close to hers, the crowd moved and pressed around them. He gulped punch from a glass, strands of his strawberry blond hair falling over his glassy eyes. "You must answer, madame."

"I will not."

"Ah, yes—what goes on between a husband and wife—none of my business." He licked his lips. "And to think I put my life on hold for you."

"I never asked you to." Justine raised her chin. "I made it perfectly clear that we had no future together quite some time ago, Mr. Blakelock."

Andrew scowled. "But you had led me to believe otherwise."

There had been a time when Justine fantasized about marrying Andrew, spending her life with him. Now their few stolen kisses and innocent hand-holding on clandestine early morning walks through the gardens and about the hillside belonged not only to the past, but to another lifetime altogether. Everything had tilted forever for Justine the moment Brandon had bedded her. New and intense feelings had swerved her emotions into a limbo of the unknown and the intricately tangled, like the tenacious flowering vines on her garden wall.

"Please, stop this. Please."

"I must tell you, I'm engaged to Mariah Marchmain. Charming girl. Utterly smitten with me, has been for a long time now. Ah, good, here she comes."

Andrew held out his hand to his fiancée who smiled brightly, her dimples showing. Her white and gold trimmed gown made her pale skin seem even more delicate.

"Dearest, you know Lady Graven." Andrew's eyes remained on Justine's.

"Of course I do!" Mariah let out a giggle, obviously unaware of his stinging tone.

"Mr. Blakelock has told me just now about your engagement," Justine said. "Congratulations to you both. Have you set a date?"

"Oh, no, not yet. Very soon though." Mariah shrugged her shoulders, her cheeks flushing. Andrew brooded over his wine glass. Mariah suddenly inhaled deeply. "Dearest, won't you come? The orchestra is beginning to play, and I do so wish to dance." She twisted her fingers in his arm.

"Of course, my darling." Andrew took her arm in his. They disregarded Justine and strode away.

A servant filled the sudden void with a tray of red punch. "Perfect." She curled her fingers around a cool cup and savored the sweet refreshment.

"Lady Graven?" That acerbic voice she knew so well slithered over her. William. Unfortunately, the slight effect of the punch was not enough to dull her senses just yet.

He leaned in closer to her, stopping her from moving forward. "I want to know how you did it, love. You seem to have him wrapped around your little finger already. Or is it around your quim?"

Justine kept her gaze riveted on Andrew and Mariah dancing. Mariah was a pixie floating in the sweet air around her fiancée.

"Wherever did you get those earrings?" William's eyes narrowed at the spray of rubies dangling from her ears. "Those are Aunt Caroline's. I'll be damned, where did you—?" He let out a hiss. Justine drained her punch. He took the glass from her hand and grabbed her elbow pulling her behind a column out of people's way.

"Lord Jeremy gave these earrings to me to keep safe for his son," Justine replied.

"Did he now?"

"It's never enough for you is it? You pillaged that house and his bank account over and over again. I wonder, do your wife and father-in-law know of any of this?"

"Sir?"

They both glared at the servant who held a silver tray filled with used glasses. William released her arm and deposited her cup on the tray. The servant receded.

"You leave my wife out of it," William said.

"Most happily."

The music swelled once more and people rushed towards the dance floor. Damn. She had lost sight of Georgina.

William crossed his arms, the edges of his lips tipped up. She smelled the liquor and the tobacco on his breath mixed with his spicy cologne. "Tell me, Lady Graven, how was your first time together?" The back of Justine's throat stung. He let out a low chuckle. "He must have been like a ravenous wolf after so many years without a woman, and to now have a wife available to him?" A couple next to them glanced over. William smiled easily.

"Or perhaps he was too intoxicated with his restorative to take the necessary actions required?" he whispered by her ear. "Pity. God knows what is really going through his muddled brain though, eh? He must be damaged after all that time in hospital, and I don't mean only the limp and the scars. Shame that. He's changed. Definitely not the same Brandon. He seems a bit, I don't know...gloomy, stiff. But it's obvious to me there is a volatile creature lurking inside. I'd watch your step with him."

"Such brotherly concern," Justine said. "You expected us to be miserable? You would have liked that, wouldn't you?"

"Are you foolish enough to think he trusts you? He'll take his fill of you then soon enough, no doubt, he'll tire of you and find a mistress. And then another. Won't be difficult. Look at all the attention he's getting this evening. You're no match for that. Few are."

Justine raised her chin, directing her gaze to the left. "I do believe your wife is first in line on that score." The moment the words spilled from her mouth Justine regretted them.

William followed Justine's gaze to where Amanda was in an animated conversation with Brandon and Thomas. Her face beamed as she spoke, the laughter flowing from her with ease. Brandon's relaxed face smiled down at her as Thomas erupted into cackles at a witty remark she must have made. Amanda's hand flew to Brandon's upper arm and rested there.

William cleared his throat. "I saw you just now with Andrew, does your husband know about that?"

"Yes, he does. In fact, I was just congratulating Andrew and Mariah on their engagement."

Lilting music, dancers' clacking steps, ringing laughter, and the din of chatter filled the hall, but William and Justine remained standing side by side silently witnessing Amanda and Brandon from across the enormous room. A muscle ticked along William's jaw.

Amanda, smiling brilliantly, her cheeks flushed, was focused on Brandon alone, and Thomas drifted away from them. Brandon leaned over closing the distance between them and spoke in Amanda's ear, and her eyebrows lifted, her delicate neck slanted. A knot twisted inside Justine. A low growl rose in William's throat.

Justine had to say it, it was too fitting. "They really do make an attractive couple. Just as I remember." William cursed under his breath.

"Will you be monopolizing your sister all evening, Treharne?" Charles's smooth voice cut between them. A burst of sunlight in their thunderstorm.

"Don't be ridiculous, Montclare." William gritted out.

"Do go find another amusement then. You've kept the girl to yourself long enough. Years, in fact, old boy. How overprotective can a brother be?"

"Phh." William left them.

"Was he being annoying, Lady Graven?"

"No more than usual."

Charles tilted his head at her. "You seem tense, my dear." He offered her a cup of punch. "Perhaps I can provide relief?"

Justine laughed. It felt good to laugh for a change this evening. "Thank you." She sipped from the sweet punch. It felt good to be flirted with rather than accosted, to be regarded as a lustrous pearl and not a mundane irritation. "Was this a rescue mission, then?" she asked.

"Something like that. Shall we dance?" He took the empty glass from her and set it absently on the edge of a nearby pedestal on which towered an enormous porphyry urn. "Come, don't refuse me."

She gave him her hand. "I wouldn't dare."

"Don't worry about Graven." Charles moved closer to her as they walked together toward the dancers, his honey-toned cologne lingering between them. "Amanda's entertaining him."

He might as well have splashed her with cold water. "I'm not worried about him." Charles led her into position as the music began again. "Actually I'm worried about you, Mr. Montclare. You must forgive me, I'm rather out of practice. I wouldn't want you to be made a spectacle of for my poor dancing."

He squeezed her fingers. "Do not fret over the steps, simply keep your eyes on me. I will guide you." That certainly wouldn't be a hardship; his gold-flecked brown eyes were captivating, his smile infectious.

Charles was indeed an excellent dancer. Once Justine forgave herself for missing a few steps here and there, she relaxed and began to better follow his lead, heeding his whispered directives whenever they were close. She laughed and danced on until the music was suddenly over. Everyone clapped for the musicians.

Charles's warm fingers took her hand in his. "Dance with me again."

She let out a laugh. "When?"

"Now, you breathtaking creature." Justine looked away from the shining glint in his eyes. He chuckled. "Your husband won't mind, my lady. I overheard him telling Amanda that he wouldn't be dancing with that injured leg of his. Consider me your partner this evening. You cannot tell me you did not find pleasure in our dance." She had enjoyed it immensely, but her head strained at the constant mention of Brandon and Amanda in the same sentence.

Thomas jostled next to them and held out his hand to Justine. "Give us a turn, Lady Graven. It would be a delight." He bowed before her. Justine grinned at Charles.

"Oh, go ahead with you." Charles placed Justine's hand in Thomas's outstretched palm.

She and Thomas danced the next piece, then Matthew claimed her for the next. She thoroughly enjoyed Matthew's constant chatter, which made concentrating on the steps less important. They applauded for the orchestra, then Charles's hand slid around hers and led her back to a spot within the line.

"All mine again," he murmured. Justine swallowed hard. Charles was very attractive and most attentive, and he knew exactly how to use his devastating appeal by lacing it with the right amount of agreeable yet mischievous looks and brief touches without ever overdoing. It was a heady combination of wickedness and protective caring. Justine was certain many young ladies fell under his beguiling spell.

The dance began. They were turning, bowing to their neighbours on the left, hands together once more in the centre, then they turned to the right. Down the long line of dancers, she spotted a mirthless Andrew partnering his sister. Georgina danced next to them with her brother, Thomas. Her smile widened and her eyes lit up when she caught Justine's attention, and she winked. Justine grinned at her.

Charles squeezed her fingertips tighter to catch her attention. "Go, go," he urged. She let go of his hand and turned right in a circle around the gentleman standing next to her before she met with Charles once more in the centre of the line. A dark, glowering figure gripping a cane amidst the spectators caught her eye, and a chill swept through her. On her next turn she glanced over once again. Brandon stood alone, his chin held high as he watched her and Charles.

"I see your husband is admiring your dancing talent from afar, Lady Graven." Charles's lips quirked. She tried to keep her attention on the dance. Charles made more clever conversation, leaning into her frequently, but she barely heard what he said. She was too aware of Brandon staring at them, glowering at them, his fingers making small jittery movements at his side. The music concluded, and she congratulated herself for having survived it.

Charles bowed before her. "A pleasure, my lady." He nodded at Brandon over her shoulder and took his leave.

Brandon took her hand in his. "The gentleman prince diverting you?"

"I have not danced in years, and Mr. Montclare is a generous and delightful partner."

His lips twitched. "Hmm."

"And Mrs. Treharne, how is she?"

He squeezed her hand. "You are a fine, delightful dancer, Lady Graven."

Justine's heart sank. He had made a distracting compliment, thereby avoiding her snappish question. He'd never replied like this before. He was placating her, and it felt false, horribly false.

A first.

She averted her gaze to the lustrous marble floor. "Thank you."

"I regret my injured leg prohibits me from enjoying this entertainment with you," he said. Her pulse quickened immediately. How could she possibly be annoyed with him and yet ignited with desire for him at the very same time?

The ladies who danced in front of them stole glances at her husband. Of course they did. He was an exceptionally handsome specimen of manhood. His tall, trim form, almost black hair, pale green eyes, and the sculpted lines of his face made him striking. The scars running down the side of his temple only added to the virile and enigmatic appeal of Lord Graven. And when he smiled, as he did now, his whole face relaxed and vibrated with a cryptic energy whose mystery you wanted to be the one to solve and hold onto.

She wanted to, didn't she?

Charles now danced with Amanda. He chattered on, but she wasn't paying any mind. Her attention was directed elsewhere.

At Brandon.

Dear Lord, if Brandon were to indulge in any lingering feelings he had for Amanda, certainly it would enrage William, and it would wound her.

Wound her?

Her stomach curled. She had thought she had been in love with Andrew but, in comparison, that was more a bond of affection and tenderness, because this, this was—

Her eyes slid to Brandon who continued to stare at her, trying to be patient, trying to gauge her thoughts. He raised an eyebrow at her.

He was maddening, unnerving.

"Justine." His voice was gentle, yet firm.

Brandon put her arm through his and pulled her close. Despite her irritation, a flutter went off in her stomach as his familiar warmth pressed against her, his rich and earthy scent enveloping her.

"My head is aching," he whispered in her ear. "Come, let's go outside." Justine only nodded.

The room was crowded with people, and the scores of lit candles added to the already stifling warmth. They went out on the wide terrace which overlooked the extensive and very carefully designed back gardens. There were only a few couples talking, strolling. The autumn night air was brisk.

"Justine, my dear, so good to see you." Mrs. Collins, an old friend of her mother's, approached them. "Lord Graven." She bowed her head, a small smile lit her face. "I heard you had married. I'm so pleased for you both."

"Thank you Mrs. Collins," Justine said. She and Brandon exchanged two or three pleasantries, then Brandon tugged at Justine's arm and they continued walking the length of the terrace. There were slim, tall, potted topiary trees on opposite sides of each of the terrace doors, and at the last door there were a few feet of space between the tree and the end of the terrace.

Brandon propped his cane in the corner and pulled her into his arms. His hands went to either side of her face, his molten gaze fell to her lips, and his mouth descended on hers, crushing her.

She pushed at his chest. "What are you doing?"

"Kissing my wife." His lips and teeth nuzzled the line of her jaw and travelled down her throat. Heat sparked deep inside her, and she clenched her jaw to constrain it. How did this happen with just one touch from him, one kiss? For God's sake, what was this?

It most certainly was a sort of madness.

Her neck stiffened against his hand. "Perhaps you're excited by the attention from all the ladies this evening?"

"I only want your attentions, Lady Graven." His lips brushed the side of her throat. "Your attentions excite me." He kissed the delicate skin under her jaw. "It's quite a combination really." He let out a low laugh between soft kisses. "You arouse me, yet you keep me calm and even. I believe you're my new craving."

"You have quite a few of those it seems," she said through short breaths.

His grip on her tightened. "I saw you with Charles just now, smiling, so very much at ease." Justine blinked up at him. His tense fingers rubbed her at the base of her skull. "I know I cannot give you that."

"And what exactly would *that* be?"

"Effortless affability. I don't seem to have it. I suspect I did once."

"In spades."

"I can give you other things," he breathed over her parted lips. His voice was full of dark promise, but a gnawing question uncoiled in her brain, and she remained stiff under his possessive touch.

"Yet you were all ease and laughter with Mrs. Treharne, enjoying each other's company so very much." She rushed to get the words out before she lost the courage, before he kissed her again, for then she most certainly would not only lose her resolve, but her wits as well.

His eyes glittered in the shadows, and his one hand slid from her neck to rest against the wall behind her. The cool air stung her skin immediately.

"Oh, she's pretty to look at, as ever she was, but I want your taste to fill my mouth." His one hand spanned her throat. "I want to make you cry out my name. I like it very much when you do that, Justine. Just the thought makes me want to lift your dress up over your thighs right this very second and..."

He whispered in her ear how he would take her on the terrace and how he was sure she'd respond. Her eyelids sank closed, her breath deepened. Raw talk like that from his mouth only churned her blood with a ferocity, and he damn well knew it. A low cry escaped her, despite her best efforts at control, and their hips pressed against each other's on instinct. She could no longer ignore the crude ache swelling within her, the heat prickling her skin, nor the hardness between his legs which throbbed right through her silk gown.

Her new lilac silk ball gown.

Because they were at a ball at a great house.

A great house filled with a great number of people. People they knew.

She pulled away from him, but he yanked her right back into his embrace, one hand pressing over her rear. His mouth descended on hers again, taking its fill.

It all became clear.

Amanda had aroused him, and now he had come to her, his wife, his legal bed partner, for his release.

How bloody convenient.

Justine shoved at his chest and twisted out of his embrace. His eyes flared, and he gripped her arms tighter. "Don't!" she said. The stinging in the back of her throat inflamed. "Control yourself."

His brows slammed together, his jaw stiffened. "Don't play games with me, Justine."

"I wouldn't know how, Lord Graven. I could learn though, if you'd like. You seem to be setting a fine example this evening."

"Brandon, there you are."

Justine's heart came to a screeching halt at the sound of that voice.

That voice that used his first name. Because she could. Because they had an intimate past, an age-old connection.

Amanda.

CHAPTER THIRTY-FIVE

BRANDON'S IRON grip on Justine's arms relaxed, and she pulled back from him.

"We've held a place for you at our whist table." Amanda's voice exuded a medley of calm, amusement, and tedium. "Everyone's waiting for you." Her cool gaze flicked over Justine and returned to Brandon with a slight smile. "You promised, Brandon."

He drew breath and released it. "Yes. We're coming." His hard gaze returned to Justine, and she squared her shoulders in response. He took her arm in his and Amanda led them to the gaming tables which were set up in a drawing room. Finally they arrived at their table. Matthew leaned back in his chair, William glanced at them, a muscle along his jaw spasming as his wife settled into a chair that Brandon held for her.

"Finally, Graven. Where have you been?" Matthew motioned for him to sit.

"I told you I'd find him," said Amanda, a slow smile curling her lips. The cards were dealt and play began.

Justine stayed through the second hand. Brandon's face was a dark mask, never giving away what he was thinking or feeling. He radiated superiority and confidence in his quiet demeanor.

William leaned back in his chair, his shoulders stiff, his eyes creasing on occasion. Justine had known these signs of his particular brand of aggravation too well over the years and did not wish to witness them now. They played for the better part of an hour. Amanda, her eyes bright, made witty, clever remarks on occasion.

The pressure between Justine's eyes had her head swimming in the smoky, warm air. She began to take small steps away from the table, straying in the directions of the open terrace doors.

"Lady Graven?" A warm hand brushed her upper arm. Charles was at her side. "You don't look well at all. Come outside at once." He took her elbow and lead her through the doors to the terrace. The cold air was a resounding slap on her skin. "Breathe, Justine." She fought back the dizziness overwhelming her, and her lungs gratefully sucked in fresh cold air.

"Better now," she said. "T'was so warm inside."

"And so bloody tedious watching others play," he said, a hand at her arm, holding her steady.

"Yes, there's that too. Why are you not playing?"

"I try to avoid it. Come, sit here." He guided her to a stone bench and took her hands in his, rubbing them. "Shall I fetch Graven?"

She shook her head. "Oh no, don't interrupt his game. Please, t'is nothing."

Charles tilted his head at her for a moment. "As you wish. I'll bring you something to drink to steady yourself, shall I?"

"Yes, thank you."

He quit the terrace. Outside the door, his deep voice boomed in conversation with a woman's then he returned. "Look whom I've found, Lady Graven."

Georgina stepped out onto the terrace. She looked absolutely beautiful with her lustrous brown hair pulled into relaxed ringlets, her ivory skin and large brown eyes glimmering against the rich burgundy of her silk dress. "Justine, darling, there you are!"

"Georgie!"

"I've spotted you then lost you at least three times over this evening." Georgina joined her on the bench pulling her into an embrace.

Justine laughed. "The same happened to me looking for you. Oh, G, it's so good to see you again."

"Keep her here, Miss Georgina," said Charles.

"I will. Bring her something strong." Georgina waved him off, and he headed back inside once more. "It's been much too long, J. Look at you, you beautiful girl." Georgina beamed at her. "I've learnt your news. Has your brother been saving you for Lord Graven all these years?"

"Something like that."

"Darling, you're the talk of the village, and I'm damn proud of you. Well done. Thank God he survived such a horrible ship-wreck. It must have been a dreadful ordeal."

"Yes." Justine held one of Georgina's hands in hers, desperate not to discuss her personal life any longer. "And you? How are you?"

Georgina pursed her lips. "Back and forth to London or to my sister's in Devon, the endless swirl of parties and civilized goings-on. Too much flirting and too many mixed signals from Matthew." She lowered her voice. "Being cool, being warm. I don't know. I don't know, Justine."

"Ah, the infatuation continues after all this time? Aren't you the constant one?"

"It's a problem I have."

Justine laughed and squeezed Georgina's hand. "I'm glad to see you haven't lost your pluck."

"Me? Never." Georgina's pretty face sobered abruptly, her heart-shaped mouth pursed together. "I must say, Brandon seems different. Rather serious, on a continual glower. And those scars only make him a touch sinister." She placed her hand on Justine's. "Is he kind to you?"

"He is. Everything he's been through has altered him, but inside he's still the Brandon Treharne I grew up with."

"Deep down inside, indeed." Georgina raised an eyebrow. "Take care, Justine. Can't be easy for you."

"It has been difficult for him. But things have been busy, which has been good, with the renovations at the house. Brandon is getting accustomed to life among the living."

"Yes, a right Lazarus sprung from the tomb," Georgina remarked. "Well, I'm just glad you're not on your own in that house any longer, and without that stepfather of yours. Oh, that was the talk of the town too, don't you know? Him being sent packing to his son's. Good for Lord Graven." Georgina smirked. "The men are playing cards?"

"Yes, with Amanda."

"I'm sure she's in the pink having Brandon back in the fold."

Justine sighed. "She went and married his cousin, though, didn't she?"

Georgina rolled her eyes. "She's given William his son and heir. You know what that means."

"No. What does that mean?"

Georgina blinked. "Oh dear, you have been out of the whirl for a long while, darling. Forgive me. It's an understanding in higher circles that once the wife provides her Lord and Master with his son and heir, she is then somewhat free to explore, as it were."

Justine's neck stiffened. "Explore?"

"Yes. Explore...elsewhere," Georgina said, her voice low. "Do you understand my meaning, *ma chére*?"

Justine's stomach rolled. The brutal information scraped through her brain as a sour taste seeped through her mouth. Amanda having an affair would be perfectly acceptable? Somehow she couldn't believe that William would find it so. No wonder she looked at Brandon as if he were the Christmas goose and with such smug confidence too.

Charles reappeared with a glass of port in one hand.

"At last!" Georgina said.

He handed Justine the glass, his eyes narrowing. "You don't look much better. Drink all of it, now."

Georgina glanced up at Charles. "Listen to the wise doctor."

Justine drank the dark ruby wine in two long swigs.

"You're still a shade too pale for my taste, eh Georgie?" Charles said.

Georgina studied Justine. "I say we get that husband of hers to take her home."

"Quite right."

"No need to make this such a drama." Justine looked up from her glass. "The heat and lack of air inside bothered me. If Lord Graven wants to keep playing he should keep playing. This is his first night out, I don't want to spoil it for him. I do feel better now, and I so want to spend more time with you, G." She handed her empty glass to Charles. "Thank you for the port, Charles."

"Of course. Be that as it may, I still think you should go home."

"I agree," Georgina said, sharing a look with Charles. "Come, Justine." Georgina rose from the bench. Charles put Justine's arm through his and led her out of the terrace, Georgina on her other side. The three of them wound their way through the crowded room and joined Andrew, who stood behind Amanda's chair.

"How goes it?" Georgina asked him.

"Brandon is making quite a sweep of it, much to everyone's displeasure," Andrew replied. Amanda's cool gaze flicked over them.

Charles cleared his throat. "I say, Graven." Brandon's dark gaze shot up at Charles from across the table. "Lady Graven had a bit of a spell before. I think she might be better off going home."

Brandon's eyes narrowed and slid to Justine. He jerked up

from the table. Everyone looked up at once and braced for the worst. Georgina's hand flew to Justine's and squeezed it.

"Oh, another round, man, give us a fair turn!" Matthew gulped at a glass of wine.

"Another time," Brandon said, his somber gaze never leaving his wife.

"Oh, let him go, Matthew, for God's sake," said William.

"To the winner go the spoils," said Andrew.

"Charles, do sit in," said Amanda.

"No. Find another."

"Andrew, sit," Amanda said.

"Once more, a fine substitution." Andrew claimed Brandon's vacant chair.

Charles turned and took Justine's hand in his. "It was a delight sharing a few dances with you this evening, Lady Graven. I look forward to seeing you again very soon. Take care."

Justine bowed her head. "You are most kind, Mr. Montclare. Good night."

Georgina kissed Justine's cheek and smiled at her. "You must come for a visit. Promise?"

"Oh yes, very soon. So must you."

A cool hand slipped around her waist and pressed into her flesh right through the thin layers of silk. Brandon lifted his chin at Charles. "Montclare."

"Graven." Charles nodded.

Amanda rose from the table, her face lighting up as she looked at Brandon. "What a fine evening it was."

"Yes." He released his hold on Justine's waist and took her hand in his, entwining their fingers. Amanda's eyes darted down to their clasped hands.

"Good night, Amanda," said Justine.

Amanda inclined her head. "Yes, good night."

Brandon ignored William and led Justine away from the table.

"Goodnight, cousin," William said as they walked past.

They retrieved their outerwear in the hall and made their way down the stone staircase toward the drive where they waited in silence in the chilly, damp air for their coach to be brought around.

"Are you unwell?" Brandon asked.

"T'was nothing. I felt light-headed, dizzy. It passed once I sat outside. Mr. Montclare brought me port."

"How very attentive of Mr. Montclare. Charles may be diverting, my dear, but he is no nice boy like your Andrew."

Justine let out a heavy sigh. "He is not *my Andrew*, Brandon. In fact, Mr. Blakelock is engaged to marry Mariah Marchmain, hadn't you heard?"

"Yes, I did. I am delighted for them both."

"As am I."

His eyes pierced hers under the light of the torches. "Are you?"

"Indeed, I am," she said. "May they find the same wealth of domestic bliss that we have." Brandon's lips flattened into a firm line.

Simms, their footman, held the door of their coach open for them, and Brandon plucked at her hand to help her inside, then pulled himself in next to her. The door slammed shut, and a moment later the coach swayed off.

"Did you enjoy your card game?" Justine asked. "Were you always such an avid player? I suppose your company this evening inspired you."

Brandon hissed in air and pulled her into his lap with one swift movement. He tugged her legs over his so that she straddled him. Her chest tightened under the fierceness of his eyes and his firm grip. That demanding grip of his lit a fire inside her, a fire she barely understood. He wrapped a hand around her neck and pulled her down close taking her mouth in a hungry kiss, his tongue searching for hers, lashing, inflaming her further. Her fingers dug into the thick lapels of his great coat.

His hands travelled down to her hips, shoving her into position over him, and a sharp breath escaped her when she felt the pressure of his hardness right between her legs, just where she ached for him. The jostling of the coach pushed her against him roughly, and she let out a small moan as the friction between them multiplied her need. He let out a heavy breath as he slipped one hand under her dress over her bare flesh. Her body jerked in his arms, and a short cry escaped her lips as his fingers found her.

"Yes, there you are," he breathed, his voice thick in the darkness.

He knew her body very well, and she immediately flooded with heat under his insistent touch. He buried his face in her bosom, and two of his fingers slid inside her.

She shuddered in his hold. "Brandon..."

"You're soaked." He let out an expletive-filled groan.

The air in the small compartment of the coach was hot and humid, pressing in on them, intensifying their urgency. His fingers claimed her depths as his thumb stroked over her, teasing, rubbing. Her arms clutched his neck and shoulders, her thighs tightened, and crying out, she came apart sharply in his grip.

"You liked that, eh, Lady Graven?" His smug, harsh tone struck her like an icy blast of winter air. Was that scorn, a taunt? Had he just proven a point? Her heart shrank. He had marked her like an animal in heat, showed her who was her master, proved to her to whom she belonged.

She twisted back from his chest, but his strength was too much for her. His one hand fisted tightly in her hair, and he brought their faces inches apart.

"Are you punishing me?" she said against his lips. "Are you trying to teach me a lesson?"

His eyes creased. "Punishing you?"

"Yes, yes, punishing me."

"What the devil are you talking about?"

"I told you you'd hate me for this marriage, you'd resent me." Her hands pushed against his shoulders. "Tonight you saw what's been denied you, and you're angry." His body hardened under her, his fingers gripped her bare thigh.

"I am annoyed about Charles and Andrew," Brandon said, his other hand releasing its tight hold on her hair. "But I don't hate you." His hands slid over her hips and pressed into her rear. Her breath caught in the darkness. The gentle yet carnal possessiveness of that gesture only set off a spiral of heat in her chest. "I don't think I could ever hate you, Justine," he whispered.

The coach rocked on the dirt covered road. The clack, clack of the wheels and the beating of the horses' hooves the only sound between them. Justine wished she could see his eyes in the dark. Brandon had addressed his jealousy and possessiveness of her, but not his feelings regarding Amanda. Again, he denied and refused.

He brushed a finger across her chin which betrayed the slightest tremor. "I've frightened you." Brandon's ribs visibly squeezed together and he exhaled. He lifted her off his lap and deposited her on the opposite end of the cushioned seat. The cold air whisked over Justine as she pressed herself into her corner of the coach. She tugged her cloak around her pressing her damp thighs tightly together. He adjusted his clothing and slumped back into his seat, covering his eyes with his hand.

"Forgive me, Justine." His voice was rough and gravelly.

She stole a glance at him. Every muscle of his body seemed cramped, constrained. A heaviness stole over her limbs, and she wanted nothing more than to disappear into the stiff cushions of the coach. He thought he had been too rough with her, too demanding, but the opposite was true, for she liked that very much. No, he had misunderstood. She may indeed be his legal wife, his possession, but Amanda was the thrill of yesterday blazing bright before him right now.

From the beginning, Justine had braced herself from confusing their physical intimacy with sentiments. Having to end things with Andrew had taught her that. It had been deeply upsetting, but she had plowed on knowing that it was smarter in future to harden herself against such an emotion that only left you vulnerable, troubled, disrupted.

However, she didn't feel troubled or disrupted now. No, more like clawed and shredded like an animal hunted and shot down, laying open and bleeding upon the ground at its master's pleasure.

Maybe she and Brandon did not share a romantic attachment, but they did have a physical compulsion for one another which was exciting and satisfying. They also regarded each other with respect and friendship. Most marriages, she knew, didn't even have that. Yes, she was fortunate. What they had between them was quite enough for a successful marriage, wasn't it?

But sharing Brandon with Amanda would be utterly painful.

She folded her arms over her chest as her brain rabidly produced images of Brandon savoring Amanda's naked body with his mouth...his fingers working to bring her to release as he just did with her...Amanda crying out his name and quivering underneath him...Brandon's face buried in her silky blonde hair...her pale, thin hands stroking the long lines of his bare back...his whispering those wicked promises in *her* ear...

Justine's eyes stung. She had begun to long for things she knew could never be hers.

Their first time together he had asked her if she wanted him. The kindness of that was not lost on her. Husbands did not ask, they simply claimed their rights whenever they desired. That was what she'd always heard, at least. He also hadn't taken her after he first learned of their marriage, and he had been so angry with her then. No, he had waited until they had gotten comfortable with one another. And from the moment she had said yes to him, he had been relentless. She liked his relentlessness, liked being driven to extremes by him, to be outside of herself.

Would she ever have her fill of Brandon? She leaned her hot face against the cold damp window pane. This was the stuff of all those wildly popular poems she had read, wasn't it? All these years going through Lord Jeremy's library she had been so very curious what the great poets were on about, tortured verse after tortured verse. She was beginning to understand.

Now it was time for her to come back down to earth. She needed to be cautious, although, as his wife it was her 'duty to submit,' as she had overheard her mother describe it often enough. But being with Brandon was no submission to duty, nor was it 'bearable' or 'rather tolerable' as her mother had also once remarked. No, Justine relished it. He engaged her in the act fully, demanded it of her, and it was exhilarating.

Her fingertip drew circles on the window. She liked the two of them having that secret knowledge of each other; it was theirs alone. Either gentle or rough, it was a magnificent catapult to some great unknown, like a wild ride on a coach where she didn't know the destination nor how to dress for the journey. He'd taught her that, and that satisfaction glowed in a secret place inside her.

She realized that for men it was a necessary physical release as well as a diversion, but for her, it was a novel experience. She delighted in Brandon's firm hands moving over her body, sinking into her flesh as if he were searching for something new every time and treasured what he discovered. Or how his lips would graze at that ridiculously sensitive spot behind her ear causing shivers to shimmer over her and linger long after.

Justine liked the after part too. Neither of them speaking, only holding onto each other, letting the sensations wash over them. Being spent and fluid as honey on a hot summer's day laying in his tight embrace was exceptional. Many times he would stay inside her after his movements had ceased, his fingers stroking her absently, the two of them enjoying their blissful haze. She savored that connection to him. She felt cherished then, for once in her life.

Her eyes squeezed shut. There, she had indeed made the mistake.

She had taken that physical satisfaction between them as sentiment, thus giving it some sort of meaning in her mind. No, that was wrong. It had to be.

Justine was certainly grateful she had an official home now, free of her stepfather and stepbrother's reign. Surely, that was more than plenty for her. It was easy not to expect more because her entire life after her father's death and her mother's subsequent marriage to Richard had been about adapting herself to low prospects. She was accustomed to it and had managed well all these years by keeping her head down, keeping quiet when necessary, and making herself useful.

She once dreamt of a life with Andrew, but that had been dashed to bits and swept away; flotsam scattered over churning waters. Just like that fateful Cornish tempest had done to Brandon's ship from Jamaica.

The coach drove through the familiar high black iron gate. She rubbed her fingers across the foggy glass window to get a clearer glimpse. The imposing central tower of Wolfsgate rose in the hilly distance, its walls glowing in the light of torches lit for their return.

Yes, she had persevered, as had Brandon. There was no need for petulance now. T'was only time wasted.

CHAPTER THIRTY-SIX

BRANDON CLENCHED his jaw as he poured himself another brandy.

He had done it again. Pushed too hard.

Once they'd arrived home she had murmured a quiet "good night." An ache had twisted through his chest at the sight of her darting up the stairs. Now here he was once again, drinking his bitterness away in the parlour alone in the middle of the night.

He threw himself in the cushioned armchair and rubbed his aching temple with one hand, balancing his full glass on his thigh with the other. Their tussle in the coach had been hasty, and there had been a note of despair about her.

He wasn't being fair. Always taking from her, demanding. Next time, if there was a next time—no, there bloody well would be a next time—Justine would have to make the first move. She had to want it just as badly as he did. He would have to bear the wanting of her until then. Dammit, constant wanting.

He gulped down the liquor, and it scalded his throat. Would the old Brandon have pushed so much? Perhaps he would have been more convincing, less harsh with his own wife. The old Brandon certainly would have enjoyed all the attention he had gotten this evening: the women's stares, the men's cool appraisals, Amanda's thirsty solicitousness.

Justine was right, of course—Amanda wanted him, but in a new, more demanding way, which had taken him aback. They weren't flirtatious youngsters anymore, their whole lives abstractly ahead of them. She was a married woman now, a mother, and had a fine place in society. The damning part was she didn't seem to mind making it obvious.

She didn't overdo it, just enough in that refined way of hers. The tilt of her head, that slight smile, a touch of her hand on his arm here and there, the perfect double-edged repartee to elicit an appreciative laugh from him along with a lingering glance. The treacherous list went on and on with that woman. He unwound the tie from his hair and sunk his fingers into his scalp. Is that how it was done nowadays?

She had showered him with her smile this evening, and he had been catapulted back to a time of glorious expectations and golden possibilities. Yes, her beauty was undeniable, and she obviously took great care with herself. *Damn, that sort of thing must be a full-time occupation.*

He should feel flattered by the attentions of such a female. She did still appeal to him, but he had been...unmoved.

He had looked into her eyes this evening, eyes that he once found so irresistible, yet tonight he saw only shining glass.

Justine's dusky velvet eyes, though, glowed with a secret heat just for him. Rich brown eyes like the coffee he used to savor in Jamaica. He could taste that rich flavor on his tongue right now, that aroma filling his senses, calling him to life. But tonight, once they had entered their house, those intoxicating eyes had been opaque in the light of her maid's taper in the hall. He had done that, he had put that resistance there, that boundary.

Congratulations.

What did he expect from his poisoned brain and polluted body bent on self-indulgence? He had spent most of the evening with Amanda and then lashed out at Justine like a jealous husband for dancing so often with Montclare. Well, he was a jealous husband, wasn't he? He raised the glass to his lips, and the heady scent of Justine's musk invaded his nostrils.

He let out a groan. She was on his fingers still. Instantly the sound of her whimpers echoed in his ears, and the memory of the silky feel of her slickness pulling his fingers in deeper overwhelmed him. His body was taut with need; now *she* was punishing him.

Bugger.

It was going to be a very long night.

CHAPTER THIRTY-SEVEN

"Look what I've brought you, Persephone."

Justine opened her palm, and her horse gobbled the pieces of apple and carrot she offered her. She murmured words of affection to the mare who snorted at her great fortune.

Justine simply couldn't sit still today. She wasn't in the mood for a book, and frankly, she had gone through most of Lord Jeremy's collection in the library by this point. Lady Caroline's spinet was woefully out of tune in the drawing room, and plucking on it seemed more like a chore than a pleasure. No, she wanted to be outside, filling her lungs with the fresh cold air of late autumn that was now blowing through the hills.

Days had worn on and nights had dragged on. She and Brandon shared meals together or they didn't. They often exchanged general information about their day without much eye contact. Frequently, Brandon was off riding or working with Davidson at the edges of the property and would have Mrs. Taggart, the new cook, prepare and pack them something cold to take along.

Justine threw herself into cleaning out the garden to prepare it for the upcoming winter months. She picked as many herbs as she could and hung them for drying. She approved Taggart's menu ideas and checked in with Molly about the housekeeping and furniture repairs.

Justine slipped her hand down Persephone's sleek brown neck and the animal whinnied. Right now feeding her horse was just as much a pleasure for her as it was for the horse.

Heavy footsteps and hard breathing from behind her raised the hair on the back of her neck. Brandon led his horse into the stable and stopped when he saw her. Free of its tie, his dark hair was ruffled with the wind, his cheeks ruddy, and his eyes bright. His horse raised his head pulling at the reigns in protest at his master's abrupt standstill.

"You look well exercised," Justine said.

His lips quirked up. "Are you talking to me or the horse?"

She let out a small laugh. She had missed this easy banter between them. "I meant you."

"I am trying to be disciplined with regular exercise and manual labour. Do you approve?"

"I do indeed." She smiled at him. He was still, taking her in with his eyes. "What is it?" she asked.

"It's just you, feeding your horse, not a care in the world." He shook his head. "Last time I tried to show you how to feed a horse you squealed and hid behind me, clutching at my coattails."

"I was ten years of age then. I've spent lots of time with horses over the years. And with Martin's help I learned to get over my fear. I enjoy spending time with them, caring for them." She cast a glance at Brandon whose face had tightened. "Bring Knight here so I can give him some treats."

He led Knight over to her, his jaw firm. The smell of horse and of a very masculine, sweaty Brandon filled the space between them. She focused her full attention on the horse. "Hello, Knight." Her hand brushed over the stallion as she offered him apple and carrot pieces which he eagerly munched. Brandon watched them in silence, a soft smile growing on his lips.

He filled the troughs with fresh water for both horses to drink from. "I was out at the eastern end today with Davidson. The new gates look good." He took the last pieces of apple and fed them to his horse. "You're probably more familiar with the way it used to be than I am. You should come see the work that's been done."

"I will. I hope you're famished after all this exercise. Molly showed Taggart how to make your favourite stew. They're both looking forward to the grand presentation."

He let out a chuckle. "I wouldn't miss it." Brandon leaned over to grab the brush that was hanging on the wall next to her. He misstepped and lost his balance. His other arm shot out and went around her shoulders, and his weight fell on her. Justine grabbed onto his torso, and he righted himself quickly, his eyes flashing over her. "Sorry," he mumbled.

"Are you dizzy?"

"No, it's not that. Quick moves are a bad decision with this knee, especially after a lot of exertion. I keep forgetting. It's getting better, but still not right." His hands slid down to her waist and curled into the fabric of her dress. His gaze fell to her mouth. They stood there in silence, holding each other, the horses' huffing and wheezing echoing around them.

She handed him the brush, and he removed the saddle from Knight. His hands rubbed over the animal's hide in long, firm strokes as he brushed him. Her fingers dug into the folds of her skirts crushing the material.

Justine's brain ratcheted back years ago to when she had first entered this stable. Her first real encounter with a horse had been with Brandon. Richard had insisted she learn to ride properly, but she had been terrified of the great big animals he and William had in their possession. Brandon had been the one to take the time to introduce her to his own horse, her hand in his.

"Don't be afraid of the horse, Justine. You must at least pretend you aren't, because if he feels that you're afraid of him, he'll be afraid of you.

"*Afraid of me?*"

"*Animals can sense things much better than we humans, and they can tell a good person from a bad one. They know, Justine. He'll see the good in you, just as the rest of us do. You show him you're his friend, and he will be. It's quite simple. Come now, try.*"

"Justine?"

She blinked up at Brandon. "I was thinking of Midnight, your old horse."

"Ah, Midnight. How he loved to run."

"You loved it too," Justine said.

"I did, it was a fine escape."

"You had taken me riding on him several times. He seemed so tall to me. A mountain. Riding Midnight I felt as if I towered over all of Wolfsgate, that nothing could touch me."

A smile lit his lips. "I felt that way myself." His soft grey-green eyes slid to hers, and her heart skipped a beat. "Another first time with me, eh?"

Her face heated, and she busied herself with rolling up the small feed bag. "I was so afraid of riding then. It was kind of you to have taken the time to get me started...riding...to get me used to the horse. It meant so much to me." Brandon's hands stilled over Knight, his head tilted to the side. "Justine—"

"You were a good cousin. I mean, you are..."

"Am I a good husband to you now?"

"Am I a good wife?"

Brandon took in a deep breath. "I can't say I really know how husbands and wives are supposed to be."

"I can't say I do either. I hardly remember my own father, and Richard and my mother weren't much of an example."

"No, they certainly weren't." His face darkened. "I wish I had paid more attention to my parents."

She stroked Knight's muzzle. "Lord Jeremy often spoke of Lady Caroline to me with the greatest admiration."

"Well, we are managing without lofty expectations, aren't we?"

"Oh, yes."

"I don't want you to feel uncomfortable with me."

"I don't."

"Or obligated."

"Are you using my logic against me now?"

"I am." Brandon grinned, his hand sweeping down Knight's side. "It's apt here, so I'm using it." The horse snorted, his head bucking up for an instant.

Justine's fingers sank into Knight's thick silky mane. Brandon stood perfectly still, his gaze locked on hers. Her hand fell from the horse and slid up Brandon's chest. Air escaped from between his lips.

"I don't feel obligated with you," Justine whispered. "For me, it's not…"

Brandon wrapped his hand around hers holding it firmly to his chest. Every particle of her being was being absorbed by the steady beat of his heart under her hand, by his firm grasp, his eyes burning into hers.

"I'm glad," he said, his voice low. He brought her hand to his lips and kissed her fingers gently. Her insides ached at the delicate contact. She missed him. Missed his touch, his deep voice, the very smell of him. His heavy gaze fell to her mouth once more.

Was he waiting for her to kiss him?

Justine brought her face closer and touched her lips to his. His breath clipped, his hand tightened over hers.

Footsteps shuffled beyond them.

"Forgive me, yer Lordship, I dinna know ye had returned." Martin stopped dead in his tracks. "Pardon, I…"

Brandon's head jerked up.

"What's this?" Another clearer, far more elegant voice rang

out behind Martin. "You two are quite the domestic types, eh?" Charles strode into the stable. "Who would have thought?"

"Montclare," Brandon said. Justine moved aside, but Brandon kept her hand firmly in his grasp.

"Am I too late to dine with you?" Charles bowed his head and winked at Justine.

A scowl darkened Brandon's features.

"Quite the contrary," she said. "Your timing is perfect. I'll let cook know we have a guest."

"Wonderful." Charles met Justine's smile with one of his own.

CHAPTER THIRTY-EIGHT

"WE ARE INVITED?" Brandon handed the invitation to Justine.

"Indeed." Charles put down his fork. "Amanda had a wonderful time at the ball, and she's excited to have our little circle of yesteryear come together again. This time at her home. Since I had stopped by Crestdown earlier, I offered to bring you the invitation myself." Charles raised his wine glass. "You will come, of course?"

"If my wife would like. Justine?"

She held the invitation in her hands studying the elegant handwriting. "I should like to go to my stepbrother's house for dinner. I long to see my nephew." She lay the invitation on the table.

"Then we shall go." Brandon drained his glass.

Grinning, Charles leaned back in his chair. "There won't be any dancing, but Amanda will surely play for us. William just bought her a new spinet. It's quite fine and does her justice. Do you play, Lady Justine?"

"When I was younger, but I confess I have not practiced in quite some time."

Charles's one eyebrow shot up. "Ah well, newly married ladies have much more interesting amusements, now don't they?"

Her face reddened, but she held his gaze. "Quite so."

"Who's being the hound now?" Brandon refilled his glass.

"Couldn't resist, Graven. Your bride blushes easily. It's charming, I like it." He raised his glass in her direction and drank.

"Her charms are only for me to like, Montclare."

Charles laughed as he refilled his glass and eased further back in his chair. "Quite so."

The great clock in the hall pinged and thumped out its even cadence, echoing through the whole house. Justine rose from her chair. "Gentlemen, I will leave you to your port." Both men nodded as she bowed her head and left the room, her skirts swishing behind her.

Charles prepared his pipe. "She's lovely."

"I know." Brandon dragged his wine glass across the tablecloth before him.

"You're a lucky bastard." Charles passed the ember tong to Brandon and puffed on his pipe.

"I am." Brandon lit his own pipe. "Why aren't you married?"

"One must spend time and effort on finding the proper candidate. And I haven't the time or desire to put in such effort at present. Even so, not one available female of my acquaintance has struck a cord deep enough to impel me to take such a step."

"You require deep to be thus impelled?"

Charles laughed. "Ach, how well you know me, Graven. No, I do not require deep, but I've decided I need to be able to have quality conversation with someone who will be sharing my house with me. And she best be plenty attractive if I am to share a bed with her in order to produce heirs." He exhaled a plume of smoke. "I am not waiting for Cupid's arrow to sweep me away—that can always be found when the mood strikes. I simply feel that the candidate for wife must not be a regrettable choice, but particular." Charles savored the word.

"Your father pressuring you?"

"God yes, that's why I keep escaping to London. At least there I can bury myself in work and avoid all this without having to lie to him about how busy I am, because things are busy. When I'm here, it's too easy to get into trouble, don't you know?" Charles let out a laugh as he filled both their glasses with wine. "You did well at cards the other night."

"I did."

"You also did well with Amanda. She had eyes only for you."

Brandon smoked and said nothing.

"She used to be your particular candidate once upon a time, eh?" asked Charles.

"That was a long time ago," Brandon said. "She made her choice."

"You weren't here, my friend. It's quite simple."

"Simple has ceased to be, don't you think?"

"Not necessarily." Charles stretched his legs, a hand smoothing down his middle. "If you still want her, you could have her. That's simple enough."

Brandon frowned at him.

"Why not?"

"She's married to my cousin whom I despise, and, by the way, and I'm married now as well," said Brandon. "What would come of it?"

"Does it matter?" Charles shrugged his shoulders. "You don't have to take it all so seriously, old man. If you want her and she wants you, you can play. Where's the problem?"

Brandon cocked an eyebrow. "You don't see a problem?"

"No, I do not."

Brandon drank. "Is that what she and William do? Play?"

"Ah, he's devoted. At least for now. But you and Amanda, you two have history between you. That can be a powerful thing, especially if it was never, dare I say, fulfilled?" Charles rubbed the stem of his glass. "You must be curious, eh?"

"Weren't we just talking about my new bride?"

"That's different." Charles brought the pipe to his lips.

"Is it?"

"Always." Charles released spheres of smoke from his lips, and they floated before him. "A wife is one thing, Graven. A mistress, quite another."

CHAPTER THIRTY-NINE

BRANDON STOOD before the fireplace in the parlour absorbing the heat of the crackling flames. The clink of Justine's brandy glass on the wooden table behind him dispelled the web of his thoughts. "Do you really wish to go to Amanda and William's dinner party?"

"We cannot very well say no," said Justine. "We shall go, get it done with, and perhaps we won't have to do it again for quite some time, if ever."

"There's a thought," Brandon muttered.

"I don't think Amanda and Andrew's father realizes the current rift between you and William. Nor does Amanda for that matter. So it's best to play the happy family for the time being, don't you agree?"

There was that word again—*play*. Such an amusement seemed odd to Brandon. Everywhere he looked he saw responsibility: his father's legacy, the house, the estate, the business in Jamaica, a new wife. Playing meant entanglements with others, and entanglements led to obligations, and mess.

To play with Amanda? Dangerous. Justine was already quite

aware of any leftover shreds of attraction he might have for his cousin's wife. Probably more than he himself did.

Even though their marriage was something he had been swindled into, the idea of betraying Justine was distasteful, especially now that he had found such satisfaction in their bed. Amanda, though, had made a statement by flirting with him at the ball, showering him with her attentions, drenching him with the finer air she breathed.

He poked at the burning logs in the fire a bit longer than necessary. "This dinner means spending an evening with the dashing Andrew, of course."

"And his fiancée."

"You realize he's gotten himself engaged only to get your attention. She's no match for you, Justine."

"I am not interested in matching anyone, Brandon. I am concerned about you, however."

He put the poker back in its place. "Dare I ask?"

"You'll see William and Amanda's life up close and first hand. It upset you your first night home and that was only peering into their window from across the lawn. Are you ready for that now?"

"I've already seen them at the ball. We spent plenty of time together."

"Yes, indeed." She rose from her seat.

"Justine, wait." He reached out and pulled her into his arms. All he had to do was to lean in another inch and a half and take her mouth.

Her pink tongue darted out, brushing her bottom lip as one of his hands slid down to her waist and squeezed. His nose trailed the side of her throat, and her pulse quickened under her skin. It was good to know he still had that effect on her.

Oh, fuck it.

He dragged his lips across the delicate skin of her neck and took her mouth gently, slowly, nuzzling the corner of her generous lips. His fingertips traced the soft, smooth skin on the side of her face. Her nails dug into his arms as her lips parted and found his. Their tongues slid against each other, discovering, pleading. His insides shifted and melted all at once.

"The fire is lit upstairs, milady," came the parlour maid's voice through the open door of the room.

Justine stiffened and pulled back from him, one hand wiping at the edge of her mouth. "Yes, Katy, good night."

"Good evenin' then."

Brandon let out a hiss. "That girl needs training."

"I'll have a word with her tomorrow." Justine smoothed a hand down her throat. "I'm quite tired. Good night, Brandon," she murmured and quit the room.

Oh, she was the Mistress of Supreme Self-Control, wasn't she? How far would she take it? Over the past weeks, he had made her body flourish with pleasure. He was sure she had to be missing it just as much as he did. But now there was this strain between them, like some sort of illness spreading its contagion.

The contamination in question being Amanda, he was sure. He leaned his weight against the mantel, and his cold flesh soaked in the heat radiating from the fire.

The memory of a trembling but clear-eyed Justine seeped into his brain. Fresh from a nightmare the other night, she had sought the comfort he could give her. There had been something confident, certain, and definitely hungry about her then, yet all wrapped up in that vulnerability of hers. A searing combination, if ever there was. That night she had trusted herself to his care, given herself over to him completely.

He liked taking care of her, relieving her of her demons. Very much. Every time he thrust his cock as deep as he could inside her he was filling himself as much as filling her; giving to her filled the empty pit inside him with something good, something real.

He tore open his neck cloth.

He wanted that back.

CHAPTER FORTY

"You're my auntie?" Two innocent azure blue eyes peered up at Justine from under a cap of fluffy golden hair.

"Yes, darling, I am your Aunt Justine. Your father and I grew up together as brother and sister. How you've grown! The last time I saw you, you were a tiny little baby." Justine's fingers stroked the impossibly soft skin of Geoffrey's chin. "You're a fine young man now."

Geoffrey's smile lit up his cherubic face. "I am going to be just like Father!" His blue eyes danced at Justine.

William took his son's hand in his. "You've met everyone now, Geoffrey. Time for bed." William gestured at the nursemaid. She swept forward, and William tucked his son into her arms.

"Goodnight, Geoffrey." Justine waved at him, and he smiled shyly as he receded up the grand staircase in his nurse's embrace. "He's beautiful, William. You must be very proud."

"I am." Without a glance, William left her in the hall and escorted his wife into their dining room.

"Lady Graven, come." Charles raised his hand out to her. Justine placed her hand in his, and he ushered her to the end of the long dining table by William who conversed with an elder gentleman seated at his left with an empty seat at his side. Her heart sank. The last thing she wanted was to have to sit close to William. A servant swiftly pulled out the offending chair for her; a punishment. She sat, a heaviness forming in the pit of her stomach.

Charles seated himself on her left. At least she would have someone friendly and entertaining to converse with, even if her husband didn't approve. Justine turned to greet the elderly man seated on her right, between her and William. Her heart stopped.

Sir Wallace's papery white face contorted into a crude expression of gratification, his thick eyebrows arched high. Here was the older man William and Richard had first promised her to.

Time had not been kind to Sir Wallace. After years of high, indulgent living, he had grown even stouter, his face quite swollen. His greenish-brown eyes were cloudy, his ruddy skin now dull, and he wore a brand new powdered wig which only made him appear more pompous than he actually was, if that were possible. His fleshy cheeks pulsed with the wine he swirled in his mouth, his thin purplish lips pursed as his leering gaze swept over Justine from head to toe. An icy shiver razored over her skin.

"My dear, a pleasure to see you again," his voice wheezed.

"Sir." She turned away from him. Andrew was seated across the table, directly opposite her across, and next to him sat Sir Wallace's daughter Lady Emily, with William at the head of their end of the long table.

Justine's toes ground into the floor. A table seating designed in hell.

Andrew nodded at her. "Lady Graven."

"Mr. Blakelock."

"Lady Graven, surely you remember Lady Emily?"

"I do, of course. Lady Emily."

In the years since they had last seen each other, Emily had grown taller, thinner, and her face now had a pinched appearance. She wore a bright coral dress in the very latest fashion, plenty of rouge and powder, and an ostentatious feather decoration in her hair that was worthy of conversation. Emily was only two years older than Justine. To think, she might have been her stepmother. Emily only smiled stiffly at her, and she dipped her head in return.

Justine's gaze darted down the long table. Georgina, Thomas and Matthew, Richard and Mr. Blakelock completed the party. Her smile slipped at the sight of Brandon seated next to Amanda at the opposite end.

A number of servants slid quietly and efficiently in between the guests filling their bowls with a creamy white soup and bringing forth carafes of the first wine. Justine rubbed the silver spoon in her fingers, wondering how she would get through the long meal. The soup bowls were soon taken, and the servants bustled in with platters of fish, beef, ragouts, green peas and french beans, and carafes of another wine. She had no appetite. The smells of the food churned her insides.

The conversations ran from the bloody uprisings in France, to politics, hunting, the theatre, and gossip about several London actors. Justine listened, smiled and commented when able. Charles often leaned closer to her to whisper a derisive remark or question the dubious intelligence of what was being said. Justine was grateful for his quick, dry wit which kept her not only entertained but distracted.

Through it all, Amanda's throaty, elegant laughter reached their end of the table. She had her head tilted toward Brandon as he recounted a tale about Jamaica. Brandon beamed a smile at her, and the sight of it ripped at Justine's skin like the sharp prick of a needle.

This was that Brandon Treharne signature smile. The one that he would always aim at whichever girl had caught his fancy.

As young girls Justine and Annie had witnessed Brandon use this particular smile with girls he was fond of. (Later that smile had been reserved solely for Amanda.) The two of them would giggle uncontrollably at how, under its spell, these girls would become absolutely paralysed with joy and rapture.

Of course, Justine and Annie had secretly hoped that one day they too would merit such a smile from a man of their liking and know that sort of joy and rapture. Had she known then that she would be receiving it from Brandon himself one day, she never would have believed it. Yes, Justine knew intimately what that smile of his felt like. A surge of wonder, an illicit promise. To see it aimed at Amanda once more...

Georgina asked Brandon a question about the food in the West Indies, and he settled back in his chair and replied. Amanda's gaze was absorbed in Brandon as if she had suffered a long thirst for the refreshment only he could provide her. Their amiable familiarity was quite evident, and they obviously still shared that sparkling affinity. After all, they had grown up together, been practically raised to marry one day.

Justine tore her gaze away from them and gave her full attention to the purplish-red claret filling her wine glass.

"Lady Graven, how are the renovations at Wolfsgate coming along?" Andrew asked as a servant ladled a spoonful of buttered green peas onto his plate.

"They are coming along nicely, and the new servants have finally found their rhythm in the house." Justine sipped her wine. "Where is your fiancée this evening, Mr. Blakelock?"

"She was feeling out of sorts today and decided it was best to stay at home." He reached for his wine glass and drank, his eyes on her.

"That is a shame. I do hope Mariah feels better."

"I'll be sure to relay your regards to her," he said, his voice flat.

"Please do."

Lady Emily sniggered loudly at a remark William had made to her, then two of them laughing.

An unusual pressure on Justine's thigh made her body seize.

Her eyes widened over a stodgy hand wearing a large engraved cornelian ring stealing up her leg. The breath choked in her throat as Sir Wallace's thick hand squeezed at her flesh.

"You're Graven's now, eh?" The old man let out a hiss of air through his thin lips. "Don't think I've forgotten that you were supposed to be my little wife, my pet."

"That was none of my doing, sir," she said. "My stepfather and stepbrother made those decisions."

His swollen hand slithered over her dark blue silk further up her thigh, and her stomach heaved. "I'm no fumbler. I would have kept your belly full on my seed. I see your husband has not accomplished that task yet. Perhaps his leg is not the only appendage of his that limps?" Wallace let out a squawk. "Those marks on his face have certainly marred his prettiness, have they not?" Sour bile seared her throat, her lungs constricted as the old man's fingers squeezed her knee. He gulped his wine and ungracefully plonked the glass back on the table.

"Sir Wallace, I must insist—"

He only leaned in closer, his fingers tightening over her numb flesh once again. "I may not look it, my pet, but I have enough energy in me to best any young buck here. More's the pity, more's the pity." He licked his reddish-purply lips, his rancid breath fuming over her. "On all fours I would have had you, my little piece, morning, noon, and night."

"Sir Wallace, remove your hand from Lady Graven's leg or I will personally dissect that arm from your shoulder. Do I make myself clear?" Charles's voice cut between them.

"You're not her husband." Wallace lips twisted. "What do you care?"

Andrew burst out laughing at a jest Lady Emily had told. The sudden cacophony jolted Justine from her numbness, and she blinked up at Andrew. He caught her gaze from across the table and sobered, his eyes narrowing.

The lines of Charles's face hardened. "I am not fond of

repeating myself, sir." His sharp, masterful tone bolted through Justine, yet she remained numb.

Sir Wallace removed his hand from her leg, scowling at them both. Justine took in a shallow breath. Andrew tilted his head at her, his brow creasing.

"There's my good man." Charles's tone remained curt. "You do not speak to Lady Graven again. You do not even look at her the rest of the evening, if ever again, do you understand? Not even a glance in her direction. Have I made myself clear?"

Wallace mumbled curses under his breath, shifted in his chair, and turned toward William again. Charles whispered encouragements in her ear, his cool hand on her arm. She grit her teeth.

"Ladies!" Amanda's clear voice rose over the hum of conversation in the dining room. There was a general pushing back of chairs and clattering of glasses and silver. Amanda took her leave of the dining room, and the women rose to follow her into the drawing room. Justine jerked up from her chair.

"Lady Graven—" Charles's voice wrapped her in its gentle warmth. "I won't let him near you again. Stay close to me for the rest of the evening. Do not be frightened. He's an old lout, and everyone knows it. Your brother is the only one who doesn't seems to enjoy his company."

"Charles—" her voice came out rough, hoarse. No other words came.

"It's all right, my dear," he said softly. "I would advise you not to tell your husband. The last thing we need is a scene."

Justine nodded at him. She completely agreed.

Charles's hands tightened into fists on the surface of the table. "I'll be in soon," he whispered, a muscle flexing in his jaw. He refilled her glass with wine and slid it towards her.

Justine seized it, taking a long swallow. "Thank you." Charles bowed his head slightly at her.

Andrew stared at them and rose from his chair as Justine

swept past Charles and made her way to the door. She ignored the fact that Andrew followed her on the other side of the table. A large hand gripped her wrist, and she stopped.

"Justine?" said Brandon.

She forced her facial muscles to relax through the prickles of cold sweat that now beaded on her temple. She pulled out a smile for her husband from the recesses of her collapsing self. His thumb rubbed her knuckles settling on the ring he had placed there, his fingers nudging it. She prayed for her pounding heart to ease its violent pace, lest its wild clamor give her away.

Brandon brought her cold hand to his lips and kissed it, but that flash of warmth did nothing to ease the numbness in her limbs. She held her breath, and with all the effort she could muster, attempted a smile as an offer of proof of her normalcy. Her knees would give way if she had to bear his searching gaze any longer.

"Release your wife, Graven," said Matthew. "You'll have plenty of time alone with her later."

Brandon frowned as he finally released her hand. Justine silently thanked the gods above. She smiled weakly and walked as elegantly as possible from the room, leaving the men to their tobacco and drink.

She entered the drawing room where the ladies were gathered. In such an elegant space—from the blue damask festoon curtains to the elaborate blue and pink floral carpet lining the floor, and the lavish blue material lining the walls to the matching upholstery trimmed with gold—one would expect elegant company to match. But instead Justine choked on the gold and blue spectacle of Amanda's drawing room the moment she walked through.

"Imagine, Lord Graven married her?" Emily pronounced loudly enough to be heard. Tittering and giggles followed.

She was very grateful that Charles had her drink that last glass of wine. There seemed to be no escape for her this evening.

"Emily!" Amanda's eyes widened at her guest, and she shook her head ever so slightly.

"She's entitled to her opinion, Amanda," Justine said. "Just as I am entitled to mine." Justine approached Emily, and the room held its collective breath. "And where is your husband this evening, Lady Emily?"

Sir Wallace had managed to marry his daughter off to a well-titled Lord from the north. It was common knowledge, however, that Emily's young and attractive husband was a card-playing *bon vivant* who only married her for the extra pocket money and to produce an heir or two under his own father's command. The husband spent most of his time wherever his wife was not, only making rare appearances with her at special events in London. It was widely known that he much preferred his mistress who was several years older than he, and, foremost, the hunting and fishing at his estate.

Emily's back straightened, her lips pursing tightly.

Justine would not be abused by both Sir Wallace and his daughter. Was it the wine that plunged her in this wave of boldness that rose inside her? So be it. She rose with its tide.

"Is he ill and indisposed once again?" Justine's voice rang out clearly. "So very curious. You really should take better care of your husband, Lady Emily. It is a wife's duty, is it not?"

A hush fell over the room.

Georgina came to her side. Amanda rose, her lips a firm line.

Justine bowed her head, and, with Georgina, moved to the far end of the room.

"Very impressive," said Georgina.

Her face was hot, her insides stung. "Was it?"

"Tell me everything, darling."

Justine had never told Georgina of her almost engagement to Sir Wallace and his and his daughter's subsequent ill will. In a low tone, she explained.

"Dear God. I think I need more wine," Georgina said.

"Unfortunately, we shall have to make do with the tea being served."

"Is there nothing stronger?" Georgina frowned.

Amanda sashayed before them, her neck stiff. "That was most unseemly, Justine. You will not ruin my party."

"Lady Graven and I are thoroughly enjoying your party, are we not?" Georgina turned to Justine.

"Indeed, we are," Justine replied, forcing a smile on her face.

Amanda cast a pointed glance at Georgina then settled her gaze back on Justine. She was going in for the kill now. "Your brother will be very disappointed when he hears about your disrespectful behavior. Sir Wallace has been a treasured friend and business partner of his for several years now. If your little snip with Emily in any way interferes with that it would be most unfortunate, Justine."

"I know all about Sir Wallace and my stepbrother, Amanda. Furthermore, my stepbrother has been disappointed in me from the moment we met. What difference would a little more make to the debris already on the pile?"

Amanda's neck stiffened. "You must apologize to her. To me—"

The doors burst open, and the men entered, and Amanda immediately swept off in their direction. Charles strode toward Justine and Georgina, a grin curling his lips.

"Mr. Montclare, you missed the show. We're going to need a drink immediately." Georgina's eyes danced at him "Get on it, would you?"

"Say again?" asked Charles. Georgina explained, and his body shook with laughter. He gestured at a servant and relayed his order. "Lady Justine. I see you are more than capable of holding your own. I like it." He grinned at her. "Very, very much."

Justine wasn't listening. Brandon, his features dark, marched through the room straight for her. Her heart stammered in her chest.

"Justine? What did Wallace say to you?"

"Pardon?"

Brandon's hand cupped her elbow, raising her off the settee. "You were seated next to him at dinner, were you not? Did he say something to upset you?"

She swallowed hard glancing at Charles. "Nothing of any significance was discussed."

"Justine—"

Amanda slipped her arm around Brandon's bicep. "Brandon, there is something Father must show you." Amanda aimed a glittering smile at him.

Indeed, *she* glittered. The pale yellow silk she wore this evening enhanced her delicate features. A diamond pendant sparkled around her throat gracing her ample bosom and matching the diamond drops hanging from her earlobes. An elegant silk turban was wrapped around her crown, long, loose ringlets of flaxen hair framing her face. Any man would be pleased to have such a stunning woman showering them with her radiance.

"Do come, he's waiting," Amanda said.

Charles handed Justine a glass of wine, and she murmured her thanks, smiling stiffly from behind her glass as Amanda led Brandon away to where her father waited for them by an open curio cabinet. Justine watched as they spoke and laughed. The two of them admired a China vase Mr. Blakelock held in his hands.

Justine swallowed more wine. It was natural between them. Just as it always had been.

"Some feelings don't ever wither and die," Andrew's husky voice was at her ear. "Don't you think?" He was perched on the arm of the settee next to her, while Charles and Georgina were engaged in conversation with William and Matthew.

"My sister is determined, Lady Graven. Amanda usually gets what she wants, always has. She does not back down. Not like I do, at any rate. Of course, if you ever feel the need for a bit of *quid pro quo*, I may be available."

"Who are you, and what have you done with Mr. Andrew Blakelock?"

Andrew threw his head back and laughed. "It's true and you know it, love." Justine drew a few inches away from him and averted her gaze. She caught Brandon's sober stare from across the room. Andrew slid down on the settee next to her, his legs outstretched. "You know as well as I that it's destiny at work with those two."

"And what does her husband think of this destiny, I wonder?"

He let out a dark laugh. "Your stepbrother—"

"You should never underestimate William."

Andrew sighed and drank from his glass as elegant notes of music rose from the other end of the drawing room. Amanda, her back perfectly straight, sat at the spinet, her fingers darting over the instrument. Brandon stood nearby with Mr. Blakelock, but he still tossed glances at her and Andrew from across the room. She could practically feel the heat of his glare as she took another long sip of wine.

"Who are any of us in the face of destiny?" Andrew murmured.

Justine straightened her shoulders and slid a hand down her silk dress. "I'm not sure I agree, Mr. Blakelock. We might as well all idle in our drawing rooms and wait for destiny to haul us through life if that were the case. Doesn't that notion of destiny go against the grain of free will?"

"And what is free will in the face of the iron will of another?" The bitterness in his tone sent a sting across her flesh.

Amanda's spirited music spun, filling the room. Justine finished her wine. She was determined to enjoy herself this evening. She took her leave of Andrew with a nod of her head and walked to a large landscape painting of a waterfall hanging in the opposite corner of the room. The painting had been much discussed over dinner. Amanda had met the artist in London.

"Moping about?"

Justine blinked up at William, then returned her attention to the canvas. "Hardly. I was admiring your new acquisition."

"Amanda has quite an eye."

"Indeed she does."

A hint of amusement glimmered in William's eyes. "What a pleasure it was to dine with Sir Wallace this evening, don't you think?"

"Most memorable, stepbrother. Thank you so much for seating us together."

"I'm glad you enjoyed yourself. It was my every intention to please you and, more importantly, to amuse myself. I heard every delicious word he said to you," he whispered.

Justine kept her gaze riveted on the brushstrokes in the painting...the icy white-blue cascade of water, the textured green foliage, the treacherous angles of the jagged rocks.

"My wife insisted on this dinner party," he continued. "I couldn't possibly let such an opportunity for my own entertainment slip by, now could I?"

"I expected nothing less," Justine said. "I must say, I am impressed that you have managed to keep in Sir Wallace's good graces."

"Well, he was quite a sore loser after we'd not gone through with your engagement, but I eased his pain in other ways." William drank from his glass. "Are you leaving soon?"

Musical notes hung in the air, and applause filled the room. "Only if you can tear your wife away from my husband, which might be difficult as she seems resolved to mesmerize and conquer."

William's eyes narrowed at her words and at the sight of Brandon and Amanda together at the other end of his lavishly appointed drawing room. "My wife enjoys indulging in nostalgia."

"Ah, is that what we're calling it now?" She let out a dry laugh. William's eyes blazed at her.

"Pardon, may I have a word?" Georgina slipped her hand around Justine's arm. William strode off. Georgina whispered, "Darling I think you should make special plans for this evening."

"Plans?"

"Yes. Tonight at home I think you should wear your finest silk chemise which I trust you own as a new bride. No, better yet nothing at all underneath a silk dressing gown and dazzle your husband."

"Dazzle?"

"Dazzle him with your attributes and charms tonight and wipe his brain clean of our delightful hostess." Georgina eyed her. "Come now, you're a married woman. You two must be..."

"G!"

Georgina tilted her head, her eyes glowed. "Well? Haven't you?"

"Yes, we have. But..."

"But what?" Georgina's eyes widened. "Oh no! It wasn't enjoyable with Lord Graven? Really? Because I have heard it can sometimes be enjoyable—"

"No, it was. But—"

"Ah, excellent!" Georgina giggled. "But what?"

Justine clasped Georgina's hands, letting out a shaky laugh. "But we argued after the ball and now we aren't..."

"No, no, no! You musn't allow your pride to drag out a simple tiff and turn it into a tangle of misunderstanding and stubbornness. I beg you, Justine. Brandon is too fine a specimen of a man to leave unattended for very long."

Justine blinked at Georgina. "Unattended?"

"Yes, that's right. You are his wife. You can and should do whatever you can to satisfy him. And do it quickly."

"Quickly? Why do you say that?"

"Amanda seems to have him in her thrall this evening. I am most annoyed by it, and so should you."

"Is it not simply nostalgia for their past?"

One of Georgina's dark eyebrows arched. "You need to do something special this evening, my girl."

"Are you suggesting I influence him with...?"

"J, it is in a woman's distinctive arsenal to show her husband her regard and appreciation by providing him with something memorable, unique, and stirring. She must dazzle him with her allurements and keep him coming back to *her*, and only her, for more of the same and, indeed, different."

Justine forced herself to take in a breath of air through her parted lips. She reached for a fresh glass of wine from a passing servant.

"Do you understand, darling?"

Justine nodded as she drank. Her brain had stuck on what the word "different" might imply.

"This should not be any kind of hardship for you, Lady Graven or am I wrong?"

Justine only shook her head as she swallowed, the liquor warming her throat.

"Hmm. I must say," Georgina's voice lowered. "There is something rather appealing about Brandon's new dark and intimidating demeanor, once you get over the initial fright, that is. I am curious how that translates to the bed—"

"Georgina!" Justine squeezed her arm tightly.

Georgina squeezed her friend's arm back. "Forgive my tongue, darling, can't help myself." Both of them returned their attention to Amanda at the spinet. She played a more melancholic composition.

"You are not wrong," Justine whispered then let out a soft giggle. "About his dark demeanor, I mean."

"Oh?" Georgina continued to watch Amanda play as her fingers pressed on Justine's arm.

"He is exceptionally intense and..."

"Hmm?" A grin began to form on Georgina's lips.

"Ardent."

"Ahh," Georgina sighed. "I do have fine instincts." The music ended, and Georgina and Justine clapped for their hostess.

"How are you so familiar with all this feminine strategy?" Justine asked.

Georgina chuckled. "Since my sister married, she has become quite a marvel of the womanly wiles. And I have been a devoted student of hers in order to prepare myself to better one day navigate married life."

Justine laughed. "Lucky girl to have such a sister."

"I had to preoccupy myself with something all those months at her house in Devon." Georgina bit her lip. "You know, underclothes are quite the fashion now for ladies in France."

A tide of laughter rose up in Justine's throat.

"Justine, you must take my advice this evening, and let me know the results, and then I will be perfectly confident to use such a stratagem myself one day should the need arise. If I ever get married, of course." She frowned. "That still remains to be seen."

"You truly expect me to put your theories to the test?"

"Amanda is not coming home with you, is she?" Georgina said and they both burst into laughter. "Then you shouldn't have any problems this evening. Justine, from what I've seen of the way your husband looks at you, all sulky and penetrating as if he's trying his damnedest to read your mind or burn through your clothing, I really don't think you're going to have a difficult time of it. Be aware. Use your particular charms to your advantage, that is all."

Justine sipped at the last of her wine. "Did you say penetrating?" They both burst into laughter.

"Have we had too much to drink perhaps, ladies?" Charles's impressive form blocked their view of La Amanda at her spinet. Both women's gazes traveled up his broad chest burnished with the gold buttons of his frock coat, past his prominent shoulders, to the angled jawline of his striking face. "Ladies?" he asked again, his blue eyes positively sparkling.

"Are we misbehaving?" Georgina blurted.

Justine's eyes widened. "Have we interrupted the concert?"

Charles grinned. "No, you haven't made spectacles of yourselves yet, but I do think you need a chaperone to keep you both in line for the rest of the evening. No more drink."

"Oh, don't be dull, Mr. Montclare," said Georgina.

"One could never be dull in your company, Miss Georgina, I assure you."

CHAPTER FORTY-ONE

"My lady?" The servant held Justine's burgundy wool cloak before her.

"Yes, thank you." The cloak fell around her shoulders, and she tugged on the edges of the thick material. The front door was pulled open, and the chill of the dark night crept over her in the front hall.

Sir Wallace brushed past, and Justine scooted back. He winked at her. "I'll be thinking of you tonight, of that you can be sure." His watery red eyes hung in his puffed face. He guffawed as he was led away by a footman at the door. Emily followed them, her face drawn.

Justine stepped back from the gathering crowd. Her head ached. Somewhere along the way to the front door she had gotten separated from Georgina and Charles. Brandon had caught up with them at one point, but now even he had disappeared as well.

She stepped into the opposite hallway and leaned against the wall for a moment to take a breath of air and settle her head in the quiet before she went back out to the busy hall. Yes, she'd had too much liquor this evening, but she enjoyed the looseness in her joints and the molten warmth in her veins.

Rustling fabric and muffled voices echoed down the hallway, and Justine turned instinctively toward the sounds. Two figures were at the other end of the hall. A tall man and a woman, his hand at the side of her arm. He planted a kiss on her cheek, then took her hand in his and kissed it as well. The woman's soft laughter echoed down the dark corridor.

Justine blinked, her mouth slackened. There was no denying that laugh. There was no denying the yellow dress reflected in the moonlight coming in from the tall arched window at the end of the hall.

Brandon and Amanda.

Brandon and Amanda together.

She spun. Everything spun.

Justine's pulse lodged in her throat as she stepped back and rounded the corner. Their footsteps grew closer, their voices louder. Her hands grazed the hard polished edges of a cabinet, and she moved around it, tucking herself over to its other side. Brandon and Amanda stopped just beyond her hiding place. He kissed her hand once more, and she murmured his name, caressing the side of his face. Justine's lungs burned.

Brandon left Amanda and strode towards the main hall. She stood still watching him, a grin lighting her face. Satisfaction. Pleasure.

Triumph.

Amanda hastened in the opposite direction toward the study where Justine knew there was a secret door that led to the other side of the great room in the centre of the house. No one would ever guess she had been on this side of the house all this time. Justine took in a deep breath, wiped at her face, and made her way to the front door of Crestdown where her husband would surely be waiting for her.

CHAPTER FORTY-TWO

"How do you know Sir Wallace, Justine?"

Brandon lit his pipe before the huge stone fireplace in the parlour at Wolfsgate. He released puffs of smoke from his mouth, his beautiful mouth. Justine admired that mouth, her brandy glass not far from her lips. She decided she wanted to feel that mouth on hers again.

Feel it demanding and giving.

Feel it drive its way desperately up her neck then down over her...

She drank as her body sank into the settee.

"You enjoyed yourself this evening, did you not?" Brandon stood over her, close, very close, so close she could smell his cologne edged with the tobacco. His brooding eyes seemed greener this evening. Fascinating how they changed tones. Her grip on the glass tightened.

"Maybe you should stop drinking." He went to take the glass from her.

"Hmm-hmm." Justine shook her head at him.

"Sir Wallace?"

"Sir Wallace what?"

"How do you know him?"

"How do I know him?" Justine sighed, a bitter smile curved the edges of her lips. "He has been a friend of Richard's for years, and William tried to make some sort of investment with him at one point."

"Yes, but you know him too, don't you?"

"Yes, I do."

"How?"

"We were almost engaged."

His forehead creased. "He's the older man you told me about?"

"Yes. You see, I'm a popular girl."

"Christ," he rasped. "The bastard seemed irritated to see us when we first walked through the door of Crestdown, and I wondered why."

"Fortunately for me, marrying him did not come to pass." She raised the glass to salute him, then put it to her lips and drank, her eyes never leaving his.

He raised his chin at her. "And they sat you next to him at dinner this evening."

"Yes. Pure William. A party favour just for me."

"What did he say to you, Justine?"

She flicked a hand in the air. "T'was nothing."

"Justine, what did he say?"

"Sir Wallace congratulated me on my marriage to you with a ripe amount of irony. I got the distinct impression the pain of losing me has cut him quite deep."

"Bloody hell." A muscle tensed in Brandon's jaw.

"He might have been a bit flippant."

"Justine—"

"Charles was there."

"Charles? I should have been there," he said. "You should have told me, at the very least. Wallace is a pig. Dammit, I'm sorry. I should have seen to it, to you." He stared at her, his gaze somber but soft. A lovely warmth enveloped her, but she pushed it away and straightened her spine for extra defense against it. That wasn't her warmth to enjoy; it was a delusion.

"The last thing I wanted was a scene at William's house," she said.

"Why do you always assume that I cannot control myself and would resort to violence, for God's sake?"

"I'm trying to protect you."

"I should have protected you this evening, Jus!"

Hearing his intimate name for her ripped at something inside her. "Your attentions were otherwise engaged," she bit out, her voice raised. His eyes flared at her. She let out a breath. "And you? Did you enjoy the dinner party given by your family in honour of your return to the land of the living?" She held her glass aloft, letting out a dry laugh. "And what a land it is, eh?"

Brandon extracted the glass from her hand dispensing with it on the end table. "I think you've had enough."

"Oh, I agree. I have certainly had enough." Justine rose. She would fight fire with her own fire. Amanda's kisses, caresses, her scent would not be the last on his skin or on his mind tonight.

Let him burn, burn as I do.

She cupped the side of his face with her hand, her thumb rubbing at the edge of his mouth with a small, gentle movement. Brandon's eyes darkened as his hand clamped over her wrist. His teeth caught her thumb, and his tongue swiped at it. A noise lodged in her throat, and his own rough intake of breath inspired her further.

It would be so easy, so very easy.

But alas, tonight was not the appropriate night for Georgina's stratagems to be put to the test. A vengeful spirit bit its fangs into her instead. She reached up on her toes and traced his lower lip with her tongue and then slid it inside his mouth. He jerked forward, his one hand sweeping up her back, pulling her body into his tight hold. His mouth crashed down on hers.

She tasted the acrid tobacco and the sweet brandy, and those familiar, beloved sensations only drove her deeper into his kiss and into his firm body. She pulled her mouth back slightly from his, her hands digging into his hair, removing the tie that held it back. Brandon's heavy breaths mingled with her own.

"Say my name," she breathed.

His hand slid up her throat, gripped her jaw, and tilted her face up at him. His eyes scorched hers in the dim glow of the candlelight. "Justine."

"Again." Her fingers tightened in his thick, black hair.

"Justine." He cradled the back of her head and drove his tongue deep inside her mouth. A groan escaped him which made her chest swell, but she tore her mouth from his, unlatched herself from his grip, and pushed away from him. Brandon's head recoiled.

"Good-night, Lord Graven."

He let out a gasp, pulled her to him once more, and shoved her back up against the wall. She cried out as his hands gripped either side of her face holding her steady. His kiss was deep and hard, and she began to dissolve in his arms, her knees weakening. Using her last ounce of bodily strength, she twisted away from him once more, but again he yanked at her torso pulling her back in.

Justine resisted and pushed at his chest, but he buried his face in her neck and sucked hard on her skin. She twisted in the opposite direction this time, but now she faced the wall. He was behind her, his one arm wrapped around her middle, his chest pressing into her back. His other hand was at her jaw, and she gasped loudly as his hot breath at her throat set her skin on fire. His brutal hardness pressing into her rear promised to satisfy a primal urge, yet also guaranteed to annihilate her all at once.

Justine pushed back and slid out from under his arm, but a strong hand clasped hers and pulled her back in. Their fierce eyes met, and Justine only shook her head. She relaxed her muscle. He loosened his grip on her hand, and she darted away

toward the door. He shuffled back a step and gave her an incredu-
lous look, his mouth gaping open as she strode from the room.

"Good night, Lord Graven, " her voice rang out from the
staircase.

Glass crashed. A stream of curses exploded in the parlour
resounding through the house.

CHAPTER FORTY-THREE

"Your Lordship, shall I—"

"No."

"Do ye need assistance, sir?"

"Go away, dammit."

Martin receded from his vision. Brandon raised the axe again and aimed it at the wood on the block. It split perfectly in two. If only this would help the pounding in his head and in his cock. Christ, what had gotten into her last night? The attitude, the teasing behavior, the surprising boldness.

It was fantastic.

Was it just the drink she had consumed all evening? That may have given her the courage to be so damned brazen, but she had been determined to make a statement. Justine had been uncharacteristically forward with him and so damned appealing doing it.

She had wanted to provoke him. It exasperated him and made him taut with desire for her at the same time. Her tongue had driven him to the edge of insanity, and the belligerence in her eyes had made him painfully hard. She had wanted him all right, as badly as he had wanted her, but she had made the choice to leave him and herself high and dry. Alone in the parlour last night, he had jerked himself to release to get some relief, but it barely made a difference.

He kicked the split wood over and tossed a larger log in front of him. He raised the axe high, it whizzed by his ear. The wood snapped and splintered. Even though Justine had downplayed it, he had seen how pale and distracted she'd seemed when she had left the dining room at the dinner party, and he felt guilty that he hadn't followed her to find out more. Then Andrew had approached him after the women had left the room.

"Wallace has said something to upset her. If, that is, you are at all interested in your wife's well-being?"

"What the hell happened?"

"I don't know exactly what he said to her as I had Emily and William prattling on at me, but it seemed quite unpleasant. Knowing him, it must have been ugly. Luckily Charles was on her other side, because he swooped in, and Wallace backed off right away."

Brandon had winced with the possibilities of what that old lout might have said to Justine, not to mention the image of Charles "swooping in."

"Do something about it, Graven, if you give a toss about your wife. And don't let it happen again. The vultures are circling." Andrew had left him with a scowl.

Andrew was right. Brandon had let Justine down, and he regretted it fiercely. Once again, he had left the field open for Charles to play the hero just when his wife needed one.

Brandon tightened his grip on the axe. What in the hell were William and Richard thinking even considering engaging the girl to Wallace? Just the thought of that old lecher ogling Justine made his stomach pitch. No one should have fantasies about his wife. Not Wallace, not Andrew, not Charles. Not even Martin whose gaze, he'd noticed often enough, remained fixed on Justine a mite too long for his liking.

No. No one. Ever.

But, of course, they did. Not only was she an attractive young woman, but her bearing was graceful and unaffected. Justine didn't exhibit the languid torpor so many women of his class strove for, believing it bespoke a cool sophistication. Her dark eyes were full of activity that made you curious as to not only what she was thinking, but how she was thinking it. Those large, expressive eyes of hers and that full mouth revealed a hidden sensuality that he had possessed.

Yes, he and someone else.

Who was it, dammit? He inhaled and brought the axe down once again. The log splintered, the pieces dropping to the ground.

The vultures are circling.

The Adonis had made a point. A good one.

More wood.

He raised the axe high.

~

"How is your head today?" Brandon asked his wife in the dining room as she filled her breakfast dish with slices of bread, and a spoonful of plum preserves.

"Sorry?" She glanced up at him from her dish. Her eyes were strained.

"From all the drink last night?"

"Ah." Her gaze returned to her dish.

Her hair was down, and thick locks of it shifted over her shoulders and across her chest. She bore a mark on the side of her throat from his rough kisses. His cock stirred in his breeches at the sight.

"This morning's walk did wonders for me."

"You went for a walk?" He moved closer to her and slid a stray piece of her wavy hair that bobbed in her eyes behind her ear. He couldn't resist tracing a trail down the edge of that delicate ear.

He managed to elicit a slight tremor from her. "Any other aches and pains?"

Justine's eyes shot up at him, and this time they were round. "Aches and pains?"

"Yes. Aches and pains."

Justine stepped back and set her dish on the table. "None." She sat down and lavished a piece of bread with plum jam. He tossed a few pieces of cheese and a hunk of bread on a dish and took a seat close to her. A smile crept over his lips, but he did his best to tap it down. He bit into the cheddar.

She sniffed at her cup of chocolate, discomfort flaring over her features, and put the cup back down. "What were you doing this morning?"

He swallowed the food in his mouth. "Chopping wood."

"That was you? I thought that was Martin."

"No."

She bit into her bread. "Impressive at such an hour."

"Indeed, I find such vigorous exercise early in the morning helps with all my daily aches and pains." He took a bite of bread and chewed, his eyes locked on hers.

"Is it your leg?" she asked.

"Primarily." He leaned forward, his forearms on the table. "It remains stiff, and the pain can be quite—"

"Disagreeable?" Justine's gaze met his.

"Quite unbearable."

"That must be intolerable for an active man such as yourself, Lord Graven. You should have told me. I could have..."

"Yes?"

"Prepared a compress of chamomile for it."

"Ah," he said, an eyebrow arching. "Do you really think such a compress would be soothing enough?" He bit into a crust of bread, chewing it slowly.

Justine patted her lips with her napkin. "I believe so, as the compress would be...

"Yes?"

"Hot."

"Hot?"

"And wet."

Oh, this woman.

Brandon's cock stirred to life in his breeches, and he squirmed in his chair. The silence in the room positively crackled. The urge to spread her on the table and take her over their breakfast dishes tore through him. He'd lick that bloody plum jam right off her nipples and pour that hot chocolate over...

Martin burst into the dining room. "Message, sir!" His loud voice broke the spectacular spell between husband and wife. Martin hastily bowed his head at Brandon and Justine then dropped a small sealed square of paper on the table. Brandon glared at him.

"'Twas just handed to me outside sir, said it were urgent."

"Urgent? Who gave it you?" asked Brandon.

"T'was a lady's maid from Crestdown."

Justine's gaze narrowed to the folded paper.

"Beg yer pardon, sir. I did na think to give it to Molly first and put it on a tray for ye."

"No matter, Martin," said Justine. Martin stole a glance at her and darted from the room.

Brandon's title was elegantly penned on its cover. He snapped open the note and read. A smirk flashed across his features then vanished.

Justine's chair scraped against the floor. She rose from the table.

"Justine, wait—" He took hold of her wrist.

"I have work to do."

Brandon pressed his lips together. His fingers loosened their grip on her wrist, and she quit the dining room.

CHAPTER FORTY-FOUR

HOW MANY WHITE tablecloths did one house truly need?

Justine's head throbbed. The walls of the kitchen linen closet where she, Molly, and Katy stood seemed to be pressing in on her. Reviewing the state of the tablecloths and napkins was a terrifically tedious job. However, she gave it her full attention, or at least she tried, in order to block out fantasies of Amanda and Brandon rekindling their bond through love notes and secret trysts. She shoved down the scream in her throat as Molly unfolded yet another white linen rectangle from the pile, this one with frayed edges.

"If you'll excuse me, ladies," Justine's voice rasped. "I need some fresh air. Do carry on."

"Of course, ma'am." Molly nodded at her and she and Katy returned their attention back to the linens.

Justine grabbed her cloak, fastened on her walking boots, and unlatched the front door. A burst of cold, clean air washed over her refreshing her senses immediately, but it did nothing to lift her spirits. She charged off through the rose garden and down the serpentine walk desperately hoping the gardens would work their magic on her as they always did. But instead of taking her

289

time, she walked quickly, needful of the exertion, barely mindful of her surroundings which were now less than lush, having succumbed to the will of winter.

Justine headed in the direction of the small hill at the eastern end of the property which overlooked Lady Caroline's folly. She effortlessly climbed the hill to a secluded spot with a grove of trees and overgrown shrubbery providing camouflage from passersby.

She hadn't seen Brandon for several hours. Usually she could hear him in the study or he'd let her know he was going out for a ride or heading out somewhere on the property, but there had been no sign or sound of him since she had left him in the dining room at breakfast.

Justine closed her eyes and leaned back against a tree. The thick knotty branches and dried leaves wavered over her in the brisk breeze. She exhaled and turned her gaze down to the folly Lord Jeremy had built for Lady Caroline.

The temple was meant to resemble an ancient ruin in the midst of the "wild" romantic landscape. Columns in the ancient style held aloft a pediment decorated with a vine of acanthus leaves. Vague sculpted figures pranced along the intentionally fragmented exterior stone wall, and a dark reflecting pool lay before it, adding to the atmosphere of mystery and intrigue. Thick vines of wisteria clambered over the gray washed stone giving the structure the air of a special, secret place that time had forgotten.

She and Andrew had regularly met at that folly to take their secret early morning walks. They would end their trysts sitting on the stone bench in its interior under the perfumed shade of that wisteria, exchanging letters and sometimes a kiss, her hand curling in his. Until William had caught them. But she couldn't think about that awful morning now.

Her breath jammed in her chest.

A figure hiked through the overgrown shrubs and greenery

down below. A small velvet hat set on loosely coifed blond hair, a fur-trimmed sapphire blue cloak fluttering in the wind.

Amanda.

Clutching her skirts, Amanda darted up the worn stone stairs of the temple and turned, a smile lighting her face. She reached out a gloved hand towards an approaching dark figure. Justine's grip tightened over the bark of the tree before her. Brandon joined Amanda on the steps, clasped her hand, and folded her in his embrace. Amanda clung to him, pressing against him, her eyes closed.

A knife ripped into Justine's middle and tore right through her.

"Here you are, what luck!" Charles's clear voice reverberated off her back. "Justine?" His hand slid up her arm. "What the devil are you—?"

She stumbled against him. His hand went to her lower back, and his front pressed against her side. He followed her gaze and muttered a curse under his breath. They both remained silent as they watched Brandon plant a kiss on Amanda's smiling lips.

Charles exhaled. "It's happening."

Justine's breathing grew shallow. A boulder squashed her soul and sank it to the bottom of the creek nearby.

"I'm sorry, Justine." Charles's face dipped down, his cheek brushing hers. "You shouldn't have to..."

Justine jerked out of his arms to face him. "What do you mean 'it's happening?'"

Charles's jaw tightened. "Let us be frank. It was only a matter of time with those two. Once he saw her again, after so long apart, it must have been difficult to keep away. You were a child then, but I was there. I know the way they used to be together."

Justine struggled for air as Charles's gloved hand travelled up her arm and squeezed. That squeeze signified a new reality that she wasn't ready for. A reality without Brandon.

It sickened her.

"It's not fair, Justine, but there it is. Dammit you shouldn't have to see this." His voice softened. "It doesn't mean he does not care for you, you know."

Justine's glassy eyes slid back to him, a sour tide rose in her belly. That knife continued shredding her veins, ripping as it went. "But Amanda is Amanda?" she asked.

"Yes," Charles muttered as he raised her hand to his lips and kissed it gently. "Of course, you don't deserve to be lied to, but it's the way of things."

His words burned right through her.

The way of things.

The way of things.

"It's destiny at work with those two."

"At least now you know," Charles said.

She blinked up at him. "Did you know? Did he tell you about this?"

"We spoke about Amanda once, he seemed curious. Graven doesn't say much about what's going on in his surely fascinating brain. Then again he doesn't have to. He's been very focused on your sister-in-law of late."

"Couldn't fight destiny," Justine muttered, the backs of her eyes stinging.

"No, obviously not." Charles's hand brushed up her arm. "Come away from here, Justine. You don't have to witness this."

Deep inside she always knew Brandon could never be hers, didn't she? But seeing it in plain sight in the glaring light of day, seeing him offer Amanda his touch, his mouth, his tenderness, tore the garden of feelings she had so well tended deep inside her. Her throat ached, a dull thudding filled her chest.

She would watch them together. Watch and learn her lesson.

She pushed Charles's hands away. "I want to see. I want to know."

"Justine!" Charles grabbed her arm tighter.

"No!" She twisted away pushing at him one final time, but she could no longer see them. They had receded into the depths of the small temple, the foliage and the shadows hiding them from full view.

"It breaks my heart seeing you like this." Charles's voice was husky at her side. His arms slowly slid around her shoulders, his lips brushed her forehead.

Justine's head swam. The pressure of his body on hers was foreign, wrong. "Stop it. Let me go." She pulled away from him. She couldn't think. She needed to think.

"Let me help you, dammit."

"Help me? How can you help me, Mr. Montclare?"

"Come, we are good friends, you and I." He pressed her hand. His expensive honey scent drifted over her, stifling her. "I can't stand to see you hurting like this. I am determined to do everything in my power to make it better."

"Make it better?"

"You have me, you know," Charles said. "You can lean on me."

Charles's dark blond hair had been swept by the wind, his angular jaw was set. He exuded calm and focus, but she was drowning, drowning in the deepest ocean, the swirling water circled now at her neck, heaving her wherever it wished. There was nowhere to run and hide anymore. She was no longer the little girl who could lose herself in the green fields, the woods, or the tower, or lock herself in her room and cry herself to sleep under the covers. She was a married woman who had to face facts and get on with it.

She glanced back at the folly. Still no sign of them, not even a swish of Amanda's skirts or the edges of Brandon's boots were visible. The two of them were probably seated on that damned stone bench, whispering intimacies, enjoying each other's touch, their gloves removed, their cloaks hastily set aside.

"Charles," her voice broke, and a tear slid down her cheek, her shoulders quaking.

"It's all right, love." His thumb wiped her tear away. "I'm here for you." His warm lips brushed the side of her face. Her eyes jammed closed, her fingers gripped the edges of his thick wool great coat. He held her tightly against his broad chest. Justine exhaled and opened her eyes again, releasing her hold on his coat. Charles put her hand through his arm and tugged her away from under the trees, away from the hill. "We should go. Let's walk on."

"Why? So they won't see us?" She wiped any trace of wetness from her hot face.

"No, because William is on his way here."

"Oh my God!" Justine's fingers tightened around Charles's arm.

"I was invited for shooting at Crestdown today. We were preparing, and then Amanda announced she was going out for a walk and disappeared. After she left ,William got a bug up his arse and wouldn't sit still. He said we should forget the shooting and go see the improvements at Wolfsgate as the weather was good. He waited for Andrew to bring their dogs. I told them I'd walk ahead and meet them here."

"He knows. We can't let William see them together," Justine said. "He will go mad."

"Don't I know it. Come." With Justine's arm firmly tucked in his, Charles turned them both in the direction of William and Andrew's route. Within minutes the men were visible, their two dappled black hounds trotting in between them.

"Put on your best happy face, love, and do it quickly."

Justine's brain rushed to form a plan of action. She would lead them back toward the house through the side park, avoiding the hill and the folly.

Charles lifted a hand in greeting to his friends. Justine let out a heavy breath and dropped her shoulders, pasting a smile on her lips.

"William, Mr. Blakelock." She bowed her head to the two men. "Good day."

Charles grinned. "There you are. I found Lady Justine here in the grove, we've had a lovely stroll waiting for the two of you."

"Lucky you," William said, his focus remaining on his dogs.

"How are you, Lady Graven?" asked Andrew.

"Very well, thank you. It's quite a delightful surprise to have such company for a change." Her fingers flexed on Charles's arm. Andrew's eyes darted towards the movement. "Shall we walk, gentlemen?" Justine infused her voice with a sprightly tone. She silently urged one leg to move in front of the other.

William threw a stick, and the two dogs shot off, eagerly racing to retrieve it for their master. He glanced at Justine. "Where's your husband?"

"He's about with Davidson," Justine replied. Charles squeezed her arm. Justine turned to Andrew. "Mr. Blakelock, how do you find our countryside after so long on the Continent? Were the countries you visited very different?"

Andrew offered her a bemused smile. "I must say I found Geneva rather exceptional. The Alps are truly extraordinary."

Justine soaked up every detail of his account of Swiss topography, every detail that took her further away from the cold harsh reality of Brandon and Amanda and what they may or may not be doing in the seclusion of that damned folly. Of William finding them together. She clung to the familiar earnest tone of Andrew's voice and allowed herself to enjoy the conversation she had initiated. Her breathing eventually returned to normal.

Within a quarter of an hour, Justine and Andrew were throwing sticks for the dogs and laughing at the animals' tumble down a short hill in their enthusiastic determination, whilst William and Charles scanned the property and the house from their high vantage point.

Andrew sprinted beside her. "Do you remember when Tiger brought us back one of father's pheasants incredibly mangled, mangled beyond recognition, instead of the damned stick?"

"Yes! He was just a puppy then." Justine laughed. "And we hid in the trees, didn't we? So your father wouldn't find us?"

"That was Annie's ridiculous idea." He laughed. "You and Annie in those skirts, and she nearly fell, yet she couldn't stop laughing. Completely absurd!"

One of the dogs jumped at her side. "And there he is! What a good boy you are, Tiger." Justine rubbed the now fully grown Tiger's head, stroking him under his jaw. The dog stretched his neck with a satisfied moan. Andrew threw the stick with a low grunt far to the left, and the two dogs bounded for it. He turned back to Justine and grinned, but his eyes widened at something behind her, his body stiffening.

Justine pivoted. Brandon and Amanda strode towards them, the dogs jumping around them. Brandon held the stick in his hand. He flung it down the hill, and the dogs leaped in the air and tore off after it, leaving their party in sudden silence.

William's arms were folded across his chest, his gaze glued to his wife and Brandon. Amanda's cheeks were rosy in the cold breeze; however, the radiance swiftly faded from her countenance only to be replaced by a sullen pout.

"There you are, sister," murmured Andrew.

"Brandon, you found Amanda. Isn't this turning into a wonderful day?" Justine barely recognised her own voice. Amanda nodded curtly at Justine, who bowed her head in return. "Brandon, I've invited everyone to ours for tea."

Andrew raised his chin at her, his lips twitching. She glanced at him and smiled.

"Anything stronger on the menu?" asked William.

"We have quite a selection," Justine replied.

William took in a deep breath through his nose. "Glad to hear it." Amanda joined her husband.

Justine wiped a stray lock of her hair from her face as Charles took her arm in his once again. She ignored Brandon's withering expression. "Come everyone, the dogs could use refreshment as well, I think." She and Charles led the way toward the house.

Andrew whistled to his dogs, and the animals bounded beside him, and without a word he left Brandon standing there on his own.

CHAPTER FORTY-FIVE

"WHAT THE HELL are you doing to me, Justine?"

A heavy, deep voice uncoiled over her. Her body flinched, the veil of sleep tearing away from her. The warm covers were flung from her body, and she winced at the cold air sweeping over her.

Her eyes blinked open. The harsh angles of Brandon's face loomed over hers in the half dark, the jagged grooves of his scars clearly visible on his skin. His one hand plunged into the mattress at her side, the other pinned her hip down to the bed. The heat of Brandon's anger prickled over her skin.

"What is it?" Justine took in a shallow breath. "What's wrong?"

"Did you enjoy your little tea party this afternoon?"

"Didn't you? I thought it was a success, especially as it hadn't been planned ahead of time. Forgive me, I was unable to ask you before I invited everyone, but I did not know where you were."

"You don't need my permission."

"I thought it went very well. Except, of course, for William glaring at you, and you glaring at Charles."

"Justine—"

"I happened upon everyone in the meadow down from the

hill. Just as you seemed to have chanced upon Amanda." Her eyes flashed up at him. "I could not be rude and turn guests from our door. What would Amanda think? We were just invited to hers for dinner. If we were to turn her and my stepbrother away for mere tea and cakes what kind of impression would that make? She is my sister-in-law after all. One does not turn away family, especially as Amanda has made such an effort. Shouldn't I play my part and make an effort as well?"

He exhaled. "Yes, but—"

"Thank goodness Taggart had baked lots of plum cakes early in the morning. What luck, eh?"

Brandon's fingers dug into her flesh. "What's come over you?"

"Must be domestic bliss."

His jaw hardened. "What the hell is going on with you and Montclare?"

"What do you mean?"

"Always laughing together, chatting. You seem to go to him all the time."

Her hand clutched the sheet at her chest. "I don't go to him."

"He goes to you then," Brandon said, his hand fisting in the bedlinen. "He's always at your side, and you don't seem to object. In fact, you seem to welcome his attentions as you did all afternoon."

"He's friendly." Justine swiped the hair from her eyes.

"Friendly?"

"What I mean is he is a friend. A very attentive one, perhaps."

"Are you being naive on purpose now? Because I know you aren't this foolish."

"Now there's a fine compliment!" Justine shot up against the pillow as far as his grip would allow. "That was a compliment, was it not?"

"The two of you keep company in my presence over and over again!"

"Would it be preferable if I met him in secret?"

"Don't toy with me, woman."

"I am toying with you? How dare you!"

His face was inches from hers now. "Was he your lover? Was it a big act all this time that he hadn't seen you in years? An act just for me?"

"Are you mad?"

"I'm trying to understand what is going on around me in my own house with my own wife no less!" The bitter tone of his voice stung.

Her hands let go of the covers, and she pulled herself up. "I could say the same!"

She hated arguing with him, hated this gulf between them. His handsomeness was twisted into a fierce scowl now, but she saw past the shadows across his face, past the menace in the harsh line of his jaw, and the glare of his scars. His eyes shimmered over her in the soft flickering light from the candle he'd placed on her night table. What she saw only caused an eruption in her chest.

Justine dug her fingers into his hair pulling his face close to hers. "Brandon, you are the wolf hiding in the woods howling. You are—"

He crushed his mouth to hers, and Justine surged forward embracing him, her tongue joining his, invading, devouring. This was the kiss she had longed for from him. A kiss that was reclaiming and retribution all in one.

Justine squeezed the firm muscles of his lower back and pressed her body into his. He shoved her down onto the bed with a grunt and ground into her. Her entire body contracted with need. She desired him, and she couldn't conceal it or suppress it any longer.

Brandon sat up on his knees, throwing his robe to the floor. His eyes seared hers as he flung up her nightdress, gripped her hips, and raising them, thrust his cock inside her. A raw moan escaped her lips as he filled her. She spasmed around him, taking him in. She had missed this potent intoxication they shared. She had missed him.

"Brandon—" Justine was engulfed in a rushing tide that wrenched any logic from her and unleashed that torrent of feeling that she had spent so much energy squashing for so long.

He gripped her hips tighter and ground himself deeper inside her, filling her with his anger, his frustration, his ferocity, bringing her to the brink. He dug into her flesh as he thrust inside her over and over again, his pelvis rolling into hers, quicker, more desperate each time. The breath squeezed from her lungs.

His raven hair hung loose about his shoulders, his eyes glittering over her. Her husband, the wolf lord, the slayer and devourer, threatened over her like a harbinger of her doom. Of her rebirth.

She wanted to free him and free herself. Her body was showing him, but she needed to tell him with her words as well. He needed to hear it.

"I want you, only you." The words rushed from her lips in the silence of the room cutting through his ragged breaths and her little gasps, and she bid them wrap around Brandon.

His eyes burned over her. She relaxed her body and took all of him. She took everything he gave her, every insistent stroke demanding from her the inevitable end. He remained above her, detached, like a cruel stranger watching her.

"You make me feel alive," Justine whispered, her throat stinging. He groaned and his movements became sharper, his hips circling and rolling into her. He knew she liked that, and he wanted her to have it. That tight knot of pleasure twisted through her. "Only you, Bran," Justine panted, her eyes stayed locked on his. He lowered himself onto his forearms. His chest rubbed over her sensitive breasts.

"Fill me." Justine's hands clung to the rippling muscles of his back as she raised her knees higher at his sides. This was what she wanted most in the world; their bodies fused together, his cock moving inside her, taking from her, giving to her. Nothing else mattered now but this.

Nothing.

A low moan escaped her chest. The intense wave of sensation rushed and receded through her body all at once as if she were at the whim of a harsh current in a churning sea.

Her eyes held his. "Don't let me go, Bran."

"Never," he breathed, his face dipped into her neck and his muscles tightened as he thrust. "Never." Her fingertips brushed over his soft lips. He bit down on her index finger sucking on the tip, and her body gave way and jolted under him, fierce pleasure shooting through her like flaming arrows torching everything in their path.

"Jus." His rough voice catapulted her deeper into that savage abyss they had created. His body was tense, his movements quicker.

Justine squeezed him tightly inside her, both her heels digging into his rear. "Let go, Brandon," she whispered, her lips brushing his ear. "For me."

His eyes slid closed, and his body convulsed inside her as he grunted loudly. He buried his head in her neck and lay on top of her, spent, immobile, one hand at her throat, the other pressing in at her side. Their heavy breaths filled the room and the aroma of their desire laced the air.

"You belong to me, Justine," he said against her delicate skin, his fingers brushing the side of her breast, kneading it.

Her heart plunged and thudded to a standstill as if under a lead weight. The hot, shimmering waves of pleasure skittered off her and were instantly replaced with cold shards of ice scraping at her skin. Justine's hands fisted in his hair, and she pulled his face up over hers with all the strength left in her spent body. His glassy eyes strained over her, his lips parted.

"But you don't belong to me," she said. "You don't."

Brandon's body stilled. "Jus—"

"You're hers," her voice broke. "You'll always be hers."

"You saw us today?"

"Yes. And at her house."

His eyes squeezed shut for a moment. "Justine, before you say or even think anything more, you must listen to me." Her lower lip trembled as cold shivers raced through her insides.

"I know how it looks," Brandon said. "But that is what I want."

CHAPTER FORTY-SIX

ACID STUNG the back of her throat. She spun her head away and arched her chest, pushing off from him. Her legs struggled to disentangle from his.

Brandon pushed his hips deeper into hers to still her desperate movements. "I mean, that's what I want it to *look* like."

Her movements stilled, but her hands remained pressed against his chest, her breathing labored. "What are you saying?"

"I am not pursuing Amanda like some lovesick puppy. I'm playing a game with her and William. I have no interest in her other than claiming my revenge on her husband. It's the most effective route with the most torment for my cousin."

The breath returned to her lungs. "You're trying to make William jealous?"

"Yes, and it's working."

"It certainly is. You've convinced us all. Congratulations."

"Frankly, I didn't really consider...forgive me. The last thing I wanted to do was upset you." His lips pressed together. "That's what I've done, isn't it?"

"You've convinced Charles and Andrew. I suppose that makes

your plan a screaming success. Today William took it quite seriously. He came to Wolfsgate to catch you out."

"Yes, he did."

"And that accomplishes what exactly?"

"Mess. A lasting stain between them. William detests mess. And now he feels the humiliation and the joy of deceit. He was behaving like a hungry dog with the scent of meat in the air this afternoon."

"And Amanda?"

"She is well and truly hooked." He raised himself on his elbows over her.

"Brandon, she's enamored with you. Maybe she's still in love with you. But if this is only a game to you—"

"She's not in love with me. She only wants a new conquest, a new toy. Perhaps that is her form of love, God knows."

"You're sure of that? She used to have feelings for you, didn't she? Don't you think it's dangerous and cruel to encourage them after all this time?"

"Don't you think what they've done to us over the years is dangerous and cruel?" Brandon raised his voice.

"You're playing with fire. I don't want William to retaliate. And Amanda is tenacious. How far do you intend to go in the name of your revenge? How far have you gone?" She couldn't resist asking in order to torture herself.

His jaw tightened. "Nothing. Simple kisses, a few embraces."

Despite her efforts to remain controlled and composed, her chest tightened and her eyes stung. She twisted her hips away from his body to release herself from his cock still pinning her to the bed, but he only buried himself deeper. She let out a slow grunt as he pressed against her centre.

"Touching her was surprisingly difficult."

"What a pity."

"Her feminine charms hold no allure for me the way they once did."

"Oh? Now you know better?"

"I do."

"I do not believe this course of revenge is worth the price for all of us, nor is it worthy of you." Her chin raised. "It's obvious she harbors expectations for you and her."

He scowled. "I don't give a toss what she expects. She'll never have me."

"Then leave it. Leave them alone."

"I'm not afraid of William."

"Maybe you should be."

His brow snapped together. "What does that mean?"

"You should be more careful how you tread with your cousin."

"What more can he do to us?" His thumb stroked her cheek.

"Let all of this go. If you truly mean it, if you don't want her."

"I don't want her, and let me say, I do not think I am Mrs. Treharne's first go at an affair. She has impressive skills."

Justine's stomach tightened. "I do not want to know."

"It is simply a game to her, and she plays it well."

"But it's not a game to William. I do not care about revenge. Do not set about destroying their family for a game. They have a child, Brandon. That boy is blameless. He needs his parents and a home. Do not be the one to tear it down."

He sighed and pulled out of her gently, rolling back onto the bed.

She turned on her side to face him. "She's still the pirate treasure you and William used to fight over, isn't she?"

As young boys, Brandon, William and Andrew often pretended to be menacing pirates on the high seas who would take Amanda, Annie, and Justine prisoner to their make-believe island fort—a flat moss-covered boulder at the creek they could all stand on at once. Brandon and William would end up fighting over whose prisoner Amanda was, and more than once Andrew,

Justine, and Annie would get bored and wander off to play somewhere else.

"No such treasure," Brandon murmured. "She's only a convenient means to an end. My pursuing her is only about what I can achieve with William."

"You've won her, and he's received your message. What will you do with your spoils of war, Captain?"

"Make her walk the plank." He chuckled as he took her in his arms. She rested her head on his chest as her fingers twirled through the crisp hairs on his skin.

"You're enjoying punishing her, aren't you?" Justine asked.

"Punishing her?"

"Isn't that part of this escapade for you? Punishing her for abandoning you and your brilliant future together?"

His hand stroked the flesh of her bare rear. "You realize that if father hadn't sent me to Jamaica, if Amanda had waited for me, if I hadn't been on that damned ship coming home, if I hadn't survived, if I hadn't been found, if they'd married you off to someone else—if, if, if—we wouldn't be in this bed together right now."

Her fingers traced a circle over his bare chest. "No, I don't expect so."

"Justine, you are something *other*, something so essential to me. I cannot do without you. I like what you and I have. Very much." His fingers seared into her hip. "I missed you, Jus. I truly missed you." He stroked the side of her face. "Now tell me about Charles."

"You men have an aversion to paying attention when women speak, do you not?" Her hand wrapped around his cock and stroked and pulled.

He grunted. "Christ, woman—"

"Are you paying attention now?" She stroked him harder, quicker.

"I am most definitely paying attention, Lady Graven." He

rolled her on her back. "Do you believe me?" He yanked up her chemise, his fingers sliding between her legs.

"I believe you, Bran. It's them I don't trust."

"Damn them." He thrust his cock deep inside her quim in one long stroke.

Justine bit her lip, her eyelids sinking as he dragged his cock out slowly and thrust back in. She moved against him, her hands pressing into his sleek back.

"You're my sweet Jus. I need you, love." Emotion washed over his face.

"Bran—"

"No more talking."

CHAPTER FORTY-SEVEN

"ARE you sure about the sixty-five pounds?"

Justine frowned at her husband from across the desk. "Must I repeat myself, Lord Graven?"

"Really, t'isn't worth an argument," Davidson said glancing up at Justine. "Let me see." He reviewed her figures as she rubbed at her stiff neck. They could have been finished ages ago.

"Sixty-five it is." Davidson winked at Justine, then glanced up at Brandon. "I really must be off now, milord. We'll meet tomorrow to discuss the new sheep, eh?"

Dear God, yes, discuss the damned sheep tomorrow. Justine leaned back in her chair.

"Tomorrow." Brandon lifted his chin at his manager as he continued writing in his ledger.

"My lady." Davidson nodded at Justine and showed himself out.

Justine tossed her quill on the desk. "Do you think I'm incapable of simple sums?"

Brandon glanced up at her leaning back in the old leather chair. "Must you take offense so easily? All I asked for was confirmation."

"Confirmation? Three times? How I managed without you for so very long I will never know. I remember a time that you and William did not do as well at sums as Annie and I."

"For God's sake, woman, we were children then." He scowled. "We wanted to chase toads and squirrels, not labor over sums."

Justine rolled her eyes.

"Do you require a prize now? Is that it?" A smirk twisted his lips.

Their governess would always turn their lessons into a contest between the boys and the girls. Justine and Annie would most often win in many subjects, and the governess would reward them with sweets.

"I'm afraid I'm all out of toffee." Brandon collected the papers that were splayed across the desk, putting them in two separate piles.

"I don't require toffee." Justine shuffled the bills into one even pile and slid them across the desk to Brandon. He filed all of them into a leather folder. His long fingers worked quickly to fasten it, and her gaze rested on the elegance and efficiency of their movements. The ledger and the heavy folder thudded into the desk drawer. Brandon slammed the drawer shut and locked it. He laid his hands firmly on the surface of the desk.

Her scalp prickled. *This damned desk.*

"What ever is the matter, Justine?"

Here in this study, William and Richard had hung over her in a severe yet gleeful manner, a unique talent they both possessed, convincing her, threatening her. Their solicitor had hovered in the doorway, his face red. Here at this desk, Richard had slapped her and William had put the quill in her hand and held it there. Here on this desk, she had signed the many marital and banking documents that had changed her life so indelibly.

The dire grimness and guilt that had haunted each one of those occasions beat through her afresh lacing her insides with ice. Such doom had pressed in on her then in this very room, in this very chair. She took in a breath and eased back in the chair, her hands sliding over the engraved arms, clutching the rounded ends.

And now?

Now in this same room, on the same desk, she was organizing a household budget with her husband, Lord Graven of Wolfsgate. Just another mundane activity for Lady Graven.

Yes, exceedingly normal, quite mundane.

She breathed out again and slowly reached out a hand and traced a line against the scalloped edge of the polished mahogany desk. Now it was Brandon's desk, as it should be. Her fingers grazed the thumb moulding over the smooth green leather writing surface and traced over the seam of gilt tooling.

His eyes narrowed over her. "Justine, are you unwell?"

Brandon's desk.

Brandon's Wolfsgate.

The tension drained from her limbs, and a small smile swept over her lips. "I'm very well."

"Are you quite sure?"

"Indeed, I am."

"You seem—"

"Shall we open one of those new bottles of Madeira that arrived this morning?"

"You want to try the Madeira?" His jaw tightened.

"Hmm. A good Madeira would be just right." She rose from her chair, fluid warmth flowing through her. "Yes, don't you think? Let's. I definitely need a glass of—"

"I need to be inside you." His eyes had darkened.

She stilled and met his gaze. "Doing sums arouses you?"

"Sums relax me. Arguing with you arouses me." His voice was low and thick. "Come here."

Justine went to him as if under the power of a mysterious force. He put an arm low around her waist drawing her close, and her hand slid over the bulging hardness between his legs. A husky breath escaping the back of his throat, and a blaze of heat flared between her legs. She touched her mouth to his, her other hand sinking into his hair as she slipped into his lap. He pulled her into a deep, hard kiss, and she was lost.

"Hmm, better than toffee..." he murmured.

She pulled at the fastening of his breeches. "I want to do it here."

Here in this room, on this desk where they had made her agree to their hateful plan.

A wicked smile tipped his lips.

Georgina's words from the ball rushed into her brain: *Give him something different.*

The heat of his hungry gaze made her entire body seize. She licked at her dry lips and slid from his lap to the floor. She released his rigid cock from his breeches, wrapped her hand around the base of his stiff length and fell to her knees before him.

CHAPTER FORTY-EIGHT

BRANDON BRUSHED his thumb over her lips, and her tongue swiped at it, then she took it in her fantastic little mouth, as she his cock up and down, her other hand at his balls.

"Bloody hell, Justine..." The blood roared in his veins.

Heaven help him. No, wait. He didn't want saving. He wanted to suffer this glorious torment. Her dusky eyes were innocent yet knowing, playful. Her mouth released his wet thumb, and she bent her head and licked at the tip of his cock, then dragged her tongue up and down the rigid shaft.

Oh yes, he was ready for death now, he was sure of it. *St. Peter are you waiting for me at the gates?* He would certainly die the happiest of men.

He let out a low groan and shifted his hips. At that, she took him in her mouth fully and sucked on him slowly while her other hand continued stroking him. His brain drained of all logic, all sense. His mouth hung open just taking in the sight of her at work over him. The wet suction of her hot, little mouth made his eyes roll back in his head. With a slight moan, she took him deeper.

He dug a hand into her hair cupping her head. "Jus...dear

God." He shuddered, his eyes locked on Justine on her knees in between his legs, her gorgeous shiny lips wrapped around his cock. He was utterly at her mercy; he was her slave.

Dammit, if he didn't stop her now, he was going to make a mess all over her and he didn't want to. What he desperately wanted was to pound into her wet quim and maybe tonight in their bed she could resume this...

This....

Look at her.

His mouth went dry. If that bloody parlour maid came in now to chat about dusting or Molly shuffled in with a tray of refreshments...Poor woman would surely have an apoplectic fit.

A small moan erupted from Justine's throat.

Holy mother of...

Detonations went off all over his tight flesh. Her hand squeezed around his base, and he grit his teeth. "Jus, stop. For the love of all that is holy, stop."

His wet and heavy cock slipped out of her glistening, swollen lips with a popping sound. Her skin was flushed, her eyes round. "You didn't like it?"

He groaned. "It was fantastic. You're fantastic. But I want to finish inside you, with you."

She let out a whimper and rose immediately, hitching herself up on the desk and wrenched her skirts out of the way.

Oh, there's my girl.

"Tell me what you want, Jus. I want to hear you say it."

A smile stole over her lips. "I want you to fill me with your cock right here on this desk."

Hell, he was a lucky bastard.

"Fill you I will." He rose.

His fingers dragged over her stockinged legs, hooking them around his hips. "Vixen." He planted his hands on either side of her and impaled her with his cock. Justine let out a sob.

His cock was so, so very happy, the happiest cock in all of England.

"Jus." He inhaled a gust of air trying to regain a slip of his sanity. "You're pure bloody velvet." She cried out with his every slamming stroke, her body jerking across the desk. "You mesmerize me over and over again," he murmured. She twisted her hips into his, and that small movement made the violence of his hunger for her even fiercer. His Mistress of Self-Control was certainly gone.

She panted hard, her eyes shining, her skin flushed, that slow smile curling her lips again. A tight lash whipped straight through his chest. His entire body throbbed with the sensations of Justine demanding, Justine unravelling around him.

Images from a thousand years ago burned through his brain. Her trembling little girl hand in his when she had been lost in the meadow for hours, and he had found her with a tear-stained face, sheep chasing her. Her anxious smile when he had lifted her up onto the saddle of his horse for the first time. And afterwards her tight embrace and nervous giggle when she thanked him for that first ride on Midnight.

Finding her hiding in the prospect room in the tower crouched in a corner hiccuping on tears after they'd brought Annie's lifeless body back to the house. They had sat there in the dust and cobwebs for a long while until she had fallen asleep in his arms, then he had carried her back to her bed.

The rose petals tangled in her mop of hair the day he had left for Jamaica. Her hushed goodbye in his ear as she hugged him quickly before darting back a few steps to stand next to Richard, her wet eyes averted, every inch the disciplined young lady.

That was his Justine. The sincere, sweet girl of his childhood. What was Annie's nickname for her? *Tina*. Now their Tina was the beautiful young woman who was his wife, his wife...His pulse roared in his ears.

At this moment, right now, here, Justine clinging to him,

writhing underneath him, giving herself over to her desire for him, he knew this was all he desired, this was where he wanted to be. He wanted to drink in what Justine offered him. Gulp it, drench himself in it. He surged over her burying himself deep.

"Tina!" ripped from his chest as he finally exploded within her. Her body stilled under him, her hands slid away, retreated.

Brandon let out a laugh and smoothed damp tendrils of hair from her eyes. He brushed her lips with his and withdrew himself gently from between her legs. He leaned against the desk breathing rapidly through the sensual storm that had pushed back the stinging in his veins. Justine pushed her skirts back down her legs and took in a gulp of air, her gaze pinned to the floor.

"Is something the matter?" he asked. She shook her head, her breath choppy. His hand cupped the side of her face. "Did I hurt you?" She shook her head again and peeled his hand from her. "Something's wrong. Tell me now, Justine." He took her hands in his and tugged at her until she sat up on the desk.

"Don't—"

His eyes searched hers. "Don't what?"

"That name, don't ever use that name for me, ever again."

Brandon frowned. His brain struggled to catch up with her. "Ah, your nickname?" After Annie died, use of the nickname had died too. "I'm sorry. We were just talking about Annie and I remembered it. Forgive me." His fingers tugged on a loose curl by her face. His lips brushed her cheek. "It was in a moment of supreme affection for you."

Justine's face remained taut, her posture rigid. She remained frozen in his arms, her gaze averted, the lines of her face drawn. "Justine, dammit, talk to me. I loved my cousin. I miss her too."

"Of course you do." She dropped her face into his chest and rubbed her forehead against him. "I'm sorry, it's childish. I just haven't heard it in so long."

"I know, love." His fingers massaged her neck. "Don't I know?"

He pulled her closer and planted a kiss on the top of her head. Her arms tightened around his middle. "But right now, this very moment feels pretty damned wonderful, don't you think?" She let out a heavy sigh but remained stiff in his arms. "Justine?" He cupped her face.

She released the tension in her shoulders, and her lips pushed up into a tight smile. She kissed his cheek and squeezed him extra tight for a moment then released her hold, the way she always used to as a child. His eyelids slid closed, and he buried his face in her fragrant hair. A rush of emotion and lavender passed through him and left him with a sensation of weightlessness.

"You were right," she whispered in his ear.

"About what?"

She bit her lip and glanced up at him. "That was much, much better than toffee."

CHAPTER FORTY-NINE

"THESE ROOMS HAVE A CERTAIN CHARM, but I can't say I've missed them," Georgina remarked.

The village assembly rooms were packed with a great many finely dressed people laughing loudly, drinking plenty, and most of all dancing. Two long lines of eager gentlemen and gleeful ladies whirled about in time with the buoyant music. A myriad of candles illuminated the long and not very wide space with as much light as possible on this winter evening.

Justine let out a dry laugh. "It may not be London. However, country charm has its own divinity."

"Divinity, indeed!" Georgina let out a laugh. "Are you referring to rustic farm hands, their eyes glistening with divine vitality from all that activity out in the fresh, invigorating air?"

"Ah, such vivid poetry," Justine said putting her hand on her friends' arm. "I think I should come for a visit to yours sooner rather than later. I can't say I've noticed any farm hands to be so full of the divine in our parts."

"You, my dear, have the divinity of Lord Graven at your side. What do you care for farm hands?"

Justine's cheeks heated. Georgina laughed and handed her a fresh glass of punch from a passing servant. "Drink, you lucky girl. So, tell me."

"Tell you what?"

"My suggestions to you at the dinner party? You did implement them, I hope? You promised a report, Justine. My own future depends on it."

Justine pulled Georgina by a pillar away from the giggling young girls that had gathered near them. She sipped on her drink. "I did offer him something different the other day."

"Oh? Yes?" Georgina's eyes sparkled.

"It had a very, very...hmm...positive effect."

"Positive?"

"He was rather taken aback and became most enthusiastic."

Her eyes flared. "Ah."

Justine leaned in closer to her friend. "In fact, I do believe the experience will stay locked in his memory for quite some time. He has been very attentive as of late. In all aspects."

"Brilliant. I'm so pleased!" Georgina clamped her hand over Justine's wrist. "Now will you trust my advice from here on?"

"You mean your sister's advice?"

"No darling. That bit was my idea."

Justine let out a laugh. "Well then, yes, I will be more open to your suggestions in future."

"Very good. Where is your husband?"

"Probably avoiding Amanda," Justine whispered.

"Ah, yes, another divine creature among us."

"Not so divine, really."

"Oh?"

"Tonight might prove to be a disappointment for Amanda, yet somehow I do not think she will easily accept defeat."

"That sounds like great amusement—Amanda rejected! Amanda shocked! We must find them."

"Wait," Justine said. "I don't want to be the hovering wife."

"J, you need to know what the devil is going on in order to protect your own interests. Always." Georgina leveled her gaze at her friend. "Never be naive and never let your guard down. These are rules to live by both in town and country. Come. Be quick."

Justine took a final sip of the sweet punch and left her glass on a nearby table. Georgina navigated them through the very crowded and very loud room, smiling and stopping to greet acquaintances. She was extremely talented at quick, friendly chatter, a wisely honed skill.

Justine's back grew more rigid every time they were stopped in the name of civility, but there was no sign of Brandon nor anyone of their circle.

"Thank God!" Charles's brittle voice cut through her mental fog. He immediately hooked his arm through hers and led her and Georgina to where there were tables and chairs. Many of their party were seated, drinking and laughing with others. Amanda, her eyebrows pinched together, a hand at her middle, her gaze averted, sat next to her husband. Georgina visibly bristled at the sight of Matthew whispering with the Marchmain sisters. Thomas leaned over a dark figure seated in a chair at the end of the table. A chill spiked through Justine.

"Damn me, don't know what's come over him," Thomas said casting a quick, uneasy glance at William. "He's not answering, it's as if he can't even hear me. 'Tis queer."

William's cold eyes flicked over Justine. "Not to worry, his wife is here to clean up his mess." He jutted his chin in Thomas' direction just as Thomas shuffled out of the way. Brandon was slumped in a chair, his legs stretched out before him, his eyes wide and glassy. He blinked long and slow, mumbling indecipherable words.

"Translate for us, Lady Justine, won't you?" William asked. Everyone tittered with laughter.

Brandon's hand reached across the table for a glass of liquor that was at his side. He lifted it off the table, but it slipped from his lax grasp and crashed to the floor. The glass shattered, splintering everywhere. The smell of liquor wafted up and mingled with the collective exclamations of the ladies in the group and the sudden hush of those around them.

Brandon's forehead wrinkled momentarily. He lapsed into languid laughter, his head rolling to the side. "Spectacular!" he said softly.

"Well, that says it all, doesn't it?" William slid an arm around Amanda's shoulders. The others snickered.

Justine extricated her arm from Charles's grip and darted to her husband. Her fingers touched his cheek. "Brandon," she whispered in his ear. "You're not feeling well, let's go home."

"Jus-tine?" Brandon smiled up at her, his facial muscles relaxed. His hands found her waist and travelled up her torso. She seized them, stopping them before they landed on her breasts. "Velvet," he murmured.

"We are leaving. Can you stand?"

"Go-o? No, stay, stay with me-e. Stay..."

"For God's sake, help her, Mr. Montclare," said Georgina. "Thomas!" Her eyes flashed at her brother.

Charles hitched an arm around Brandon. "Come, Graven." His face snapped up in Thomas' direction. "Get his other side." Thomas smashed his lips together and put an arm around Brandon's middle. They hoisted him up and held him until Brandon found a measure of balance on his own feet.

"Tragic isn't it, darling?" William's voice sliced through them. Even though he addressed his wife, his voice was loud enough to be heard by all present. "My cousin always had a fondness for indulgences, but this must be an exotic sort he picked up in the Indies. God only knows what barbaric debaucheries he indulged in with the natives in those two long years on that island, eh?"

Murmurs and whispers cascaded across the table. "Indeed," Amanda remarked, her hands clasped in her lap.

"Good thing he has his wife to clean up after him." William drained his glass of its contents.

"Enough." Justine's voice was sharp.

Amanda averted her gaze. William planted a lingering kiss on his wife's bare shoulder. She remained perfectly still.

"Love your scent, Jus." Brandon's soft voice floated in their candlelit bedroom.

"Rest now, Brandon. Close your eyes."

"Stay...stay with me."

"I won't leave you. Sleep now." His head was in her lap, and she stroked his hair as his breathing finally evened out, his chest rising and falling deeply. He hadn't closed his eyes at all in the past hour. He was in a trance, under a spell far from her reach. A shadow settled over her heart as her fingertips traced over his scars.

He'd been in good form the past months taking lots of exercise, actively involved in the house, the estate. He had enjoyed his strength returning, his independence. She hadn't seen any signs of a grave depression or the usual melancholies, no drowsiness or confusion. Not like before, at least. Just the occasional withdrawal here and there, but even those had been fleeting. Truly, no indication that he had been indulging again. Could she have been that blind and he so cunning?

Justine gently rolled his upper body from her lap onto the pillows and tucked the thick covers over him. She removed her dress, her jewelry, and half-heartedly splashed water on her face. She peeled back the covers and got into bed next to Brandon, wrapping an arm around his bare waist. Her forehead sank against his shoulder, but sleep would not come.

She wiped at the tears that spilled from her eyes. Outside strong winds heaved and heavy rain drummed against the window. She listened in the dark. She waited. She was sure he would come this evening. Especially now. She took in a deep breath, closed her eyes.

There.

The Graven wolf howled through the claps of thunder.

CHAPTER FIFTY

"No! It's no use, I tell you! Jump! Jump! Let go!"

The following night the nightmares had returned with a vengeance.

"Brandon, you're dreaming. Wake up. I'm here with you." Justine's honeyed voice seeped through his consciousness.

He was covered in a sheen of perspiration, his one fist pounded the mattress, twisting in the linens, his legs jerked and kicked. The fingers of his other hand gripped her throat. Gasping, Justine clasped his wrist.

His eyes unsealed, his stiff body slackened, and he let out a wheeze, his hand loosening around her. He tore his hand away as if he had been burnt by the contact with her skin. "Dear God. Did I hurt you?"

"No, no." Justine took him in her arms. His cold, damp flesh flinched under her touch for an instant then his arms tightened around her.

He buried his face in her chest. "I can feel the remnants of it inside me. I can feel it."

Her fingers ran through his hair then swept down his cheek to linger on his jaw. "How does it feel?"

His weary eyes slid closed. "Too good, all warmth and soft-ness. A lull so seductive, it promises everything." He exhaled heavily and glanced up at her. "I'm sorry, Justine. I'm sorry. I'm so sorry. Here I am helpless and broken again, with only myself to blame."

"Shh," she whispered.

He held onto her tightly, his breathing shallow. He savored the weight of her body pressed against his. "I've disappointed you, and I've most likely embarrassed you as well."

"No. No, you haven't. Do you remember anything from the other night at the assembly rooms?"

He took in a deep breath and pressed a hand over his brow. "I remember Amanda becoming angry with me when I'd kept my distance. William seemed pleased by her irritation, and he ignored her as well. I chatted with other ladies of our acquain-tance. I should have quit their dull company, but I lingered, intent on a final flourish." His hands shook slightly.

"It doesn't matter now."

"Yes, it does, dammit. I've disappointed you and that matters to me. I'd begun to like waking up in the morning looking forward to a day full of prospects, not thinking only of that one thing, craving only that, being its slave. I'm a disaster."

Her tense lips brushed the side of his face. "You're no such thing. Sit up. Drink some water." His weary glance settled on the cup on the side table. "Am I nagging again?" Her lips curved into a slight smile. "I am trying to reform, you know."

"Don't, I like you as you are." He pushed himself up, took the cup of water in both hands, and drank.

"We'll go for a walk outside later today if you have the energy. Davidson will be up soon. I've given the servants the day off, so we are alone."

Brandon handed her the cup and sank back onto the bed once more. "Don't go," he whispered. "Please." He closed his eyes, one long, sinewy arm hooked over his face. His other hand reached out and clasped Justine's keeping it close to his chest.

What had he done? *Fool.*

CHAPTER FIFTY-ONE

A BITTER TASTE flooded his mouth.

He stared at the small bottle in his hands. The bottle was empty. The bottle that he'd kept hidden in the hat box in his dressing room. The bottle he regarded as a solution, a victory, a relief, was now nothing more than a relic of hollow, dirty disappointment, an accolade of shame in this hot, sweaty tournament with himself. He thought he could keep this little survival stratagem a secret, didn't he? Just a drop here and there for that persistent ache in his leg and a little extra pleasantness besides. Had he taken it before the dance? He couldn't remember now.

Bloody hell, why couldn't he remember?

He marched back into their bedchamber and flung the bottle into the fire. He was weak and selfish and small in the face of that accursed tiny bottle; a burden to Justine, a millstone around her neck. He was dragging her down into his foul, polluted waters. She was clean and clear as the crystalline turquoise sea of the Caribbean that had struck him with such awe.

Maybe he should end this and put himself back on a boat to Jamaica.

But what the hell would that solve?

Nothing.

He got back into their bed and took her sleeping form in his arms inhaling the warm scent of her skin. Any fantasies of running off were the narcotic talking, seducing him into crawling into a hole to languish in some artificial web of serenity.

His father had put him on that boat in the first place in order to grow up, to learn the meaning of hard work, to understand the significance of a commitment to a goal and then to truly appreciate its rewards.

Being an investor in a sugar plantation and sugar export operation was a new business venture for Lord Jeremy. He had wanted Brandon to learn the business firsthand and be his representative there, not merely to sit back in his armchair at Wolfsgate and amuse himself with the dividends.

Brandon, of course, had considered it to be a vile, bitter form of exile. Only later had he understood. Wolfsgate had been in a shambles when his father had inherited. Brandon's grandfather, Malcolm had been an extravagant sort and a great card player and had almost driven it into the ground. Lord Jeremy, however, with his single-minded determination and his business acumen had resurrected Wolfsgate and all the Graven holdings. Brandon had then reigned over it as its young prince, much to William's great resentment.

When Lord Jeremy had floundered in the early years trying to make sense of the mess his father had left him, Richard had been doing well on his own, and so William had become quite proud of his station in life. Even if Wolfsgate and its title could never be his, at least he and his father had their own wealth and social standing. But when Lord Jeremy's wealth eventually eclipsed Richard's, the brothers grew even more estranged, and William's competitiveness with Brandon intensified.

As Brandon grew older, Lord Jeremy must have seen the signs in him that reminded him of his own father. It burned him deep in his gut when his own son began to exhibit a casual disregard for the riches and the properties they had. After Annie died, Brandon's interests had shifted towards superficial entertainments with his circle of friends with Amanda feeding his arrogant, juvenile sense of self-importance. Too many parties, too much drink, and those card games, so many card games.

Brandon was Jeremy's only child, the sole heir of Wolfsgate, and he refused to allow his son to piss it all away. Lord Jeremy had decreed that Brandon needed to prove himself worthy to be the Lord and heir of such an estate.

After much argument, Brandon had gotten on that ship to the Indies, landed in Jamaica many weeks later, and literally smelled poverty up close for the first time in his life. He noticed right away that the businessmen who brokered the operation on the island looked at him with derision and waited for him, the young, green nobleman, to make a fool of himself. He'd felt the shocking onus of disrespect for the first time in his life. Brandon's charm and personality were of no worth in Jamaica, and that had been jarring, a blow.

He was on his own. He had gritted his teeth and took on the challenge to prove them and himself wrong. Couldn't he be practical and responsible just like his father if he had to be? It was only then that instead of considering the responsibility of Wolfsgate as a nuisance, he began to see it as an opportunity, then a privilege, and later, an honour.

Brandon learned everything he could about the business and found he actually liked it. Soon enough he began to offer his own ideas, a few of which had been approved and implemented much to his satisfaction.

After two years in Jamaica, as had been Lord Jeremy's terms, Brandon shook hands with his partners and the overseers and boarded a ship to return to England. He was eager to see Wolfsgate and his father once again. He wanted to share his triumphs and failures with him man to man and to finally make amends for his past behavior. But that splendid dream had been shattered into bits on the rocky coast of Cornwall in a violent squall.

Brandon swallowed past the lump in his throat. That shipwreck had certainly swerved his life in a very unexpected and dark direction. It had deprived him of so much, yet it had brought him to Justine. She was his family now, and he would fight to preserve that family, to protect it, but he had to be strong and clear-headed to do that.

Yes, she was his family.

Not just his cousin's stepsister or his father's sort-of-ward. No. She was his wife. His other half in the typhoon that was his life. Not just a pretty accessory on his arm at social events or the prescribed female who would produce his heirs, she was his partner. He could converse with her, exchange ideas with her. And no matter what excrement he'd waded into, she had been there with an outstretched hand to support him, tug him towards dry ground. Like she'd just done with this rotten relapse of his.

She was his wife, his lover, and not just to provide relief in his bed. No, it was much more than that. Christ, so much more than simply a stroke of pleasure. His heart thudded in his chest. Being with her, in and out of bed, was nourishment, sustenance. He needed that and only from her. He couldn't imagine not wrapping himself around her in their bed in the stillness of the night, her soft breathing filling his ear, her warm skin against his.

All they had was each other. His muscles tightened at the thought. Justine had once remarked that they had been given a second chance at life. Those words seared through him now like a fiery sword. His second chance included the gift of Justine. He would do everything in his power never to disappoint her.

No, never again.

$\sim$

LATE IN THE afternoon of the next day the nausea had passed and the sweating and itchiness had begun to subside, but Brandon's restlessness and anxiety were still intense after only a short, uneasy sleep the night before.

"I'm no physician, but I truly believe fresh country air can cure most ills," said Justine. "Come, let's have our tea then go for a walk." He agreed.

The skies were thick today with that dull, white grey that signaled snowfall was imminent. Their boots crunched over the frozen twigs and rocky soil on the cold, hard ground. Brandon squeezed her arm. "You truly enjoy the country very much."

"I do." Justine put a gloved hand on his arm. "When mother and I first came to Wolfsgate, it seemed like a fantasy come true, a veritable wonderland."

Brandon let out a small laugh. "Did you expect fairies to be flying about?"

"Upon first hearing the name 'Wolfsgate,' I expected ghosts and savage beasts amidst castle ruins. I was sure it would be the most macabre, sinister place in all of England."

"I think the place is full of ghosts and savage beasts," he murmured.

"Maybe it is full of ghosts, but not savage beasts. Not anymore."

"I believe Wolfsgate has better prospects with you as its mistress, Lady Graven."

"I must confess I can scarcely believe I am its mistress. I still remember the thrill of first seeing the gardens blooming in those rich purples and blues, the lush green of the meadow, the endless hills, the creek, the extraordinary folly, the mysterious woods at the edge of the property. All of it filled my starved imagination.

"Before Mother and Richard married, we had been living in a small house in London. It was dark and narrow, and I was confined to the nursery. That's all I remember of it. Richard and William's house in town was grander and quite formal. Whereas

Wolfsgate was all wide open spaces filled with light and colour and endless promise."

The glow from her eyes radiated warmth through him. "Promise?"

"There was so much to discover. Annie always knew where to spend a few precious hours to run, play, to hide. We could imagine and do whatever we wished. Simple breathing the air here was pleasure enough for me. It must sound ridiculous to you, but there it is."

Something in his chest caught at the sight of her eyes sparkling with excitement and her cheeks flushing that shade of deep rose. "It's not ridiculous at all. I'm glad you feel that way about Wolfsgate."

He decided he wanted to give that back to her, more than anything in the world. To make Wolfsgate a pleasure, a sanctuary for her once again, and not the prison it had once been for her. Brandon's ribs squeezed tight. He would make their home her land of enchantment once again. He removed the glove from her hand and kissed her fingers. She blinked up at him.

"Wolfsgate has been your refuge," he said. "I envy that, for I resented it for quite some time. Mother died here and later Annie, and it became infected with sorrow for me. Father chose to deal with his pain with work. Always working, always so busy. As I got older I only itched to escape it and all the responsibilities it required of me." His voice trailed off, and he shook his head.

"Brandon—"

"I assumed that everything would always be waiting at my pleasure. When I left Jamaica to come home, I thought I would find the estate, the house, Amanda, even Father in the same condition I had left them. Imagine." He scoffed. "What an idiot I was. No plans, just whims. Father, of course, had offered me a plan, and part of me hated him for it."

"You followed his plan. And you did well."

He took in a gulp of air. "I must have been a thorn in his heart. I regret that exceedingly."

"He was proud of you. He loved you, Brandon," she said. It was so simple for her, these emotions, her belief in them.

Justine let out a laugh and reached her hand out. She looked up at the sky. "It's snowing!" Thick flakes floated in the cold air and bunched on their eyelashes.

"We're close to the stables," Brandon said.

"Are you tired?"

"Come, Justine." He tugged on her arm.

The snow fell thicker coating their cloaks and hair in white sparkles. Brandon pushed open the heavy wooden door.

"What's this?"

A grey mare and a dark chocolate stallion stared at them. Persephone and Knight stamped their feet in their stalls.

"New horses for my lady," Brandon said. "Now that you ride so well I thought you might like—"

Justine lunged at him. She wrapped her arms around his neck and squeezed him tightly. He pressed her into his chest, and his eyes closed as he took in her rose scent and her little breaths. Her wild heartbeat drummed straight through his own.

She planted a kiss on his mouth.

"You're welcome, love."

"Why didn't you tell me?" She wiped at her eyes.

A faint smile curved his lips. "I wanted to surprise you. I even swore Martin to secrecy."

Justine approached the new horses. "Aren't you beautiful?" she murmured, stroking the mare.

"Come, Justine." He led her to a corner of the stables where bales of hay were stacked. "We can admire our new beasts from here." He pushed a few bales to the side, removed his coat and shook it out then laid it down over the hay dry side up. Justine took off her cloak and shook it out as well.

Taking her hand, he pulled her down to the hay, holding her

close, and they settled on their backs, her cloak over them, listening to the extreme quiet of the snowfall and the horses whinnying softly and stamping in their stalls.

"A country symphony." Justine laughed turning into his chest.

"Now there's enchantment for you."

She smoothed a hand over his chest. "Brandon, tell me about Jamaica. I can't even begin to imagine it."

"Colour, that's what I remember. colour shimmering in the heat of the constant sun. The tall, lazy palm trees, the unusually shaped mountains thick with green, the bright, colourful clothes the natives wore. Of course, the deep dark colour of their skin and their blinding smiles were something to behold. They are a joyful people, and it was quite a switch to get accustomed to, I can tell you. I liked it. Singing and laughter could be heard all hours of the day and night."

"Wonderful."

"It is, yet it struck me as so very odd in the beginning. Damn me, that heat was overwhelming, sticky, oppressive. But then there are the winds coming in from the sea that fill the house with their hazy energy. Bathing in those clear waters was physic enough. And so much fruit, fruit of all sizes and colours. Fruit with every meal, in almost every dish. Never tasted anything like it before." He chuckled. "Spicy and sweet together."

"That I would like to try."

His gaze heated over her. "I think we already have, don't you?" She made a small noise in the back of her throat, and he shifted her in his arms.

"Tell me something now," he said, his blood quickened with the memory.

"Yes?"

"The other day when we were together in the study, I got the distinct impression you needed to exorcise some sort of ghosts on that desk. Am I correct?"

Justine bit her lip as her hand smoothed down his shirt. Brandon squeezed her arm. "Justine?"

"William worked in there, at that desk, and I grew to hate being summoned there to be informed of some new turn of events regarding my future. I never knew what was coming next nor how it would affect me, and I had to accept it no matter what it was. It is where Richard and William told me I was to marry Sir Wallace, and also where they informed me of my having to marry you."

"So it was an exorcism then?" His lips brushed the side of her hair. She nodded and settled into his chest. A low chuckle escaped his throat. "Did we expel the ghosts?"

"Yes," she whispered.

"Any other rooms in the house need exorcising?"

She pinched his waist. "Are you mocking me?"

"Ow! Absolutely not. As your husband it is my responsibility to relieve you of any burdens, is it not?"

She raised herself on her forearms and met his amused gaze. He brushed her generous lower lip with his thumb. "Tell me."

"The wine cellar."

His eyes narrowed. "The wine cellar? Why?"

"I'll tell you. After you relieve me of that burden."

"Whatever my lady requires." His one hand wrapped around her neck, and he pulled her to him and took her mouth in a languorous kiss. "I am most happy to comply." His lips dragged across her jaw. "To submit." He kissed her throat. "To yield." His greedy hands found the curve of her breasts and tugged away the fabric at her bosom. "To satisfy her every desire."

"What a thoughtful husband you are, Lord Graven."

"Is there anywhere else where you require my assistance, madam?" His thumbs rubbed her nipples.

"The folly." She arched her back.

"Absolutely." He bent his head and took a nipple in his mouth and sucked on the tip. She let out a whimper.

"And you, Brandon?" She combed her fingers through his hair keeping him close. "Do you have any requests? We've covered the kitchen, your parents' chamber, my chamber, the parlour."

His lips brushed hers. "The great oak tree."

"Hmm."

"I do have another."

"Where?" she asked, her breathing now irregular.

"My old bed," he said. His tongue lashed across her other nipple. "Yes, definitely. That bed."

Her eyebrows snapped up, and she pulled back from him slightly. "Have you entertained on that bed?"

"I tortured myself with fantasies on that bed. Utterly ridiculous fantasies." He sucked on her breast, kneading the other as she held her breath.

She dug her fingers in his hair. "Why were they ridiculous?"

"Because my reality today is so much better than I could have ever imagined back then as a smug, young fool." Her mouth found his and they kissed hungrily. "Jus, I want to give you so much," he murmured against her lips. "But I'm not sure it's enough."

Her forehead creased. "Brandon you give to me all the time."

"No, I don't."

"Yes, you do. Every time you smile at me or take my hand. Every time you laugh in appreciation of my wit." Her hand stroked over his at her breast. "Every time you touch me, you give to me."

His eyes flashed. "Yes, but you should have— "

"Clothes? Jewels? A roof over my head? New horses?" You've provided me with all that, not to mention a title, Lord Graven. I like this, Brandon. This, right now."

"I want to give you more." His tongue trailed behind her ear.

A shiver stole through her, and her hand slid down his

breeches until it found his hardness. "Lord Graven, I thought you were controlling your urges."

"My urges for you are particularly strong these days—the one happy aftereffect of the opiate. It ceaselessly demands satisfaction." He glanced up at her. "Is Martin working today? He's always hanging about."

She shook her head. "He had to help his aunt with a repair at their cottage."

"Good. I have to taste you right now," he breathed against her lips. "Then I'm going to take you." The dry straw crunched underneath their bodies. "And I won't be gentle."

Her eyebrows lifted at his words, and his hands disappeared under her skirts exploring her every curve, and she melted helplessly. "Turn over, Jus," his voice was thick, his hand pressed at her waist. She did as he asked.

Brandon raised himself up, lifted her skirts, his breath spiking at the beautiful sight of her bare rear. He slowly caressed her soft flesh until she squirmed with need, then his fingers slid in between her cheeks and she whimpered. "You're magnificent," he murmured. Her fists tightened in his cloak as his fingers glided through the wetness between her legs. Once slick with her juices they glided back up to tease her tight bud.

She cried out at the sweet invasion. "You like it there, don't you?"

"So do you, my love."

He explored her secret flesh with his fingers and his mouth until she pleaded with him in muffled words and moans. He bit a cheek, and she groaned raising her arse higher for him, her thighs trembling. He forgot everything else. There was nothing but this, this giving to Justine and her yielding to whatever he gave her. He finally released his throbbing cock and thrust inside her sleekness, ending their torture, ripping his breath away.

"Jus..." He let out a hiss of air.

Her harsh panting breaths filled the stable with every quick, hard thrust he gave her.

"Christ, Justine..."

A sharp need to see her face and watch her finish overtook him. He pulled out of her, turned her around and pressed her flat to the ground. Raising her legs high against his chest, he thrust back inside her, both of them groaning. He held her hips steady and plunged into her hard and fast. She cried out, her release seizing her, her fingers biting into his arms, and he followed.

Justine wrapped herself around him, brushing his face with her lips. The dull smell of hay and the pungent odor of horse settled over them. Her fingers absently tangled in his hair. The softness in her full eyes filled him with a ripple of warmth.

He folded her in his embrace and kissed her, and she clung to him. Something shifted inside his chest just then, and he stilled and closed his eyes in an effort to contain it.

Yes, he had to keep it safe.

CHAPTER FIFTY-TWO

CHARLES DISMOUNTED FROM HIS HORSE. "I must speak with you, Lady Graven." He marched toward her, his boots crunching in the fresh snow outside the stables. The snow had stopped and had left behind a startling, pristine white landscape; a thick field of powdered diamonds glinting in the afternoon sun.

"Whatever for?"

"How is Graven? Is he doing any better?"

"He's sleeping now." She smoothed her mussed hair behind her ears.

After having fallen asleep in Brandon's embrace in the stables, she had woken up to the rumble of horses' hooves approaching. She'd carefully untangled herself from his arms, smoothed out the hay from her skirts, adjusted her stays, and threw on her cloak, slipping through the opening of the stable door as quietly as possible.

He pressed his lips together. "I wouldn't have come if it weren't important."

Justine led him away from the stables. "Go on."

"I came to warn Brandon."

"Warn him?"

"I saw William today. He insinuated to me that he had put quite a bit of laudanum in Brandon's drink the other night at the assembly rooms."

Her heart tripped.

"He was quite proud of himself."

She winced. Of course, William. Why didn't she see it? Instead she'd believed that Brandon had indulged in his addiction once more. It was a perfect plan. Perfectly William.

Her eyes leveled at Charles. "My stepbrother confides in you, does he?"

Charles tilted his head at her. "Did you hear what I said?"

"Yes. I heard you."

Charles frowned and glanced back at the stables. "Amanda distanced herself from him immediately."

"William was counting on that reaction," Justine said. "He's punishing the two of them for their flirtation. She was mortified by the sight of Brandon in the throes of euphoria, wasn't she? How William knows his wife."

"Yes, she spent the rest of the evening squirming yet glued to her husband's side."

"Then he accomplished two goals," Justine said. "That and Brandon's public humiliation."

"And yours."

"I don't give a damn about anything except Brandon's well-being."

Charles sighed heavily. "Please be careful and stay away from them both."

"I always try to stay away from my stepbrother, Mr. Montclare." Her eyes narrowed. "And I believe I will be staying away from you as well."

He pulled his head back, his mouth tightening. "I'm sorry you feel that way."

"I think you should leave."

"I wanted you to know that I think William's overstepped.

Something's different in his attitude towards Brandon. It's harsher than the usual sibling rivalry there always was between them. I can't explain it, I just know. At least William's reined in his wife for the time being."

"What does that mean?" Justine asked.

"You know Amanda."

"I cannot say I do. I knew her as a girl, but we have not been in each other's company for quite some time."

"Amanda is perpetually dissatisfied no matter what she's been provided with. William indulges her for a time, and she settles with him after her current distractions fade." Charles bit his lip. "Those two have a peculiar bond. Her moods tend to vary between excitement, displeasure and irritated boredom and only he knows how to navigate them. More power to him."

"You seem to know Mrs. Treharne very well."

A muscle pulsed in Charles's jaw. "I should go. Do be careful. If you need anything—"

"I do not need anything from you, sir."

"Justine, please." He reached out and took hold of her hand. She pulled away.

"What the hell is this?" a menacing voice boomed. Brandon, his features tight and dark, stood just beyond her and Charles. "What the hell are you doing here?"

"I came—"

"You came to see my wife. Again. Obviously her being my wife is no deterrent to your passions. So desperate to get between her legs, are you?"

Charles's body visibly tightened. "Graven—"

Brandon's cold gaze was as hard as iron. He had not slept enough, and Justine knew the prickling torment was now scalding his insides.

Brandon snapped his head at Justine. "Did you think you could play me for a fool? Was this all a big game for you and William? He knew he'd be in trouble if he married you off to anyone else. So why not to me? Half-dead, broken Brandon. Wouldn't matter to him, would it?"

"Brandon—"

"What the hell are you on about, Graven?" Charles asked. "Insulting bastard! You're mad, you know that?"

"It's Charles, isn't it?" Brandon's eyes bored down on Justine. "Yes, your friend, indeed."

She flushed. "Brandon, please! Stop."

"Graven, listen to me." Charles wedged himself between Brandon and Justine. He touched Brandon's arm, but Brandon shoved it away. "I came about William. You've got to stay away from Amanda. Did you really think he was going to sit by and allow you to amuse yourself with his wife for old time's sake?"

"I did it for his benefit, you idiot," Brandon said. "I'm not interested in any affair with that woman."

"Are you quite sure?" Charles asked. "Because it certainly hasn't seemed that way to the rest of us. Especially to your wife."

"Stop this!" Justine raised her voice.

"And you've made it your priority to know my wife's mind have you?" Brandon shot back.

"I have witnessed her experiencing the Brandon and Amanda spectacle. Painful, my friend," said Charles. "And yet she continues to put on a brave face and stand by you. Why, I do not know."

"Gentlemen, please!" Both men ignored her.

"I find it fascinating, Montclare, how you happened to be at my wife's side at every turn of said spectacle. And I find it even more fascinating as you were the one who had encouraged me to pursue Amanda. All those amused looks you've been giving me over these past weeks—there I thought it was your smug understanding and approval of my flirtation. When in truth, it was your derision. You were mocking me whilst enjoying your ploy. Always the master player." Brandon's eyes slid to Justine. "What do you think of your *friend* now, Justine?"

Justine's head jerked towards Charles, and his jaw tightened at her cold glance.

"Nothing to say for yourself now, Montclare?" Brandon's one eyebrow lifted. "You've had a hand in all this so that you could get under my wife's skirts, haven't you? Just for a laugh, eh?"

"Dear God," Justine said, her shoulders slumping.

"I did not come here today with the intention of pressing my affections upon your wife. I came for your benefit," Charles said, his voice hard. "William is not finished with you, Graven. I am sure of it. He is incensed. I have come to know the signs. I felt badly for you the other night. It was appalling of him to use your weakness against you. That's why I came here today, not to amuse myself with your wife, but to warn both of you." Charles's hands smoothed down his great coat, his face tight. "I realize you are not well. I shall go."

Charles took a step towards Justine. "Have a care, dear girl. I beg your forgiveness for abusing your friendship. I regret it deeply." He bowed to her and without another glance mounted his horse and rode away at a gallop. Justine held her breath, her eyes remaining on Charles and his horse until the woods seemed to swallow them up.

"The bastard," Brandon said on a growl. "I am distracted with Amanda, and he insinuates himself into your heart, and you begin relying on him. First Andrew, now Charles." Brandon shook his head at her. "Not such an innocent girl, are you? You've been lying to me about who you are all along." His voice had lowered ominously.

Her heart thudded in her chest. "I have not lied to you. And Charles is not in my heart nor in my bed. There is only you."

He closed the distance between them. "Then explain what I know to be true, because I felt it inside you, or rather—" he smirked "— I did *not* feel it." His words blistered on her skin like hot coals. "Have I upset you, my lady?" he breathed, his tone bitter. His hands gripped her upper arms, his eyes simmered. "You've been lying to me."

"I've never lied to you, Brandon."

"Bollocks!" His one hand slid around her neck yanking her close, his mouth inches from her own. "Am I not enough for you? You need your first love or a fresh model with no scars, no limp, no compulsive fixations to better satisfy you?"

Her fingers dug into his sides. "You are the only man—"

"Oh, Justine." His nose glided along her jaw and icy shivers crawled across her back. "The game is up." His voice was so cold, brutal. A sneer.

"There is no game." Tears filled her throat, her fingers curled into his shirt. "No man has touched me the way you have. Ever."

"'The *way* I have?' My clever girl." He took in a shaky breath and hissed out air as he shoved her away. "I do not know what to believe anymore. The one thing I do know is that I cannot bear you lying to me, Justine. Not you. It's killing me." A moan heaved from his chest.

"Brandon, please listen—"

"I want to believe in you. I do." He pressed his palms to his eyes. "Because you're all I see." His hands fell from his face revealing heavy, red eyes. "I feel things for you, things I've never felt before." His voice broke. "It scares me, it hurts."

"Brandon—"

He raised his chin at her. "Ultimately, I am to blame. I gave Charles a free path to you by being so focused on my vain, pathetic scheme with Amanda." A derisive smile curled his lips, and he took several steps back. "But still you will not confess to me. Why? Protecting your lover? You are so very cruel. That, dear girl, pains me more than the knowledge that you have lain with another." He charged away from her moving through the snow.

Justine couldn't move, couldn't breathe, couldn't think. Everything had changed in the flick of an hour's time; the snow obliterating the landscape into shapeless, colourless mounds, and the many bitter truths disconnecting them, destroying the tenderness between them.

She trudged through the dense snow as quickly as she could following Brandon's path to the house. He had slowed down at the front staircase, his limp now pronounced, the discomfort etched on his shoulders.

She froze.

William stood in the open doorway. "Have I come at a bad time?"

CHAPTER FIFTY-THREE

"WHAT THE HELL are you doing here, William?" Brandon stopped abruptly. Justine rushed up the stairs behind him, her fingers digging into her husband's arm.

William smiled and proceeded them into the house. "I had to check on you, cousin. That was quite a turn you had the other night, quite a sight to see. And everyone did see it, didn't they?" He tossed his hat on the bench in the hall. "You're sullying our family's good reputation with all this peculiar behavior. Look at you." He gestured with an elegant hand at Brandon. "There's something positively tattered about you." William's eyes glinted, his teeth dragging along his lower lip. "You are the talk of the village."

"I don't give a toss," Brandon said.

"Maybe you don't, but I do. We share the same last name, and I have a wife and son to think of and business investments to consider. A family, a future. Do you think I'm going to stand by and allow you to destroy what I've built because you cannot control your pathetic impulses?"

"You put the laudanum in his drink, didn't you?" Justine said.

Brandon's eyes widened. "Is that true?"

William grinned at Justine. "What an intelligent slut you are."

"Don't you dare speak to my wife that way!"

"I'll speak to her any way I like. You, however, will stay away from *my* wife."

A brittle smile slowly spread across Brandon's face. "You didn't like that did you? She wants it badly from me."

Justine's breath snagged in her throat. "Brandon—"

"Rest assured, cousin. I do not want your wife. Making her prance for me and watching you squirm was all the entertainment I required. She is not half the woman my wife is."

"Indeed?" William narrowed his eyes at Brandon and lowered his chin making the hard line of his jaw more distinct. "Your wife gave me quite a headache once upon a time." William's lips twitched. "You know about Andrew, but did she tell you the truth of it? Hmm?"

"I don't want to hear anything you have to say."

"I caught them on a lover's walk, don't you know? Exchanging love letters, kisses, passionate murmurings at the folly. Seems they had a regular *rendezvous* there for quite some time."

Brandon gritted his teeth.

"I put a stop to it, like a good brother should." William sniffed. "Poor sod, she tried to get Andrew to marry her out from under my nose because she didn't want me choosing for her."

"You wanted to use her for Wallace," said Brandon. "A fine choice."

"It would have been a respectable one and a good investment in our future. But she outmaneuvered me in quite a stellar way. Didn't you, Justine?" His gaze settled on her, his lips rolling. "She didn't leave me many options. But luckily I managed to save our family's reputation by marrying her to you."

"I don't know what you're implying, but I—"

His head tilted at Brandon, a dry laugh escaped his throat. "You don't know?"

Brandon's eyebrows snapped together and he lunged at William, shoving him against the wall, his lips twisted in a snarl.

"Stop it! Stop it!" Justine cried out.

"You and your wife belong together." William laughed. A bitter, cold laugh. "I should add matchmaker to my list of talents."

"Stay away from Justine! You and Montclare, stay away from my wife and from me. Or I swear to God—"

"Ah, defending her with such violence, how touching. I'm finding this most entertaining. I'm quite pleased that now people know what the real Lord Graven of Wolfsgate is like," William said. "No longer is he the prize of the county. From trying to seduce his own cousin's wife, to his peculiar, unseemly behavior at a simple village dance. And now attacking his cousin who only wished to defend his wife's honour and his family name. You have no shame."

"Get out, damn you!"

William adjusted his clothes and smoothed back his hair, his fingers gripping the ends of his waistcoat momentarily. "As we are family, a duel would be unfortunate, ridiculous. Anyhow it's a tedious business nowadays, rather *démodé* for my taste."

Brandon seethed. "Leave, damn you. You are no longer welcome at Wolfsgate."

William shifted his weight and raised his chin. "There is a price for that particular favour."

Brandon raked his hands through his hair. "What are you on about?"

"One good turn deserves another," William said. "Ten thousand pounds in my account by your Christmas party next week. Or I publicly blame my bruises on you and your ongoing squalid habits, and," he pointed a finger at Justine, "I'll make something else public knowledge while I'm at it to sweeten the pot."

"What are you...?" Brandon sucked in air. "You poison me, humiliate me in public, then you come to my house and threaten me?"

"Yes. If you don't give me that money, I shall make it known that Justine had a lover before she was a properly married woman."

The air in the room changed direction and stalled into a split second of deafening, suffocating silence in that cold hall.

William glanced at his stepsister, that familiar sneer on his lips. "Ah, you didn't tell your husband about *him*, did you?"

"William, please," Justine breathed.

"Tell me what?" Brandon asked his pale eyes trained on William, his body still.

"About her *other* romantic plaything." William licked at his lower lip. "Here all alone at Wolfsgate, it seems the poor girl was quite bored after Andrew left. She needed another playmate, another distraction, since I no longer allowed her to go to any parties after I caught her with Andrew. Once I had arranged things with Wallace, though, the slag found a way to spoil those plans. She bed the stable boy. Martin—that's his name, isn't it?"

Brandon's limbs locked. The air burned in his lungs.

William's iron gaze pierced Justine for a moment then slid back to Brandon. "Well, I couldn't very well marry her to Wallace after that, could I? He had been so looking forward to plucking her blossom. He most certainly would have made it known and would have demanded a refund for used goods. Imagine his disappointment, his wrath upon their wedding night. No, I simply could not take that chance."

"William..." Justine's voice was barely above a whisper.

William's eyes glimmered at his stepsister. "I see she made sure Martin is here with her again, under your roof, under your nose, in your stable. She certainly spent a lot of time with him in that stable, didn't you, Justine?" His gaze returned to a stone-faced Brandon. "Riding lessons," he said, drawing out the words, relishing them. "She had so much opportunity for practice. She must be very good at riding, eh cousin?"

"Get out of my house and off my property." Brandon's words flared with fire.

"William...William..." Justine breathed, her eyes brimming with water.

"Shh." William flicked his fingers at her and shook his head. She dropped her hands to her sides, straightened her shoulders, her breathing labored. The two of them stood, inches apart, their eyes locked in a dark, warped, ages old battle of both victory and defeat.

"Out of my house now!" Brandon shouted. Justine's fingers curled into her skirts.

William raised his chin at his cousin. "You have until the party. Ten thousand pounds." He snapped up his hat, flung open the door, and strode out.

Justine stared after her stepbrother, her eyes opaque, drained. She reminded Brandon of a cornered and wounded animal with nothing left to lose. He took a step toward her.

She shot out the open door.

CHAPTER FIFTY-FOUR

BRANDON FELL BACK against the wall, struggling to regain control of his breathing.

Justine and Martin?

Impossible. No.

And yet...

It made a horrible kind of sense. No wonder she wouldn't confess it. But to make him hire the boy? To keep him on? His stomach churned. How could she? How could he have misjudged her so? He pulled his hands through his hair. Gusts of icy wind rushed over him. The door was open. She had run away. Run away rather than face him.

He had to hear it from her.

He took off after her, easily following her tracks in the snow, leading him through the woods on the western edge of Wolfsgate.

She was doubled over heaving, a mass of retch over the white snow before her. He approached her, reaching out a hand, touching her back.

"No!" She jumped from the contact. "Don't." She pulled away, a wild look twisting in her eyes.

"Justine..."

"You must hate me now," she whispered.

"No, I don't hate you."

"I disgust you."

"No! I only want to understand. I am trying to understand. You must have been very lonely, very desperate to..." He couldn't say it.

"It doesn't matter." She wiped at her mouth.

"Yes, it does. You matter to me."

A pained, cold expression passed over her face. "You'll feel differently when this settles in your head." Her voice was low, controlled.

"I already do feel differently, Justine. I do."

A sob escaped her throat, her palms flew to her temple. "I'm sorry, I'm so sorry."

"You were lonely, Martin was a friend, a companion," he said through gritted teeth.

"Dear God, I beg of you, Brandon. Stop."

"He cannot work here any longer. I cannot have that. How could you have kept him on?"

Her hand covered her eyes for a moment, then came away. She took in air. "He had no work, the family needed...it was only that, please believe me. I've never betrayed our marriage, Brandon. Never." Tears streamed down her face, she turned away from him and wiped at her cheeks with the back of her hand.

"I believe you. Please stop crying. Come, let's go."

She glanced up at him and shook her head, gulping in more air.

"Justine—"

"I cannot."

"You will!"

"There's no help for it." A tiny wail escaped her lips filling the air between them, rising through the ice-laden trees.

"Just like Annie. Stuck in the rocks, the floodwaters dragging you under." She raised her chin. Defiance. Control. "Once again, I am too late," Brandon muttered.

She shook her head. "No."

"I cannot pull you out, cannot get air into you."

"I should have been the one that died that night!"

"Don't you dare. Don't you dare repeat those awful things William said to you then. Annie chose to go to the creek. She decided all on her own. Richard and William always treated you badly. My father and I left you here unprotected—"

"Dear Lord, please stop."

Brandon ground his boots into the snow. "Was it an ongoing affair?" he asked, his voice just above a whisper.

"No." Justine's eyes remained on the frozen ground, her arms wrapped around her middle. "Just the once." She became unnaturally still once more, her eyes round. Brandon's breath stung in his throat at the sight. Was she remembering what it was like with Martin?

"How did William find out?"

She sniffed in air, her gaze darting to the ice laden trees. A painful memory for her, too embarrassing to discuss. He must have caught them in the act, seen them together. Martin and Justine kissing, the two of them writhing on the... The muscles jumped under his skin, and his flesh seemed burned from the inside out.

All this time Brandon had indulged himself in feelings of paranoia and jealousy, thinking the worst possible things about Justine with Andrew or with Charles. He had wanted to punish her, wanted to wipe that memory of her first time from her body with his own. Yet it had been the unassuming stable boy to whom she had first given herself. Indeed, it was plain they shared some sort of bond. His hands pressed into his temple where the pounding in his veins threatened to split his head in two.

Another thought pierced his soul, and the blood drained from his face. "Did you love him? Do you still?"

"We had only been good friends." She cleared her throat. "It was a terrible mistake, and it never should have happened."

"Did you do it to stop the engagement with Wallace?" He had to ask. William had planted that rotten seed in his brain and now he had to ask, had to know if she had purposefully decided to take Martin.

"No."

"William made you break off with Andrew. You must have been desolate. It's obvious Martin cares for you very much."

He rubbed over his mouth with the back of his hand. Images of Martin's hands caressing her secret places, his lips discovering her soft skin, Justine clutching his thick, muscular body close to her own, the boy whispering passionate words over her as he thrust inside her for the very first time, the two of them in the throes of their shared pleasure—all of it pummeled his heart, robbed him of air, twisted his gut.

Had they been together in her bed where he had lain with her? In the stables where they had just been together? Wherever it happened it must have been fraught with intense, desperate emotion. It had been obvious to him from the first that Martin was infatuated with Justine, but it was more than that, wasn't it? The boy was completely in love with her.

Brandon's mouth swirled in acid and his blackened heart hammered all the way up his throat. Her body was still, her large dark eyes glued to his. She braced herself for his judgement. "Whatever has happened here, my family bears the responsibility. We failed you, Justine."

"Brandon, you have saved me from myself. Being with you made me feel alive again. Safe. I didn't think I'd ever feel that. But with you—" He held his hand up between them in an attempt to stop her words from singeing him further. A lethal elixir of venom and nausea swirled in the back of his throat.

Silent tears spilled down her face once more, she wiped them away. "I know everything will be different between us from now on." Her voice was fragile, yet clear. "In your eyes I will be forever used, sullied, repulsive. I have been living in a fantasy thinking this would remain a secret. From the first time you and I laid together, I knew it, I feared it. Of course, you must have realized. Of course, you became suspicious and did not trust me. Soon you will come to despise me as well, and that is the one thing I could never bear."

"I could never despise you, Justine," Brandon said. "For God's sake, we both have our scars. Do mine make you despise me or care for me any less? Do you despise me for playing my hand with Amanda? Of course you don't, because you are too generous. I hurt you, did I not? And yes, this hurts too, but dammit, it no longer matters." He raised his eyes to the tops of the snow covered trees wavering in the icy air. "It should not."

"It does!" she bit out. "You will always feel the bitterness of this deception."

"No, Justine, you are wrong."

"I am not wrong in this." Her voice was even, controlled.

"You are, dammit! I love you." The words rushed out of his mouth. His heart skidded in his chest. "I love you."

Justine's face paled. "No, don't say that. Don't say that now. You only feel responsible for me like when we were children, but we're not children any longer, Brandon. No longer simply cousins. I am so sorry you were deceived over and over again, so very sorry. I do not want to be the reason for strife between you and William. He will always hold something over our heads, and you do not deserve this. It is best if you free yourself from me. You must. Yes, you must go and be happy."

Christ, the very idea of separating from her unhinged him.

"Go? Go where, goddammit? I've been happy with you. William and Richard may have convinced you all these years that you are nothing, unworthy of love, but I am telling you, you are, and I love you." He stepped closer to her. "You are starved for it, Lady Graven, starved, just as much as I am."

Their hard gazes locked on each other for an unholy second, their breath cold vapors filling the space between them."

The thick, dense snow cracked and snapped under Brandon's boots. "This strife between me and my cousin goes back years and for a number of reasons, none of them having to do with you. He has always resented you and has always enjoyed tormenting you, but that has no bearing on us. You are staying with me, and I with you."

Justine shifted her gaze past the drifts of snow on the ground, past the green trees now plastered in thick white, and overhead to where grey slabs of cloud dragged across the sky. "Stay with you... as your cousin."

"As my wife."

"You cannot possibly want that now."

"Do not tell me what I want."

"I could live quietly somewhere else."

"Never. Don't you dare abandon me. I'm utterly stranded without you," he whispered, inches from her. "I need you, and you need me, too. Now more than ever. We will keep our past in the past, and we shall both recover from it."

"Be honest with yourself, Brandon. It will be easier, cleaner if we put an end to this now." She took in a breath and leveled her gaze at him. "Do you remember what you said to me your first night back at Wolfsgate? We are both 'the tossed off, the rejected.'"

"Yes?"

"That is truly what I am, what I have always been. But not you. You must lead your new life out in the world, a life full of prospects—"

"You listen to me, Justine Traherne. When you found me, I was broken, unable to function or take care of myself. I was dirty and sickly, behaving like an animal. Yet you took me in your arms, you washed me, fed me, cleaned my sick for God's sake, put up with every vile, nasty thing that came out of my mouth."

"Yes, that's it, you see?" A strained smile etched over her mouth, her voice controlled. "That is obligation, but you owe me nothing. You must—"

"My life does makes no sense without you in it. I cannot pick up where I left off years ago, and I do not want to. I thought revenge would make it all meaningful, but that was foolish, childish even. I want to be with you. I want to have our life, together."

"You should not have to settle for someone like me, Lord Graven."

"Someone like you?" He let out a strangled laugh. "Someone like you? You are strong and as hardy as these evergreens under all this snow and ice. Through the bitterness of every winter, the wilting heat of summer year after year, you fucking persevere, you endure. Your colour remains fixed."

Her eyes slid closed and her body tightened as if his very words had slammed up against her and she had to fight their force. She clutched at the cloak around her. The heartbreak stamped on her face was that of the lost, sorrowful little girl she once was. Both at her mother's funeral, and then years later when she had gripped his arm at Annie's burial, choking back her tears.

He was desperate now to fold her in his arms, press her to his chest, and expel every last vestige of hopelessness from her and fill her with his hope, his belief in her, in them.

"My Lady Graven, you are not alone anymore."

She lifted an eyebrow. "I've always been alone, and I accepted it as my destiny a long time ago. I had grown quite accustomed to it until you relieved me of it for this small while, and it was so, so very lovely. Yet somehow I always knew it could never last."

"No." The savage tone in Brandon's voice made her eyes flare.

"Everyone leaves me, Brandon. My parents, Annie, Lord Jeremy, you, when we thought you were dead."

"I came back, you brought me back."

There were no more tears in her eyes. "Over time your disappointment will eat at you, and I could not bear it if we were to only exist politely leading separate lives in the same house or if you were to continually punish me somehow without being able to help yourself. Nor could I bear it if you found someone else, someone better."

"There can never be anyone else. You have me. I am your husband. You have me, Jus, and there's an end to it."

A cold wind gusted over them, and she gulped at the air.

"Let's go home," he said.

"Brandon—"

Give her a challenge, dare her.

"I am canceling that ridiculous Christmas party."

"No! Don't do that." Justine's hands tightened into fists at her side.

"Of course I am. You are in no fit state to play hostess to a house full of idiots celebrating a holiday, and I could care less."

"No, you cannot cancel it. You know how important this event is for Wolfsgate. It always has been."

"And?"

"And...I want to do it."

"Why?" He shifted his weight on his legs, his hands on his waist.

"Do you want William to think he has brought you to your knees?"

"Bloody hell." Brandon's hard gaze bore down on her. "Look at you. You've had a lifetime's practice at soldiering on, haven't you? It's how you've survived. That's what you know. Yes, just as I said—evergreen."

"William is expecting an answer to his ultimatum, is he not? Are you going to give him the money he wants?"

"Of course not. He keeps using the fine notions of family honour and reputation as his almighty weapons, but we'll use it against him. No matter what money he gets it will never be enough for him. Why the great need every so often? Amanda had a healthy dowry from what I remember, and his own income was good. He continues to be a success from what I've heard. There has to be a better reason why he wants my inheritance at his fingertips. I'm not convinced it's only a matter of his childhood rivalry with me. I've been making inquiries in the village and in town about his expenses. I should know more within the week." He raised an eyebrow. "You're sure about the party?"

"Quite sure." She wiped a stray lock of hair from her face. "I've been looking forward to it. We could discuss all this again after the party."

"Very well. Let us go home then." He stretched out his hand to her. "It's quite cold out here now." His voice was low and gentle.

Justine's weary gaze rested on his hand and then darted up at him for a moment. She placed her hand in his, and Brandon exhaled, the tension dissolving from his frame as her cold slim fingers settled in his palm. He rubbed them, warmed them, entwined them with his.

CHAPTER FIFTY-FIVE

BRANDON'S great grandmother had made the Wolfsgate Christmas Tea a tradition, and his mother had succeeded in making it a cherished and highly anticipated event on the social calendar of the local nobility.

Lord Jeremy had canceled it after his wife's passing, but now with a new Lord Graven in his place and his new wife at his side, it needed to be done, and Justine had seen to it with a great deal of satisfaction. She had enlisted Georgina to help her plan a Christmas Tea that Lady Caroline herself would have been proud of.

"I can't say I remember too much about her parties," Justine said to Georgina, "just the fuss and clatter about the house for days and days. We were so young then, but I do remember how the tree cuttings smelled so fresh in every room, how everything sparkled and Lady Caroline sparkled right along with it."

"Well, Lady Justine, this is now your party. You will leave your very own sparkle on it."

"I hope so," Justine murmured as she reviewed the list of the silver. "There's so much to do."

"Not to worry. You have me, my friend." Georgina straightened her shoulders. "Once we finish with the menu and the silver, we must arrange for holly branches and garlands and swags of greenery, and on and on we go. Oh dash, you know a sugar sculpture would be fantastic as a centrepiece—a replica of the house?"

"No. Too ostentatious." Justine handed her Taggart's menu notes to review.

"Come now, Lord Graven's in the sugar trade, after all." Georgina studied the menu.

"Let's focus on the greenery and the fruit bowls. You shall have free rein to festoon every painting, doorway and window in the house."

Georgina shot her a look over the menu. "Promise?"

Justine smiled. "Absolutely."

CHAPTER FIFTY-SIX

"THE NECKLACE IS READY, LORD GRAVEN."

The jeweler placed a leather box ceremoniously on his shop table before Brandon and snapped back the top with a flourish. The delicate arrangement of small diamonds and emeralds glittered at Brandon. When he first saw it last week, he knew it would lay beautifully against the exquisite bones at the base of Justine's throat, one of his favourite places on her body. Gliding his fingers over those intriguing, smooth hollows made her pulse charge to life. And his. Every time.

"Oh yes, that will do quite nicely." Brandon closed the leather box.

He couldn't wait to clasp it around her neck this afternoon before the party and see her smile again. Smile for him.

All week she had been avoiding him. She had tried to sleep in her old bedchamber, but he wouldn't permit it. Instead, she woke up very early every morning quitting their room whilst he still slept. No matter, Brandon was determined to keep Justine focused in the present with him. His thoughts ran crystal clear on this point. He had every intention of keeping her as his wife.

Although the knowledge of her and Martin stung, it was a

relief to finally know the truth. He was determined to put the incident away and make it not matter.

Mr. Easton, the jeweler placed the leather box in a small pouch and slid it toward him.

"You will send the bill to my attention, Mr.Easton, and I shall pay it directly."

"Very good, sir." Easton pursed his lips together. "If only my other clients were as considerate." The jeweler grimaced slightly as he rubbed his hands together. "Forgive me sir, I would not mention it, but there was a time or two when Lady Graven would take care of Mrs. Treharne's account with us."

Brandon's head tilted. Justine had once paid for Amanda's purchases? "Come again, sir?" Easton's pale cheeks reddened under Brandon's severe gaze.

Mr. Easton leaned over the table. "Mrs. William Treharne's account has been in arrears for quite some time. I have tried communicating with the lady, but alas, she has not responded. I fear I must take some other course of action shortly which, I would rather not do. The Treharnes are a great family. Your late father, indeed, was the finest patron—"

"Yes, yes."

Easton coughed. "It is indeed an honour that a fine lady such as Mrs. Treharne enjoys the wonderful selection of jewels I offer, and as a lady of such fine taste it is perfectly understandable that she cannot help herself when she sees a piece she is so very fond of. I would not wish to deny Mrs. Treharne such a pleasure in future, you understand, sir."

"No, of course not," Brandon said. "Mrs. Treharne comes here herself and makes purchases? Not Mr. Treharne?"

"We haven't seen Mr. Treharne for quite some time. I have several times brought my collection to Crestdown as per the lady's request. She has excellent taste. "

"Indeed, she does." Brandon shifted his weight onto his good leg and gripped his cane tighter. "May I see the bills, Mr. Easton?

Thus, perhaps, this matter could be resolved quickly." Brandon's blood raced with the possibilities within reach.

"Sir, I do not wish—"

"Mr. Easton, let me assure you, I appreciate your taking me into your confidence," Brandon said, his voice low. "I sincerely hope to assist my cousin in any way I can."

"Indeed, sir." Mr. Easton pressed two fingers to his lips as he briefly bowed his head. He disappeared into a back room and swiftly returned with a sheaf of papers. "The total figure is just here." He sniffed as his bony finger pointed to an absurdly high sum.

Brandon wanted to laugh out loud, but he checked the reflex. He only offered the grateful man a brief, easy smile. "Very good, Mr. Easton. You shall be hearing from my cousin shortly, I warrant."

Mr. Easton's face beamed. "Thank you, my lord. Thank you, indeed."

With Justine's gift in his possession and a smirk slashing his lips, Brandon crossed the noisy square, dodging the hawkers and the beggars, sidestepping the large patches of ice and the murky black puddles, and finally reached the Fang & Feather. He threw open the doors and spotted Davidson in the far left corner, gesturing at him.

"Tell me," Brandon said, settling on a bench. "Because I think I know what you're going to say."

Davidson let out a dry laugh. "Ah, bloody hell, milord, don't spoil me fun now."

Brandon pressed his forearms into the wooden table. "I was just with the jeweler, and it seems the poor man's been having a terrible problem with Amanda Treharne's credit. And yet he says my cousin has not stepped foot in there for ages."

"Ale, sir?" An eager girl hovered at his side.

"No," Brandon replied without a glance, and the girl shuffled off.

Davidson slapped his hand on the table and leaned in closer to Brandon. "The lady's in debt all over the village—finery for herself, finery for her house, but most especially, it's the card games at every party she attends. She's wildly popular there."

"I did get that impression," Brandon said. "But I did not think it ran so deep."

"In fact, they quit London earlier than usual this season because of it."

"That must have been a blow, imagine the shame." Brandon rapped the table with his knuckles.

"Seems she was in debt before they married, and lo and behold, all her debts were cleared immediately after."

"Were they?"

"Yes. However, just before you came back from the dead, her debt had mounted once again, and only half of it was cleared." Davidson lifted his mug to his lips and drank. "The other half is still in arrears, mounting, demanding to be paid."

CHAPTER FIFTY-SEVEN

BRANDON'S MANSERVANT brushed down the back of his frock coat then smoothed the fabric down over his shoulders, but Brandon's attention was riveted on Justine across their chamber. She sat at her vanity table in her dressing room, a robe tied carelessly about her, her hair thick and loose down her back while she opened her perfume bottles.

"Leave." He jerked his chin sharply at the servant. The young man bowed and swiftly quit his dressing room.

Brandon's pulse hammered as he watched Justine trail a small glass wand up and down an arm daubing her skin. She dipped the wand in the bottle once more and slid the wand at her throat and down her other arm. The scent of roses filled the air. How could the scent of a flower be so bloody intoxicating?

His hand swept down his necktie as he moved through the chamber toward her. She met his gaze in her looking glass offering him a small smile. He brushed back her hair from one shoulder, his lips grazing her skin. "Such a scent."

"It's only roses, nothing extraordinary."

"Hardly. On you, that is exactly what it is—extraordinary." He planted a kiss behind her ear, her skin quivering under his gentle touch. "I have news. My inquiries in town bore fruit. William is not in debt."

She turned in her chair. "Oh. But then...?"

"Amanda is." Brandon's eyes relaxed over Justine as she absorbed the news.

"Amanda?"

"For years now, general overspending and then more at the gaming tables. Her father was always a very conservative fellow, I can't imagine he would put up with this from his daughter. Social disaster. I don't think their living could cover a Duchess's spending, and I'm sure she kept it from him. William, personally, has no debt. Never has. He's always been quite fastidious on that point."

"This has been about Amanda all along?"

"William must have promised to save her from herself. I wonder, she agreed to marry him thinking she would finally be out of debt and yet also be able to continue to live that good life without displeasing her father any longer. William has always enjoyed the finer things, but not to excess. That's why I found his need for so much money curious. My thoughts also went to his possibly needing capital for a new business venture, but, again, he was always careful never to overextend himself. And Charles confirmed to me that William has not been engaged in any new, overly-ambitious enterprises of late."

"Strange that he would marry such a self-indulgent creature," said Justine.

"Love is a great tormentor." Brandon's gaze fell to her mouth. "But our local Duchess is unable to free herself from the bonds of her addiction, and William's resources have their limits. It makes sense that he would need to find other resources, thus dipping into mine."

"He's been protecting her all along."

"Like the good husband that he is."

"Yes." Her fingers absently touching her throat.

The muffled sounds of curt voices and bustling footsteps boomed from the hallway. Musical instruments being loosened and prepared echoed from downstairs.

"Damn, I don't like all this commotion in my house."

Justine laughed. "Oh, it will all be over by this evening." She turned back to face the looking glass.

He stilled, something in his chest tugged at her words. They were eerily akin to what she had told him earlier in the week, weren't they?

"We can discuss all this again, make a decision after the party."

"It's only a tea," she said. "A formal one, but only a tea. Cling to that."

"I shall cling to a great many things." He opened the drawer to the chest and took out the velvet box placing it on the table before her. "This is for you. Merry Christmas, Lady Graven."

Her gaze fell to the box, her brow pinched together.

"Open it." He fingered a lock of her hair at her shoulder. She snapped open the hinge, pulled back the lid, and the necklace gleamed at her in the candlelight.

Justine's eyes widened as she fingered the bright green stones and the crystal clear diamonds. "Oh, Brandon," her voice shook.

"Does my wife like her present?"

"It's very..."

"Breathtaking, like you."

"Brandon—"

"Do you like it?" he breathed.

"You're so kind."

Brandon let out a laugh as he took the necklace from the box. "Kind would be offering you a cup of chocolate or an extra wool blanket on a cold winter's night." She drew her hair out of his way, and he laid the necklace around her throat and clasped it there. He brushed his lips at the nape of her bare neck, sensing her tremors under his delicate touch.

"You honour me," she breathed.

"The honour is mine." His fingers lingered at her throat, tracing a line down to her collarbone, then drifted over her bare shoulder. She made a slight noise in the back of her throat. "It's beautiful. You're beautiful." His voice came out hoarse. Her eyes filled with water.

"'Beggin' your pardon." Lizzie hesitated in the doorway.

Justine's hand darted to his at her shoulder. "Go, Brandon. Lizzie needs to deal with my unruly hair." She wiped at her eyes.

He smirked and leaned in close to her. "I like your hair unruly," he whispered in her ear as he ran the back of his knuckles gently down the side of her face. He left the women in the dressing room, but turned to take a final glimpse of his wife's reflection in the looking glass.

Lizzie ran a brush through a thick strand of that beautiful, coppery brown hair. Brandon's heart beat heavy and full inside his chest. Justine's dark eyes were luminous, her cheeks flushed, the necklace shimmering at her throat.

CHAPTER FIFTY-EIGHT

JUSTINE SMOOTHED down the silk of her deep emerald gown. She was continuing in the Graven family tradition this afternoon, and a flare of pride glowed inside her that she could do this for Wolfsgate, for Brandon.

"I love you."

Her hand went to his beautiful gift at her throat. The back of her eyes stung as his precious words rushed through her. He was only being comforting and kind, wasn't he? They were good friends and close companions. Anything else would be...

She knew what it would be, so she decided she wouldn't think about it. Not now at least.

"There, finished." Lizzie released the last ringlet. "You look beautiful, milady."

"Thank you, Lizzie."

"Much prettier than Mrs. Treharne could ever be, even though she has that fairy princess hair and those doll-like eyes. You're glowing, you are, 'cause you have a good heart, and it shows. 'Tis rare, that. I was only in service at her house a short time, but she seldom had a kind word. I'm right glad I had to stop working there last year."

Justine blinked at the girl's stream of words about Amanda. "Well. I'm glad you're here with me, Lizzie."

"So is I, ma'am." Lizzie stacked Justine's jewelry boxes in the drawer of the vanity. "Mrs. Treharne weren't ever mean, really, but cold, as one is to servants, I suppose. But she could be especially cold to her own husband."

Justine handed Lizzie hair pins. "Oh?"

"He was ever so attentive to her, always bringing her little presents and such, being thoughtful, but she wouldn't pay him or his presents much mind. Once in a while, but not all the time. When it fancied her. She had her moods. Other presents she liked better, and t'would act like a giddy young thing whenever she received them." Lizzie let out a giggle as she organised the hair brush, combs, and pins on the table top.

"Other presents?"

"Yes," Lizzie faced Justine, eyes wide. "Presents that t'weren't from her husband."

"You mean, from another man?"

Lizzie grinned, her cheeks pink. She was telling the greatest secret in the world. "From that handsome friend of his Lordship's, the blond one—"

"Mr. Montclare?" Justine's hands gripped the edges of her cushioned seat. "Are you sure, Lizzie?"

"Oh yes ma'am, I saw one of his notes me'self. She'd left it open under a jewelry box by mistake. I know how to read, and I couldn't help me'self when I saw it. And there was his name at the bottom—Charles."

"Lizzie!"

"I wouldn't really call it a love note, ma'am," she whispered, "He did express certain ideas that perhaps were not appropriate for a young girl such as me'self to read upon." Lizzie let out a snort.

Justine put her hand to her middle. Gifts and erotic notes

from Charles to Amanda. Over a year ago. The two of them together right under William's nose.

"Have you spoken of this to anyone else?" Justine asked. Lizzie's face tightened as she shook her head. "You must not, ever, Lizzie."

"Yes ma'am. I mean, no, no I won't. Am I in trouble? I've been indiscreet! Oh goodness. Forgive me. I'd never...Oh dear, I am a foolish girl! She is your brother's wife. I am so sorry, ma'am. I did not think." Lizzie's hands flew to her mouth, her entire body stiffened.

Justine put her hand on the girl's arm. "Lizzie, I appreciate your telling me, as I do care about my brother's happiness. Rest assured, I would never come between them." Justine's voice was calm and soothing. Lizzie's shoulders dropped. "But it must remain our secret. It must. Do you promise?"

Lizzie nodded, her eyes wide as saucers. "Promise."

CHAPTER FIFTY-NINE

"LADY GRAVEN and I welcome you to Wolfsgate." Brandon raised his glass high. "Merry Christmas to all!"

Standing next to her husband, Justine raised her glass. The entire first floor was trimmed with garlands and swags of evergreens, the fresh, crisp scent filling the house along with the rich perfume of heated spices from the mulled ale. The rooms were ablaze with a multitude of candles and a multitude of faces.

"Here! Here!" Cups and glasses clinked together as murmurings and ripples of laughter filled the hall. The musicians began to play once more, and the melodic strains of the French horn, trumpet, clarinet, and bassoon rose through the house.

Justine took her husband's arm, and they moved through their guests in the great drawing room. "I must speak with you," she whispered in his ear. He took her hand in his and led her to a quiet corner and she shared with him Lizzie's information about Amanda and Charles.

A grin lit his face. "William has been so focused on solving her debts that he hasn't realized that his wife has been entertaining herself with one of his friends. Or more."

"Is it still going on between them?" Justine asked. "Both she and Charles turned their attentions to you and me at the same time. What perverse..." her voice trailed off.

"We're the new playthings in the neighbourhood, don't you know? And if, as you say, they've been at it for a year, they're probably bored with one another now. I know Charles. That's always been his way. He would usually linger at the end instead of making a clean break."

"Dear Lord."

"You're not feeling sorry for William now, are you?"

"God, no," Justine said. "He's very smart. He had to have known what he was taking on when he decided to marry her. But he had to have her."

Brandon let out a short laugh.

"What is so amusing, Brandon?"

"Well, I can't say I knew what I was taking on with you as my wife."

"Lord save us, you didn't even know you had a wife."

"My point exactly." His thumb stroked her cheek. "I do so love irony, don't you?"

"Rather delicious, I must say." Her face warmed under his touch.

"Hmm." He brushed her lips with his. "We've got William now, Jus."

Justine's fingers clutched at his waistcoat. "Please, Brandon, tread carefully. Whatever you do, he might still find a way to use it against you."

"Still so worried?" Brandon ran his hands down her arms. "Now I can threaten him with exposure, and he will retreat. He won't want his name or his wife's reputation in the mud for all to see. That's what all this has been about, hasn't it? You must trust me."

His lips tickled the skin behind her ear, and the shiver that raced through her instantly propelled her to the sensation of being in his arms and giving herself over to such small intimacies. He gave her that smile, and her breath caught. So damned handsome, so full of the promise of good things.

Remember this. This moment. This feeling.

He kissed her hand and left her, taking a piece of her with him.

Someone played the spinet, and Justine took in a breath of air as the melodic tones of the fine instrument filled the house. So beautiful. Thankfully, she had arranged for it to be tuned last week.

"There you are." Georgie bustled into the dining room.

Justine's hand went to her middle. "Who is playing? Such a fine talent."

"Mariah Marchmain along with a rather ill-tempered Andrew Blakelock at her side."

Georgina joined Justine at the table and checked on the delectable offerings—platters of iced cakes and sweet meats, sugar biscuits, small mince pies and gooseberry tartlets, boldly colored jellies, and bowls of oranges and apples. Movement caught Justine's eye by the servants' hallway off the dining room which lead to the cellar stairs. She approached, but hushed voices stopped her in her tracks.

"Enough, Charles. I do not care any longer."

"Oh, I'm sure you do, lady mine," came Charles's voice.

"I'm not your lady, sir."

"Turn of phrase, love and indeed, I am most fortunate that you are not."

"How dare you!"

Justine darted over to Georgina. Luckily the dining room was empty except for them.

"Are you offended by that?"

"You've grown quite tedious."

"That goes both ways, Mrs. Treharne. Be assured, I have seen the error of my ways. Enjoy the rest of your evening."

Georgina and Justine only stared at one another. There was a scuffle of sorts, and they immediately turned and busied themselves over a great china vase of holly, ivy and bay branches Georgina had prepared the day before. The stamping of a woman's delicate shoes on the parquet receded from the room. Georgina turned slowly. Charles stood over the great table plucking sugar biscuits.

"Are you mad?" Georgina exclaimed. His head snapped up at her, his face a mask.

"Georgina, quiet!" Justine said.

"Have you been carrying on with Amanda?" Georgina asked.

Charles's hard gaze flicked over her. "Stay out of it, Georgie."

"And I repeat—are you mad?" Georgina crossed her arms. "How could you do this to one of your good friends?" He shifted his weight and said nothing. He returned his attention to the table, picked a sweetmeat and chewed on it. Georgina moved in closer to him. "And yet you have been hovering over Justine the past few weeks, at the very same time?"

"That's not exactly true," Charles said swallowing.

"Isn't it?" Justine asked.

Georgina's eyes were fierce. "Are you such a rogue, Mr. Montclare?"

"Georgina..." He brushed off the powdered sugar from his fingers.

"That bored with your life?"

"Stop this."

"Or are you simply that insatiable?"

Charles's eyes flared. "Shut it!"

Georgina's hands gripped her hips. "I most certainly will not. How dare you speak to me that way."

"I've known you since the day you were born, little mouse. I'm like your own brother."

"I caught you out just now, Charles Montclare, and you have the gall to speak to me like I'm the naughty one?"

"Naughty? Really, Georgie? We're not children any longer." Charles bit out.

"That is plainly obvious," she shot back. "Is it done with now?"

"You overheard us, didn't you?"

"Is it done with, for good?"

His lips pressed together in a firm line. "Yes, dammit. It's been over for quite a while, but now it's official. Is that sufficient for you?"

"Was it worth it?" Justine asked.

He trained his gaze on her, his posture stiff. "What, exactly?"

"Being naughty with La Amanda?" Georgina asked.

"Christ, the two of you!" His eyes darkened, and he let out a heavy breath. Several couples entered the room, strolled by the table, and decided on sweets from the colourful selection. He gripped Georgie's elbow and Justine's arm and led them out of the dining room to the hall by the staircase.

"Truly, was it worth all the bother?" Georgina whispered. "Will you now be forever dissatisfied with the rest of womankind for none will ever compare to her?"

"What a mouth!"

"It starts with my brain, darling," she retorted.

"Hmm." His eyes narrowed. "A gentleman does not discuss such things, especially with young ladies."

"A gentleman, indeed." Georgina's brows knit together for a moment. "Was possessing Amanda's perfection for even a short time so very worth the risk?"

His shoulders dropped. "What perfection? Is that what you think? You too, Lady Justine?" He crossed his arms. "Oh, she's far from perfect."

"Then why?"

"You really want to know, Miss Georgina?"

"I'm all fascination, Mr. Montclare. Educate me."

Charles followed Justine's gaze to Andrew and Mariah at the

spinet, Amanda and William standing nearby. "She is, of course, a great beauty, but what I enjoyed was the chase. She likes games, as do I. In the end that's all it was really. I never expected nor wanted more. She's married, after all. Soon enough the game became wearisome."

"A game that included me?" said Justine.

Charles's jaw clenched. "That was Amanda's idea."

"Pardon?"

"She wanted Brandon, so she asked me to distract his wife. The crazy thing is," he leaned in closer to the women. "William asked me to do the very same. To dally with Lady Graven in order to annoy Brandon. Imagine my surprise and delight." Charles let out a heavy sigh.

"Bloody hell!" Georgina said.

"Tsk—Georgie," Charles said. "It's mad, eh? I must admit I found it amusing in the beginning, but it began to vex me. Brandon's been through a hell of a lot, and Lady Graven, you did not deserve such treatment. You do not deserve to be trapped in their twisted webs."

"Neither do you," Georgina said.

His head jerked up. "Pardon?"

"You do not deserve that sort of twisted rubbish either."

"Don't I?"

"Why should you be their puppet, Mr. Montclare?" she asked.

His lips parted, and he studied Georgina as if taking her in for the first time.

"Charles?" Georgina touched his arm.

He shifted his weight, a hand smoothing down his waistcoat. "Yes—I mean, no. I won't be their puppet."

"Congratulations, then." Georgina turned her head slightly to smile at Lord Marchmain and Mr. Blakelock as they passed.

Charles leaned in to her. "Congratulations for what?"

She smiled at him. "For extricating yourself from her and that vile situation, you idiot."

His eyebrows darted up. "Should I say thank you?"

"If you like."

"And now do you hate me, Miss Georgina? Are you going to run off to your little circle of friends and discuss Charles Montclare's disgusting, roguish ways and plot the downfall of Amanda Treharne while you're at it?"

Georgina bit her lower lip. "Absolutely not."

"Absolutely not what? You don't hate me or you—"

"No, Charles I don't hate you."

"Should I believe you?"

A smug smile lit Georgina's face. "Everyone already knows you're a rake, Mr. Montclare, and I do not delight in spreading nasty rumours. Furthermore, I consider you a friend. I would never hurt you intentionally."

"Well, I am most grateful for your friendship and care, Miss Georgina." Charles bowed his head at her. "And yours, Lady Graven. I realize I do not deserve your generosity, but I do beg your forgiveness for my behavior. Please know I value your friendship and I hope that in future we may—"

"I will consider your request, Mr. Montclare," Justine said. "Rest assured, this shall remain between us."

"Thank you." A small smile lit his lips. His gaze darted between the ladies. "May I ask, do you both really think she's perfect?"

"No," Georgina's gaze travelled over Charles's finely tailored waistcoat. "She does though. Her demeanor is overwhelmingly annoying. I have this recurring fantasy of releasing the pins from those coiled ringlets, sending her jewelry sailing, misaligning ribbons on the trim of her dress, seeing unsightly red splotches mar her ivory skin—"

"Georgie, hush!" Justine squeezed her friend's arm.

Charles laughed. His brightly lit eyes settled on Georgina. "That I'd like to see. Truly. I would pay money, in fact, to witness that."

"Oh, I'm sure you would," Georgina said, an eyebrow lifting. "Scoundrel."

His finger brushed her nose. "You're a funny thing, aren't you?"

"Hilarious." Georgie cleared her throat. "Shall we go through?"

He tucked her arm in his. "You do realize, however, that being seen with me, a vile rogue, may tarnish your reputation?"

"Ah, I do not have a reputation, Mr. Montclare. Not just yet."

"It would be my pleasure to oblige you in such an endeavor, Miss Georgina."

CHAPTER SIXTY

THE GUESTS SHOWED their pleasure and approval of the Graven Christmas Tea by leaving behind a dizzying array of plates, bowls, glasses, and cups everywhere. Demolished jellies and wafer and cake crumbs, sugar, and empty platters littered the great dining table. Thankfully, their guests also left plenty of gifts for the underprivileged children of the village for Justine to distribute.

From the open door Justine watched the last coach make its way down the drive in the darkness of night . She closed her eyes and inhaled the fresh cold air in her lungs. She was exhausted and dearly looking forward to removing her shoes and dress and collapsing into bed at long last.

"Very fine party, Lady Graven. Well done," William's voice rose behind her. "Well done, indeed."

Justine remained motionless under his cold, assessing gaze.

"I underestimated you," William said, the lines of his face relaxed.

"Oh?"

"You make a perfectly respectable Lady Graven. I always thought you'd only amount to a second-rate imitation. Yet this evening I watched you, and you were very gracious and attentive to all your guests and to your husband." He leaned in close to her, his woodsy aroma invading her nostrils warning her she was now in different territory. The acid in Justine's stomach rose, her knees locked.

"Does he like it, Tina? Fucking you," William breathed. "Does he like it? Or does he pound into you every time trying to erase me?"

Justine's heart thudded. William tilted his head at her, his eyes taking her in. "Are you frightened now?"

"No," she replied. "I know that's what you want."

William only raised his chin at her. She wanted the last word. *Just this once. Just bloody once.* "The answer to your first question, William, is also no."

His eyes glittered over her. "No?"

"We don't think of you at all when we're fucking."

"Oh, Tina. You are remarkable indeed." William's brittle laughter rang out.

"Get away from my wife," Brandon's growl rose between them.

William turned to face his cousin, his neck stiffening. "There you are. Our agreement?"

"There was no agreement and there is no money for you, you bastard. Not ever."

William's face darkened. "You know what this means, don't you?"

"I know what it means—for Amanda," Brandon said. "This has all been about Amanda, from the beginning. Her pleasures, her debts. No more. Find a way to take care of your wife's little problem on your own."

William took in a breath. "There is no problem."

"I've seen the bills, cousin, looked into the rumours. There's a big problem."

"You did what?" William's eyes narrowed.

"Then there are her things with other men."

"Things?"

"Sorry, did I say 'things?'" Brandon said. "I meant flings. Your wife's flings with other men."

"You bastard!" William launched himself at Brandon.

With a grunt Brandon pushed Justine out of the way and shoved William back against the wall. "Yes, William. While you've been working hard to save her reputation and your own by clearing her debts, the ungrateful bitch has been entertaining herself with other men. I suppose you've been too busy to notice? But you noticed how much she wanted me, didn't you?"

"Brandon, stop!" Justine yelled, stumbling back.

William sputtered and flung himself at Brandon once again. William punched Brandon in the chest, and Brandon's fist landed on the side of his cousin's jaw, knocking him back. William cursed, staggering to the side.

"What is this? What is going on?" Amanda rushed into the hall, her eyes wide, her cape in her arms. "What are you doing? Thank God everyone's left and no one's here to witness it!"

Brandon burst out into laughter, releasing his hold on his cousin. Justine rushed to her husband's side.

William wiped his hair from his eyes, glaring at his wife. "Wait for me outside." She only stared at him, her cheeks flushed. "Do as I say! Go!" Amanda turned on her heel and charged out the door.

William staggered to his feet, brushing at the side of his mouth. "All I ever wanted was to protect this family."

"No, you wanted to protect your interests, your name," Brandon said. "Our definition of family, cousin, is quite, quite different."

CHAPTER SIXTY-ONE

LIZZIE SMOOTHED out Justine's dress while her mistress sat before her looking glass removing her bracelet. The lady's maid noticed him and stopped in her tracks, clutching the gown.

"Go," Brandon said, his voice low.

Lizzie bowed and darted from the chamber.

Brandon shut the door behind her, pressing his hand against it. His necktie hung loose, his shirt open, revealing his bare chest. Justine raised her head.

"Did William upset you?" he asked.

"No."

He came up behind her, his gaze fixed on her reflection in the glass. "He has a peculiar way of speaking to you."

Justine's fingers worked the clasp of the bracelet. "He always has. I don't think that will ever change." The clasp unhooked.

"He called you Tina."

Her lips pursed as she lay the bracelet on the marble top of the chest. She said nothing.

"He seems to know how to hurt you, and I want to hurt him for it."

"Brandon—"

"I know. You don't want me to."

"You promised me you wouldn't."

"And I will not break that promise because it is important to you. Because you are important to me."

He wanted to relieve her suffering, he wanted to relieve his own. He had no other words, there were no other words, only—"I love you, Justine."

She gripped the edge of the chest, her body swayed slightly, her forehead creased.

His heart ached. "Look at me. Please look at me." She finally raised her head and held their reflection in the glass again.

"Only you," he whispered. His fingers brushed the rubies and diamonds that hung next to her throat. The earring swung and he unscrewed it from her lobe and let it drop from his long fingers, crashing onto the marble table top. The tip of his tongue traced a line of wet fire up her neck to her other ear, and there he bit the soft lobe, eliciting a whimper from her. "Only you." Brandon released the other earring, and it too plummeted to the table with a crash.

His eyes darkened as he leaned his head close to hers. "Look at us." His fingers drew her face towards the glass once more. "What do you see?"

Her lips parted, but she did not speak. Her lower lip trembled.

A smile crept across his mouth. "Don't you see it, Jus? Can't you feel it between us? I can."

She swallowed, her eyes shimmered with wet.

"This is us," Brandon whispered. "No one and nothing can take that away, sweet thing. Not ever. Not things that happened in the past way before us, not people's poisonous tongues today nor tomorrow. Nothing." His lips brushed her cool cheek and her chin lifted. "You have to believe in it, Justine. I do. You made me believe. With your goodness, your strength."

He turned his face into her neck and drank in her rose scent once more. "Let me be strong for you now, as a husband should. You need me to be," he murmured against her skin. "I love you. I love you." Brandon swept her hair from her neck and his fingers traced a feather-light line down her shoulders. "I've never felt this before." His eyes darted up to hers in their reflection. "Never." His mouth sank over her skin and he felt a shiver race through her. "Let us have this." He soaked in the pools of her silky brown eyes which remained riveted on his. "Do we not deserve it?"

Her body stilled as if a new thought had occurred to her. A new resolve. Her fingertips brushed his lips then went to her chemise, and she pulled it over her head, freeing her body from the fine material. It dropped to the floor.

The energy in the room changed, it was potent and powerful and it charged through his veins like a bolt of lightning. Justine stood before him gloriously naked but for his necklace glittering at her throat. He was going to combust here and now. His heart pressed against his ribs.

"Take me, Brandon," she said in the half shadows. "Right here, I want to see us."

The air was sucked out of him as if a tightly wound rope that bound him had snapped and he was at long last let loose. Her fingers clutched the ends of the dresser as he unfastened his breeches. He raised her hips and brought himself to her entrance on a groan, and slid inside her.

Joined. Union.

She let out a low moan, and he leaned over her back, planting a kiss on her soft skin. He was starved for her. "Justine..." It came out as a warning, because he didn't think he could hold himself together too much longer. The blood pounded in his head and in his cock.

"Fill me, Brandon," she breathed.

He drew himself up, and his one hand dug into her hair pulling her head back. She gasped, her back arched, her eyes melding with his in the looking glass. He rocked inside her as fully as he possibly could. Every particle of his being cried out for more, more of his woman. His eyes shut for a blinding instant.

"Look at me," her husky voice insisted through his carnal fog.

Brandon raised his hooded gaze to hers in the mirror. Her lips were parted, her velvet eyes steadfast and swirling in desire.

Desire for him.

"This is our revenge," she said. "Our satisfaction, together."

Brandon's chest burst. He drove into her slickness and buried himself to the hilt, then pulled out slowly, relishing every sensation that ripped through him.

"Give me all of you, Bran. I want to feel you everywhere."

A grunt escaped his chest and he lost the last scrap of control he had left. He wrenched her hips higher and thrust deeper, moved faster, his eyes never leaving hers in the glass. She gasped for air as she pushed back into him. The necklace on her throat made thudding sounds against her chest, the dresser jerked and shuddered, the earrings and the bracelet shaking over its marble surface.

Justine yielded fully to his violence, welcoming it, needing it just as much as he did.

"Only you, Jus. Tell me. Tell me you believe me."

"Only you, Brandon. Only you..." A loud cry escaped her.

That desperate, wild sound blasted the ache in his chest and vanquished it once and for all as the rising tide of sensation overwhelmed them both. He gave himself over to it, to her.

CHAPTER SIXTY-TWO

"Where is she, Molly? Where the hell could she be?"

Molly's face creased. "I dinna see her, sir."

The sun was setting and a bitter wind battered the window panes. Justine had not been seen all afternoon. It had been hours, in fact. "Where's Simms?" Brandon asked for his new stable hand, his lips set in a firm line.

"Not seen him either, sir."

Brandon had just come back from the stables, the freezing air still stinging his face. Justine's horse, Persephone, was missing.

He cursed under his breath. Had she left him? She was stubborn, but no, no impossible. They had made love last night for what seemed like hours. Spoke. Laughed. It had been perfect. Perfect.

Was that her way of saying goodbye?

His throat constricted. That trace of sadness, that distraction was still in her eyes. It was something she couldn't yet let go of, and he couldn't wipe it away just yet.

He tore up the stairs to their chamber and went straight to her dressing room. The doors to the closet hung open. His pulse thudded as he pushed one door back. Bloody hell. It had been full of frocks last night. Today it gaped at him half-empty.

No.

He stepped back and darted to the vanity. The surface was clean, not a dainty object out of place, only her two perfume bottles, and that small Prussian blue enamel box of her mother's stood still on the surface.

He tugged opened the drawers one after the other and dumped the jewelry boxes on the table, snapping them open. His mother's earrings, the bracelet, the new emerald necklace. All of it. Still here. Her mother's ring. The box for the wedding ring he bought her that day in the village was empty.

His eyes went to the enamel box. He lifted off the top. *Dammit to hell.* There it was. Justine's wedding ring. The one he had chosen with her trembling at his side. The one she wore every day. He slumped against the table.

"Milord?" Molly clutched at her hands in the doorway.

"She's gone."

"No, sir."

"Did she tell you?"

"She said no such thing, she wouldna leave. This is her home!"

Brandon shoved the vanity against the wall knocking over the perfume bottles. The boxes shifted from their pile, tumbling, rubies, diamonds, and emeralds spilling over. He charged past Molly out of the room and out of the house.

"LORD GRAVEN?" Georgina stood in the parlour of her family home, her face flushed. "Welcome. Please sit...."

"Where is she?" he breathed.

"Pardon?"

"Justine, where has she gone?"

"Gone?"

"Is she here?"

"No, she's not here."

"You must know something. You must have helped her."

"Helped her?"

"Tell me."

Her eyebrows drew together. "Forgive me. I do not understand. Justine is gone?"

"There's no sign of her, she's taken clothes, left her jewelry behind, even her wedding ring."

"Are you certain?"

"Are you certain you know nothing?" His ragged voice boomed.

Georgina's hands curled into fists at her side. "It cannot be!"

"She hasn't said a word to you?"

"Not a one. She seemed happy at the party, even though somewhat distracted. I assumed it was nerves, excitement, fatigue. Are you sure she's not out visiting?"

"I wouldn't have come if I wasn't sure," he shot back through gritted teeth. "She's sent no message to you, no—"

"No, nothing. I will come with you—"

"Stay here. Perhaps she will contact you or come herself."

Georgina's large brown eyes tightened. "Have you done or said something to upset her?"

He gave the girl a hard stare. "I would never do anything to harm or frighten my wife, Miss Georgina. I only want her home safe where she is loved."

Georgina clasped her hands together. "She has said nothing to me to indicate that she was even considering such a thing. If she had I would have dissuaded her, you can be sure of it."

Charles Montclair entered the room. "Graven? What are you doing here?"

"Lady Graven is missing," said Georgina quietly.

"Missing?" Charles turned to Brandon.

"Have you seen her or spoken to her since the party, Mr. Montclare?" asked Georgina.

"No. We only spoke that once with you, then later when we took our leave."

"Yes." Georgina glanced up at Brandon's hard features. "Lord Graven, in such a dramatic instance, if she has chosen to leave, would she not even turn to her stepbrother?"

"No."

"Your estate manager? She has told me that—"

"I have seen him, he is searching for her himself."

Georgina wipe a hand over her brow. "I must confess, I know of no other acquaintance of Lady Justine's whom she would trust in such an instance. She is friendly with several of your tenants, though, is she not?"

Brandon exhaled. "Yes. There is one tenant. Dammit, there is one in particular."

CHAPTER SIXTY-THREE

She knew that howl.

It was not the wind, it was *him*.

He was here.

Here for me.

Yes. Yes, do come.

There was a glimmer in the twilight before her. She tried to raise her hand, but it would not comply with her wishes. The light only dimmed, paled. His gold eyes shone but for an instant, making her heart throb. His cry filled the air again, breaking over her, taking her breath away.

I am with you.

The gold flickered and vanished.

Stay.

Only white filled her vision.

Don't leave me.

He howled once more.

White...

Only white.

CHAPTER SIXTY-FOUR

BRANDON GALLOPED over the hard frozen ground toward the tenants' cottages. Toward *him*.

She had trusted him years ago. She trusted him still. He'd seen it in both of them every time they'd been in each other's presence. It was quiet, simple. It was there. A bond.

Martin.

She could trust Martin to help her leave. Maybe they had left together. Maybe he'd been right all along and the world truly was a mad, mad place, and he was cursed to live in it, resurrected or no.

The drifts of endless white snow in the dark sparkled at him under the cold glow of the moon. Knight cut through the eerie quiet of the frozen woods bringing them closer to the tenants' cottages. She could still be there, before heading off somewhere early the following morning. Beads of sweat prickled along his spine. He barely noticed the drifts of white his horse charged through. An icy net spread over his chest pulling tight.

Let me not be too late. Let me find her.

Knight pulled on his reins giving a subtle tug of his head to the side. Brandon's eyes focused before him instinctively, his back stiffened as he listened, his legs firm against his horse. Another animal had to be about.

A heavy whisper, a shuffling movement, crunching in the snow. All his senses tuned to every flick of—

Knight whinnied and pulled again. Brandon's fingers tightened against the reins. Two eyes glowed in the distance, yellow gold, flickering. His breath caught. His heart pumped wildly in his chest.

Could it be?

The gold eyes vanished, but he heard the creature shifting warily in the snow, appraising him. Was it...

A neigh shuddered through the air, and the vision manifested before him, but it was no apparition, it was real. Persephone. Alone, bare in the snow, watching him and Knight, bobbing her head, her thick black mane whipping in the wind.

Brandon slid off his horse and approached her slowly. "Here, girl. That's it." The horse snorted at him, shook its head from side to side, its eyes wide. She was agitated. What was she doing out here alone and with no saddle?

Persephone snorted, her hooves stamping restlessly, crunching in the stiff icy snow. She stamped back a few steps and trotted to a grove of ice-laden trees in the distance. "What is it, girl?" He plodded after her, Knight's hoofs behind him.

His flesh prickled with ice.

A mound of black lay like a large immoveable stone under the frozen branches. Persephone snorted and neighed, bobbing her head over the black stone.

Brandon's heart tore through his chest. He ran, fell on his knees, his hands clawing over the motionless figure, digging into the icy woolen fabric, pulling at the cold softness underneath. The full mass of copper hair fell over his arm, and the breath caught in his lungs. His hand went to her cold face, his shaky fingers brushing over her icy lips.

The wind rushed through the trees leaving an eerie shriek in its wake. Chunks of snow fell on the lifeless body, and he pawed at them like a creature possessed, preserving its most cherished...

He exploded.

"Justine!"

~

"LADY GRAVEN'S CONDITION IS SERIOUS," Dr. Langham pronounced. "She has a broken arm, several broken ribs, and there are bruises all over her back and legs. I cannot rule out the possibility of serious injury to her back. Fortunately, you were careful in moving her to the Shaw's cottage in their cart and not on your horse, but I cannot yet be exact as to the severity of her injuries."

"Why has she not yet woken up?" Brandon's voice was lifeless, his eyes locked on Justine's still form in Mrs. Shaw's bed.

"That is another point of concern. If her head knocked against that tree or a frozen rock on the ground hidden by the snow, she may have an injury in the head. There is some swelling, but it is not over a large area, thankfully. Neither her neck nor her spine broke, and that in itself is a miracle. There is something else, my lord." Dr. Langham tilted his head at Brandon and moved deeper into the room, further away from the tenants hovering in the Shaw's small doorway.

Brandon's jaw tightened, his strained eyes prickling with a thousand shooting pains. His legs filled with molten lead as he followed the doctor. He leaned his hands on the back of a chair bracing himself. "Tell me. Be done with it."

"Lady Graven may be with child."

That molten lead now poured through him incinerating every nerve ending. Words would not come.

"There was some bleeding," Dr. Langham said.

"Bleeding?"

"Yes, but I cannot be sure if it is enough to constitute alarm.

We can only wait. I am sorry. Pray she awakens. Pray for that," the doctor said. "I will give Mrs. Shaw instruction as to her care. This is most important, sir—Lady Graven must not be moved. Do not under any circumstances, attempt to take her back to Wolfsgate. She must remain here in this bed until she awakens and we know better what her injuries are. Do you understand?"

Brandon nodded. His hand shot out and gripped the doctor's arm. "A child?" Brandon rasped.

Langham put his hand over Brandon's, a slight smile curved the edges of his thin lips. "Yes, my boy. A child."

Brandon sank into the rickety chair by his wife's bedside. Her face was pale, her body unbelievably still except for a gentle inhalation and exhalation of breath. Her broken left arm was bound, her slender fingers peeking through the binding. Brandon touched the worn quilted blanket at her chest, his shaky hand traveling down to her belly and resting there.

"A child," he whispered. The word sounded foreign to his ears as he released it from his lips. Deep inside he was thrilled, wild with joy, but he bound that joy tightly with thick iron chains and shoved the weighty mass down into the dark pit of his being.

He let the numbness overtake him once more. *Yes, only that for now.* Otherwise, he would fly into an explosive rage or shatter into a million pieces, he wasn't sure which.

His beautiful Justine hovered between life and death in a musty dark room in a tenant's cottage. He covered his eyes with his cold hands as the raw truth seeped through him. The door creaked open, and his body flinched.

"Pardon, your Lordship, I've brought you some fresh tea," came Mrs. Shaw's careful voice. "Martin's here, sir. He has something to tell ye. Says it's important."

Heat roared through his body. *Martin?*

Gripping his cane, Brandon jerked up from the chair. "Have the boys brought the extra wood from Wolfsgate for your fires?"

"They have, sir." The older woman clasped her hands

together. "I'll keep her warm, don't fret now. I won't leave my lady alone. Doctor's told me all I need to do. If there's any change in her, I'll send for ye. Lizzie is on her way, as well."

With a final glance at his sleeping wife, Brandon quit the room. The ache in his knee shot through his thigh and grimacing he leaned on the damned cane. He closed the door behind him, and his tight gaze leveled on Martin.

He hated that Martin was doing anything for Justine.

He hated him.

Martin posture was stiff, his lips pressed together.

"How dare you even show your face here? How dare you?" Brandon spit out. Martin only glared at him, raising his chin. "Was she coming to you?"

A muscle along Martin's lean jaw pulsed. "I don't know what you're talking about, milord. I came here 'cause I found her saddle. It's been cut."

"Cut?"

"And a pin were inserted to weigh down on the horse, more like so' her ladyship wouldn't be able to control the animal. Found the wound on the horse to match." Martin's hands tensed at his sides as he took a step closer toward Brandon. "Simms is gone. He musta been ready and waiting in the stables and saddled the horse for her ladyship. I wasn't there, was I?" Martin held out a crumpled paper. "I found this in the stable."

Brandon snatched it. His eyes poured over a badly scribbled note insisting Lady Graven come to a tenant's cottage over an ill baby.

"There is no ill babe anywhere," Martin said through gritted teeth. 'Twas all a fiction to draw her out, to have her ride in the snow at a gallop and make that saddle tear apart and twist her."

Brandon's insides hardened. "Do we know where that bastard is?"

"He's gone. Mr. Davidson's looking, asking about in the

village. Dunno more." Martin's face was flushed, his eyes turbulent. "Someone else put him up to it."

Brandon's brow creased over the crumpled note in his hand. His thumb stroked the paper. Dark ivory, the same rag texture. He had received love letters on this very same paper a hundred years ago, and another just recently, hadn't he? Brandon crushed the paper between his hands.

"'Tis from Crestdown, in'it?" The vehemence in Martin's tone pounded in his head. "There's only one person who's ever hurt her, only one," Martin seethed, his voice raw, his eyes pooled in black pitch.

"What are you on about?"

"I know, sir," Martin said slowly, those black eyes even blacker. "I was there."

Brandon's cane clattered to the floor as he snapped up Martin's shirt collar in his fists and held him fast. "What do you know, you shit? What do you know?"

"The evil thing her brother did to her." Martin's haunted voice hung in the stale air between them.

The grim loathing on the young man's face seared Brandon like a stinging slap. "Why should I believe anything you have to say?"

"I was there in your grand house. I saw. I heard it all." Martin spewed the words as if releasing fire from his soul. "Do you really not know the truth, Lord Graven?"

"What truth, damn you?"

Martin lips twisted. "All you fine people so busy hiding the truth, running' from it. You're all still flesh and bone like the rest of us, aren't ye?"

Brandon shook Martin, shook the doors of hell. "Tell me."

"'Twas two years ago. I were in the kitchen at Wolfsgate. Molly was givin' me apples to bring home to the boys, and that's when I heard the carrying on. I heard them fighting in the study. Them both yelling at her, her crying. I rushed out to the hall, saw her run up the stairs. Then he chased after her."

Brandon's throat stung. He shoved Martin against the wall, his face inches from the lad's. "Who? Who chased her?"

"Your fine cousin, her stepbrother." Martin's dark eyes locked on Brandon. "I went up a few stairs. The door slammed behind them, him yelling at her more. Then the door broke open, and I heard feet running, heavier steps after, then a hard slap, and a crash on the floor.

I ran into the room at the top of the stairs, leaving the door open. She was sobbing, pleading with him. Suddenly she burst down the hall runnin', she musta gotten away from him. But she tripped on that bloody carpet and fell. I heard a rip, him pullin' at her dress. He was muttering some shite, mocking her. Cursing her. And then came that God awful crop lashing on her flesh."

"No."

"I heard it." Martin averted his gaze. "But it's her scream I'll never forget. Full of shock, full of sadness. He kept jeering on at her. Then his voice went all soft, and he were calling her Tina, telling her that he only wanted to take care of her, and of you, but she wouldn't let him. That she had to do what he wanted."

Brandon's body shook. "No..."

"There was all this strange whispering and sobbin'. All I could hear was her begging him, saying 'no, please no,' over and over." Martin choked on a breath and lifted his smoldering black eyes to Brandon's. "She knew what was comin'."

Brandon's pulse jammed in his neck. His knees locked. He pressed harder against Martin, pleading for more, pleading for no more.

"Then there was another scream." Martin's wet eyes glinted in the shadows of the room. "But this one was different, 'twas full of terror, full of pain."

Brandon's grip on Martin tightened, his knuckles white. "No!"

Martin let out a long hiss of air. "Yes, Lord Graven, yes. From my pathetic hiding place I heard your cousin grunting over her like a rutting pig."

Brandon's vision dissolved into a blur.

"Then she were silent."

A sharp slash pierced Brandon's gut ripping it wide open.

"T'was so hideous that silence," Martin breathed.

"No!" Brandon roared, his head fell against Martin's chest. *William.*

Always so clever. Spinning lies from threads of truth. He had woven his tales and ensnared Brandon into believing them all.

"We understand each other, don't we, Tina?"

Nausea roiled in his gut. How could he not have seen it? Her nightmares, her initial hesitation in bed, and then her sudden eagerness to experience it all, even his aggressiveness, as if she wanted to only plunge ahead and forget.

Forget.

Forget something so vile, a horror. Forget something that had been branded onto her spirit and onto her very body. Her beautiful, innocent body.

His speeding brain called up her constant anxiousness over William's retaliation, her tight-lipped patience with his own jealous rants over Andrew and Charles and Martin. She had swallowed it all in order to keep the bloody peace, and thus she had sacrificed her true, fine character. First to Andrew and then to Brandon, letting them think ill of her; that she was less than she actually was.

Brandon's brain ticked through all the times he had seen William and Justine together before. Both of them always remained cool and detached, keeping out of each other's way except for basic social pleasantries with barely a word spoken or a look exchanged unless necessary. If words were exchanged, they were brittle ones. Days ago William had spoken to her in an eerie way, used her nickname, even touched her. She had not seemed shocked nor surprised. She had swallowed it all down.

This was the secret William constantly used against her to his advantage, holding it over her head like an executioner's sword twisting it this way and that.

A noise rose in Martin's throat. "After he were done with her, he ran down the stairs, but he heard me open the door. He stopped and came at me. Like a demon he was, his eyes wild and wet with tears, his face red with scratches. He said if I told he'd come after me and throw Auntie Keren and the boys out of their home, leave them with nothing. And he'd tell everyone I had done it to her.

"Oh, I didn't care about meself, but I couldn't put the Shaws in danger. I was enough of a burden to 'em. And I couldn't have her be so humiliated. So, I agreed. God forgive me, I agreed." He let out a wail. "Who would've believed me anyway? Who would ever believe the bloody truth?" Martin let out a bitter laugh as Brandon's body sagged, his fingers digging into Martin's shoulders.

"Out the front door, the demon ran," Martin continued. "She were lying on the floor of that hallway weepin' silently. I hid and watched her. I knew she wouldn't want me to see her that way. All I wanted to do was..." Martin's breath hitched, he swallowed hard and sucked in air.

"She sat up slowly, crawled into her room, and locked the door behind her. Didn't come out for days. I rolled up that bloody carpet and burned it, I did. Didn't want her remembering every time she had to see it or tread on it. She noticed it missing later, but never said a word about it, and neither did I." Martin's watery eyes drifted beyond the room. "I couldn't protect her then, and I didn't protect her now."

"It's my job to protect her." Brandon seethed. "It's my job. Dear God!" He shoved at Martin's shoulders.

"You failed," breathed Martin. "I failed. Won't happen again. Never again. No."

"William told me that you and she had been together—"

"Of course, he did! And you believed him?" Martin's body bucked against Brandon's hold. "I adore her! She has been nothing but a kind, good friend to me. An angel. You don't deserve her! She knows that bastard better than all of you do."

The room swirled around Brandon, he stumbled against the wall. His head sank in his hands. Justine had taken the weight of his world on her delicate shoulders and suffered a long hell for it. William had made her lie to Andrew for his own benefit and had done it again when he forced her to lie to Brandon about Martin. He continually punished her, made her pay a heavy price for defying him over and over again.

Was that why when Justine had learned that Brandon was still alive in hospital, she brought him back to Wolfsgate to be her real husband? Not only to save his life and fortune, but to save herself from William as well? Had she feared that he would come back for more? Find a new way to humiliate her?

He would have.

Brandon steadied himself against the wall. He wouldn't let that happen. She hadn't left him. Their life together was real, she had been the one who first chose to make it real. He pushed back from the wall.

There was no Wolfsgate without Justine.

There was no him without her.

He would fight for her. Fight for them both.

CHAPTER SIXTY-FIVE

"COME SIR, SHE'S AWAKENED!"

Mrs. Shaw, her face flushed, was at the door. Brandon brushed past Martin and his aunt and went to his wife's bedside. Justine's eyes were open.

"Justine?" Brandon put a hand against her face. Her eyes slowly moved towards his voice. "I'm right here darling, you're safe. You're at Mrs. Shaw's cottage. You fell off your horse. I found you and brought you here."

"It hurts," she whispered.

"Where, love?"

Her face tensed. "Everywhere."

Brandon bit the inside of his cheek to stem the fury in his blood. Thank God she was awake and talking with him, but she was so weak, and he was helpless to do anything about it. She needed him now. She needed him to be strong and sensible.

He swallowed past the dry rocks lodged in his throat. "Dr. Langham needs to know where you hurt in order to help you. Your left arm is broken, but he set and bound it, so have a care."

Her round eyes darted down to her arm, her pale bottom lip trembled. She was going to be fine. She had to be. He couldn't lose her. Not now. He had so much to make up for. Mrs. Shaw entered the room and raised the blanket from the bottom of the bed. Her gaze darted to Brandon for a moment. He nodded at her.

"Can you wiggle your toes for me, Lady Graven?" Mrs. Shaw asked in a soothing tone.

"Toes?"

Brandon gently tucked her hand in his. "Yes, love."

A smile illuminated Mrs. Shaw's face. "Aw, that's nice now." She nodded at Brandon as she smoothed the blanket over Justine's legs again.

"Martin, fetch Langham," Brandon said. "He'll want to see her right away."

"Yes, milord."

Warmth flooded Brandon's chest easing his rigid limbs and joints. He planted a kiss on Justine's hand. "You're doing fine, my love." Brandon forced his lips to form a slight smile. "It's good to see your eyes open, Jus. I can't tell you how I missed them, those beautiful velvet eyes."

"You're worried."

"I'm relieved. I have you back," he said through the needles in his throat. He leaned over her and touched his lips to her mouth. "That's better."

"Brandon..."

"I thought...I thought for a time that you were gone, Jus. First I thought you had left me. Half your clothes were gone, your ring."

"Lizzie's been in a fit of cleaning and mending. Once the message came, I rushing and left the ring."

"Georgina and Charles hadn't heard from you. Then I thought you might've come here. When I saw Persephone wandering alone in the woods, saw you crumpled in the snow, I thought I had lost you all over again. I'm so grateful to all that is holy that you have returned to me." His voice shook, and his hand gripped hers tighter, his eyes stinging. "I can't lose you. I can't."

"I heard…"

"Let me have this," he said. She bit her lip. He got into the bed and stretched out alongside her. His hands cautiously roamed over her. "I have you back." He kissed her cold fingers and rubbed them. "I have you back, my sweet thing."

They laid together quietly until Dr. Langham finally arrived. The few breaks, the sprains, and the large number of bruises seemed to be her only injuries. Everyone heaved a collective sigh of relief.

"And the child?" Brandon asked Langham when he finally emerged from the room.

"There is no more evidence of any bleeding. I've told her. She's in a bit of a shock over it, I think," Langham pinched the bridge of his nose and adjusted his spectacles. "I'll check in on her tomorrow. She will stay here for a few more days. I don't want to take any chances."

Brandon saw him out. He looked in on Justine. Mrs. Shaw was with her, adjusting bedclothes and blankets, preparing her medicine.

"Sir, Mr. Montclare and a lady are outside to see ye," young John whispered hovering in the doorway.

Brandon squeezed the boy's shoulder as he passed through and flung open the door. Georgina and Charles stood outside, the hoods of their cloaks covering their heads as the snow flurries fell thickly about them.

Georgina rushed to him. "Lord Graven, how is Justine? Is she all right? May I please see her?"

"She's awake now, just a few broken bones and plenty of bruises. Go to her."

Georgina bounced up on her toes, her stricken features brightening. She glanced back at Charles for a moment and then immediately entered the cottage, the door clanging behind her.

Charles stood motionless. "Say it was an accident. Say it, dammit." Brandon only shook his head and glowered at Charles. "No. No. He couldn't have done this, not to his own sister."

"He did do this," Brandon said. "And more."

Charles turned his head away and sucked in air. "Christ! How could he go this far?"

"Because he's always shown nothing but contempt for her. We need to stop ignoring that fact. And he has had nothing but contempt for me for a long time. Now she's my wife and she's carrying my child."

Charles paled. "Dear God, did it survive?"

"So far, yes."

Charles moved closer, his mouth a hard line, his eyes narrow. "Bloody hell, I warned you, Graven."

"You dare come here tonight to show your dramatic sympathies, your bloody concern?" Brandon asked. "Such a bastard! All along you were playing a role in William's intricate little plot."

"You played your own game, Graven, let's not forget."

"Pity for you I never had any intention of putting my cock inside Amanda. You didn't count on that though, did you?"

"Graven—"

"You assumed she'd suck me right in, and I'd be thrilled, grateful even. You were so wrong. You do well to remember that Justine is not so pliable to one such as you, dripping with honeyed compliments and florid attentions."

Charles's eyes flashed. "Ah, your wife appreciated the attention, I'll have you know. How did you think she felt watching you and Amanda catching up on old times over and over again?"

Brandon knew Charles was right and he hated himself for it, but this very second he hated Charles more. His fist shot out, landing on Charles's jaw. Charles fell back on the snowy ground cursing. He managed to get up on his knees, and Brandon stood over him, the two of them breathing heavily.

Charles stood. "I loathe myself for my role in this deception."

"As well you should."

Charles wiped the side of his mouth with the back of his hand. "I truly like Justine."

"I'm warning you, Montclare."

"No, you idiot, I mean she's a fine, good woman, intelligent. I could not in all conscience go through with my original plan of seduction."

"Bloody hell—"

"I'm being forthright here!"

"Should I be impressed?" Brandon scowled at him. "Are you saying you actually have a conscience?"

"Yes, dammit!" Charles brushed the snow and grime off himself. "I've come to realize that self-indulgence truly reeks after a while.

Brandon lifted an eyebrow. "Oh? And how did you come to that brilliant conclusion?"

"It was seeing you with Justine. She enters a room, smiles at you and you're...different. Her concern for you and desire to keep you safe, happy, and comfortable are obvious. And you for her safety and happiness. It's as if there's some sort of secret language between you that only the two of you share and understand." He wiped a hand over his face. "It surprised me."

"Surprised you?"

"That I liked it!" Charles said. "Look at me. I keep running around in circles. Same circles, different players. Like I did with Amanda."

"I do not want to hear this."

"No, I need to tell you, Graven. I pursued Amanda after you left England, and she enjoyed it. I fell hard or thought I had. But she chose to marry William. He beat me to it, asking for her hand. I do not take loss well."

Brandon wiped his brow with his arm. "He just struck a better bargain, more like."

"Yes, probably," Charles said. "Then about a year ago she

became flirtatious and wouldn't take no for an answer. I wanted her, always did, but I wanted to punish her too. So I took her. At the end of it, I knew I'd be the one able to walk away free. She'd still be married to William."

"Montclare, really." Brandon's jaw hardened.

"They're not unhappy together, you know. She has a great affection for him, she's simply greedy in many different ways."

"I don't give a damn."

"I was looking for a way out. Then when I saw you and Justine together—"

"You decided you wanted to change up for my wife?" Brandon asked.

"No! Well, yes—but that's not my point here." Charles's palm went to his temple. "I realized how your wife loved you, and what that was—the bloody grace of it. A man could endure a great deal if it meant he'd have someone at his side the way Lady Graven is at yours." He cleared his throat, his eyes meeting Brandon's dark gaze. "And then I felt small and piteous, not to mention deceitful to the both of you and, dare I say it, to myself in the end. Forgive me, Brandon. I beg you."

"Now you would have me believe your attraction to manipulation has suddenly lost its lustre?"

"Yes, that's what I'm saying."

Brandon smirked and untied his horse's reins. "You're too good at it though. It'll be difficult for you."

"You got over your compulsion didn't you?"

"The struggle never ends Charles, be forewarned." Brandon heaved himself up into his saddle.

Charles tightened his lips together. "Where are you off to? Is there anything I can do?"

"I must pay my cousin a visit." He rubbed the side of his horse's neck.

"Now?" Charles asked "Are you sure?"

"Quite sure."

Charles's eyes narrowed. "What are you not telling me?"

"Get out of my way, Montclare." Brandon drew on his reins.

"Hang on, Graven. I'd better come with you and prevent you from getting sent off to gaol for murder." Charles unfastened the reins of his horse at the post.

"I don't think William will be too pleased to see you," Brandon said.

"No matter." Charles cocked an eyebrow. "I've got you at my back, haven't I?"

CHAPTER SIXTY-SIX

BRANDON SHOVED at the ornately carved doors of Crestdown and marched through the long front hall. One enormous candelabra held a mass of candles flickering their wan light across the gold-trimmed walls. Melting snow and water shook from his boots and cloak. Charles strode in behind him.

Amanda's eyes widened at the sight of them, her hands clutching the polished handrail. "What are you doing here?"

"Where is he?" Brandon's voice echoed in the long hall. His harsh tone made her face tighten.

She swept down the stairs, her head held high, the gold-painted flowers along the stairwell glimmering in the dim light as she passed. She reminded him of an overwrought actress making her debut on an excessively decorated stage.

What do you want?" She frowned at the puddles on the parquet floor.

"Your husband has much to answer for," Brandon replied. "Now where is the bastard?"

Charles leaned into the drawing room. He pushed open the ornate doors of the dining room. He shot Brandon a look, and Brandon charged down the dark hallway toward the library.

"Has something happened?" asked Amanda.

"This is going to get ugly, I suggest you go back upstairs." Charles followed Brandon.

The library door was closed, and Brandon turned the handle, but the door was locked. He tried it again more forcefully this time. Strangled voices rose from within the room, and Brandon kicked at the ancient door handle. Amanda screeched from somewhere behind him.

The bolt gave way, the wood splintered, and the door bounced ajar. Martin held William in a chokehold with a knife at his throat. Blood stained the front of William's shirt at his chest and side, and his wrists were tied behind him.

"William!" Amanda's voice rang out.

"You started without me, Martin," Brandon said.

"Christ!" Charles pulled Amanda back.

"He must bleed like the animal he is for hurting her," Martin declared as he shook William. "For that lash you gave her. For that scream of hers that filled the whole house. Can't you still hear it, Mr. Treharne? I bet it comes to you in yer dreams, eh? A scream like that never fades from memory. It's in my dreams."

"Dear God, who is he talking about? What is going on?" Amanda stumbled back into Charles. He steadied her and shoved her to the side with a warning look.

Martin lashed the knife across William's arm and drew a line of blood. "I heard her crying when she thought she be all alone in the world." Martin's eyes blazed over William. "And every night after for months. Now this, today. No. You must be stopped. And if none of you fine gentlemen will do it—" Martin's burning gaze flared at Brandon and Charles "—He is one of your own after all. I'll do it." He dragged the blade over William's chest this time, and the blood seeped from the torn flesh. The knife halted and remained at the artery in William's neck.

William moaned, his body stiffened, then twitched. His head fell forward and his legs buckled, then surged up again.

"No better than a pig," Martin hissed.

Brandon moved closer. Martin's head snapped at him, his eyes wide. "Time's over for the gentleman's way. He must pay for what he done. With blood." Martin drew the knife into William's shoulder and dragged it down his arm. Blood poured from the ripped flesh, and William grunted. Amanda shrieked once more. Charles darted forward.

Brandon held out his hand to stop him. "Judge and jury then, it works for me. You hold him, Martin. I'll ask the questions. Charles, you keep Mrs. Treharne out of the way." Martin brought the knife back to William's neck.

Brandon stood before his wretched cousin. "Why did you do it? Why did you call her out and have Simms cut her saddle?"

William's eyes struggled to focus on Brandon. Martin pressed the knife in on William's flesh. "Answer!"

"What have you done?" Amanda's shaky voice rose up.

William's dazed eyes raked over Brandon, his breath labored. "You have her in your bed, don't you? Why should she bear your merry-begotten? A precious heir for your precious Wolfsgate?"

Amanda's hands flew to her mouth.

A bitter laugh ripped from Brandon's throat. "You put her in my bed, William. You bound us together by marriage. You put that quill in my hand and hers. May I take this opportunity to say thank you for my wife, cousin."

William struggled to meet his gaze. He grunted, stumbling against Martin.

"I know what happened in my house when I was away. I know what you did to her. How could you? She was part of your family."

"She is not my family! Her and her mother—interlopers, the two of them."

"She was a girl who only had you for her protection, who depended on you for everything."

"She is nothing to me." William raised his face higher

grunting with the effort. "She resisted my wishes at every turn, kept pleading for you. She had to do as she was told."

"Bloody hell," muttered Charles.

William's head hung from his shoulders. A hiss and groan of breath heaved from his bloodied lips. "Did I ruin her for you?"

Brandon backhanded William hard across the face, then again across the other cheek, the splitting cracks ricocheted around the library. Blood and saliva splattered against the leather bound tomes that lined the ordered shelves. Brandon's eyes glittered over his cousin. "That's what you wanted, wasn't it? To ruin her for everybody?"

A sneer twisted William's face as he hung his heavy eyes on Brandon. "Yes!" He spit blood on the floor, a cracked laugh tumbling from his bloody mouth. "I've had both your women, and that gives me great satisfaction."

"I'm going to be sick," Amanda moaned.

Brandon shot Martin a look then threw a punch at William square in the face. Blood gushed from William's mouth soaking his teeth. He choked and heaved for air.

"Tell me he deserves to live, sir." Martin scored William's flesh with the knife once more. William howled.

"Please, oh please, stop!" said Amanda.

"Listen to that, William," Brandon said. "Surprisingly enough there is one person begging for mercy on your behalf. Or maybe she's only thinking of herself yet again, eh? Quite touching either way."

"No mercy for this beast," said Martin.

"Yes, he is a beast, and he deserves to suffer and more for everything he's done, but you don't deserve to hang for it, Martin." Brandon's teeth dug into his bottom lip. "Although I would dearly love to assist you in his demise."

William's body swayed. More of Amanda's muffled cries rose up.

Brandon sat up on the ornately carved rococo desk and

crossed his arms. "Let us bargain, cousin. Are you listening?" William grunted and his eyes flickered up to meet Brandon's. "Martin releases you. Martin disappears. You and your wife go on and lead your interesting life together undisturbed in London. You stay the hell away from me and my wife, you stay away from Wolfsgate, and the entire bloody village unless I allow it at some point in the distant future. Furthermore, we never discuss this again. Every single one of us in this room is honour bound to utter silence."

William twisted in Martin's hold, his face black.

"Perhaps Martin should have some more fun with you? I'll join him for good measure while you take your time to consider your decision. I find I'm in the mood for blood this evening."

Amanda let out a sob. "Brandon!"

"This deal also includes any retribution against Montclare," Brandon said. "Frankly, you gave up that privilege the minute you and your wife set him on Justine." Brandon leaned in closer to William's gnarled face. "Do you hear? Otherwise I will let it be known that Amanda not only carries a great deal of debt and is unable to pay, but also has a long list of paramours. And we all know how that would play out, don't we? Points for the mystery lovers, demerits for the husband, and as for the lady..."

William wrenched his body in Martin's hold. "Goddamn you!"

"He already has, cousin. From getting on that ship to come home, my mad imprisonment in that hospital, to my wife now lying in a stranger's bed with broken bones and a hundred bruises. Luckily she regained consciousness before I came here, so I am in a somewhat generous mood. Now—" Brandon sat back against the desk. "Think again."

"Was there a babe inside her?" William asked, his voice low.

"Bloody hell, man!" Charles exploded. Martin pulled tighter on the ropes.

Brandon sucked in air, his lungs burning. "Yes. And my child lives inside her despite your efforts. He survived and will be born."

William stopped struggling against Martin. His strained gaze fell to the floor.

"Are we all agreed?" Brandon's voice surged.

"Agreed." Charles said.

"Y-yes," Amanda sobbed.

"Sir—"

"You heard me, Martin," Brandon said.

Martin's face tightened. "Agreed."

"William?" Brandon pulled his cousin's head up by his hair. William only grimaced. "Not a word to my wife ever. Not a look. Nothing." Brandon shot Amanda a scowl. She nodded at him.

"Yes," William spit out. Amanda's shoulders dropped, her hands trembled at her mouth.

"And Martin disappears," Brandon said. "I leave with him here tonight, and you do not follow him, you do not look for him. Ever. He ceases to exist for you, is that understood?"

"Yes, goddammit," William said. "Get your dog off me!"

Brandon lifted his chin at Martin, but the lad's eyes narrowed in response.

"Martin," Brandon said, his voice low. "Let him go and come away. We're leaving Mr. and Mrs. Treharne to their eternal happiness."

"My lord—"

"Do as I say, dammit."

Martin's face hardened, and he took in a deep breath holding it in. He cut the ropes binding William and slowly lowered the blood-covered knife in his hand. He shoved William forward, and he landed face down on his desk.

"See to your husband, Mrs. Treharne. Remember, not a word about this evening if you want your dark secrets to remain within our family circle."

He took hold of Martin's arm, but there were shuffling move-ments and a muffled noise that made him swivel back.

"Brandon!" yelled Charles.

William held a pistol aimed straight at him. "You're not going anywhere!" William's voice was thick, the heavy pistol shaking in his hold. "Do you really think you can threaten me? Force my hand?" He raised the pistol higher. The air was instantly sucked out of the room.

"What's the party for, boy?" Richard's thin voice quivered from the doorway.

"Fa-ther?" Geoffrey asked, his eyes round, his little hand in Richard's, a finger in his tiny red mouth.

Amanda screamed, and a cracking blast exploded.

CHAPTER SIXTY-SEVEN

ACRID SMOKE CHOKED the small library. Brandon grabbed Martin and pulled him down to the floor with a thud.

Charles and Amanda lunged at her son. "No!" she screamed.

Brandon crawled over to his uncle's crumpled body. He touched his neck to find his pulse, but it was no more. Richard's old wig lay lopsided on his head, a frozen look etched over his distorted, paper-skinned face. Blood seeped quickly from his chest, staining his faded blue silk dressing gown.

"He's dead," Brandon said.

The smoldering pistol hung from William's hand and dropped with a loud thud to the desk.

Charles thrust Geoffrey into his mother's embrace. "Mummy!" The boy's breath snagged in his tears.

"Oh, my darling boy. Hush, hush now." Amanda clutched her son as she moved back toward a wall of books.

William sank to his knees before his father's bleeding corpse, his eyes drowning in his face.

"Mummy! I want Grandfather!" Geoffrey's tiny hand reached out.

"Hush, my love." Amanda kissed Geoffrey's forehead, her hand sinking into his hair.

"Now there are more secrets to keep in the family, are there not?" Brandon asked. "William, do you agree?"

"Yes," William said without looking up.

"And if you want my and Charles's cooperation in keeping these heavy secrets, keeping your family from scandal, you must comply."

William raised his bleary eyes at Brandon.

"It is common knowledge that Richard had lost his senses. You will say he had a fit, was wandering the house. It was dark, you mistook him for an intruder. You were frightened for your family's well-being. Martin, where did you get the knife?"

"The kitchen. Came in through there," said Martin.

"Excellent. Give it to me." Martin gave him the bloodied knife. "Let's make this theatre really believable for the good doctor, eh?" Brandon placed the knife by Richard's hand on the floor. "There, Richard threatened you with a kitchen knife. You took defensive action."

Geoffrey's muffled crying filled the room.

"Say you sent for me and Charles. We will bear witness to your account," Brandon said glancing at Amanda.

"Yes." She nodding stiffly, her blue eyes clear.

"Where are Andrew and your father?" Brandon asked.

"In town."

"All the better."

William's eyes remained on his father's lifeless body. "Dear God!" William closed his eyes.

"Ah, it's too late for you to look to Providence now, there's no time for that," Brandon said. "Do you agree?"

"I do," William muttered, his jaw sagging.

"For the sake of clarity, I shall repeat myself. I will forgive your attempts to kill my wife and me and Martin and Charles tonight. And I will do this one last thing: I will clear your debts in the village so you can leave here directly. The gambling debts are your responsibility." Brandon turned to face Amanda. "Do you understand, Mrs. Treharne?"

"I understand," she said. "Thank you."

"Answer me, you devil," Brandon said to William. "There shall be no revenge, no retaliation between us, do you understand?" William mutely looked up at him.

Brandon leaned into him. "You don't deserve to live for what you did to Justine. If it were up to me alone I would kill you. But I will not because it would make my wife unhappy, and I want to live a long and happy life with my wife and child without your stain on my hands. I cannot bear the sight of you."

William gaped dully at him.

"They saved our son from your pistol, do you hear?" Amanda shouted.

William's weary, leaden eyes slid to his wife then back to Brandon. "Paid in full."

CHAPTER SIXTY-EIGHT

"HAVE MORE TEA MA'AM. Your medicine is in it, 'twill do you a world of good for the pain." Justine took the cup from Mrs. Shaw's hands and drank more of the bitter, lukewarm fluid. Mrs. Shaw took back the cup and handed Justine a cloth.

"Do you know that I am with child?" Justine asked.

The woman smiled down at Justine. "Isn't it wonderful, Lady Graven? You're to be a mother. Mother to the heir of Wolfsgate." Mrs. Shaw's soft face beamed at her. Justine swallowed, the bitterness of the medicine still coating her mouth. Her head sank back into the pillows.

Mother to Brandon's baby? It was inevitable, but barely hoped for. In fact, she'd never let herself hope for it. It was too precious a desire that she kept locked in the deepest place inside herself.

A baby would certainly cement her and Brandon's marriage. He had even told her he loved her. Wasn't that every girl's dream to have a fine man declare his love to her, to claim her for his own, and for her to bear his child?

But everything between her and Brandon was blemished, scarred. William had once again resolved everything in his favour, and she would have to bear Brandon's disappointment forever over William's poisonous lie of a love affair between her and Martin. She could never tell Brandon the truth. The truth was unspeakable and would spell disaster for all of them. It had already spelled disaster for Martin, and that was a blistering wound. No, she would never risk Brandon's safety or that of their child's at the altar of William's cruelty.

A heavy tear fell from her eye and slid down her cheek.

"Why do I not think that is a tear of joy, Lady Graven?" Mrs. Shaw's voice poked at her chest.

She glanced up at her and wiped the tear away. "It's too late now."

"What do you mean by that?" Mrs. Shaw plucked the cloth napkin from Justine's fingers and dabbed it over her cheek.

"It is a long and intricate story, complicated by someone who won't stop interfering, and, I fear, never will."

"Be that as it may, you are married to a fine man, and he loves you," Mrs. Shaw voice was firm. "Lord Graven was destroyed when he brought you here, absolutely ravaged. Him watching over you, and you lying there like a broken doll beyond his help. I never seen the like before, and doubt I ever shall again." Her brow furrowed and her shoulders stiffened. "'Tis a rare thing when a marriage has such affection. You have that. Be grateful for it and don't ever turn your back on it. And don't ye tell me I know not what I speak of, ma'am. I know of menfolk. Had me fill."

Justine's head sank back against the pillow. "Does not a man's ardour fade?"

Mrs. Shaw took a seat in the chair by the bed, her lips in a firm line. "To be sure. But not for all. Not him. Not the way he looks at you, speaks to you. No, not him. He's like his father before him, that one. Eyes and heart for only one woman. Oh, he adores you. I warrant he doesn't give you a moment's rest in that bed of yours." She laughed softly, a hand at her mouth.

A physical ache spiraled inside Justine at the memory of the sensations of Brandon's body pressing in on hers...his touch over her flesh...the tang of his salty skin on her tongue...his unfettered groans of satisfaction as he moved inside her. Her face heated.

"Hmm." Mrs. Shaw chuckled. "I see you agree with me."

"Still, he won't want the baby." Justine bit her lip.

"Why ever not? Excuse me for asking ma'am, but is the babe Lord Graven's?"

"Of course it is."

Mrs. Shaw's eyes bulged at her. "So why wouldn't he want his own child, I ask you?"

"Does he know?"

"Of course he knows. Doctor's told him. He was quite moved." Mrs. Shaw waved a finger at her. "You are making me quite cross, you are, milady. No, ma'am. You are wrong. He wants this child. Why wouldn't he? Whoo!"

"It's a matter of trust, Mrs. Shaw. I have reason to believe he mistrusts me and—"

"You are wrong. I refuse to hear another word about it." Mrs. Shaw raised her eyebrows and her hands high in the air. "Wrong!"

CHAPTER SIXTY-NINE

BRANDON WAS PLEASED to see the colour had seeped back into Justine's skin, giving her back the freshness that always marked her. He had been relieved to hear from Mrs. Shaw that there had been no more bleeding. There was still hope for their babe. He clung to that hope as he'd clung to the broken mast of the shattered, wrecked ship in that fateful tempest years ago.

He laid down on the bedcovers next to her, and placed a small bouquet of pink viburnum from their garden in her hand.

Charles and Martin had left William's house and gone on to Wolfsgate to wait for him. He had stayed on at Crestdown to assist William and Amanda with Dr. Langham's visit and Richard's corpse. Once home, Brandon made arrangements for Martin to board the next ship to Jamaica and head for his office there. He wrote out a letter of introduction on the young man's behalf to his chief manager.

Martin refused.

"Are you mad?" Brandon asked. "After everything we've been through tonight? After what you did to him? You know William cannot be trusted. He might one day seek his revenge on you for your little stunt. That one such as you bested him will rot inside him forever. I gave my word that you would vanish."

"I will not—"

"This is for all of us, Martin. Most of all for you. You have no real family here, no prospects. This is a good opportunity for you, a new start. For God's sake, man, take it."

Martin turned his face away from Brandon's heavy gaze.

"Lady Justine would want this for you," Brandon said hoarsely, his hand raking over his throbbing scalp. "Do it for her."

The resignation swelled in Martin's eyes, and he finally nodded. He shrugged on an old blue wool cloak of Brandon's that Molly had fetched for him, and he took the satchel she prepared for him in which there was a loaf of bread, cheese, sausages, and small pies. In the courtyard of Wolfsgate Brandon handed him a pouch of coins and the letter.

"Mr. Montclare and Mr. Davidson will take you to Southampton and book passage for you," Brandon said. "It is a fine place, Jamaica. A beautiful island. You may find it strange, certainly exotic, but it will be an adventure, Martin, a new life. Your hard work will be rewarded, and I will be glad to have you there on my behalf." He put his hands on Martin's shoulders and squeezed. "You are a fine young man, and I thank you for defending Lady Graven, for having a mind to her all these years." He took his hand in his and shook it.

Charles and Davidson waited for Martin in a carriage at the end of the drive. They would meet with a hired coach in the next village.

Martin raised his chin at Brandon as he adjusted the leather strap of the satchel over the bulky wool cloak. "You'll not forget the flowers. You'll give them to her. You'll tell her—"

"I will. I promise."

"Be good to her, milord. She's..." He pressed his lips together, his chin trembling.

Brandon had always felt keen annoyance and stabs of jealousy over Martin, and now he only felt the highest regard for him. Martin had been Justine's only witness to the truth, had protected her darkest secret, had been her steadfast, loyal friend. He had appreciated her precious worth long before he had, and Brandon admired him for it.

Brandon raised his hand in farewell.

Martin turned toward the waiting carriage. His wool cloak billowed behind him. Brandon watched as the gloom of the cold night swallowed an exceptional grieving young man from his sight.

CHAPTER SEVENTY

"BRANDON?" Justine's small voice perforated the darkness.

"Jus?" He raised himself from her side. "How do you feel?"

"Better." She smiled weakly at him, the strain in her eyes easing when they caught his gaze in the glow of the firelight.

"What's this?" She fingered the pink blossoms, her eyes softening. "They're lovely."

"From Martin. He wanted you to have them. He wanted you to know that he will never forget you." Her clouded eyes darted up at his. "He's left."

"What do you mean he's left?"

"I sent him to Jamaica."

"Why?"

"He attacked William last night. Wouldn't let him go. We struck a deal so that all this is kept between us without retributions." Brandon sat on the side of the bed.

"No retributions? Truly?"

"Yes, love. I am satisfied on your behalf as per your urgent and repeated requests for peace. Last night's events were heavy enough, indeed."

She studied his taut expression. "Tell me of these heavy events?"

"Another time, Jus."

"Brandon, please."

Brandon frowned and took her hand in his. "William tried to shoot me with his pistol, but he ended up killing his father instead. I pushed Martin out of the way, and Charles covered Geoffrey, who had been with his grandfather."

"Oh my God!" She squeezed his fingers tightly. "Whatever William is, he truly loved his father."

Brandon rubbed the back of his neck. "Amanda was there as well. She knows he's responsible for this." Justine's lips parted as if to speak. "Shh, love. The result is that Amanda is humbled, William is in shock, and Richard is where he should be. The child is safe, and Martin is far away from all of them and onto a new life." He let out a sigh. "He's a good man. He deserves a new start. Perhaps now, you and I can finally start ours without inter-ference at long bloody last."

"Ours?" she murmured into the fragrant flowers.

"Our life together." He turned over her hand in his and touched his lips to her palm, then her wrist. His grey-green eyes rested on her. "With our child, Lady Graven."

"Brandon..."

"All right, Justine, say it. I'm ready for it now." He crossed his arms at his chest.

"There's no need for—"

"For what, Jus? Go on."

"For your kindness."

Brandon's head fell back and he laughed.

"What is so funny?" Justine winced with pain as she struggled against the headboard. "Why are you laughing at me? We're having a serious conversation, and you're laughing?"

"I see my Mistress of Supreme Self-Control has returned."

"What?" Her brows knit together and she planted her arms at

her sides into the bed to lift herself higher, but it was useless. "Brandon, you're not listening to what I have to say." She fell back on the pillows once again.

"No, Justine, you're the one not listening—to me or to yourself." He leaned over her. "I'm not going to let you finish this ridiculous denial you've conjured in your head. I cannot bear it, and I swear, if you go on I'll either laugh or explode in a rage.

"I love you. It's not kindness or obligation, it's bloody love. It's all the times you've held my hand and helped me walk the straight and narrow. All the times you've stood with me through the drama of the past months. You bathed me, dressed me, fed me, put up with my temper and my mania. Made me laugh, worked beside me day and night without complaint. Encouraged me in all things. Poured me a glass of brandy when I didn't deserve it, and then another and another." He let out a sigh, and her gaze darted down to their hands.

"It's the passion I feel for you in the middle of the night in our bed, when I reach for you, and you press against me. Any time of day when you give me that half smile. Even when you're mad at me, and your eyes get all fiery and you stomp away, and then you come stomping right back just to try to get the last word in." A grin curled the edges of his lips as the sweet pressure of her fingers squeezing his hand warmed his skin.

"But—"

"No." His thumb stroked the inside of her wrist, and he tilted his head at her. "Justine, please. I know that William lied to me about Martin. I know what he did to you. That he forced himself on you. I know."

Justine blanched, her gaze dropped down to the delicate flowers in her hand.

"They were trying to force you to marry me," he whispered. "And you refused?"

She nodded.

"So he assaulted you."

"He was so angry with me. He—"

"He humiliated you, hurt you in the worst possible way."

All the miserable, horrible cards were on the table now. No more hiding. She could finally be free of it. Be free of the fear, and all the lies crafted upon that fear. Justine's grip on the flowers tightened. Her lower lip quivered.

Brandon's nostrils flared. "What is it?"

"After, he told me he was pleased that I could no longer marry properly. That any man in his right mind would always be suspicious of me and eventually turn me out. He had made it so I was only fit to marry you in your mad, half-dead state. That if you were ever to return home and bed me, my...condition would be a humiliation for you."

"What a clever little bastard." Brandon took in a deep breath. "We proved him wrong. We've deprived him of that satisfaction, just as you said."

She glanced away, but he drew her face back to him. "Let me say this once and for all, Justine. You told me once that you are not worthy, that you're tarnished. That's not true. You're stronger than those words, those ideas. You've pulled yourself up and walked on after all the things he's done to you. You've faced him since, been in the same room with him, been civil to him in public and alone, carried yourself with great dignity. You've taken care of yourself, gone out into the world, not scurried away into a hole somewhere and given up. That takes an unbelievable amount of strength." He wiped at his face, his eyes shining.

"Do not assume how I feel about it. Do not attempt to give me an easy excuse to reject you as any other man might. I'm not any other man. I'm the manic egotistical bastard who adores and admires you." He squeezed her hand. "I'm the man who loves you."

He clutched her hand, brushing it with his lips. "You are bright and clean. The bright and clean I've barely ever known and have always lacked. I'm not letting go of it for anything in the world. You took a risk in bringing me home and living with me. And you were right to enjoy what we have had between us, to reach out and grab at life. You are so bloody brave. I want that too. I want to truly live, to be that brave. I want us. Us, together."

Brandon stretched out next to her on the bed and brought their entwined hands to his chest, his molten grey green gaze locked on hers.

"The passion I feel for you when I touch you deep, when I'm moving inside you, isn't just what my cock needs from a woman. It's what I need from you, from your sweet body and your beautiful spirit," he whispered roughly against her ear. "We are lovers, you and I. Between us it is gentle and wild, frenzied and sweet. It's good, and we make that together.

"That's what we are, Justine—lovers, husband and wife, partners in this enterprise called life." He leaned up on an elbow over her, his warm eyes soft and full. "Do you want it too, Justine?"

Her chest heaved, her eyes were wet. "I want it too."

His fingers gently tugged at the bodice of her nightdress and he stroked the warm satiny skin along her collarbone.

"Know this, my love," he whispered. "When I made you mine that very first time, whatever came before simply fell away."

She let out a cry, and it set his heart spinning.

"And the baby—" Brandon's lips formed a smile against her cheek. His hand travelled under the thick quilt and down her torso to rest on her belly. "Oh, Jus," he sighed. "There aren't words to describe that. At least I haven't found them yet."

The smile lingered on his lips, its warmth radiating over her skin like the hot summer sun. He snapped a small flower from the bouquet and tucked it in her hair, then his finger traced the edge of her face down to her chin.

The tears finally escaped her eyes, and her fingers curled into the thin wool fabric of his sleeve. Her fingers released their grip on the flowers, and her hands tucked around his middle. "Hold me, Bran," she breathed in his throat.

"What is it, love? Tell me."

"After I fell off the horse, I heard the wolf howling in the woods. I heard him, Bran."

"I heard him too."

" For the first time, I wasn't afraid. It was a comfort, because I knew."

"What did you know?"

"I knew then you would come for me, Brandon. I knew you would find me because he would lead you to me."

"He did, my love. He did."

CHAPTER SEVENTY-ONE

A BITTER WIND blew every so often to remind him that high winter had arrived and he should not be outside for too long, but it could not be helped. He hadn't gone to his uncle's funeral, he had brought his wife home to Wolfsgate instead. But today he had wanted to see his uncle's grave. To know that just as Richard was buried in the ground, so were the horrible events of that night. His gloved hand stroked the head of Annie's angel as he turned to leave.

Charles waited for him by his horse. "Everything go as planned?" Brandon asked.

"Yes, he got on the ship. We stayed until it sailed." Charles' lips pulled in and settled into a firm line.

"Good."

"How is our happy couple?"

Brandon sighed. "William's quite altered. I suppose killing your own father does that to you. Not to mention having your son witness it."

"For God's sake, I don't think I shall ever forget it," Charles muttered. "He could have killed the boy. And Lady Graven? Is she home now?"

447

"Yes, she's home and much improved." Brandon unfastened the reins of his horse from the post.

"May I see her?"

Brandon only tilted his head at Charles.

"Please, Graven. I would like to see for myself that she is well."

"Would you now?" Brandon smirked at him as he mounted his horse.

"I do feel a measure of responsibility here. I should have woken up to it sooner, then perhaps William wouldn't have gone directly after Justine. He and Amanda both played me for their own purposes, and I foolishly allowed it."

"That's who you are though, Charles. A player."

Charles let out a huff. "I want to reform. Am I not allowed?"

Brandon settled in his saddle, a grin passing over his lips. "Montclare, for some reason my wife likes you and has even asked about you, so I will not deny your request. Come along. Georgina's with her now."

"Is she?" Charles pulled his frock coat tighter about him under his cloak and mounted his horse.

Brandon's lips twitched. "Yes, which means, you will grovel to them both and beg forgiveness for your horrid behavior, and I will be greatly entertained by the spectacle."

Charles only grinned.

CHAPTER SEVENTY-TWO

"What are you doing?"

Justine's hand jumped to her throat where she had just clasped her new emerald necklace. She flushed. "Admiring your Christmas present."

A smile curled the edge of his mouth. "I came to say goodnight. I know the hour is late, but I still have some correspondence to go over." He stared at the necklace. He stared at her staring at her necklace in the looking glass. "You like it?"

"Very, very much."

He absorbed the warmth radiating between them. The small scars on her temple had whitened now and were barely visible. She never complained about them, his beautiful, un-vain wife, but they bothered him. Those tiny scars reminded him of all that she had endured. His lips touched her temple as his hand pressed in on her lower back.

"Brandon, do you think Martin will be happy in Jamaica?"

"He's a hard worker, Justine, and quite responsible for one so young. There, his hard work will be rewarded accordingly, and I know I can trust him. That is extremely important to me and a huge relief, because I don't know if I will ever be able to brave that crossing again.

"You told him to write immediately upon arrival?"

"Yes, to keep you and Mrs. Shaw calm. He'll let us know that he's still in one piece and found all as he should. It's been over a month since he left."

"Then another such before his letter arrives here," Justine murmured. He squeezed her hand.

He found he liked being able to give her assurances about Martin, pleased that he could honour the genuine bond the two of them shared, even though Justine was not completely aware of its true profoundness.

"I'd like to see it one day, you know. See it with you."

"See what?" The smile began to curl his mouth once more.

"Jamaica. I want to see coconuts dangling from palm trees and feel the sun beat on my skin, smell the sea from every window, and sleep outside on a veranda in the breeze." She let out a soft laugh and turned back to face the looking glass.

Brandon closed his eyes. Her laugh was a heavenly chime that echoed in his chest. He moved closer to her, and her fragrance shifted around him. "Perhaps, yes, perhaps we shall go one day."

"I can hardly believe Christmas has come and gone, New Year's as well," she said.

"Hmm." Two of his fingers stroked the emerald gemstones at her throat.

"I had no present for you, Brandon."

"Justine, you've given me the best present of all." His hands went around her waist and slid down below her belly. Her roundness was now evident. "The absolute best gift." Brandon held his breath. It was the first time he had touched her so intimately in a long, long while; since her accident, since she finally, finally told him everything. She leaned back against him. "Are you quite tired this evening?" he asked her, his mouth at her ear.

"No, I had a long nap this afternoon. Why?"

He brushed back the hair from her shoulder and planted a kiss on a fading bruise on her smooth skin. "I thought you might like to exorcise the wine cellar this evening? Or perhaps my old bedchamber?" His hands swept up her torso and cupped her full breasts stroking them with his thumbs. "Gently, of course."

Justine bit her lip, her hands covering his at her chest. "When will you be finished with your correspondence, my lord?"

BRANDON HAD WOKEN UP EARLY, the rose dawn streaming through openings in the thick curtains covering their windows. His fingers trailed a lazy pattern on Justine's naked body sprawled next to his, the bedlinen twisted through her legs and arms as they were every time. His hand found the scar on her lower back. He leaned over and kissed it then traced it with his tongue. Her beautiful body stretched against his, and he smiled to himself.

His hand travelled over her rear, her hips, and then slid between her legs. He couldn't help himself, he wanted her all the time. Giving her pleasure especially excited him; he lost himself in it. She mewed in her sleep, her lower body twisting toward his hand. He pushed back the covers and spread her legs wider, her one knee falling open for him. He slid his body down the bed, the promise of her musk enflaming his hardening cock as he kissed and suckled on her gently.

That excruciating surge of anticipation beat through him as he savored her soft cries, her hips rocking up to meet his demanding mouth, her fingers digging in his hair, tugging, making his scalp tingle. He smiled as he licked and nipped his way over the smooth flesh of her thigh, her rounded belly, her luscious breasts, her pebbled nipples glistening under his tongue, to her pleading lips. Her arms wrapped around him.

"Good morning, my Lady Graven," he whispered. She

grinned at him, kissing him. "Bloody hell, I miss being inside you."

"As do I," she breathed.

He stroked her full breasts, bringing one then the other to his mouth. "Look how they've changed. Damn me, how will they be months from now, do you think? More to look forward to." He suckled them, his tongue lashing over the hardened nipples.

"They feel different too. When you do that..." She squirmed in his embrace.

A soft chuckle uncurled in his throat. "Are you hungry for your husband, my lady?"

"Very hungry, my lord."

He moved down her body once more, drinking deep of this rich, rich wine.

CHAPTER SEVENTY-THREE

HERE IN THIS BEDCHAMBER, where she had once mourned the loss of Lord Jeremy and dreaded a new and unknown fate, she and Brandon were now leaving the shadows behind them and chasing a new life together.

"I love you, Brandon," she confessed against the damp skin of her husband's throat. His fingers dug into her flesh.

He raised himself over her, his eyes bathing her with something more than pleasure and satisfaction. Something glorious in its magnificence and powerful in its delicacy. His beautiful eyes were no longer haunted, no longer withdrawn, nor cold. He took her in his arms and held her as she settled.

Her fingers traced lines down his firm arm. "I have a question for you."

"Hmm?"

"When did you know?"

"Know what?"

"When did you know you loved me?"

Laughter rumbled in his chest. "When do you think it was?"

"I say it was when I took you home from the assembly rooms,

when you had been afflicted with the laudanum. In the coach you held me close and mumbled the sweetest things."

"Did I?"

"Yes, you did. Am I correct?"

"No."

"All right then, surely that time in your study when I first..."

"Like what you did to me in the wine cellar last night, you shameless piece?"

She pinched his waist. "Yes."

"I'm disappointed in you, Jus." His hand slid between the cheeks of her rear, and her breath caught.

"When was it then?"

His fingers teased her delicate flesh. "Why do you require this information?"

"I want to know. I'm curious." Her fingers grazed his chest as her one leg hitching over him.

"It was that morning you took me to the cemetery. When you slipped your hand in mine at my father's grave and we stood there together quietly."

"But that was when you first came home!" She raised herself up.

Brandon's clear, steady gaze held hers. "I knew then, Jus. Looking back on it, I fell in love with you right then. And you?"

Her eyes darted up at him, and she bit her lower lip.

"Confess, wench." His finger slid inside her rear even further. She let out a whimper as the tingles spread through her. A wicked grin curled the edges of his lips as he pressed in.

Her back arched. "When you took me on the kitchen table."

Brandon shook with laughter.

EPILOGUE

"My godson is an angel, pure and simple," said Charles.

"Indeed he is," said Justine. "All newborns are angels."

"Oh no, Justine. Some can't stop crying or demanding attention. Little Jeremy here is all serenity."

Brandon scoffed. "You should stay the night then and experience our evening 'serenity.' The chit gets troubled after his midnight feeding and has a sore time falling back asleep, and the rest of us follow."

"Don't listen to them, Jeremy. Do not give them one bit of consideration." Charles leaned over the baby's crib and rubbed the babe's tiny arm with his finger. "You are absolutely perfect."

"He is, isn't he?" Brandon rested his hand on Charles's shoulder.

"He is indeed." Charles grinned at Brandon.

The summer sun burnished the lush front lawn of Wolfsgate. The large tent Brandon had arranged for his guests to his son's christening did a fine job of keeping everyone cool in its shade. They drank their fruit punch and wines and enjoyed their luncheon feast at Justine's finely dressed table *en plein air*. Fillets of beef, roast chickens, boiled potatoes, salads and colourful jellies, custard tarts and iced cakes adorned the new crisp linen over the long tables.

"I envy you, you know," Charles muttered as they left the babe in Georgina and Justine's care.

"I know."

"Seeing that child, knowing he's a part of you and your wife, it's startling. You've created a new life, Graven. We talk and talk about spawning heirs, but we don't really think about what that means, do we? Sweet Jesus, he's a little person cut from your very own cloths."

Brandon sent a silent prayer of thanks up to God and his mother's spirit for the hundredth time that his wife had survived giving birth to their son. His anxiety had run high the final weeks. The night Justine's water had broke, he had sent for the doctor and Mrs. Shaw directly. His heart had burned anew with the stinging memory of his mother's fatal suffering.

In the hours of Justine's labor his pulse had drummed a rhythm of dread through her crying out, her grunting and heavy breathing. It drummed on even when the babe's cries pierced the air, even when Molly had shouted out that it was a boy. His leaden heart had jammed in his chest, and he'd remained rooted to the wall. Dr. Langham and Mrs. Shaw had to assure him repeatedly that all had gone well and that Justine was in good health.

Then an uncontrollable urge to see and touch his wife for himself sent him running. He had burst into the room. His beautiful Justine was exhausted, pale, drenched with perspiration, and yet she grinned and held her hands out to him, his name on her lips.

When Brandon had finally held his son in his arms, this tiny warm bundle yawned and stretched and nestled further in its blanket. Holding this small weight in his hands, he had not felt anxiety over this new, extraordinary and strange responsibility, but an unexpected exhilaration. It was not unlike the euphoria he had once known, but this sensation was real and true and filled his blood to bursting.

This was a euphoria to last a lifetime.

When Justine had drifted off to sleep after a feeding, and the babe was still fussing at her side in their bed, Brandon had brought his mother's music box. As a young boy, he had taken it from her chamber the day they had buried her and kept it for himself, but now he'd brought it out for his son.

He had sat on the floor, leaned against the bed, and unlocked the small gold box, releasing the soft strains of music into the room. He leaned his head against the mattress and breathed deeply. The bittersweet memories of his mother swept through him with every note.

He knew that now he was at the dawn of a startling new life and wanted it marked with his mother's melody. More importantly, he wanted to vanquish that music's former wretchedness and transform it into something else, something beautiful once again. Brandon turned and reached up to the child. His son's fist had sprouted open and clasped onto one of his father's fingers. So tightly. Ever so tightly.

Now, at little Jeremy's christening he felt settled into that new, beautiful life.

He turned his eyes from the sun as Charles clasped his shoulder. "It's beginning to make sense now, I think," he said.

"What's that?" asked Brandon.

"The notion of marriage."

"Ah, I'm impressed with your rapid progress on the subject, Montclare."

"Too right." Charles's mouth broke into a grin. "Quite impressive."

"Make a wise choice though. Don't get carried away by a pretty face, a fetching figure or an enticing income."

"Oh, shut up. You've spoilt it for me you know, you and

Justine. I look at the two of you and see what a marriage could be, and I am full of pathetic envy and high ideals."

"If that's what you want, do not rest until you find it. You have razor sharp instincts, man. Have some faith, patience, and do not be persuaded otherwise."

"Faith," Charles muttered as they watched Andrew, Georgina and Justine laugh together. "Any word from William?"

"Not a one. They've been in London for almost a year now. Amanda sent a silver bauble for the baby's christening."

"That was civil."

"Justine was touched by it. She has greater faith than I."

"Indeed." Charles drained his wine glass.

"Perhaps one day our children can come to know each other. Andrew remains a friend, no matter his sister and brother-in-law's course."

"He's always been a good sort," said Charles, folding his arms across his chest as the trio approached them.

Justine rushed to Brandon and curled her arm through his, squeezing it. "Brandon!" Her cheeks were full of colour, her lush dark eyes sparkled up at him. The air caught in Brandon's lungs. Would that exhilarating delight in his wife ever cease?

Never.

His fingers entwined with hers and he brought their hands to his chest.

"Mr. Blakelock has just told us the most wonderful bit of news," Georgina said.

"Has he now?" Charles' eyes flashed as Georgina slipped her arm through Andrew's.

Georgina glanced up at Charles. "He has indeed. Tell them, Mr. Blakelock."

"It's Amanda," Andrew said. "She's with child."

Charles shot a look at Brandon. "Ah, and life goes on."

"And so it does."

Justine's face tilted up at him. "Fresh beginnings are the very best, I think."

He brushed her soft cheek with his fingertips and planted a kiss on her warm lips. She sighed against his mouth.

It felt good, so very good, standing here in the glow of the hot summer sun with Justine pressed against him, their friends with them to celebrate the naming of their first child. Dear God, how he wanted to plant another babe in her womb. And another.

Last night they had finally made love again for the first time since her confinement and little Jeremy's birth. It was slow and gentle and glorious. She had trembled in his arms for a long time after, and then he took her again. This morning there had been more of that rich, sweet wildness. Her taste was still on his tongue now.

Brandon raised his head at the sky and smiled at the sight of thick masses of clouds gathering in the east. A summer storm brewed, and it would surely arrive by nightfall.

He knew that if he heard the howl of the Graven wolf in the din of this evening's rains and winds, he would not be disturbed. He would know the animal was finally at peace, for he had proven himself loyal and true. He had persevered through the dark, deceptive shadows of such a long winter and found a new peace of his own making. Tonight, the wolf's cry would mark that passage of theirs at long last.

His gaze darted over his guests and his magnificent property. Georgina laughed at something clever Charles said, and Charles smiled smugly. Brandon slid his arm around his wife's shoulders and drew her closer.

Even now in the glaring heat of the August sun, the evergreen trees which dotted the edges of Wolfsgate stood vibrant and tall, strong and tenacious, full of the sap of life.

*The
End*

BOOKS BY CAT PORTER

- LOCK & KEY SERIES -

LOCK & KEY

RANDOM & RARE

IRON & BONE

BLOOD & RUST

LOCK & KEY CHRISTMAS

LOCK & KEY - THE COMPLETE SERIES BOXED SET

FURY

MC Romance Standalone Spinoff

- LEGENDS OF MEAGER SERIES -

Prequel Series to Lock & Key series

THE DUST AND THE ROAR

THE FIRE AND THE ROAR

THE YEAR OF EVERYTHING

DAGGER IN THE SEA

Mediterranean Romantic Suspense Adventure

WOLFSGATE

Historical Romance

ACKNOWLEDGMENTS

I COULD NOT HAVE MADE THIS DREAM COME TRUE without a great many wonderful, supportive and very smart people who deserve my big hugs and my sincerest thanks:

To editor Jennifer Roberts-Hall for her insights, her dreams, her beautiful friendship, her generous heart, and all the laughter day and night across oceans and continents and many time zones.

To the amazing Najla Qamber for her artistry in creating a truly magical and wonderfully unexpected cover and for collaborating with me over and over again in our very own time zone.

To Jovana Shirley for her patience and beautiful handiwork in the first edition.

To my wonderful betas Adele, Alison, Angela, Archie, Carolyn, Danette, Deana, Natalie, and Rachel. Your eagerness, enthusiasm, and feedback always made me smile, gnash my teeth, and kept me moving forward. Thank you for answering all my questions and putting up with me. Your insights and generosity are treasures to me, and I would be lost with you.

To Chas Jenkins, Jessica, and Steffi for their support and guidance. Big smooches to all the book blogger and Facebook book groups for their support and enthusiasm. The amazing work all these wonderful women do mean so very much to me as an author and a reader and always will.

To my aunt Stella with whom I shared a passion for romantic reads. Growing up, every summer when I would visit she would let me raid her vast secret library of Harlequins and historicals that was stashed under her bed and in the shadowy depths of her basement opening up a whole new world to me, along with the classics I was reading at school and was falling in love with. This was another kind of love, though. Auntie, this book is all your fault. Well, sort of. (I have Winston Graham's wonderful *Poldark* series to thank for that, too!) Love you. And of course to my mother who would roll her eyes at us, yet for most of my adult life was constantly urging me to write a historical- "you know you want to, just do it already!" I wish you and dad were here to finally see it happen.

But most of all, it has to come down to my three children who not only put up with my long, crazed hours of writing day and night and all my emotional wackiness as I live these creatures of my mind, but encourage me to do it. Their generosity and gentle reminders to feed them a real meal, bake them a treat, resolve an argument, help them with their homework, or simply to play with them gives me the temerity and resolve to keep plugging along even on the days when everything looks and feels so damn grey. You're my everything. And to my husband for supporting the circus that is our lives.

To my readers, this is truly nothing without you. Thank you for letting my words whisper in your ears and in your hearts. Thank you for reaching out to me, for the laughs, the smiles and the sharing. Thank you for your reviews. You make it all worthwhile and all the sweeter.

Visit my Wolfsgate boards on Pinterest that I hope you enjoy as much as I do pinning them into creation. Thank you for reading, and if you have a moment please do leave a review wherever you may roam for all are very much appreciated and are very important for readers and writers alike.

xx C

ABOUT THE AUTHOR

CAT PORTER was born and raised in New York City, but also spent a few years in Texas and Europe along the way, which made her as wanderlusty as her parents. As an introverted, only child, she had very big, but very secret dreams for herself. She graduated from Vassar College, was a struggling actress, an art gallery girl, special events planner, freelance writer, restaurant hostess, and had all sorts of other crazy jobs all hours of the day and night to help make those dreams come true. She has two children's books traditionally published under her maiden name.

She now lives on a beach in Porto Rafti, Greece with her husband, three children, and three Cane Corsos, freaks out regularly, still daydreams way too much, and now truly doesn't give AF. She is addicted to reading, classic films, cafe bars on the beach, Greek islands, photography, Pearl Jam and U2, bourbon she brought home from Nashville and whiskey she brought home from Dublin, and realllllly good coffee. Writing has always kept her somewhat sane, extremely happy, and a productive member of society.

for more more more
www.catporter.eu

See my inspiration images for Wolfsgate on the Wolfsgate Pinterest Board

Email me at catporter103@gmail.com

facebook.com/catporterauthor
twitter.com/catporter103
instagram.com/catporter.writer
amazon.com/author/catporter
bookbub.com/authors/cat-porter
pinterest.com/catporter103

Made in the USA
Las Vegas, NV
02 March 2024